# Breath
## OF THE
# Giant

**STORY & ART**
TOM AUREILLE

**COLOR ASSIST**
TAREK ABDEL RAZEK

**FairSquare**
COMICS

*Thanks to Max and Julia who helped me breathe life into this story.*
*Thanks to Tarek for his help on colors.*
*For Vince.*
Tom Aureille.

**BREATH OF THE GIANT** First Printing.

This title is a publication of FairSquare Comics, LLC.
608 S Dunsmuir Ave #207, Los Angeles, CA 90036.
Copyright © FairSquare Comics. All Rights Reserved.

Originally published as "Le Souffle du Géant."
© 2021 Sarbacane, Paris. Translated and released under exclusive license.

The story and characters presented in this publication are fictional.
No portion of this book can be reproduced by any means without the express consent
of FairSquare Comics, LLC.

**CEO & PUBLISHER** | Fabrice Sapolsky
**BRAND AMBASSADORS & CO-OWNERS** | Kristal Adams Sapolsky, Ethan Sapolsky
**ENGLISH ADAPTATION** | Fabrice Sapolsky and Nikki San Pedro
**DESIGN** | FairSquare Studio
**CONTACT** | fairsquarecomics@gmail.com, +1(323) 405-9401

**COMICS FROM THE REST OF US**
WWW.FAIRSQUARECOMICS.COM

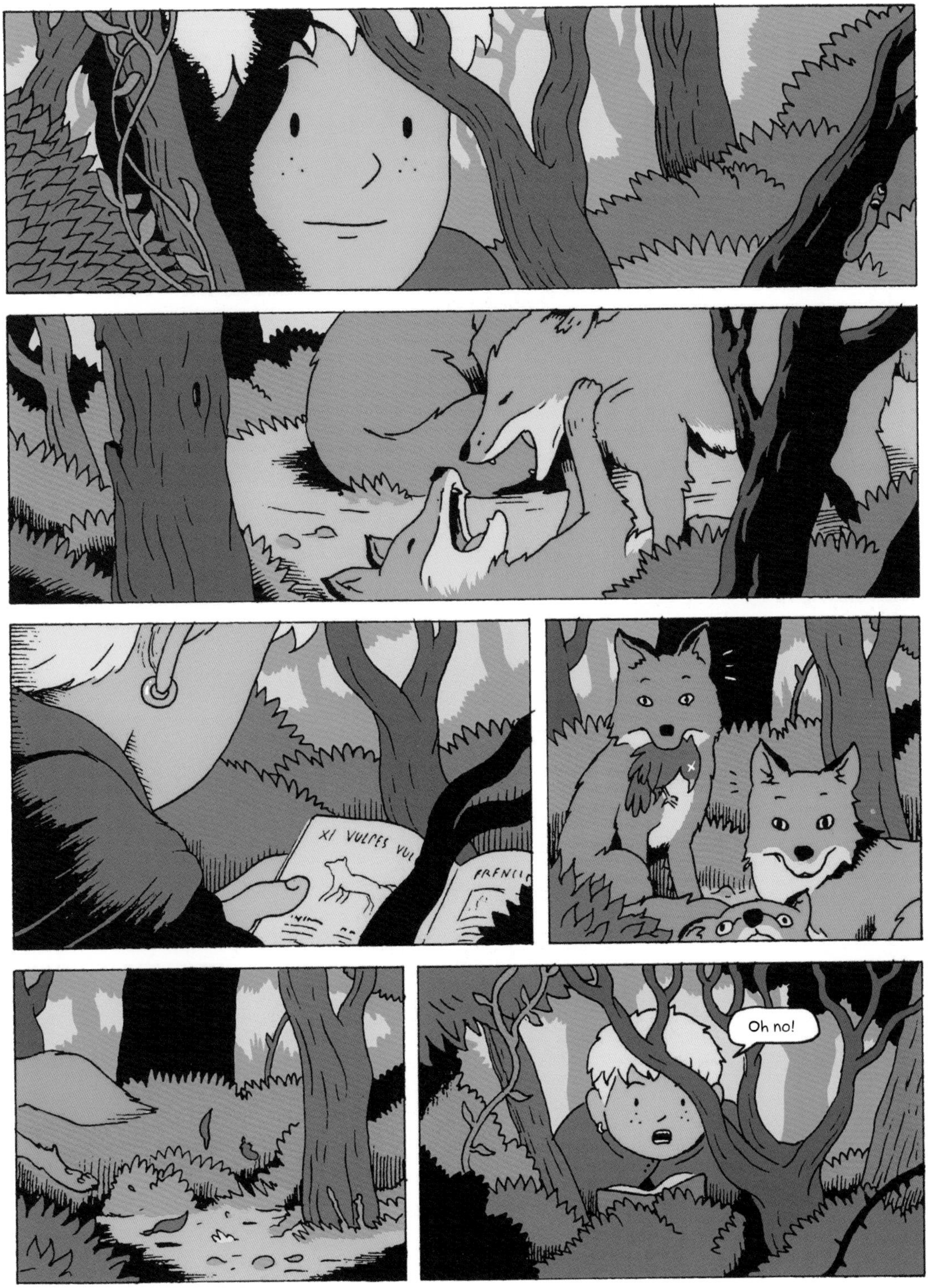
Oh no!

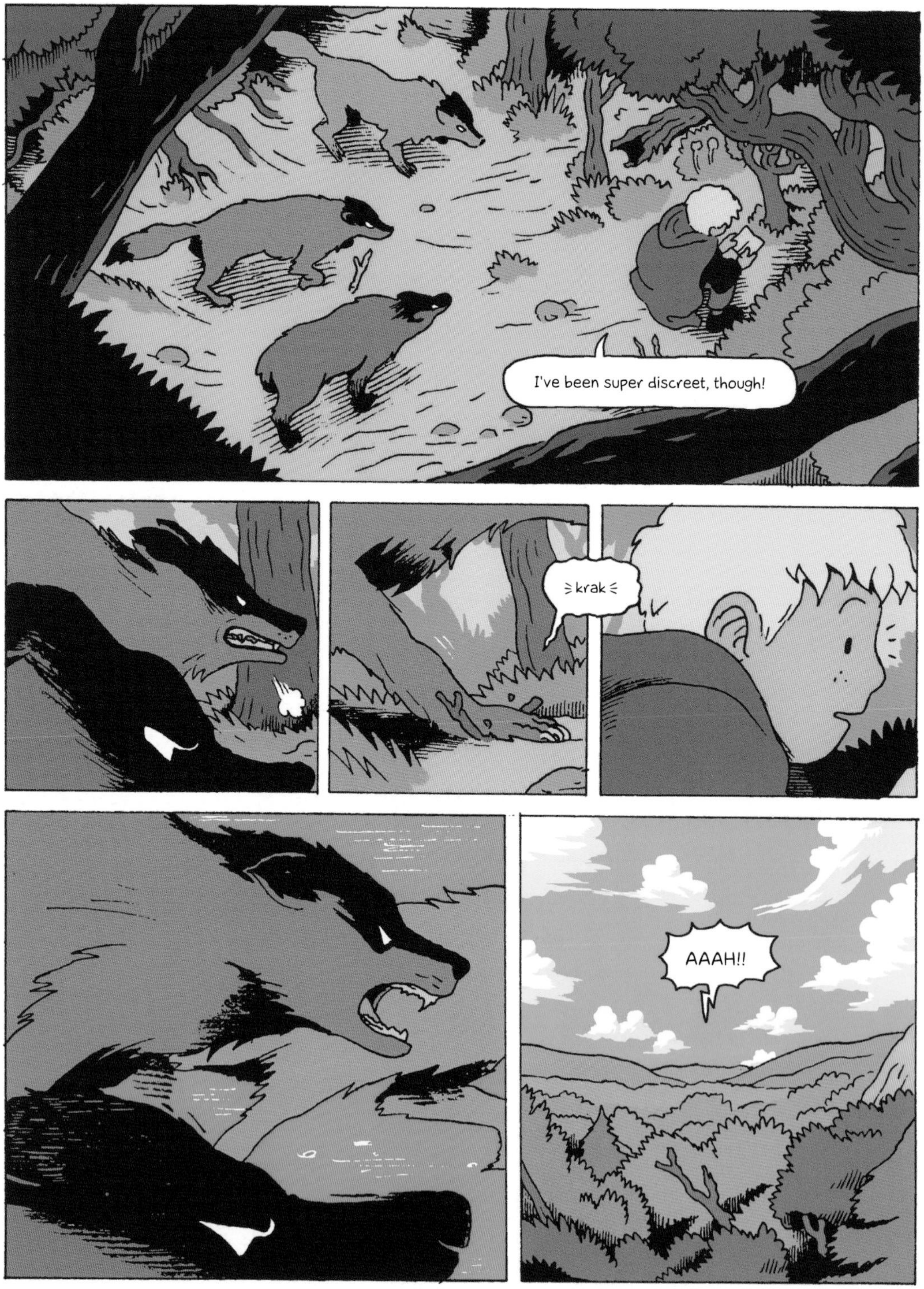
I've been super discreet, though!
krak
AAAH!!

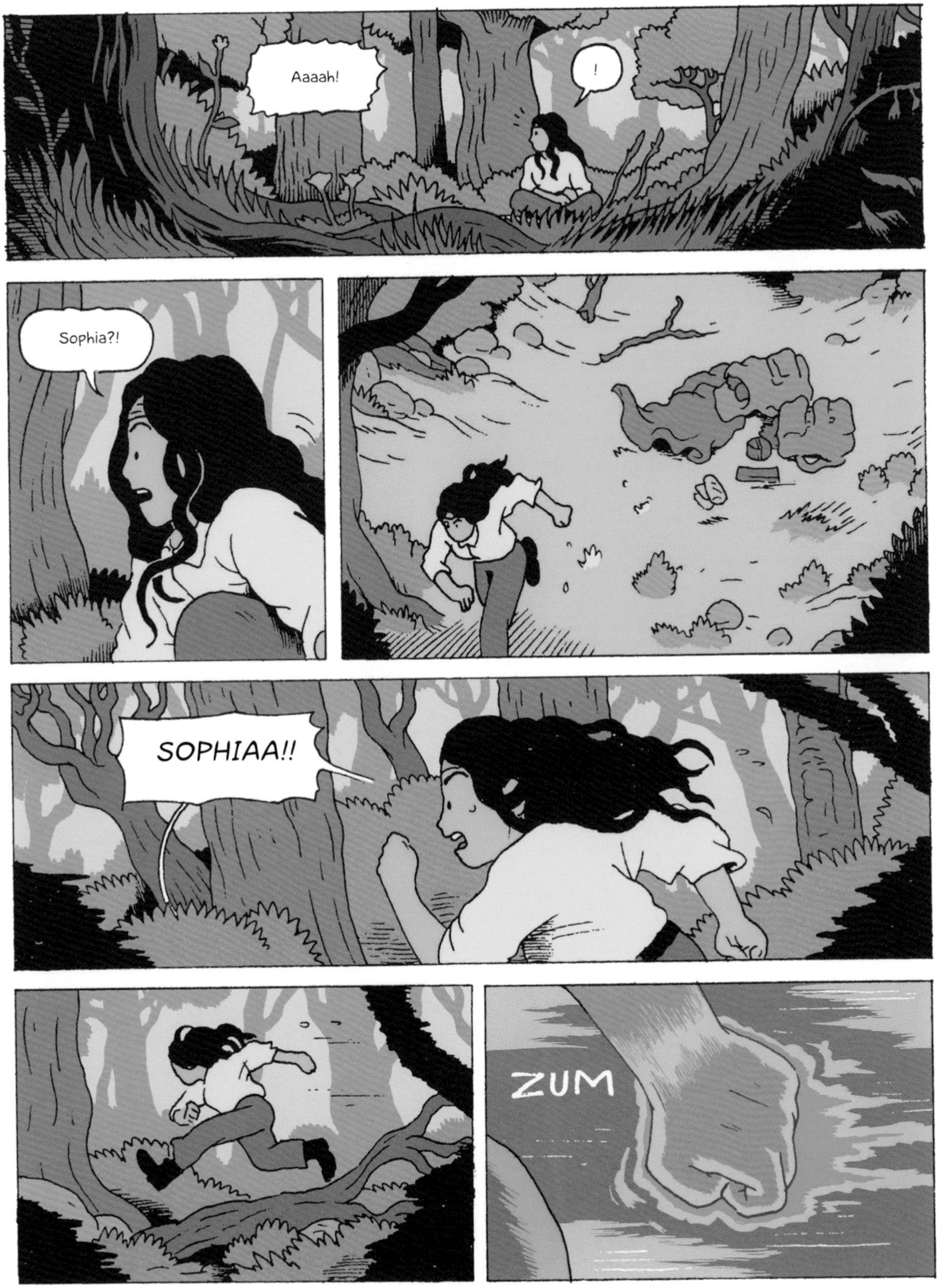

Aaaah!
!
Sophia?!
SOPHIAA!!
ZUM

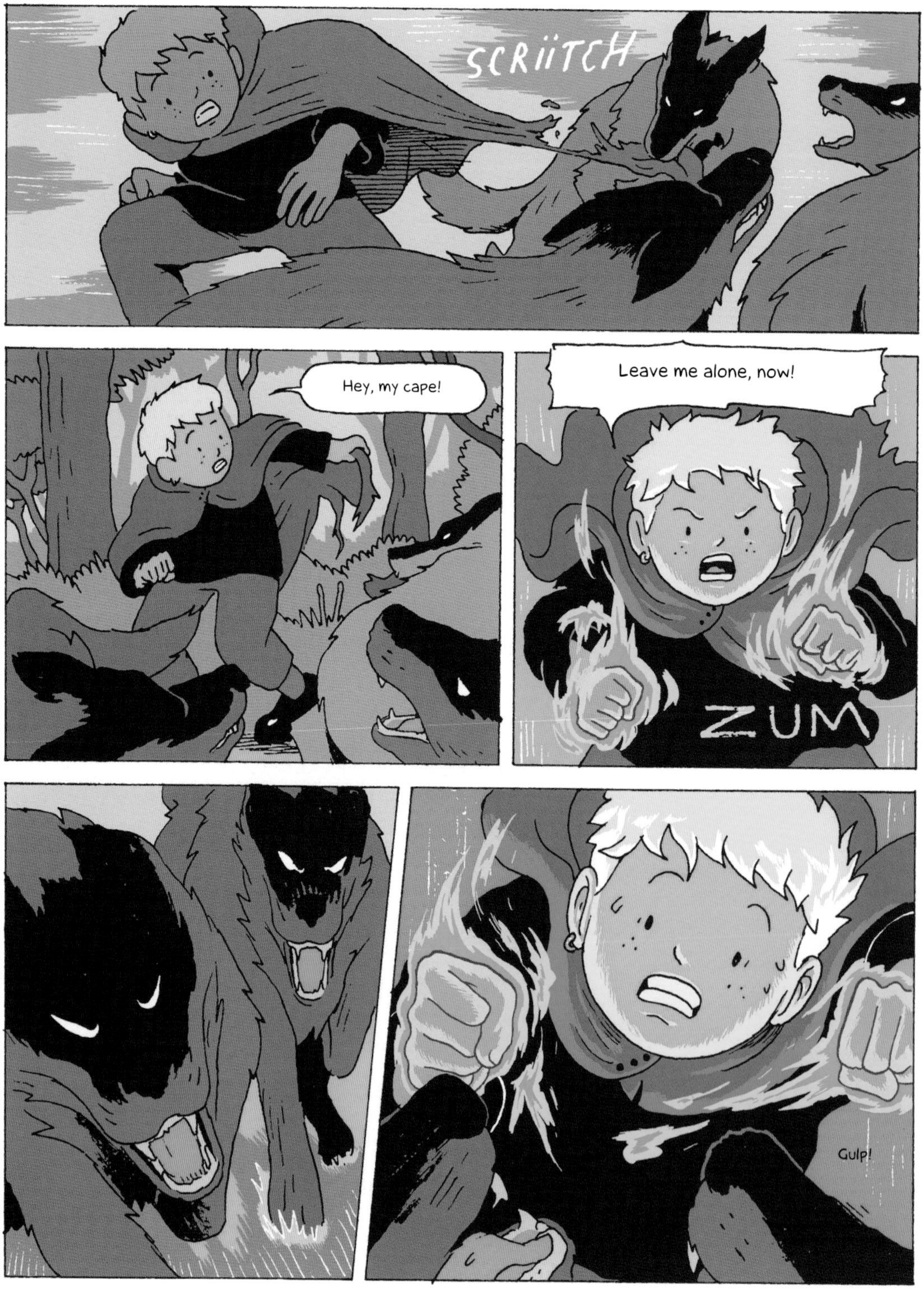
SCRÜTCH
Hey, my cape!
Leave me alone, now!
ZUM
Gulp!

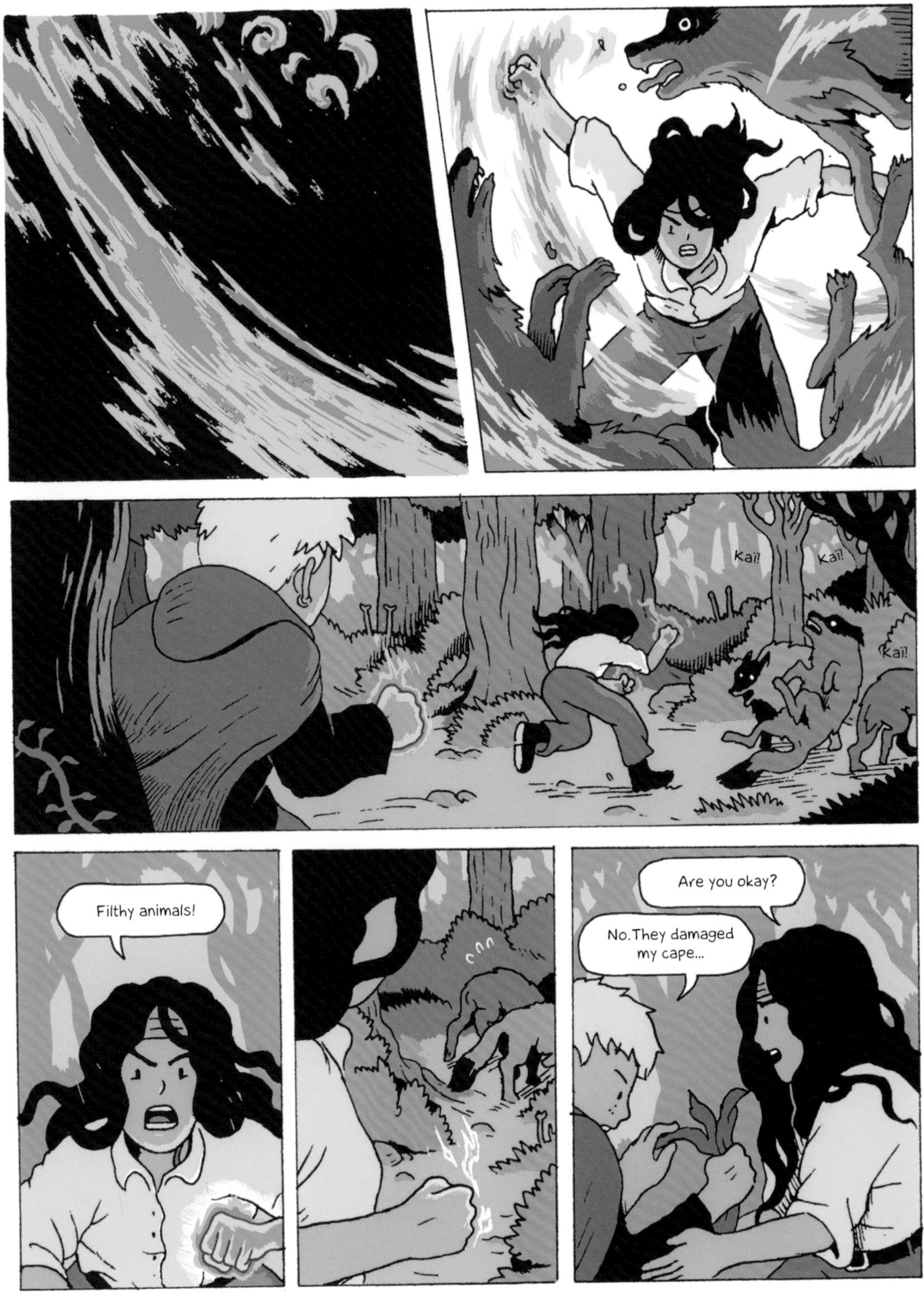
Kaï!
Kaï!
Kaï!
Filthy animals!
Are you okay?
No. They damaged my cape...

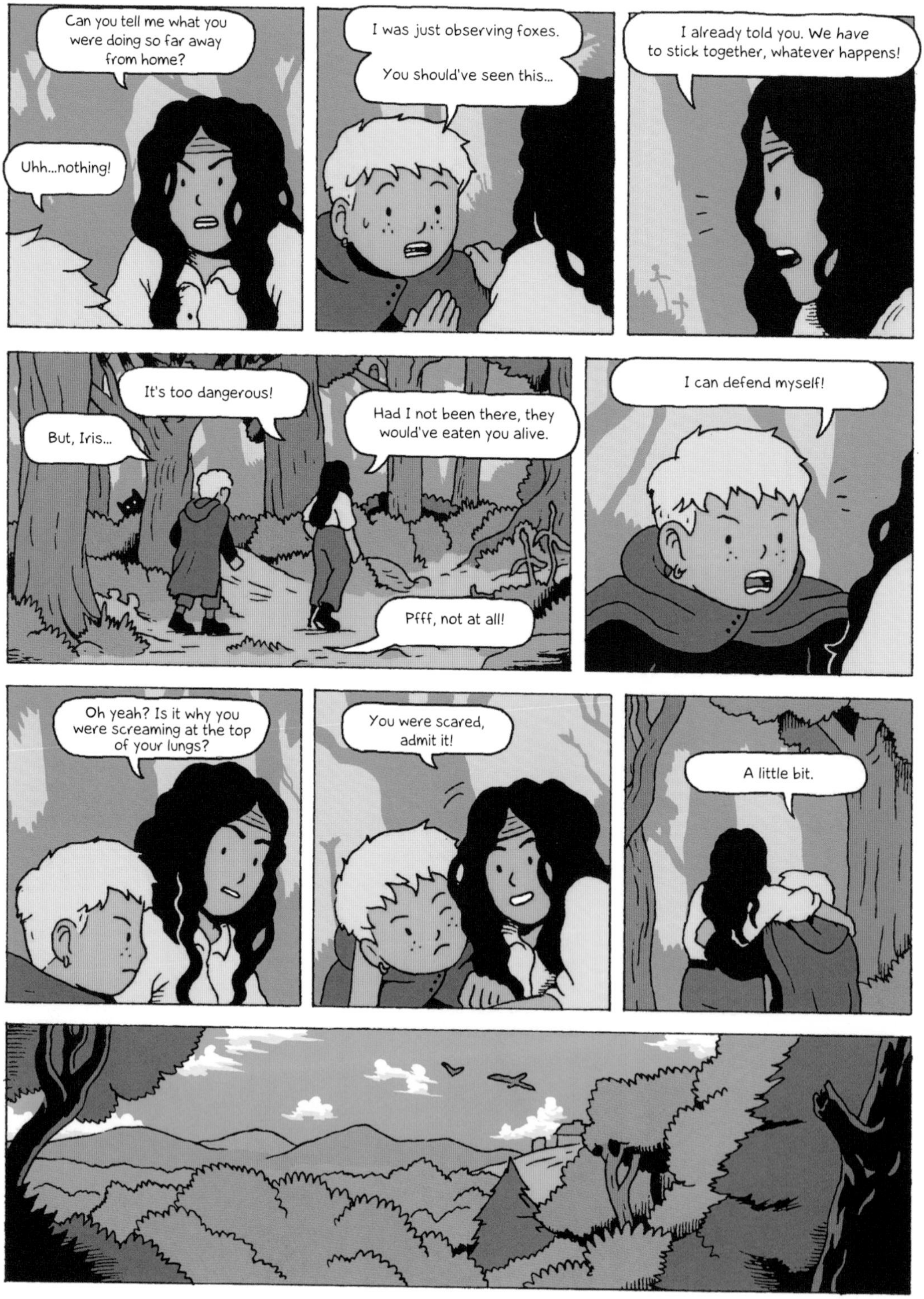
Can you tell me what you were doing so far away from home?
Uhh...nothing!
I was just observing foxes.
You should've seen this...
I already told you. We *have* to stick together, whatever happens!
But, Iris...
It's too dangerous!
Had I not been there, they would've eaten you alive.
Pfff, not at all!
I can defend myself!
Oh yeah? Is it why you were screaming at the top of your lungs?
You were scared, admit it!
A little bit.

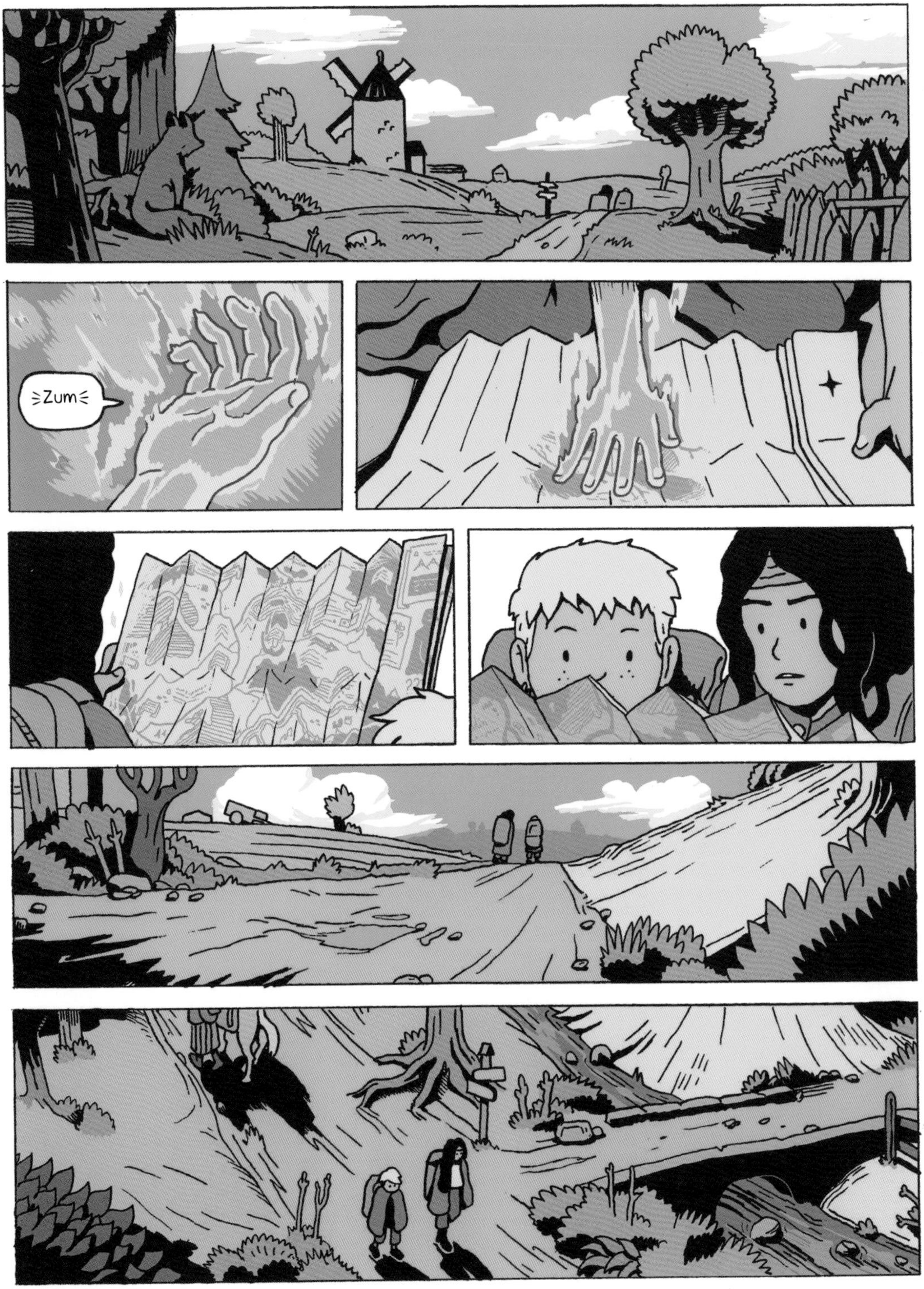
Zum

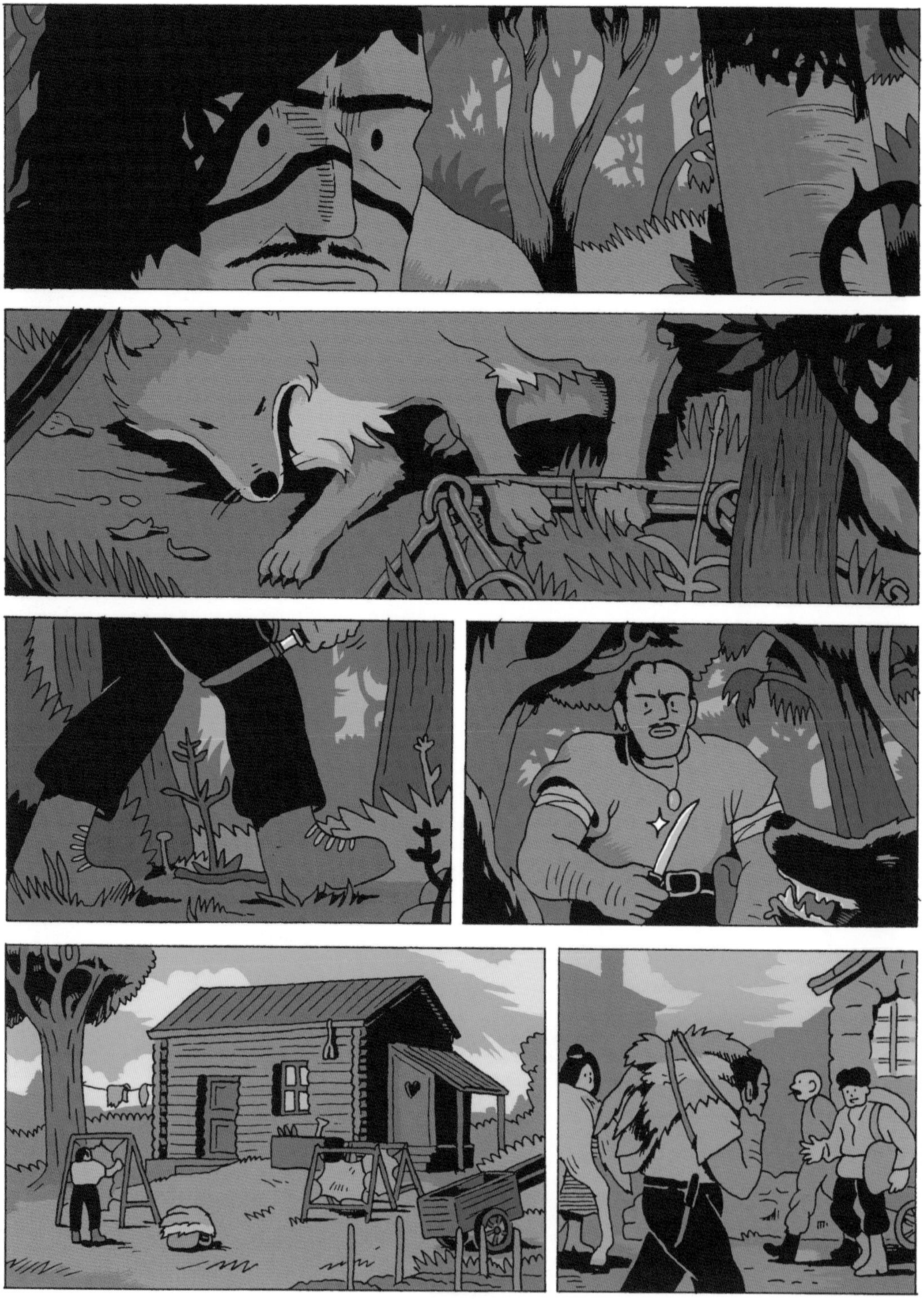

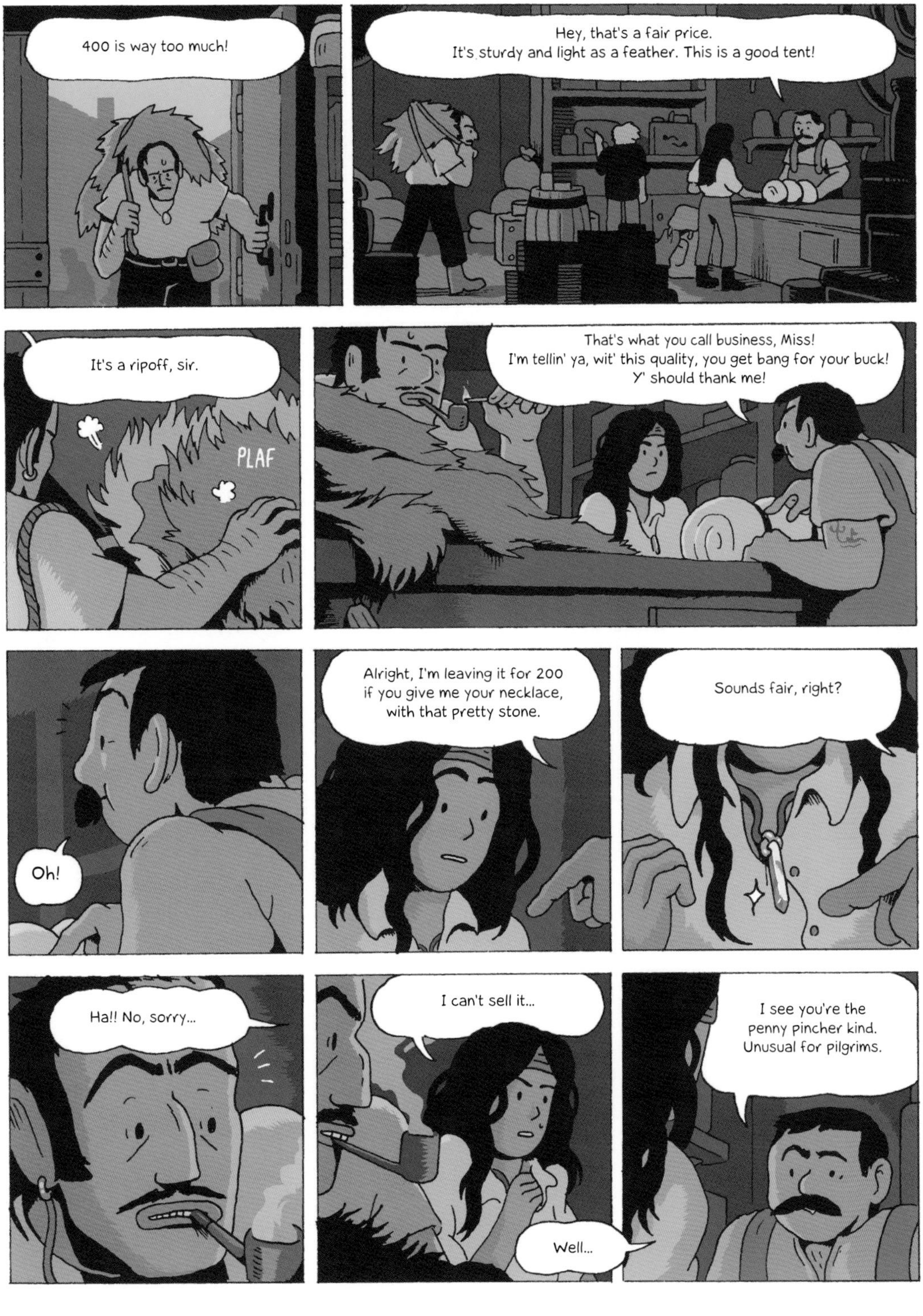
400 is way too much!
Hey, that's a fair price. It's sturdy and light as a feather. This is a good tent!
It's a ripoff, sir.
PLAF
That's what you call business, Miss! I'm tellin' ya, wit' this quality, you get bang for your buck! Y' should thank me!
Oh!
Alright, I'm leaving it for 200 if you give me your necklace, with that pretty stone.
Sounds fair, right?
Ha!! No, sorry...
I can't sell it...
Well...
I see you're the penny pincher kind. Unusual for pilgrims.

What's wrong with you, man?! Why are you staring at me?

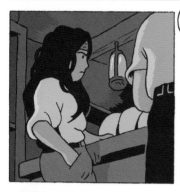

Alright. You have it for 400.

There!

Come on Sophia, let's go!

Farewell, thanks.

I can buy it all for 600, is that good for you, Fagus?

Did they say where they were heading?

Towards the Holy Lands of the East, they said.

But I assume they didn't tell the truth.

It's not really my business actually...

See you round, Fagus!

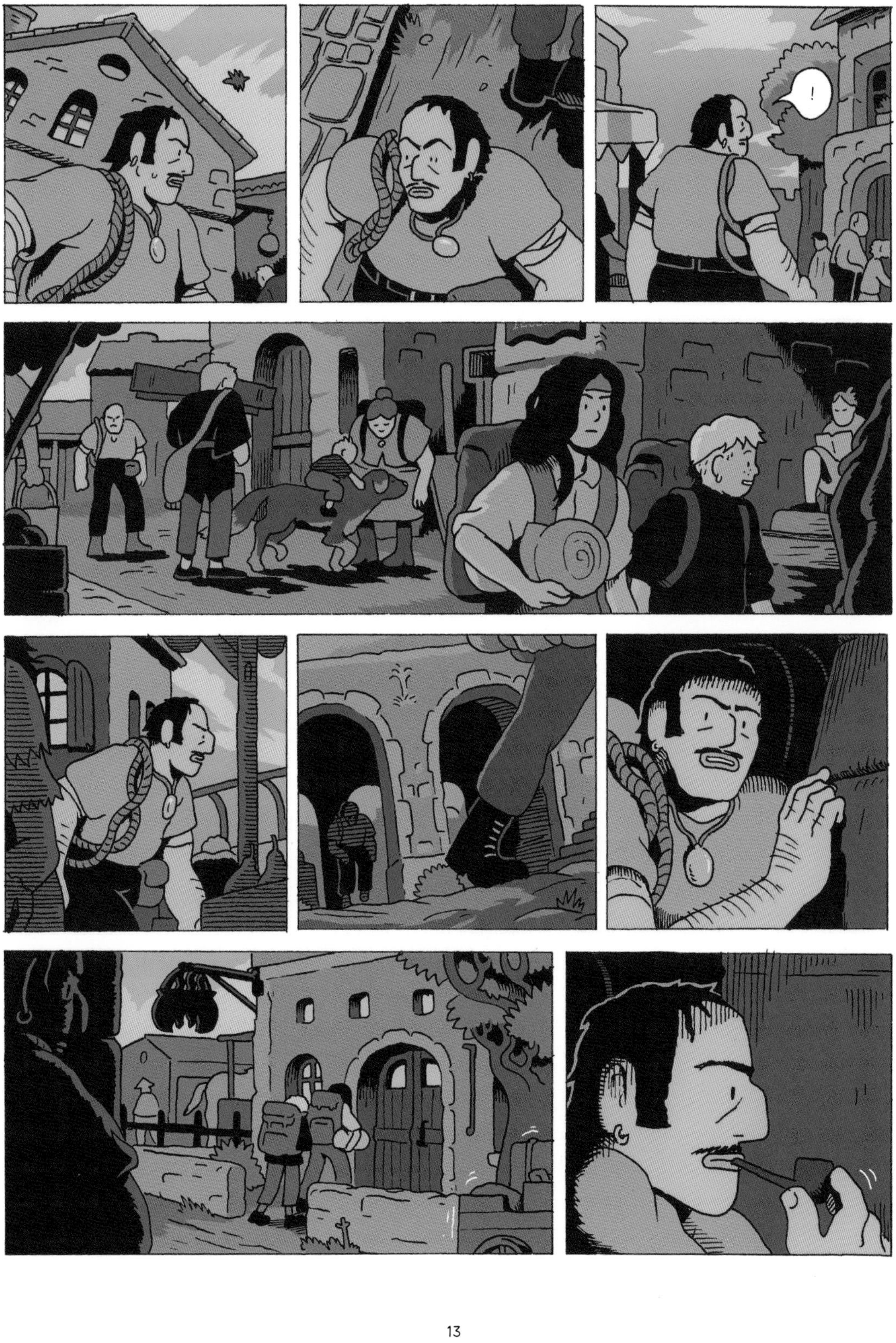
!

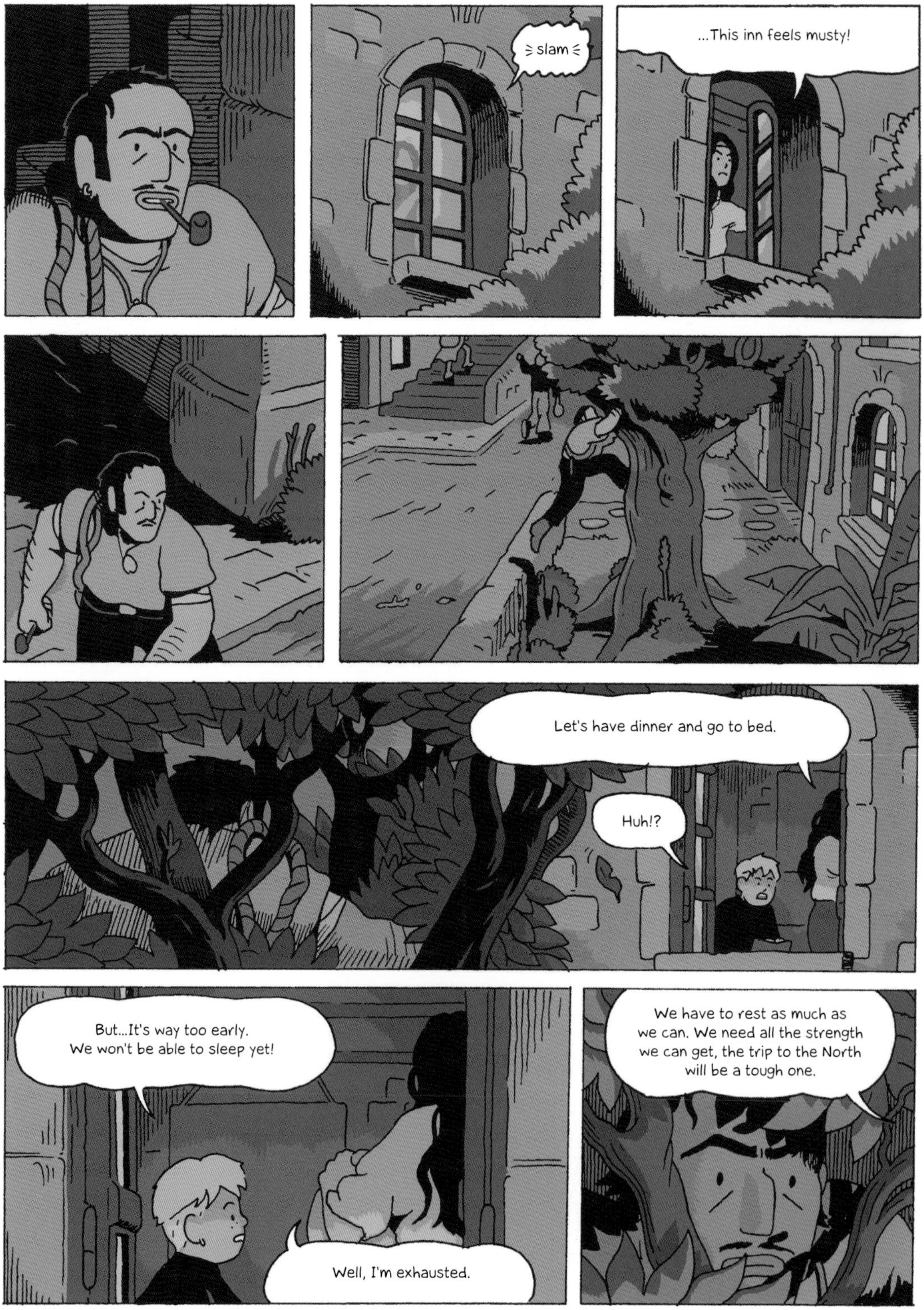

≷ slam ≶
...This inn feels musty!
Let's have dinner and go to bed.
Huh!?
But...It's way too early. We won't be able to sleep yet!
Well, I'm exhausted.
We have to rest as much as we can. We need all the strength we can get, the trip to the North will be a tough one.

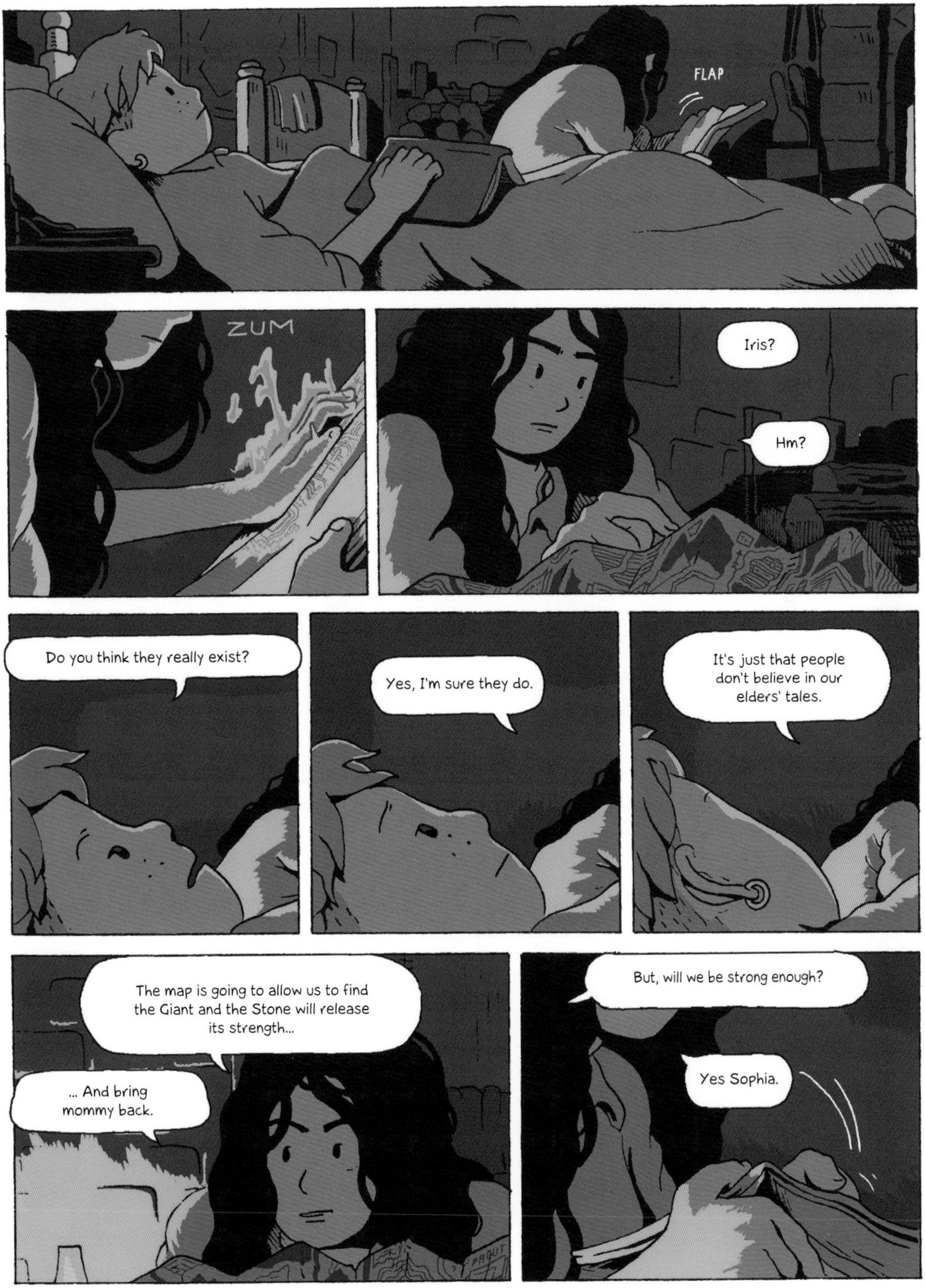
FLAP
ZUM
Iris?
Hm?
Do you think they really exist?
Yes, I'm sure they do.
It's just that people don't believe in our elders' tales.
The map is going to allow us to find the Giant and the Stone will release its strength...
... And bring mommy back.
But, will we be strong enough?
Yes Sophia.

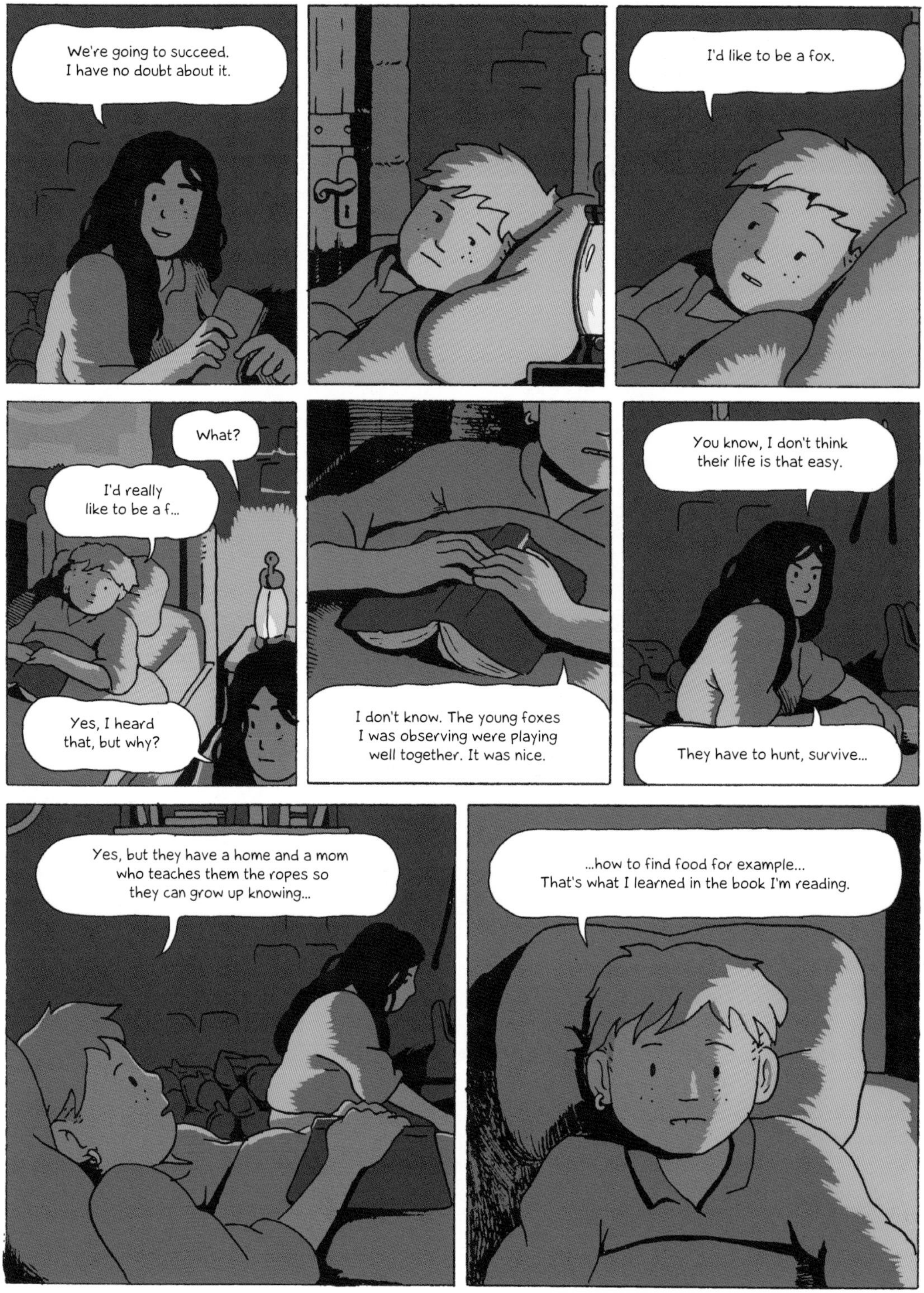
We're going to succeed. I have no doubt about it.
I'd like to be a fox.
What?
I'd really like to be a f...
Yes, I heard that, but why?
I don't know. The young foxes I was observing were playing well together. It was nice.
You know, I don't think their life is that easy.
They have to hunt, survive...
Yes, but they have a home and a mom who teaches them the ropes so they can grow up knowing...
...how to find food for example... That's what I learned in the book I'm reading.

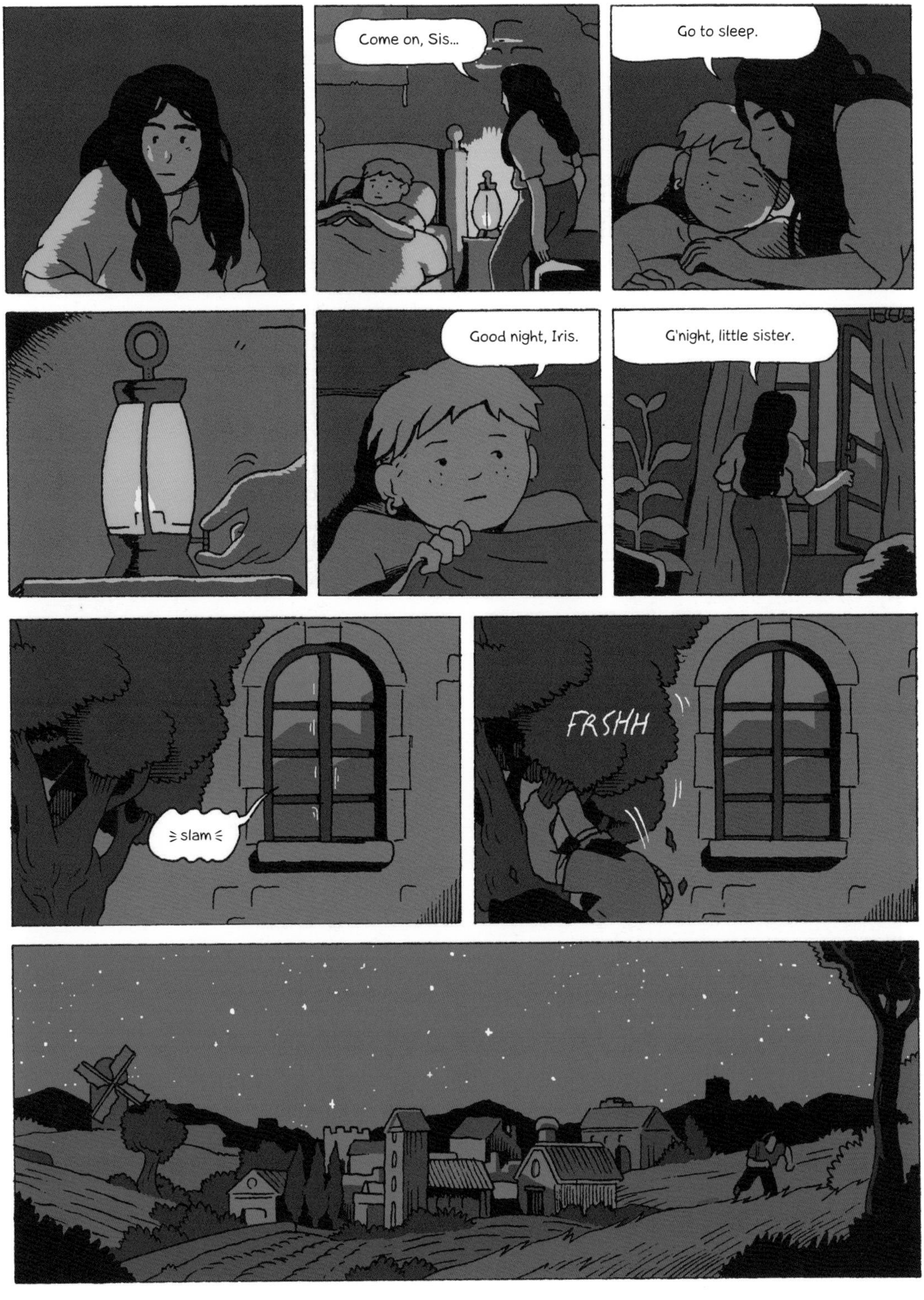
Come on, Sis...
Go to sleep.
Good night, Iris.
G'night, little sister.
slam
FRSHH

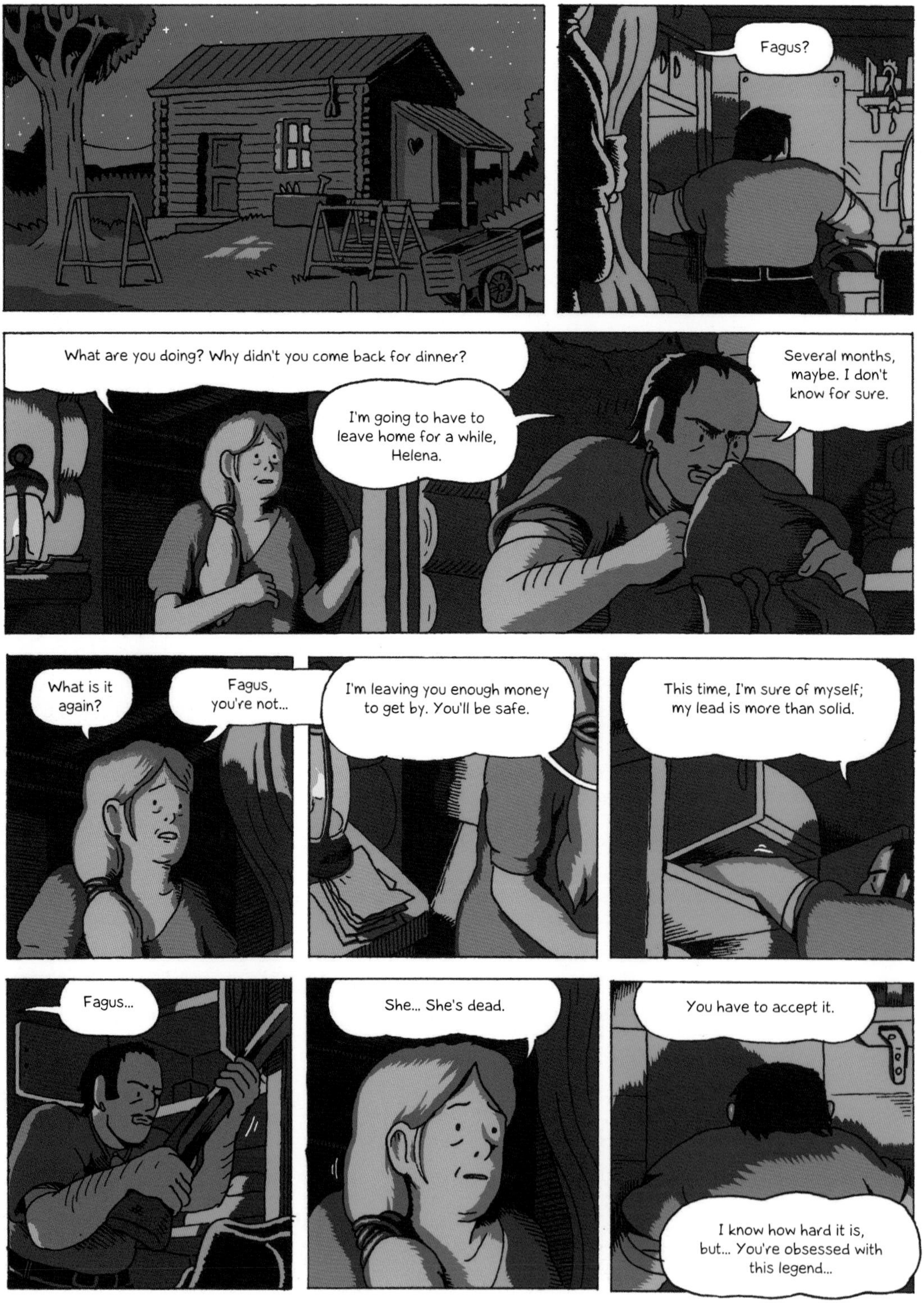
Fagus?
What are you doing? Why didn't you come back for dinner?
I'm going to have to leave home for a while, Helena.
Several months, maybe. I don't know for sure.
What is it again?
Fagus, you're not...
I'm leaving you enough money to get by. You'll be safe.
This time, I'm sure of myself; my lead is more than solid.
Fagus...
She... She's dead.
You have to accept it.
I know how hard it is, but... You're obsessed with this legend...

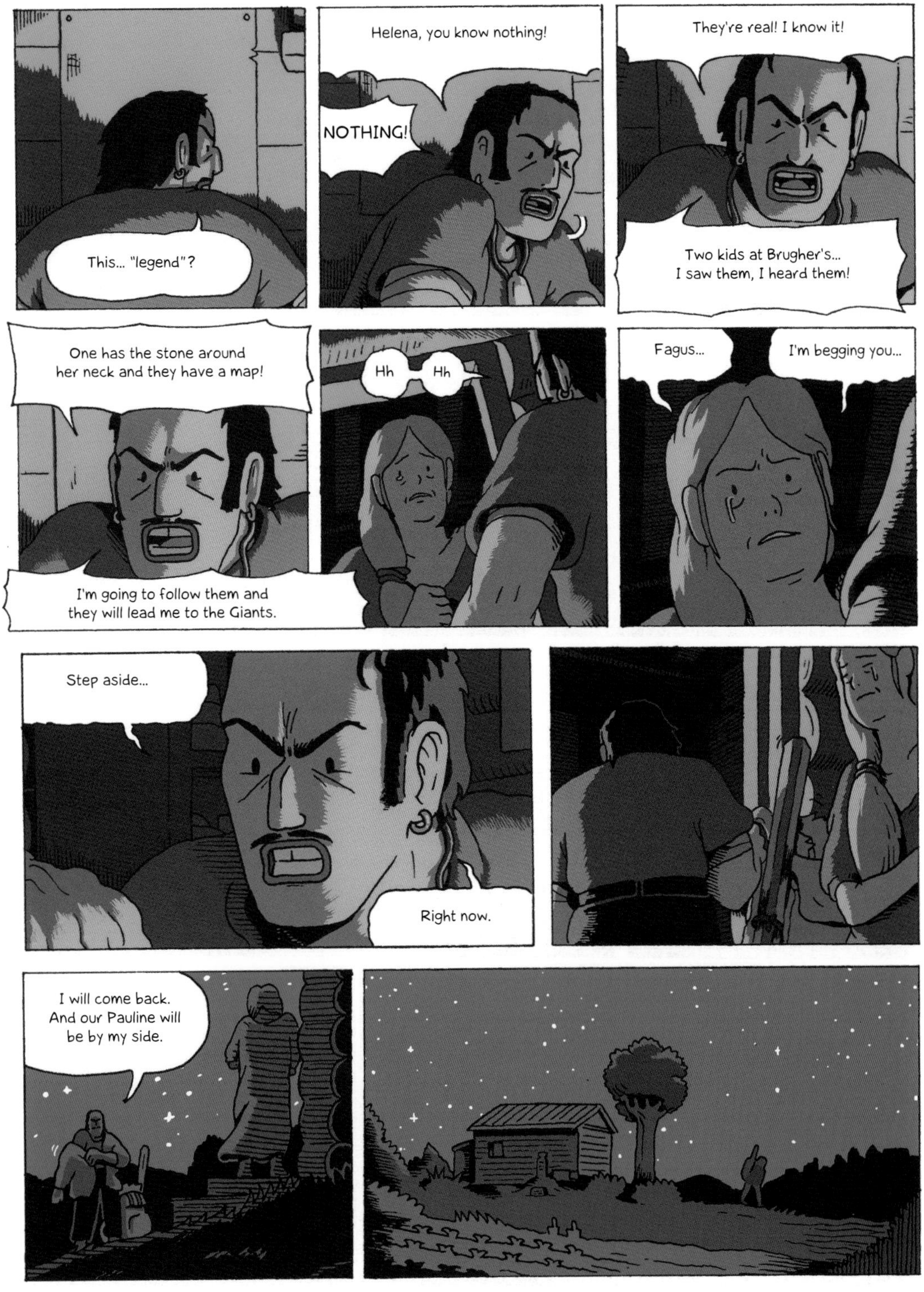
This... "legend"?
Helena, you know nothing!
NOTHING!
They're real! I know it!
Two kids at Brugher's...
I saw them, I heard them!
One has the stone around her neck and they have a map!
I'm going to follow them and they will lead me to the Giants.
Hh Hh
Fagus...
I'm begging you...
Step aside...
Right now.
I will come back.
And our Pauline will be by my side.

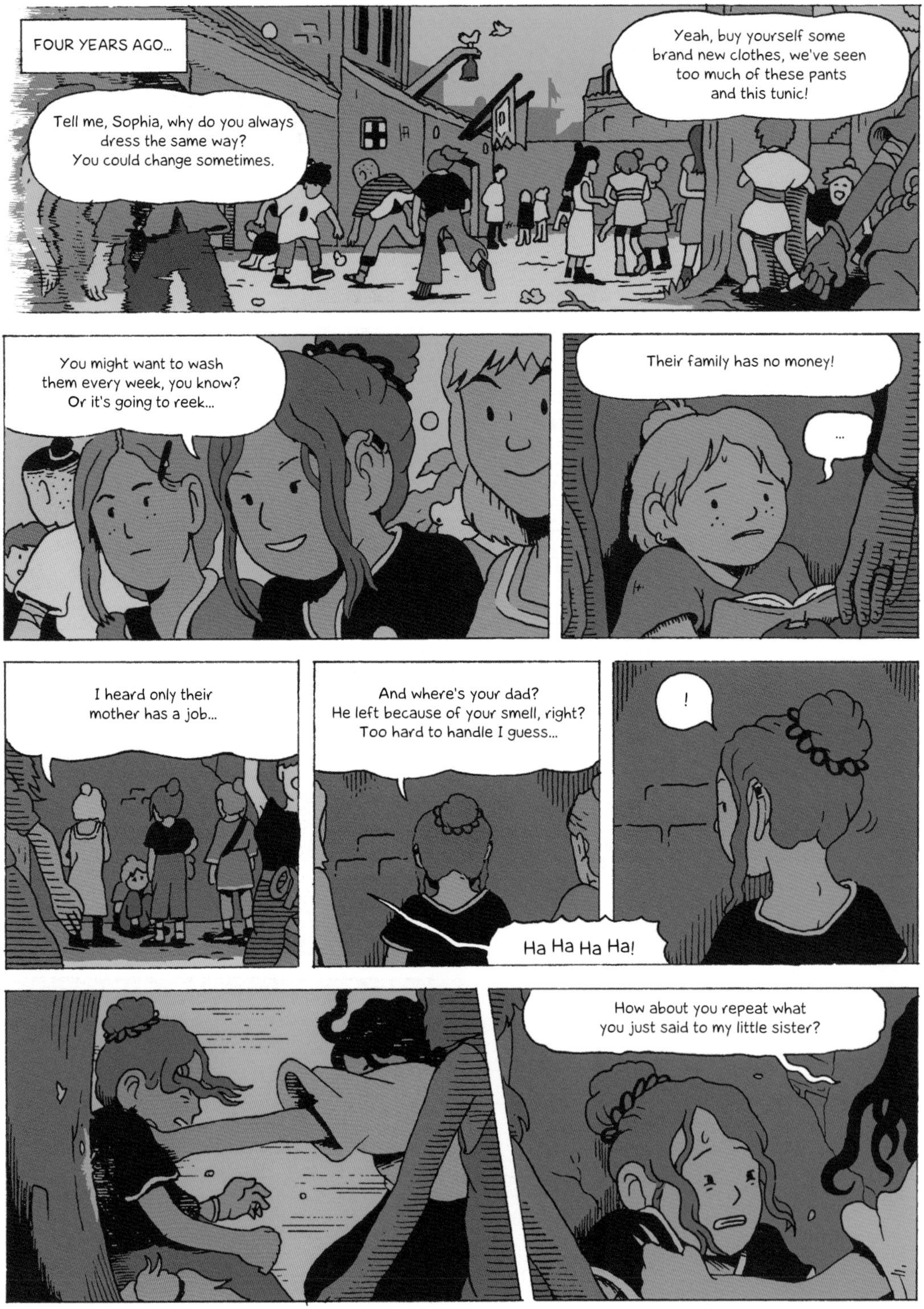

FOUR YEARS AGO...
Tell me, Sophia, why do you always dress the same way? You could change sometimes.
Yeah, buy yourself some brand new clothes, we've seen too much of these pants and this tunic!
You might want to wash them every week, you know? Or it's going to reek...
Their family has no money!
...
I heard only their mother has a job...
And where's your dad? He left because of your smell, right? Too hard to handle I guess...
!
Ha Ha Ha Ha!
How about you repeat what you just said to my little sister?

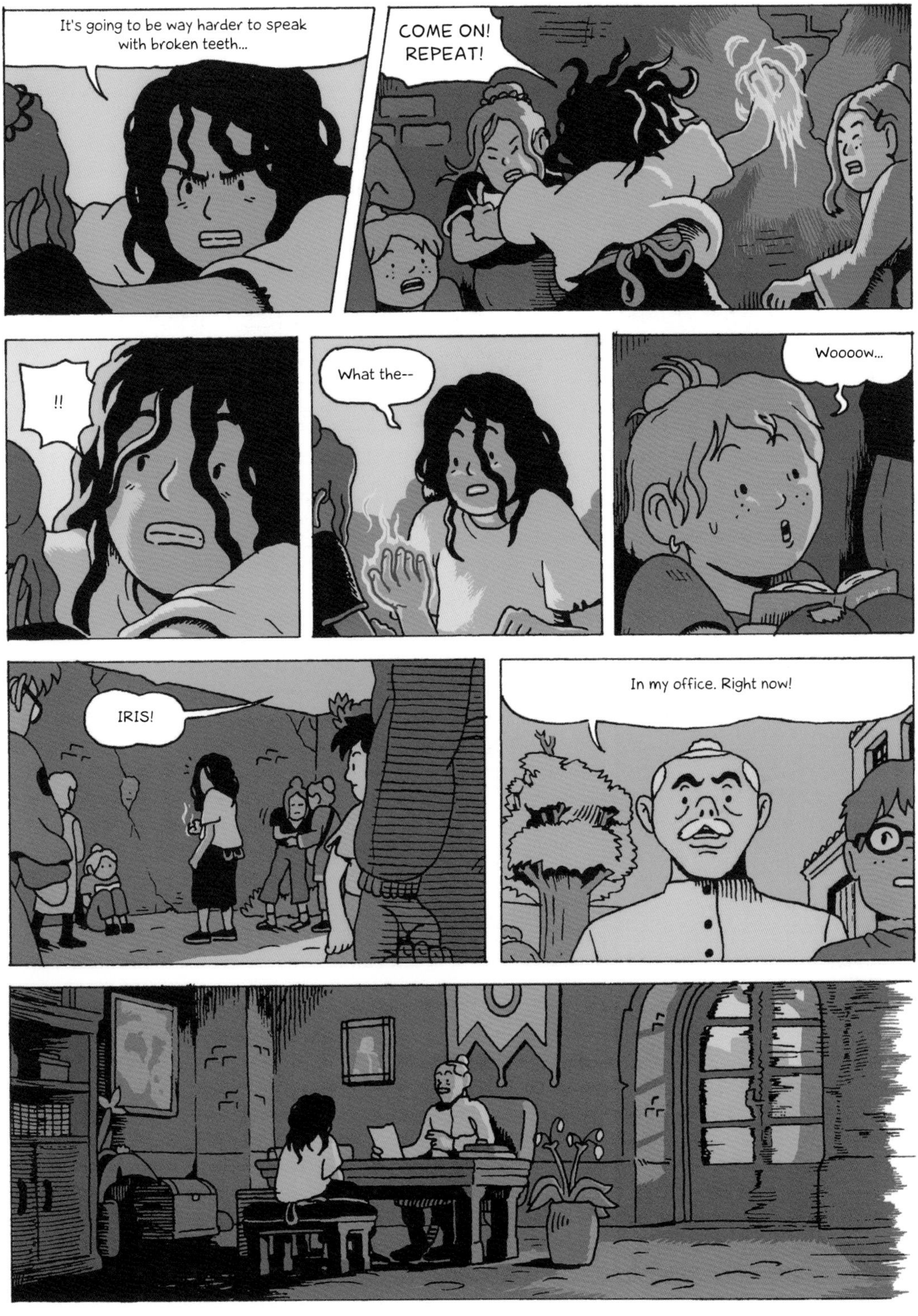
It's going to be way harder to speak with broken teeth...
COME ON! REPEAT!
!!
What the--
Wooow...
IRIS!
In my office. Right now!

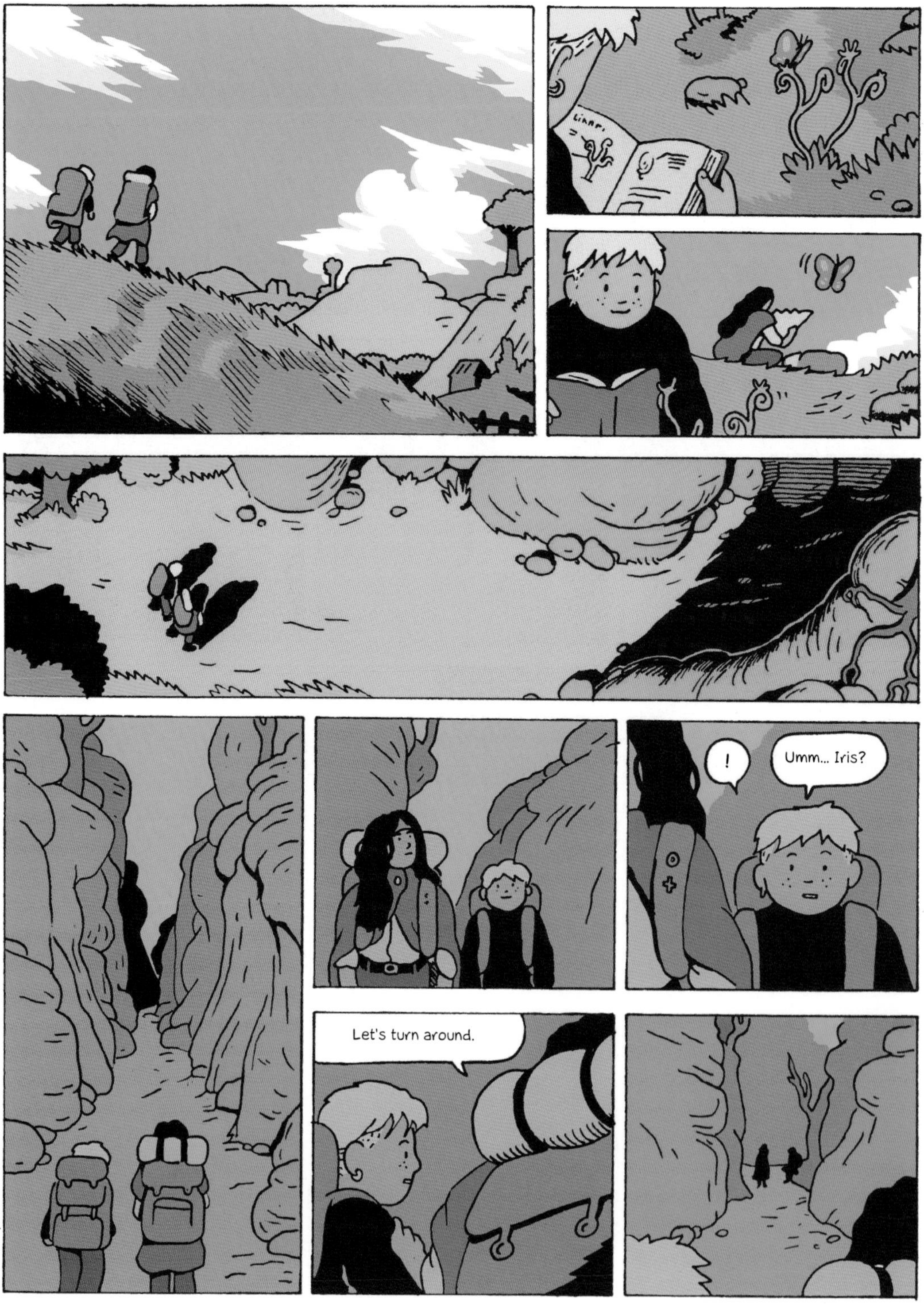
!
Umm... Iris?
Let's turn around.

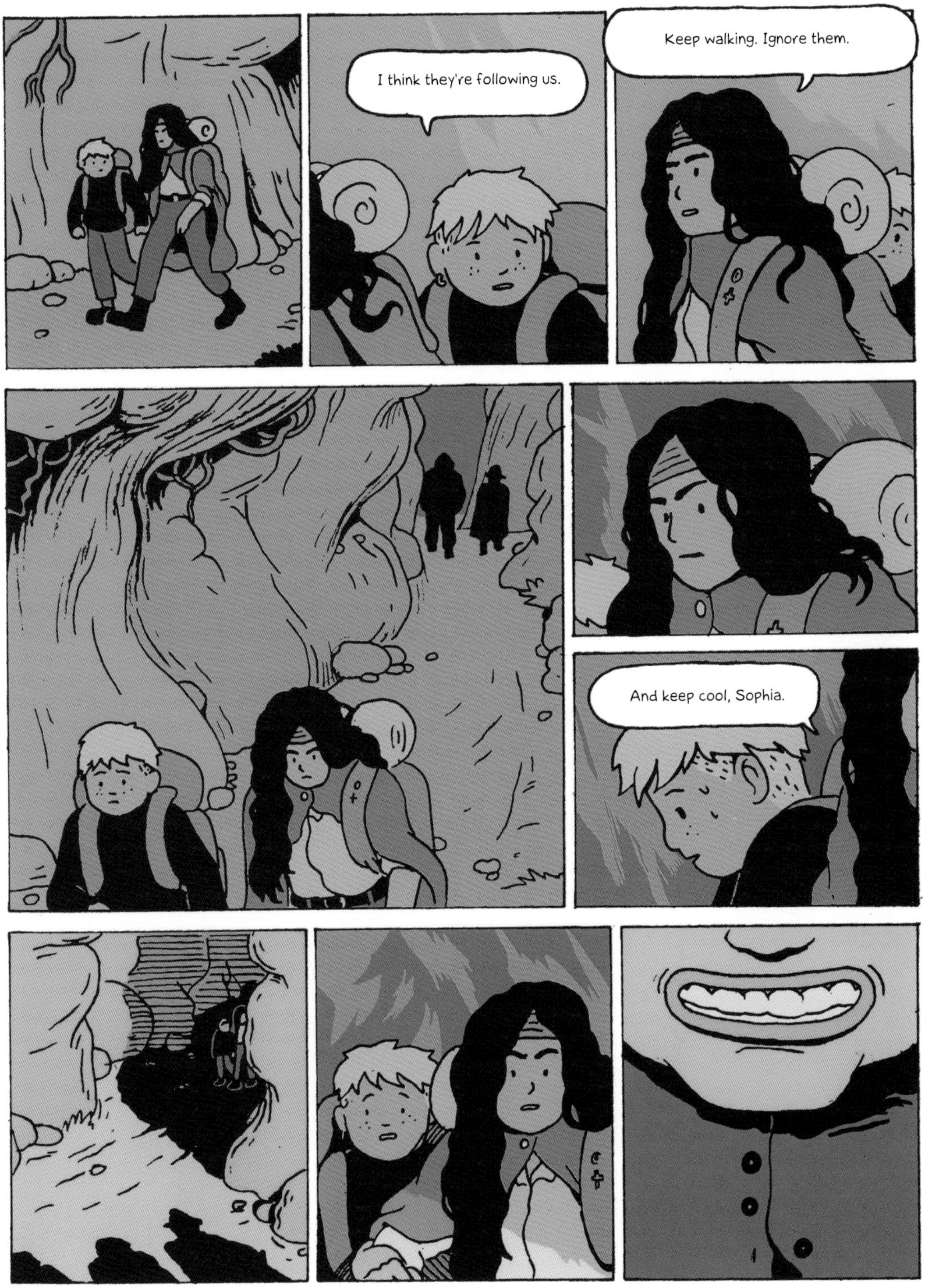
I think they're following us.
Keep walking. Ignore them.
And keep cool, Sophia.

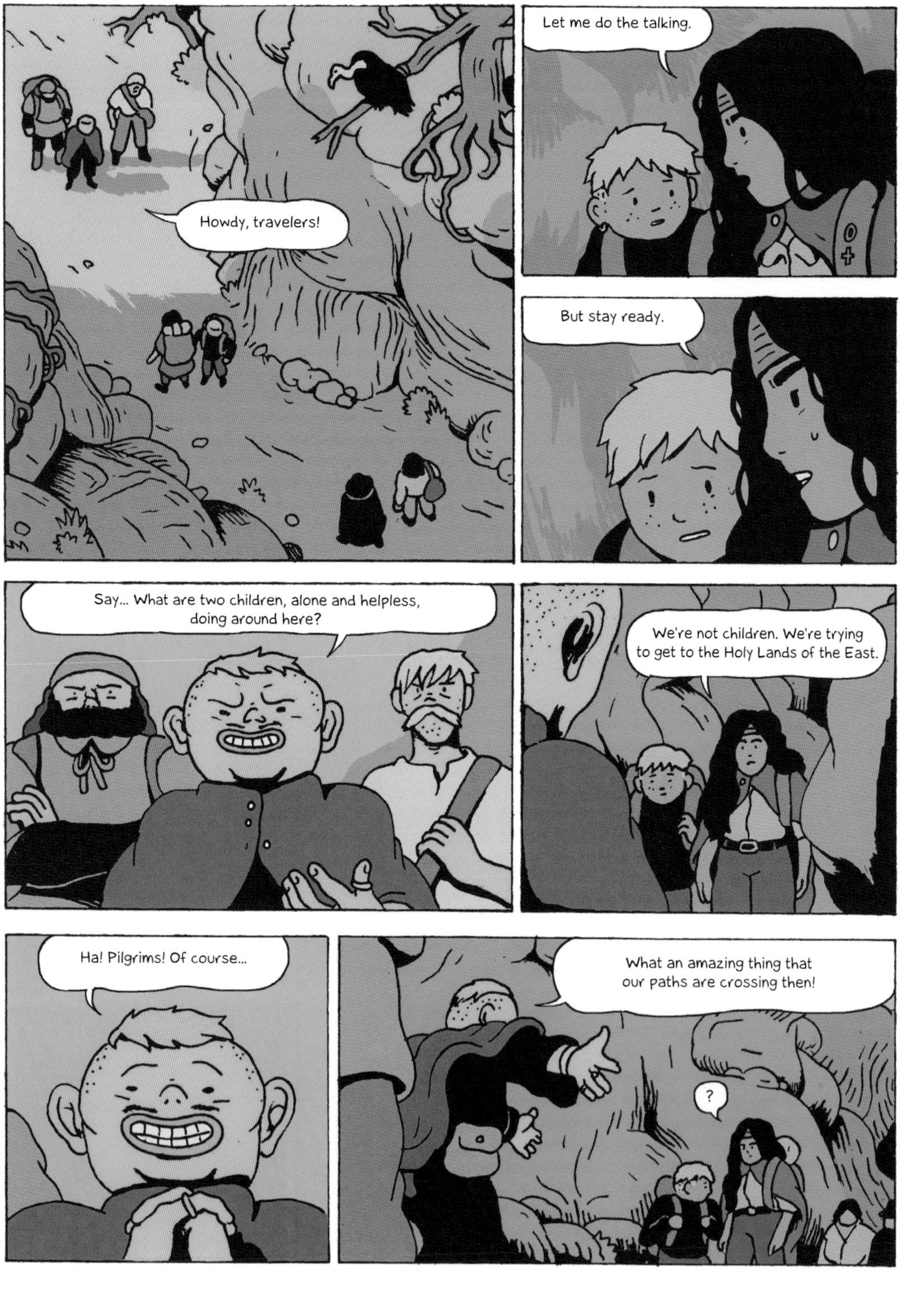
Howdy, travelers!
Let me do the talking.
But stay ready.
Say... What are two children, alone and helpless, doing around here?
We're not children. We're trying to get to the Holy Lands of the East.
Ha! Pilgrims! Of course...
What an amazing thing that our paths are crossing then!
?

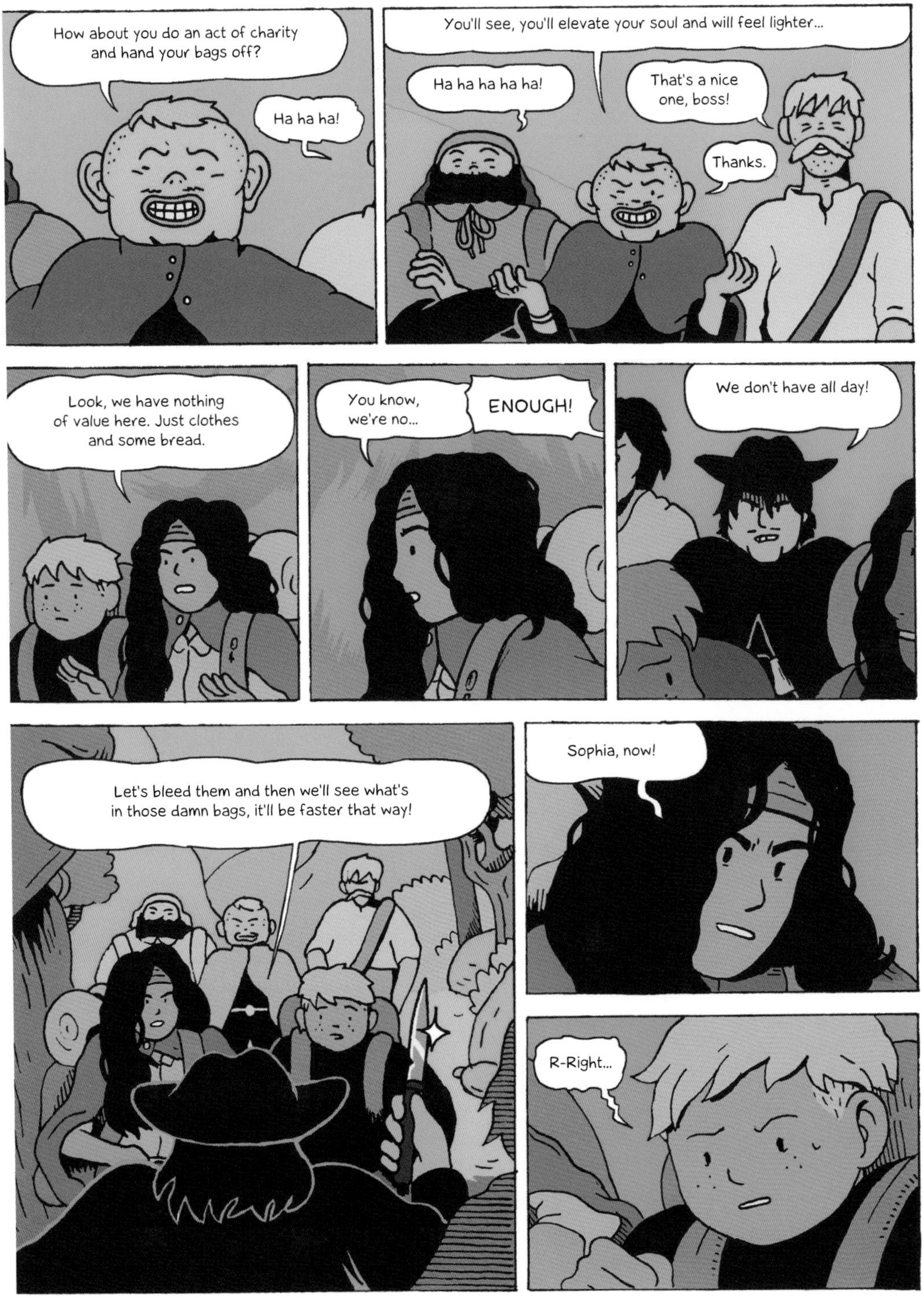
How about you do an act of charity and hand your bags off?
Ha ha ha!
You'll see, you'll elevate your soul and will feel lighter...
Ha ha ha ha ha!
That's a nice one, boss!
Thanks.
Look, we have nothing of value here. Just clothes and some bread.
You know, we're no...
ENOUGH!
We don't have all day!
Let's bleed them and then we'll see what's in those damn bags, it'll be faster that way!
Sophia, now!
R-Right...

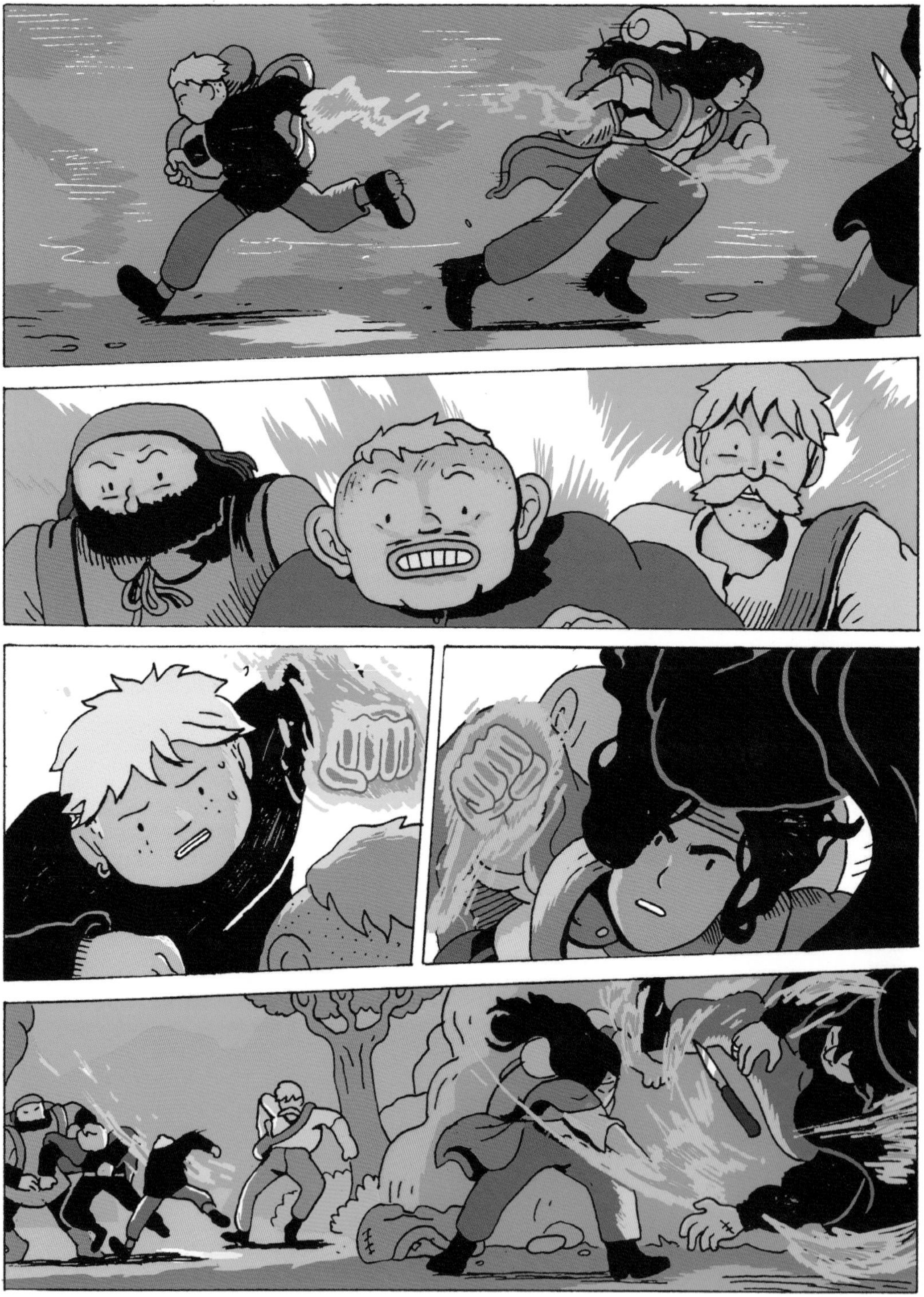

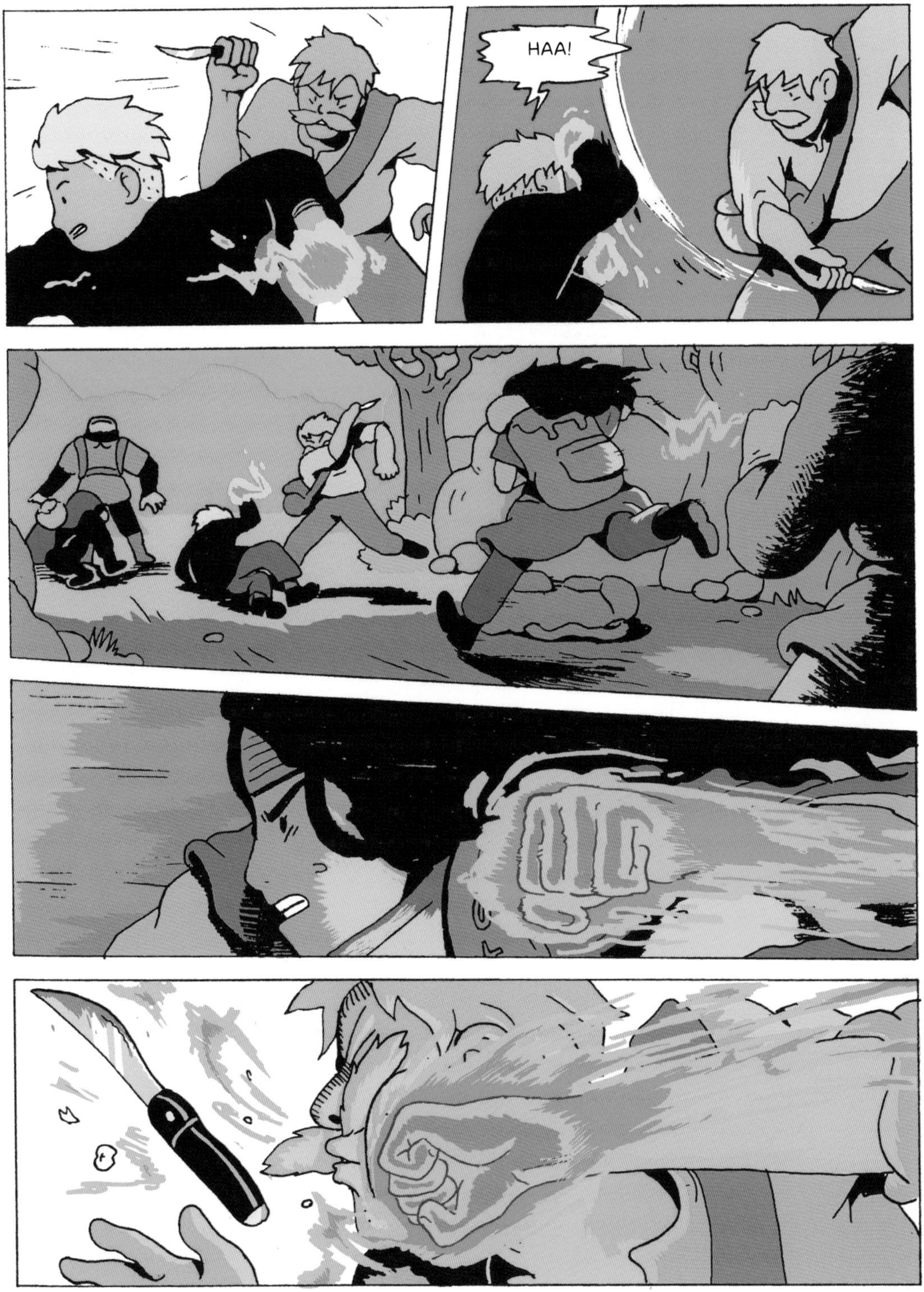
HAA!

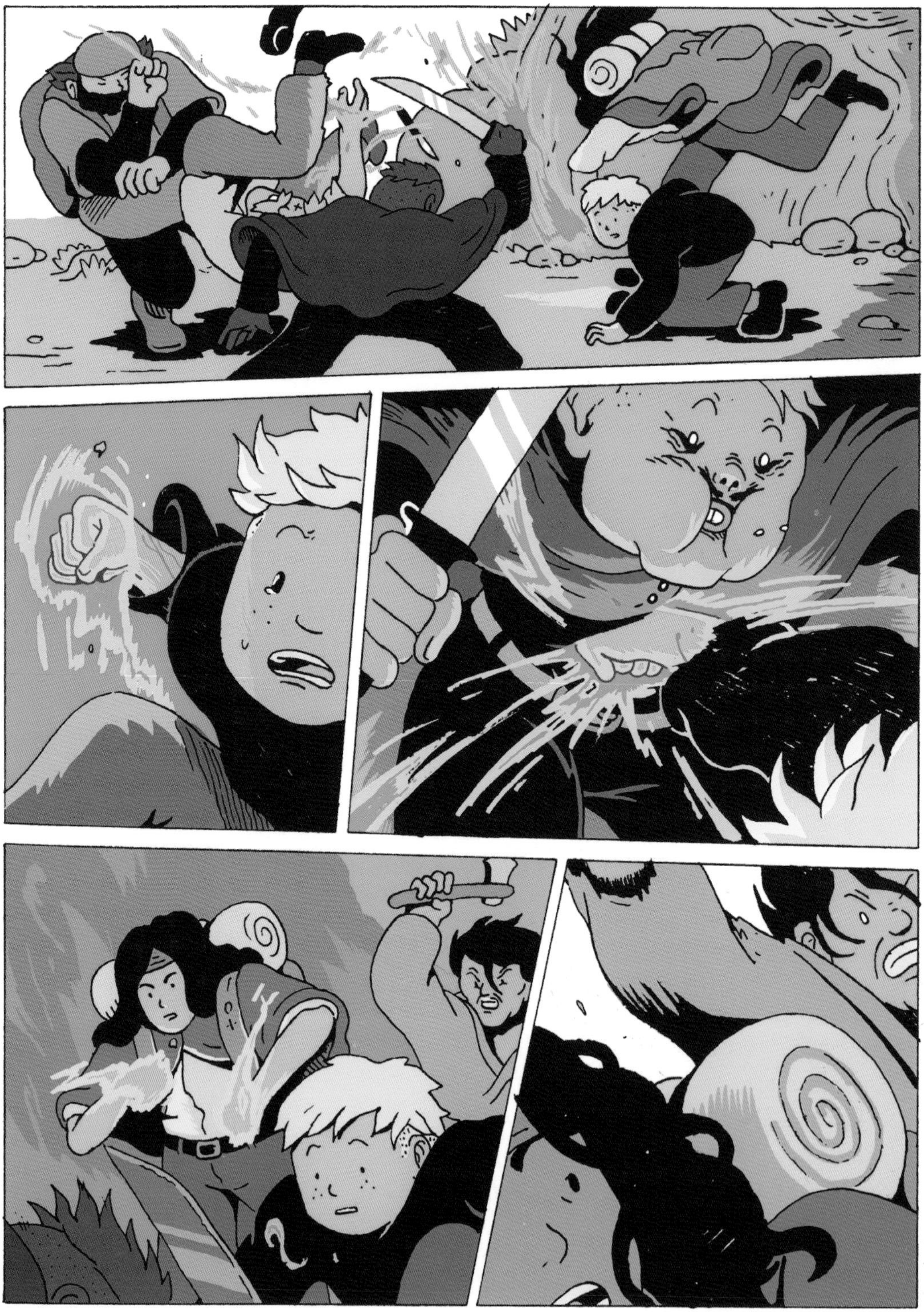

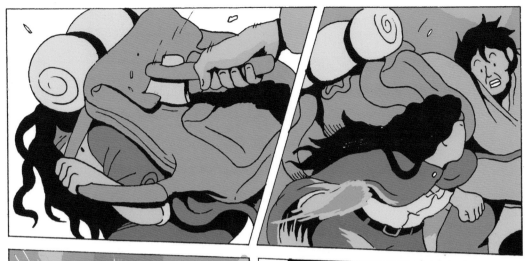

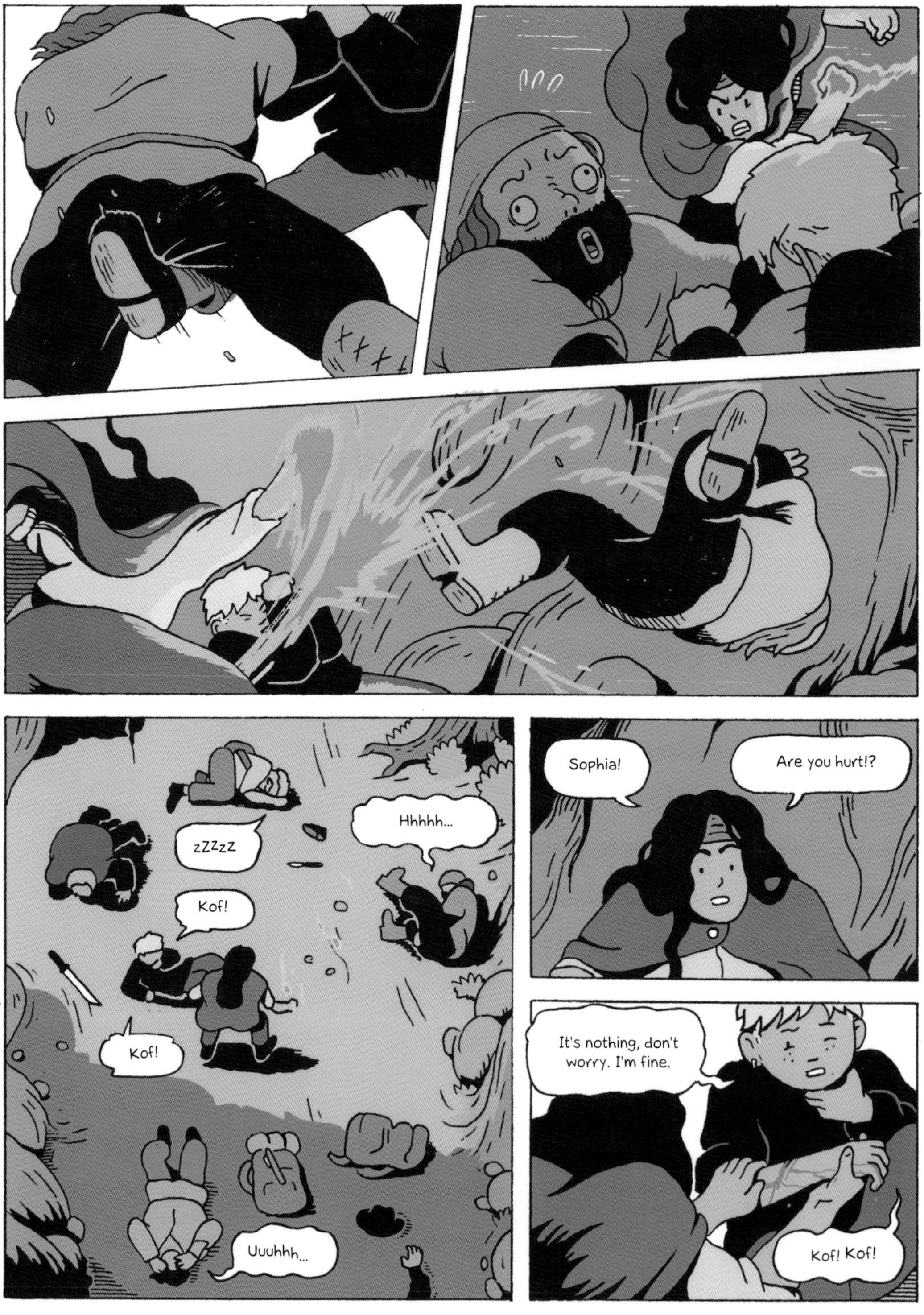
zZZzZ
Kof!
Hhhhh...
Kof!
Uuuhhh...
Sophia!
Are you hurt!?
It's nothing, don't worry. I'm fine.
Kof! Kof!

I should have something here.

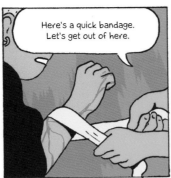

Here's a quick bandage. Let's get out of here.

Hey!

I've never seen pilgrims who know how to fight with breath control. You're not going east, are you? You're going north.

Poor fools...

Go ahead, throw yourself into the mouth of the wolf!

...

Hehehehe.

Maybe you'll see your loved one again, it's very likely.

But it won't be in this world! I hope you're ready for the afterlife!

Shut up...

Iris...

What's certain is that you'll freeze to death in the mountains!

SHUT IT!

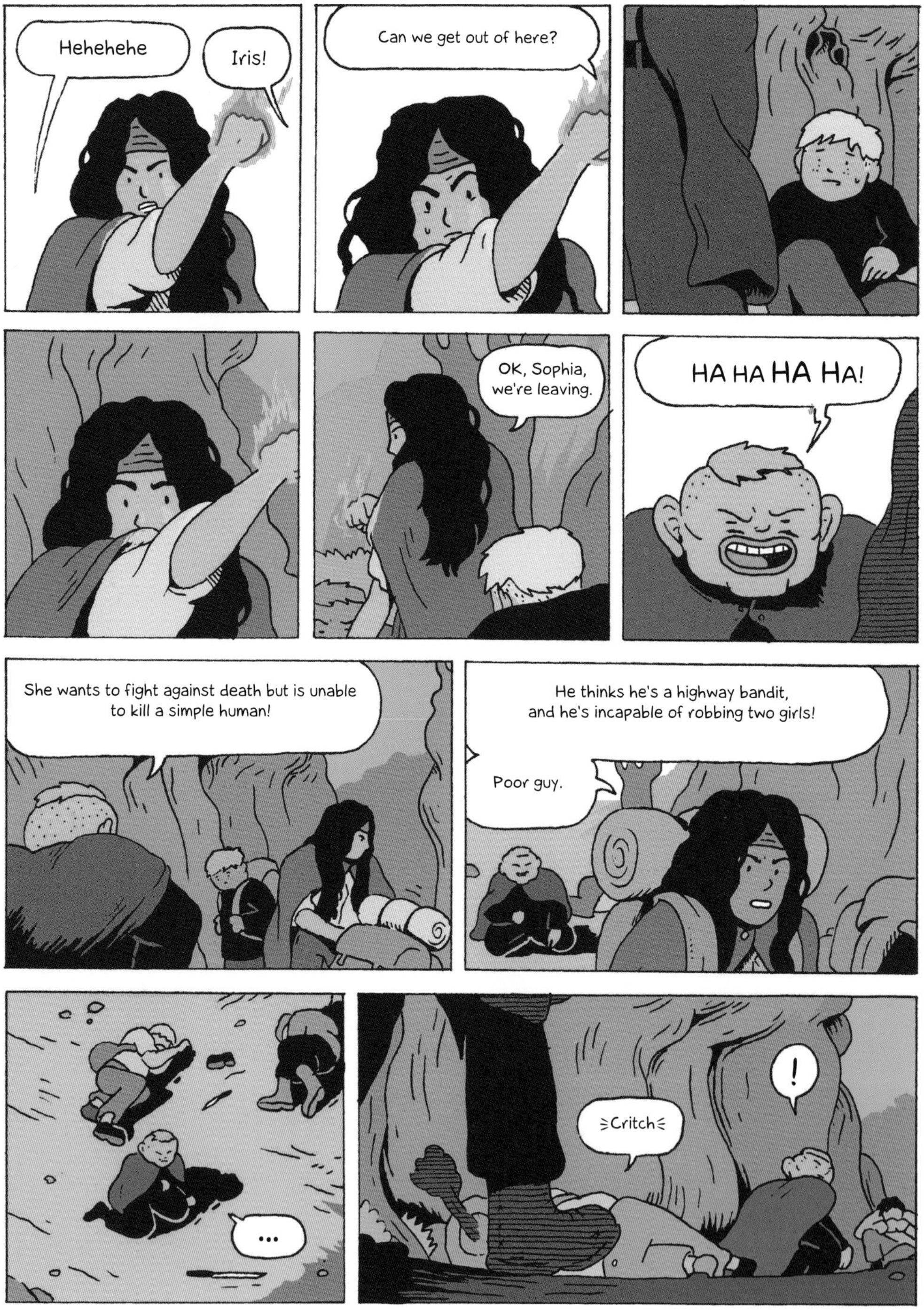
Hehehehe
Iris!
Can we get out of here?
OK, Sophia, we're leaving.
HA HA HA HA!
She wants to fight against death but is unable to kill a simple human!
He thinks he's a highway bandit, and he's incapable of robbing two girls!
Poor guy.
...
Critch
!

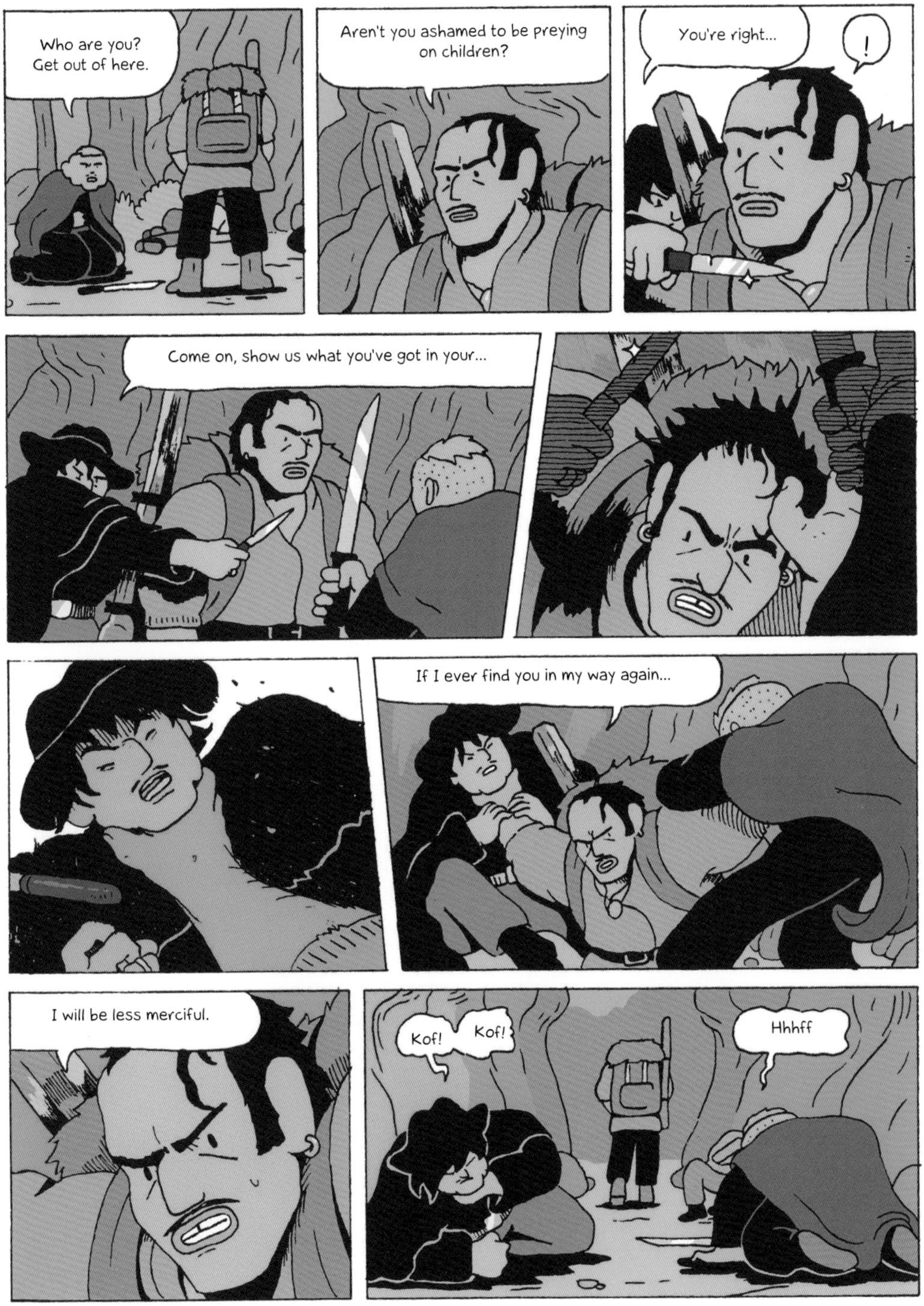
Who are you?
Get out of here.
Aren't you ashamed to be preying on children?
You're right...
!
Come on, show us what you've got in your...
If I ever find you in my way again...
I will be less merciful.
Kof!
Kof!
Hhhff

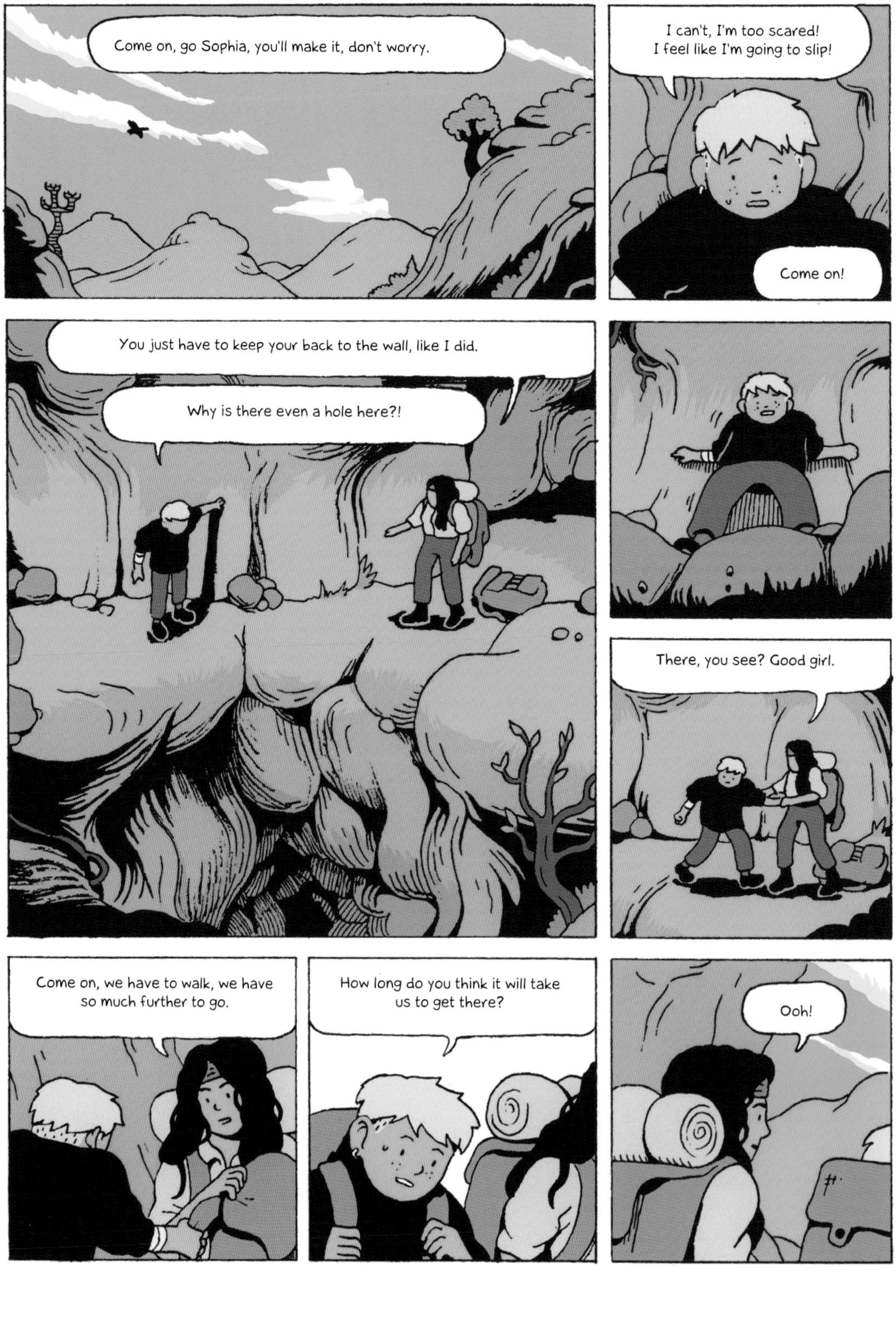
Come on, go Sophia, you'll make it, don't worry.
I can't, I'm too scared! I feel like I'm going to slip!
Come on!
You just have to keep your back to the wall, like I did.
Why is there even a hole here?!
There, you see? Good girl.
Come on, we have to walk, we have so much further to go.
How long do you think it will take us to get there?
Ooh!

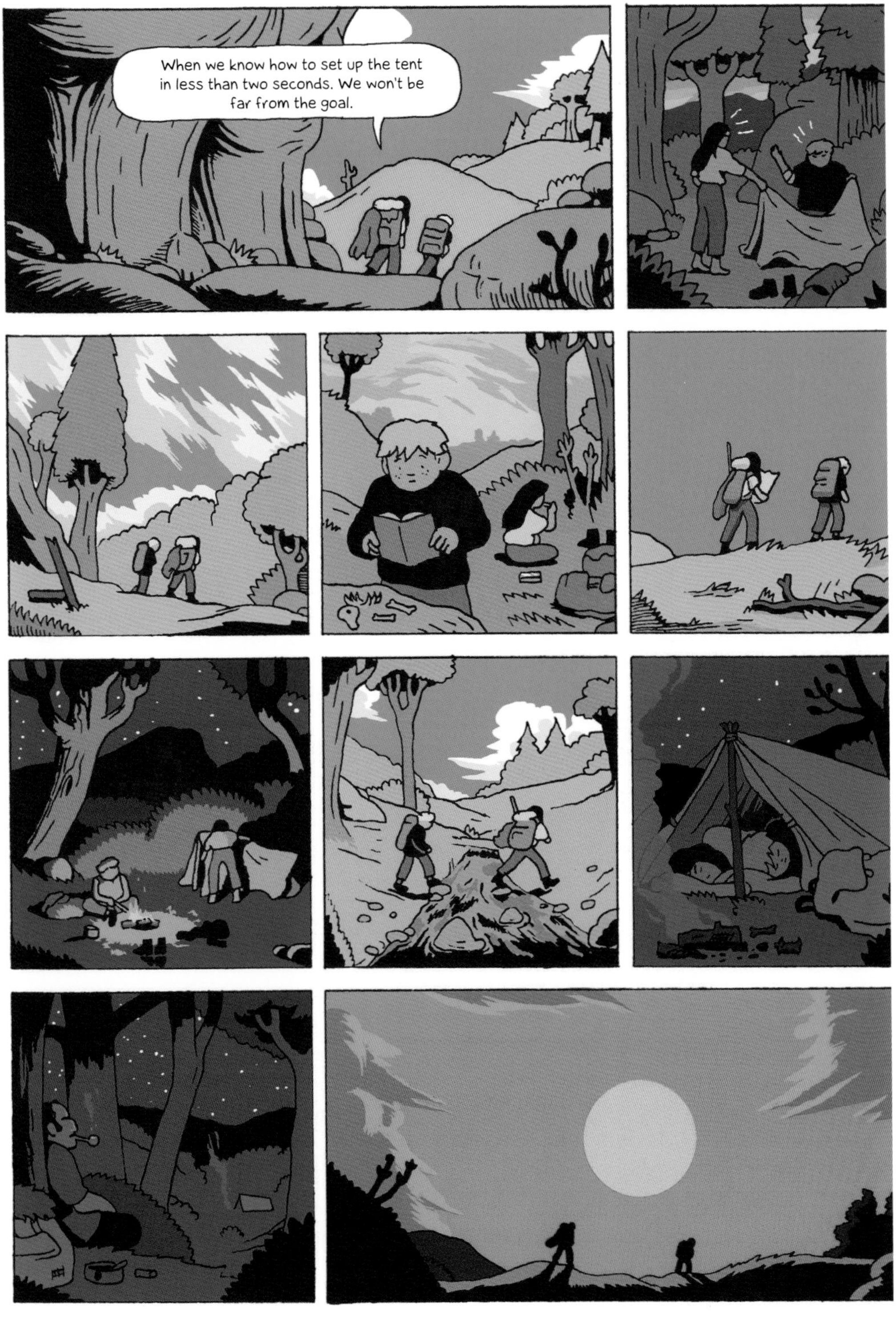
When we know how to set up the tent in less than two seconds. We won't be far from the goal.

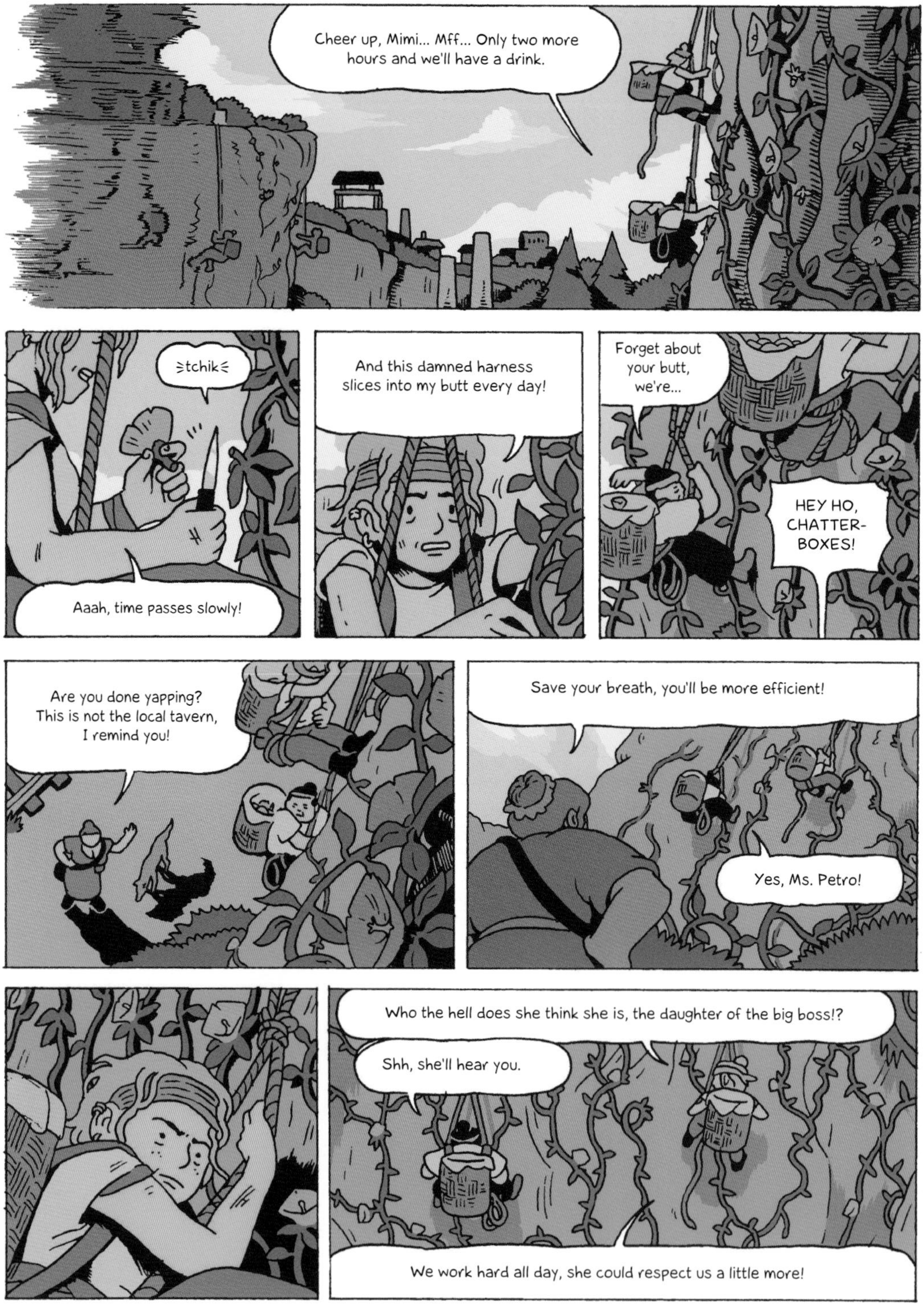
Cheer up, Mimi... Mff... Only two more hours and we'll have a drink.
≥tchik≤
Aaah, time passes slowly!
And this damned harness slices into my butt every day!
Forget about your butt, we're...
HEY HO, CHATTER-BOXES!
Are you done yapping? This is not the local tavern, I remind you!
Save your breath, you'll be more efficient!
Yes, Ms. Petro!
Who the hell does she think she is, the daughter of the big boss!?
Shh, she'll hear you.
We work hard all day, she could respect us a little more!

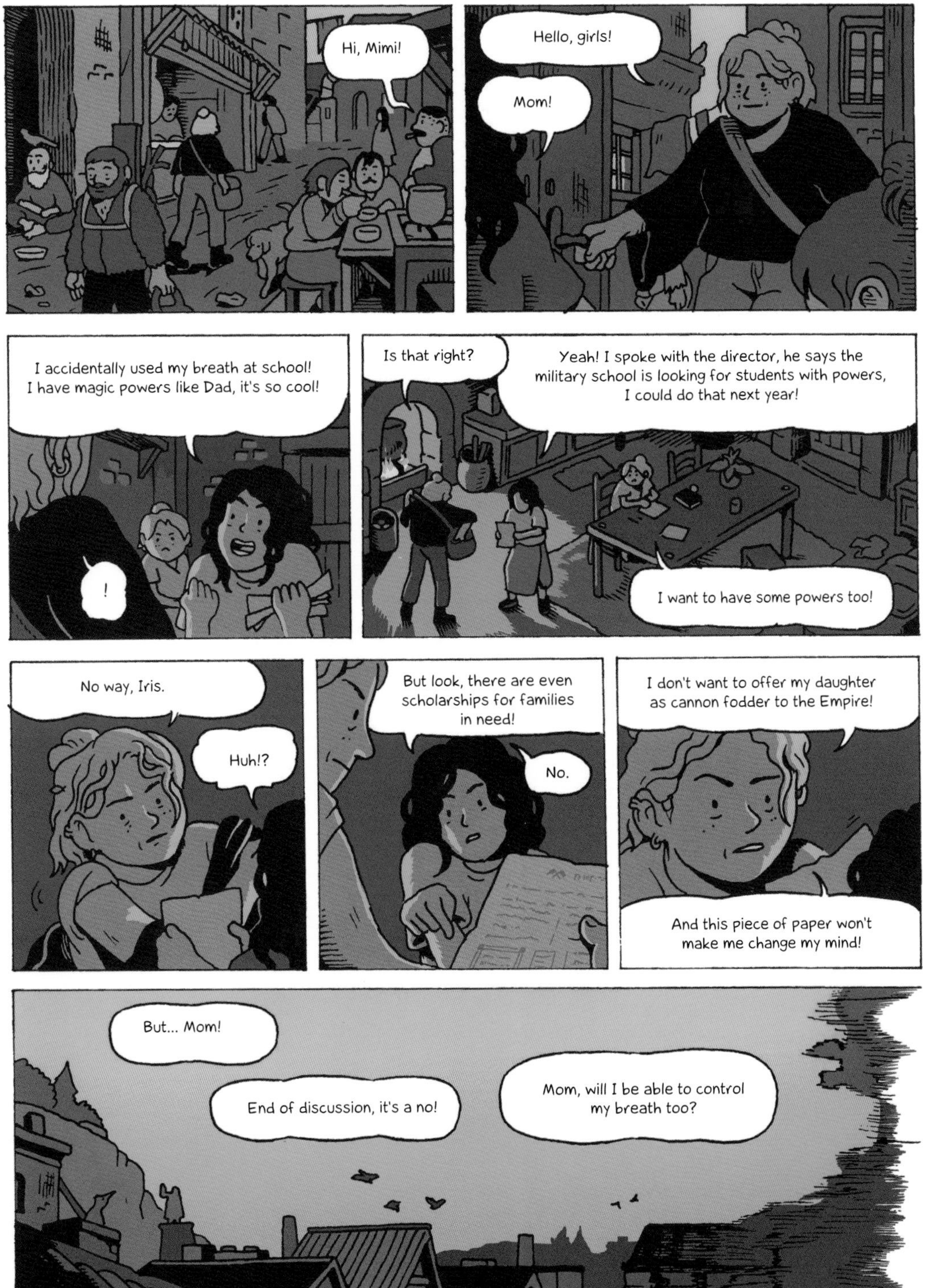
Hi, Mimi!
Hello, girls!
Mom!
I accidentally used my breath at school! I have magic powers like Dad, it's so cool!
!
Is that right?
Yeah! I spoke with the director, he says the military school is looking for students with powers, I could do that next year!
I want to have some powers too!
No way, Iris.
Huh!?
But look, there are even scholarships for families in need!
No.
I don't want to offer my daughter as cannon fodder to the Empire!
And this piece of paper won't make me change my mind!
But... Mom!
End of discussion, it's a no!
Mom, will I be able to control my breath too?

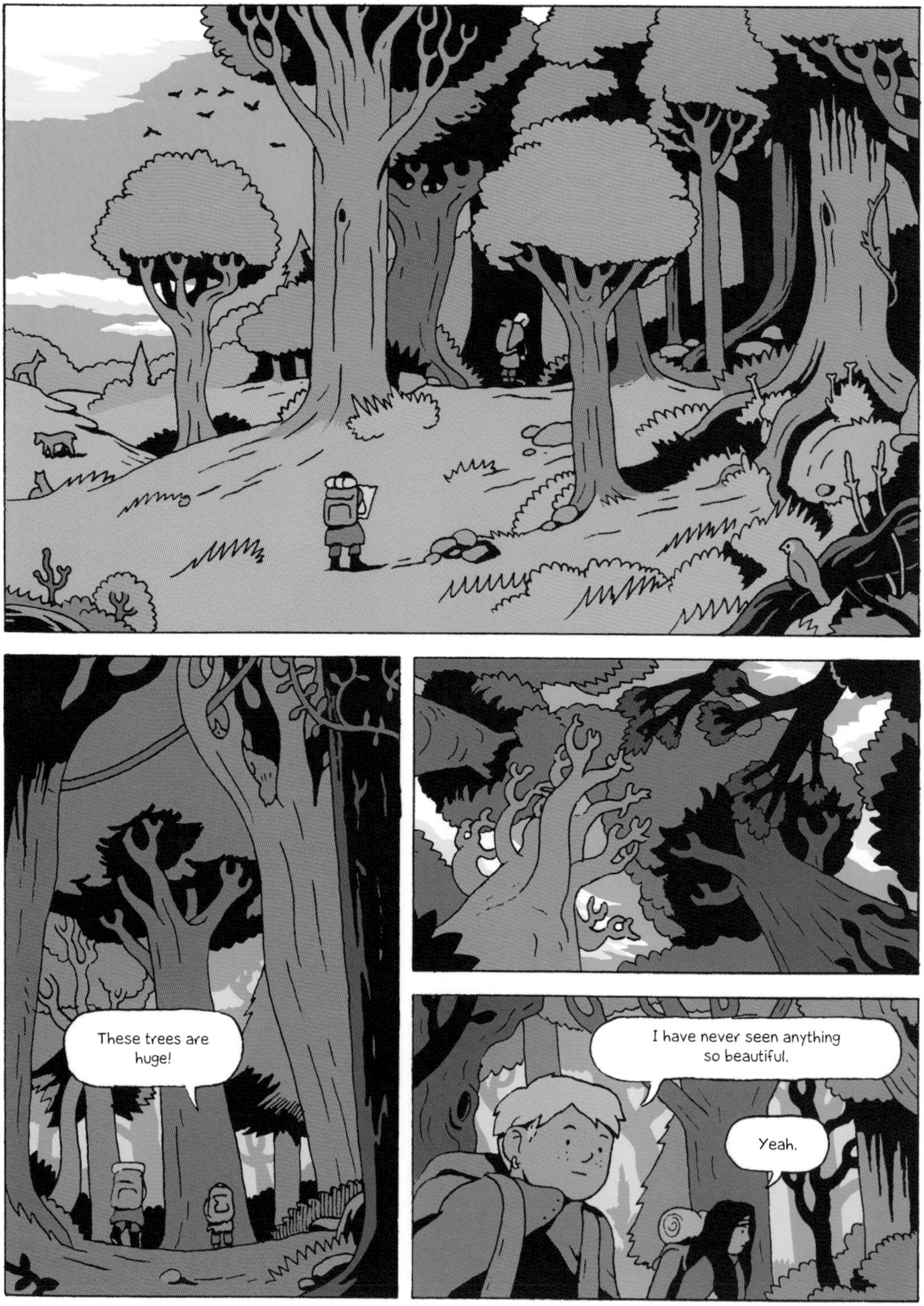
These trees are huge!
I have never seen anything so beautiful.
Yeah.

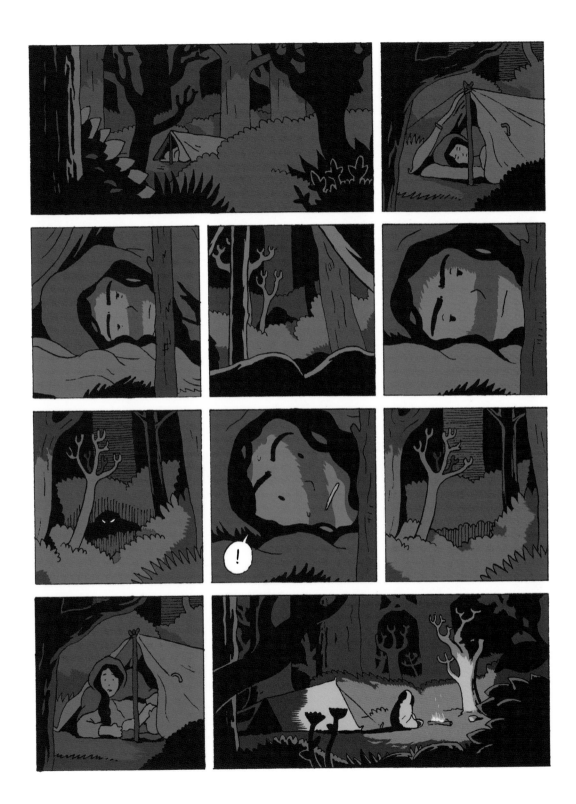

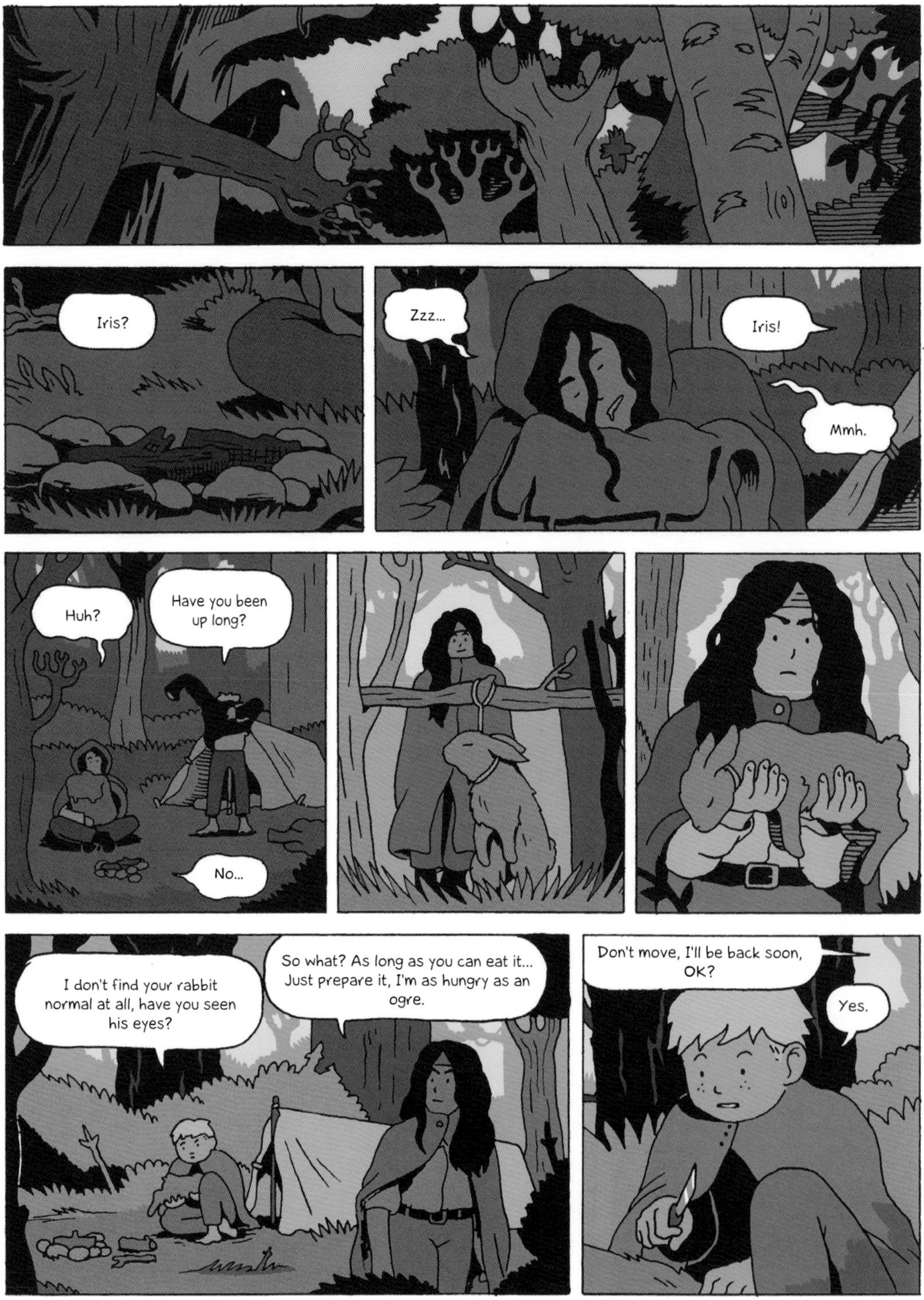
Iris?
Zzz...
Iris!
Mmh.
Huh?
Have you been up long?
No...
I don't find your rabbit normal at all, have you seen his eyes?
So what? As long as you can eat it... Just prepare it, I'm as hungry as an ogre.
Don't move, I'll be back soon, OK?
Yes.

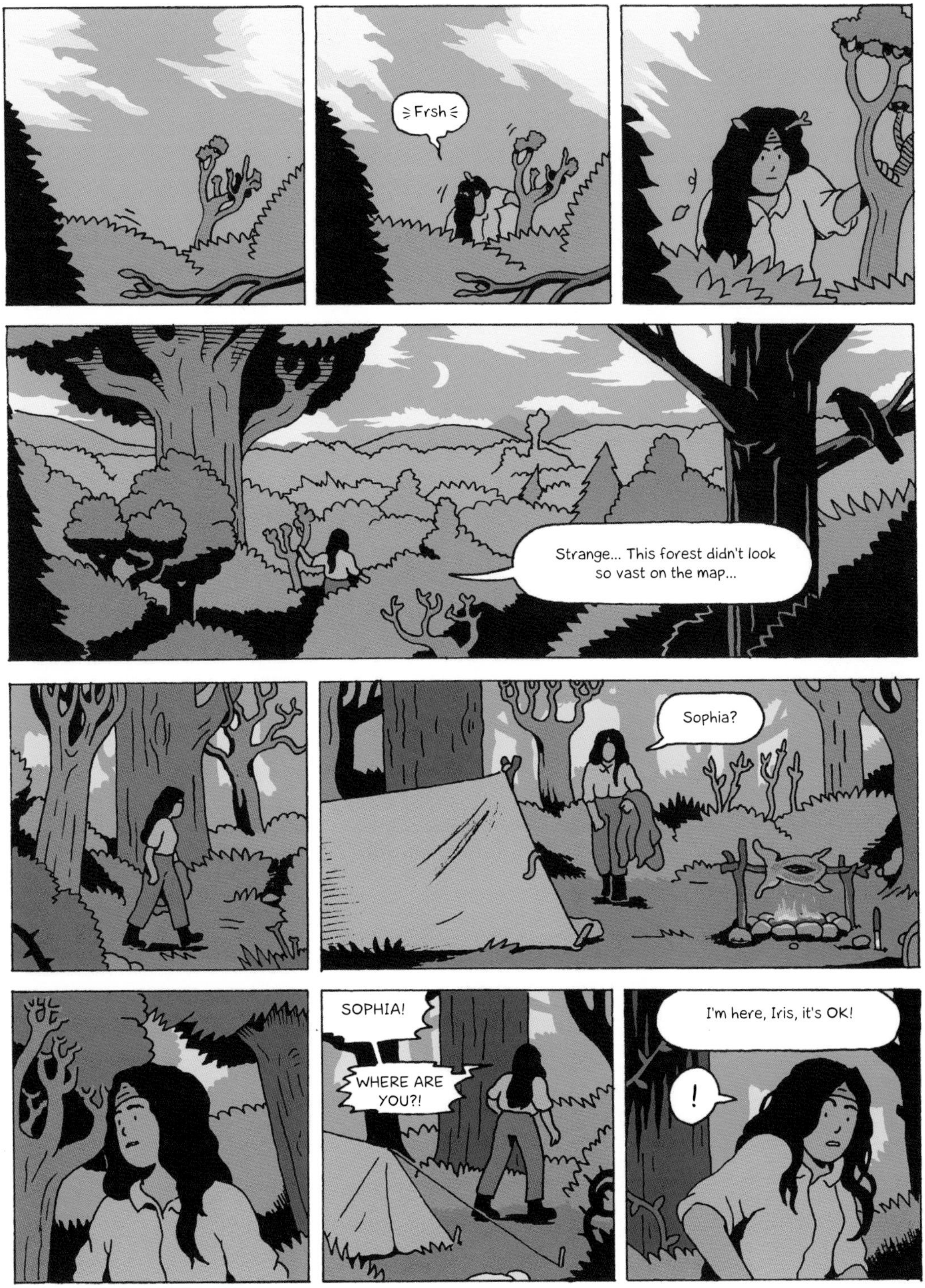
Frsh
Strange... This forest didn't look so vast on the map...
Sophia?
SOPHIA!
WHERE ARE YOU?!
I'm here, Iris, it's OK!
!

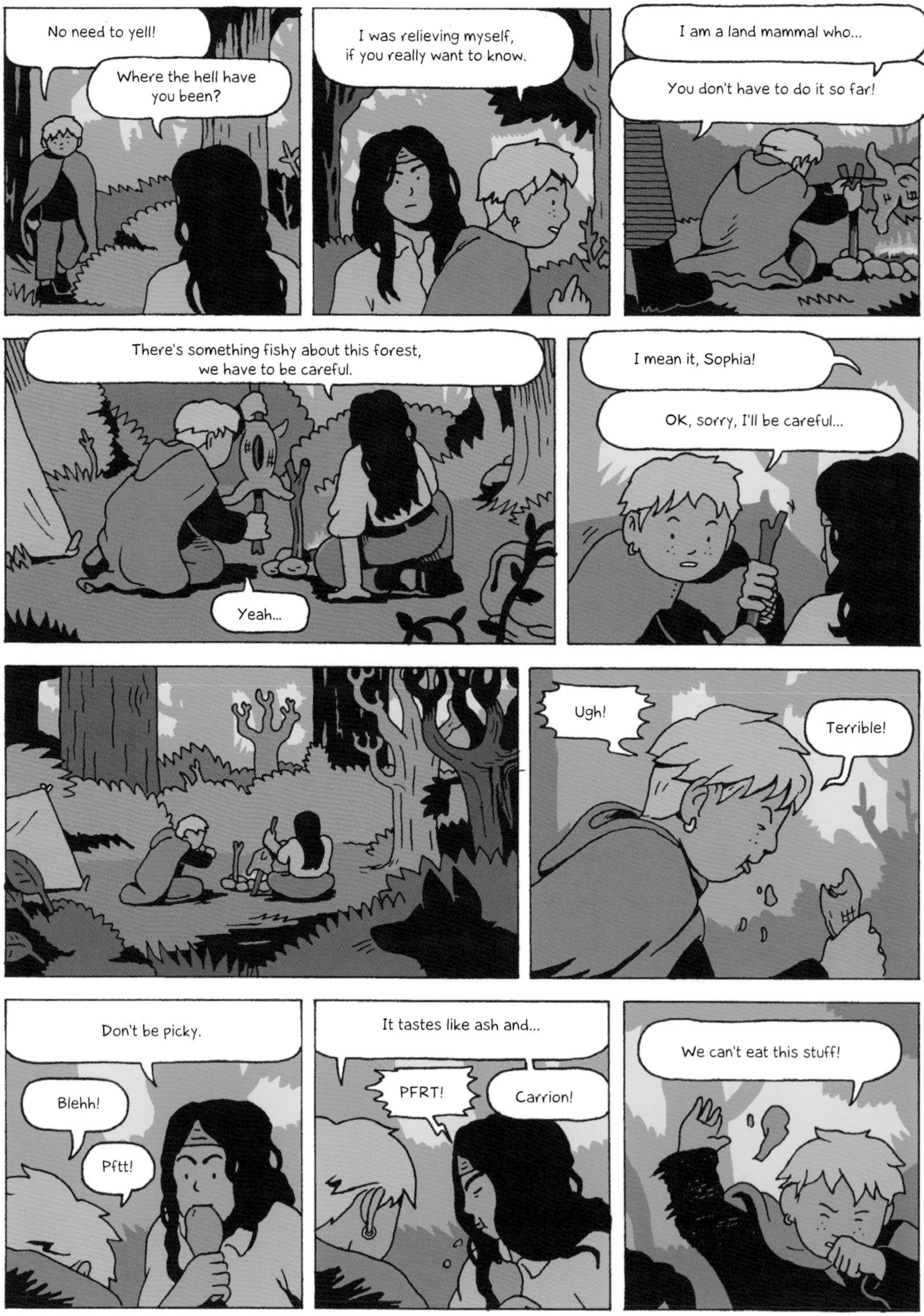

No need to yell!
Where the hell have you been?
I was relieving myself, if you really want to know.
I am a land mammal who...
You don't have to do it so far!
There's something fishy about this forest, we have to be careful.
Yeah...
I mean it, Sophia!
OK, sorry, I'll be careful...
Ugh!
Terrible!
Don't be picky.
Blehh!
Pftt!
It tastes like ash and...
PFRT!
Carrion!
We can't eat this stuff!

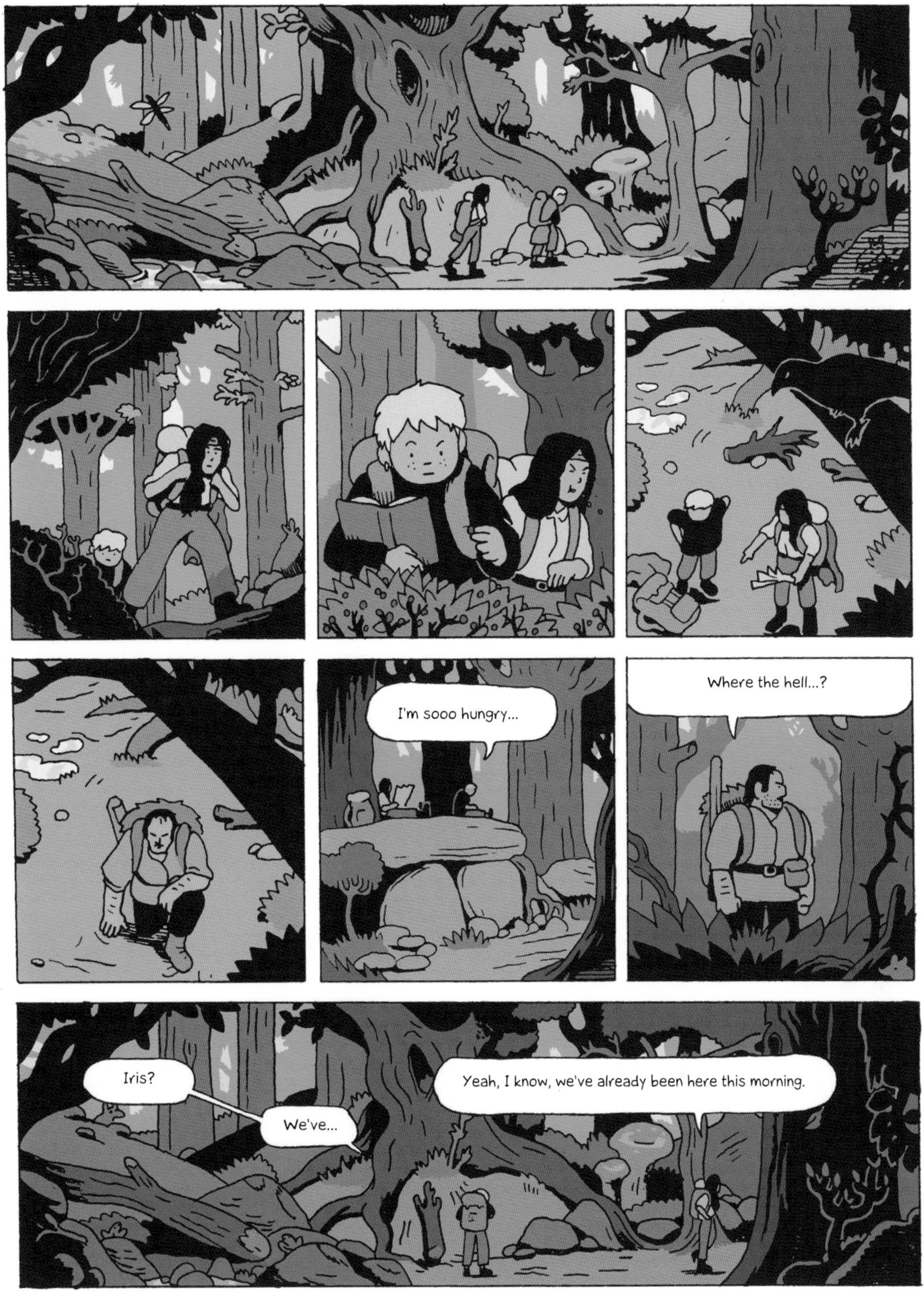
I'm sooo hungry...
Where the hell...?
Iris?
We've...
Yeah, I know, we've already been here this morning.

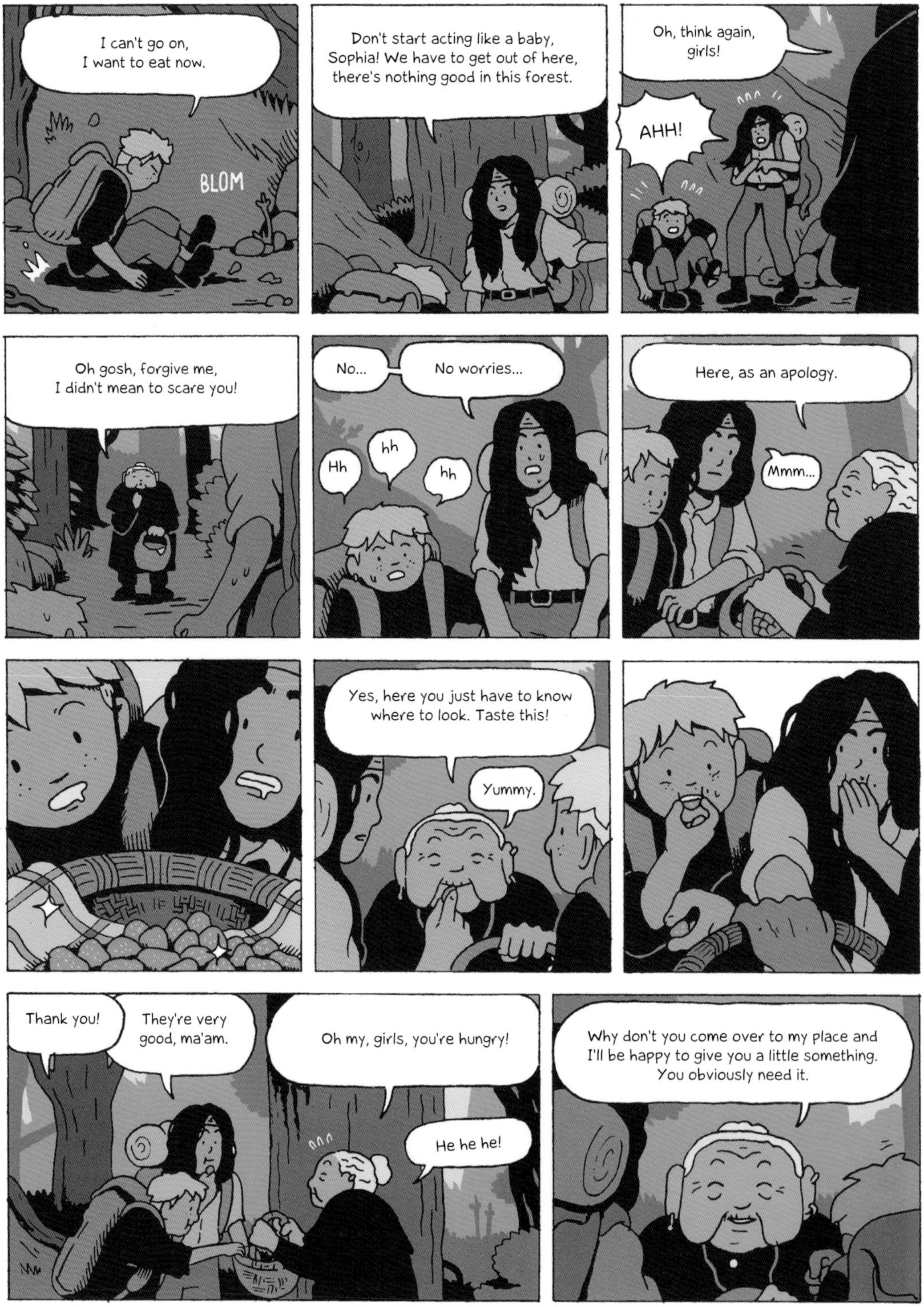
I can't go on,
I want to eat now.
BLOM
Don't start acting like a baby, Sophia! We have to get out of here, there's nothing good in this forest.
Oh, think again, girls!
AHH!
Oh gosh, forgive me, I didn't mean to scare you!
No...
No worries...
Hh
hh
hh
Here, as an apology.
Mmm...
Yes, here you just have to know where to look. Taste this!
Yummy.
Thank you!
They're very good, ma'am.
Oh my, girls, you're hungry!
He he he!
Why don't you come over to my place and I'll be happy to give you a little something. You obviously need it.

Save some space, it's only the appetizer!

It's delicious, Mrs. Mel, thank you!

Yes, thanks but...

Tut tut tut tut, young lady!

No "but." At your age, it's important to eat well!

Besides, you are not going to take away my joy of welcoming and sharing a little chat with you!

I live alone here. A few travelers pass by from time to time, but it's still quite rare.

It must be said that beyond this forest, there is nothing more. Except for the Northern Lands and the legends that surround them.

And I imagine that you are not here for the pleasure of visiting the region either, are you?

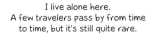

We are on a pilgrimage. We are going to the Holy Lands of the East.

Come on...

How about that! You're passing through here on your way to the East? Come on, come on... What's the point of hiding the truth from me?

I may be a little old, but not yet gone!

CLONK

Mrs. Mel, the Giants...

Have you seen them before?

You know, my girls, there are a lot of myths about this.

From gossip, exaggerations or lies.

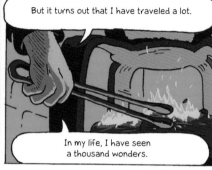

But it turns out that I have traveled a lot.

In my life, I have seen a thousand wonders.

The Giants are one of them.

Like all these travelers, you want to see a deceased loved one again, don't you?

If you tell me your story, I will tell you about the Giants.

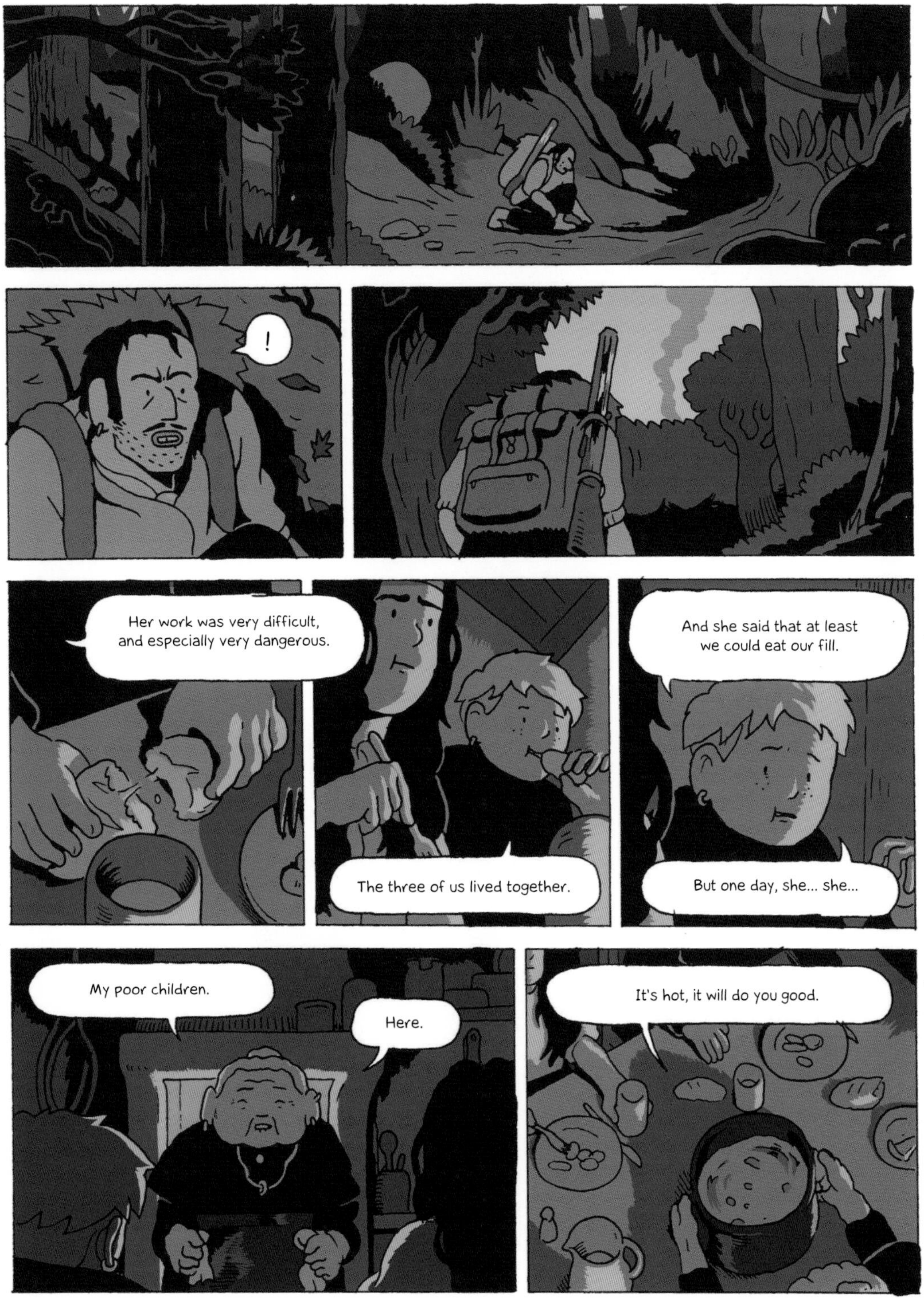
!
Her work was very difficult, and especially very dangerous.
The three of us lived together.
And she said that at least we could eat our fill.
But one day, she... she...
My poor children.
Here.
It's hot, it will do you good.

Fresh pasta!

What's next, fatty?

I work harder than you do and I have to make your lunch on the way home?

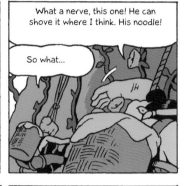

What a nerve, this one! He can shove it where I think. His noodle!

So what...

... maybe it's not so bad that mine is gone!

zip

You bet! Leaving you alone with two kids to look for Giants that never existed...

≥ krk ≤

At least mine is still here...

Oh!

!

Damn it...

Did you slip!?

The rope!

Quick! Grab onto what you can, I'm coming to help you!

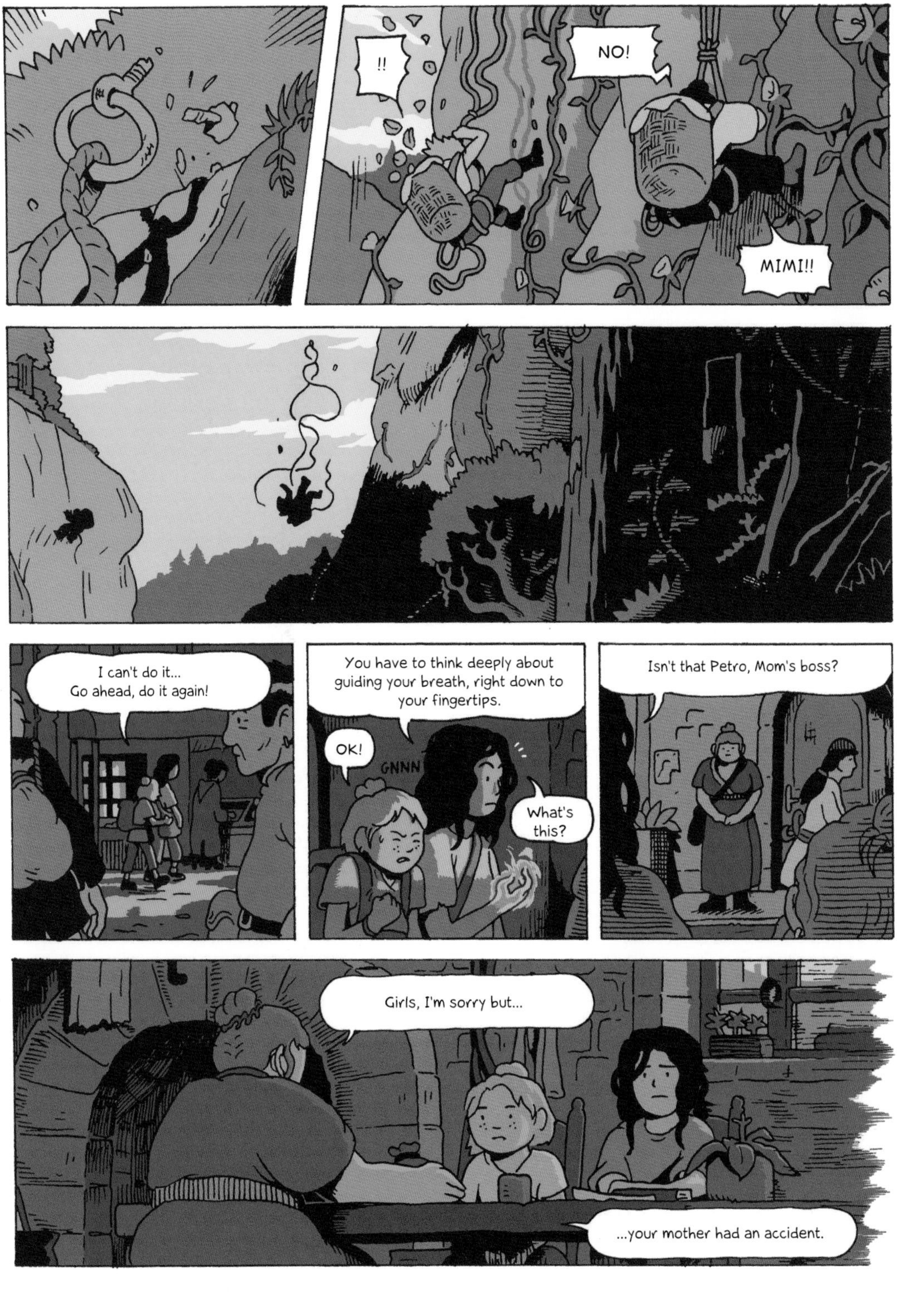
!!
NO!
MIMI!!
I can't do it...
Go ahead, do it again!
You have to think deeply about guiding your breath, right down to your fingertips.
OK!
GNNN
What's this?
Isn't that Petro, Mom's boss?
Girls, I'm sorry but...
...your mother had an accident.

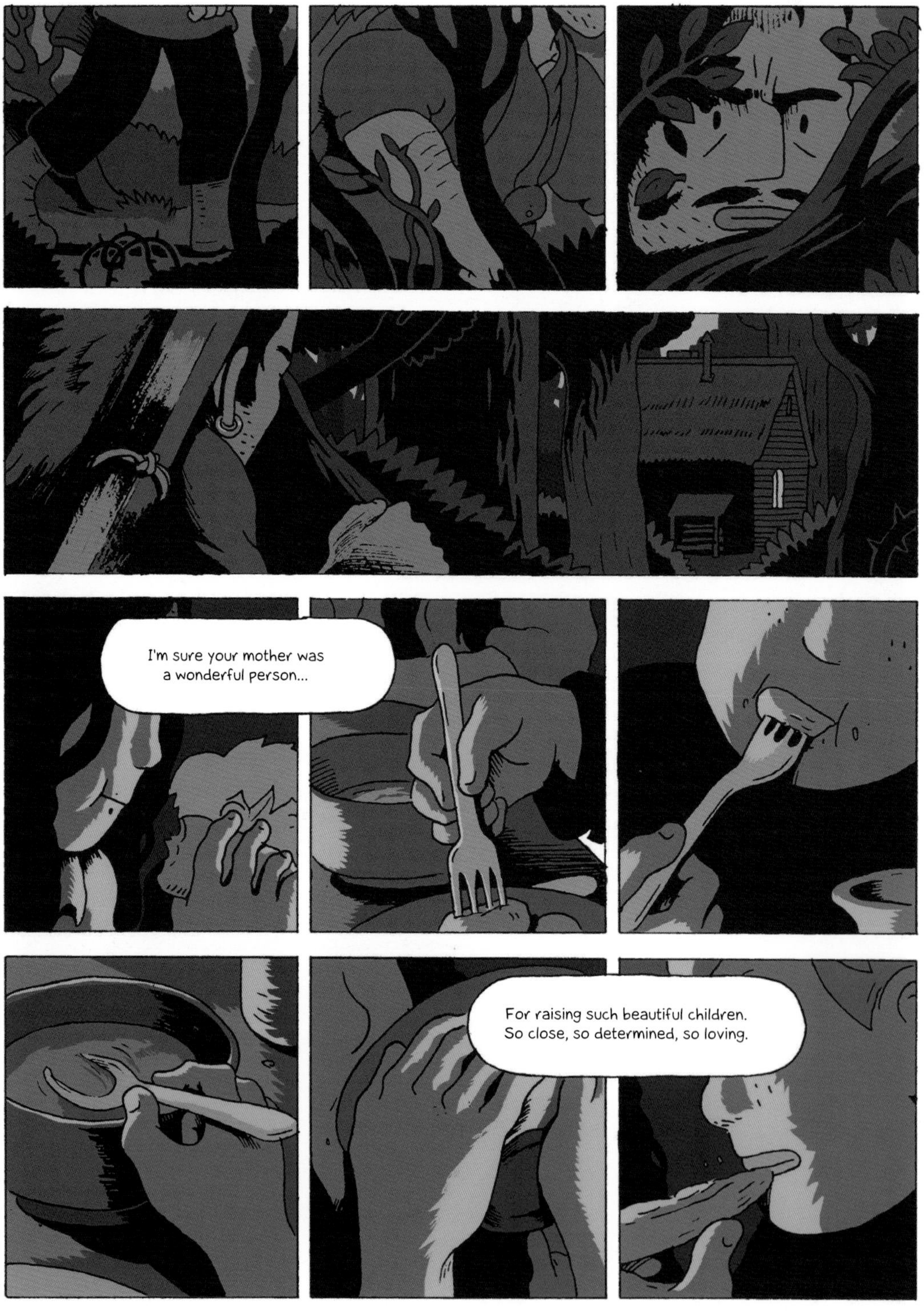
I'm sure your mother was a wonderful person...
For raising such beautiful children. So close, so determined, so loving.

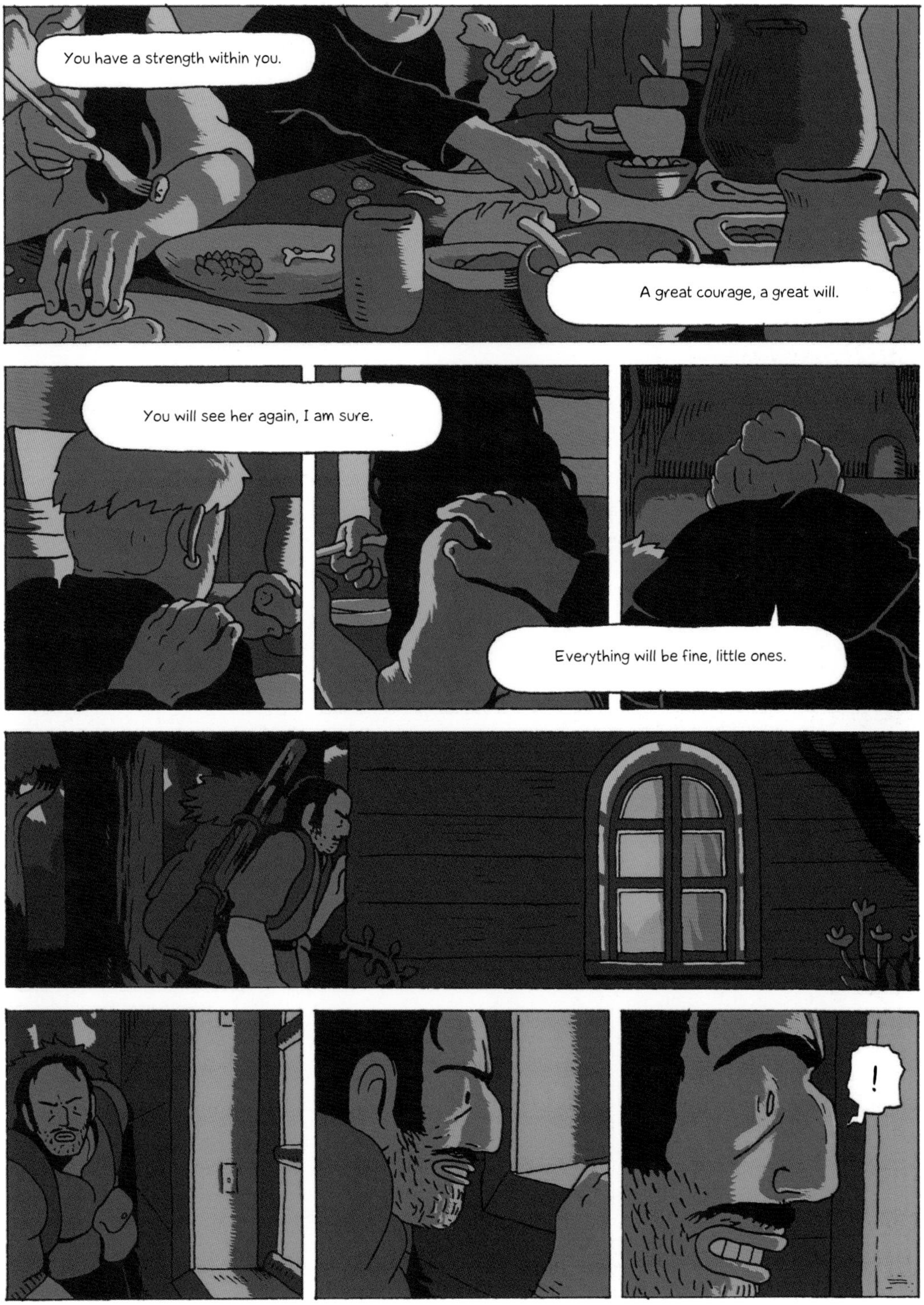
You have a strength within you.
A great courage, a great will.
You will see her again, I am sure.
Everything will be fine, little ones.
!

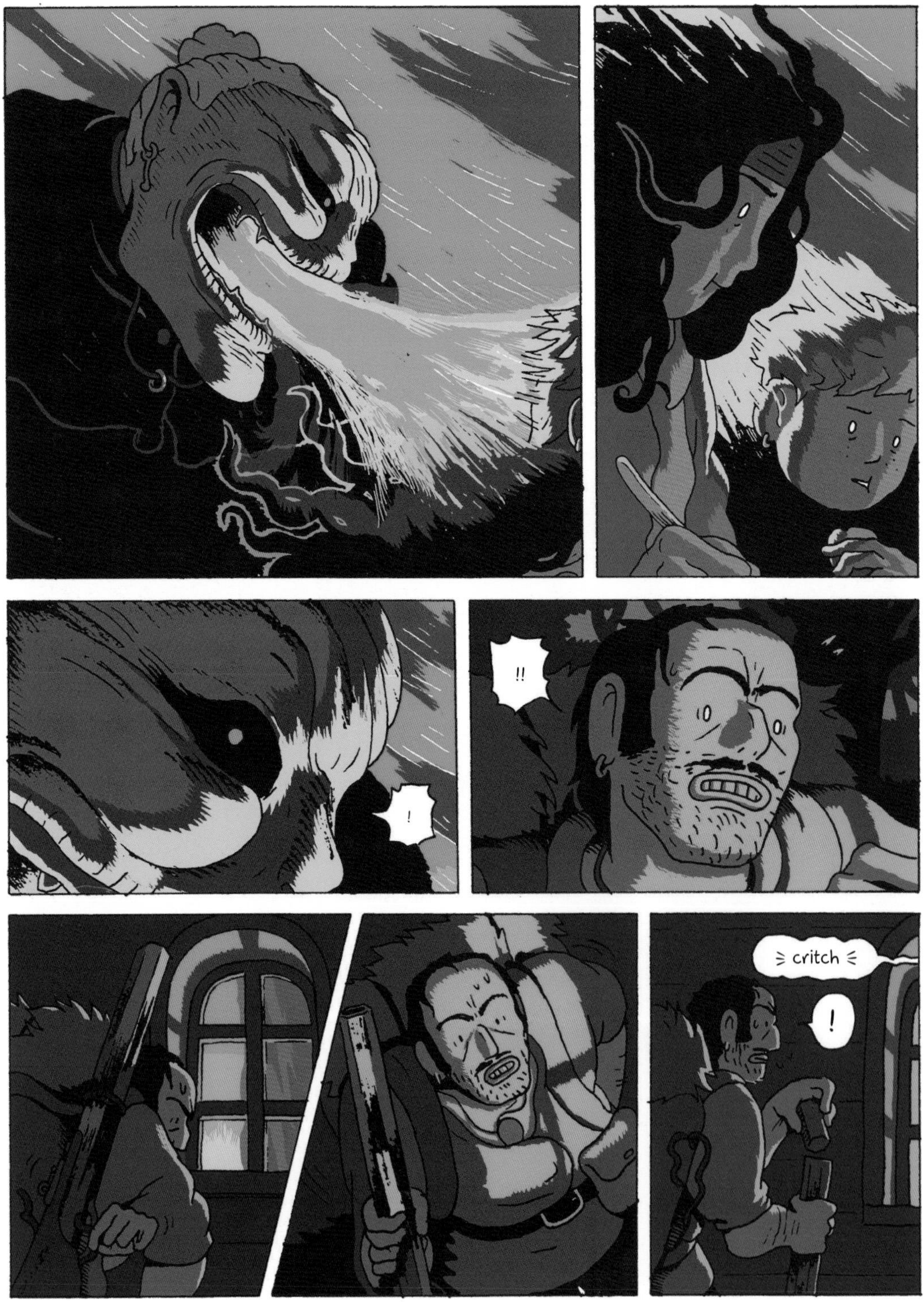

!
!!
critch
!

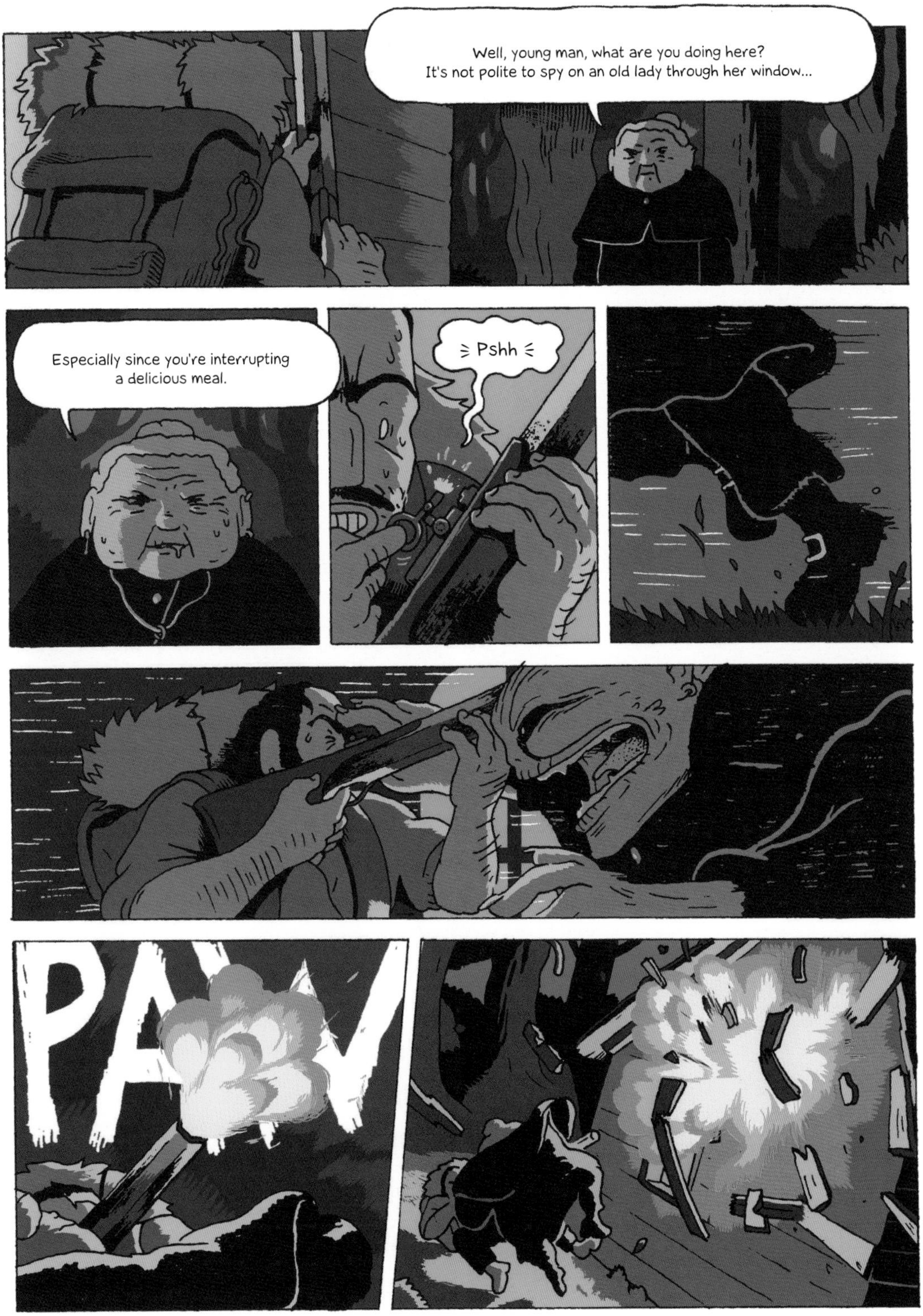

Well, young man, what are you doing here? It's not polite to spy on an old lady through her window...
Especially since you're interrupting a delicious meal.
Pshh
PAW

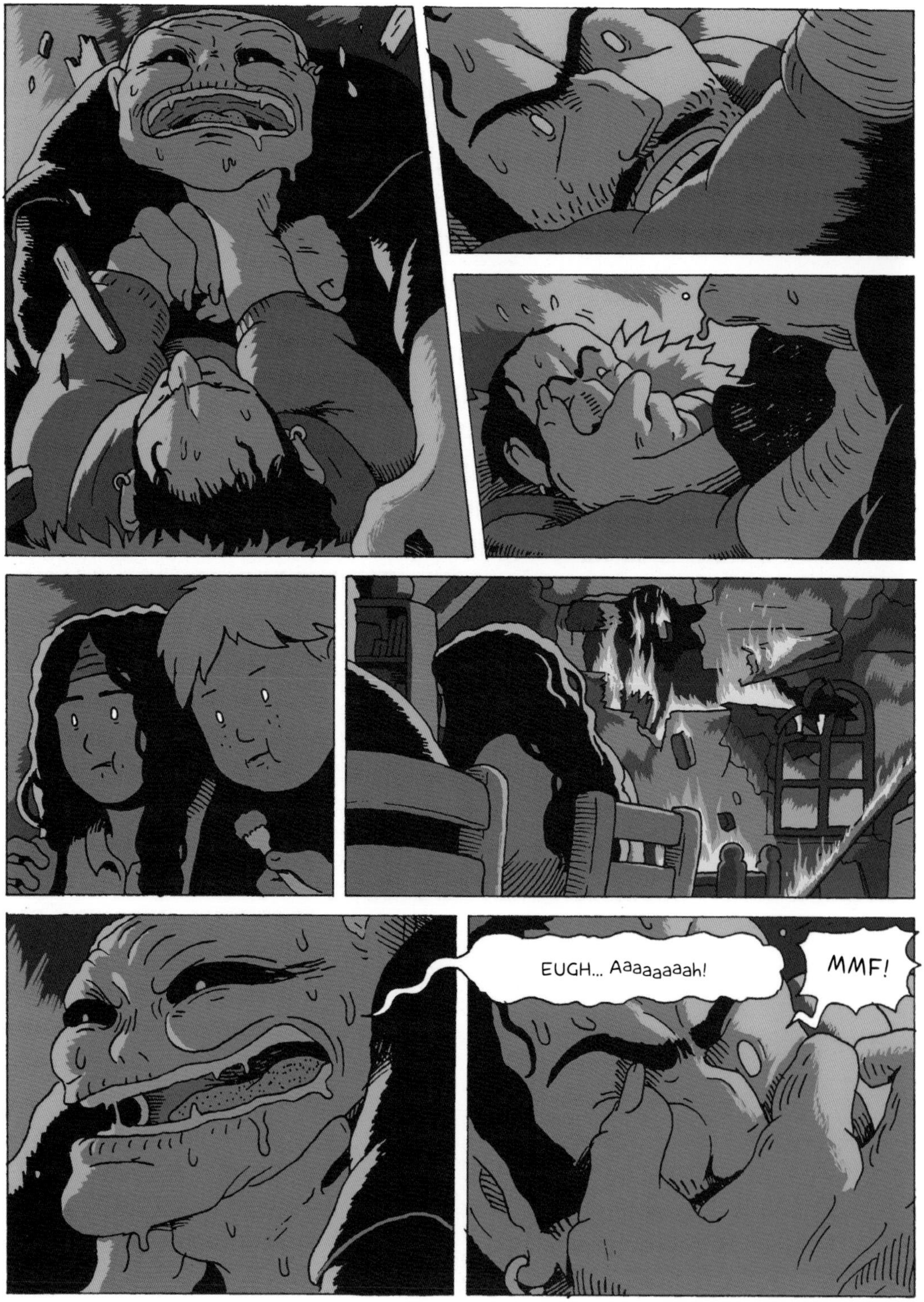
EUGH... Aaaaaaaah!
MMF!

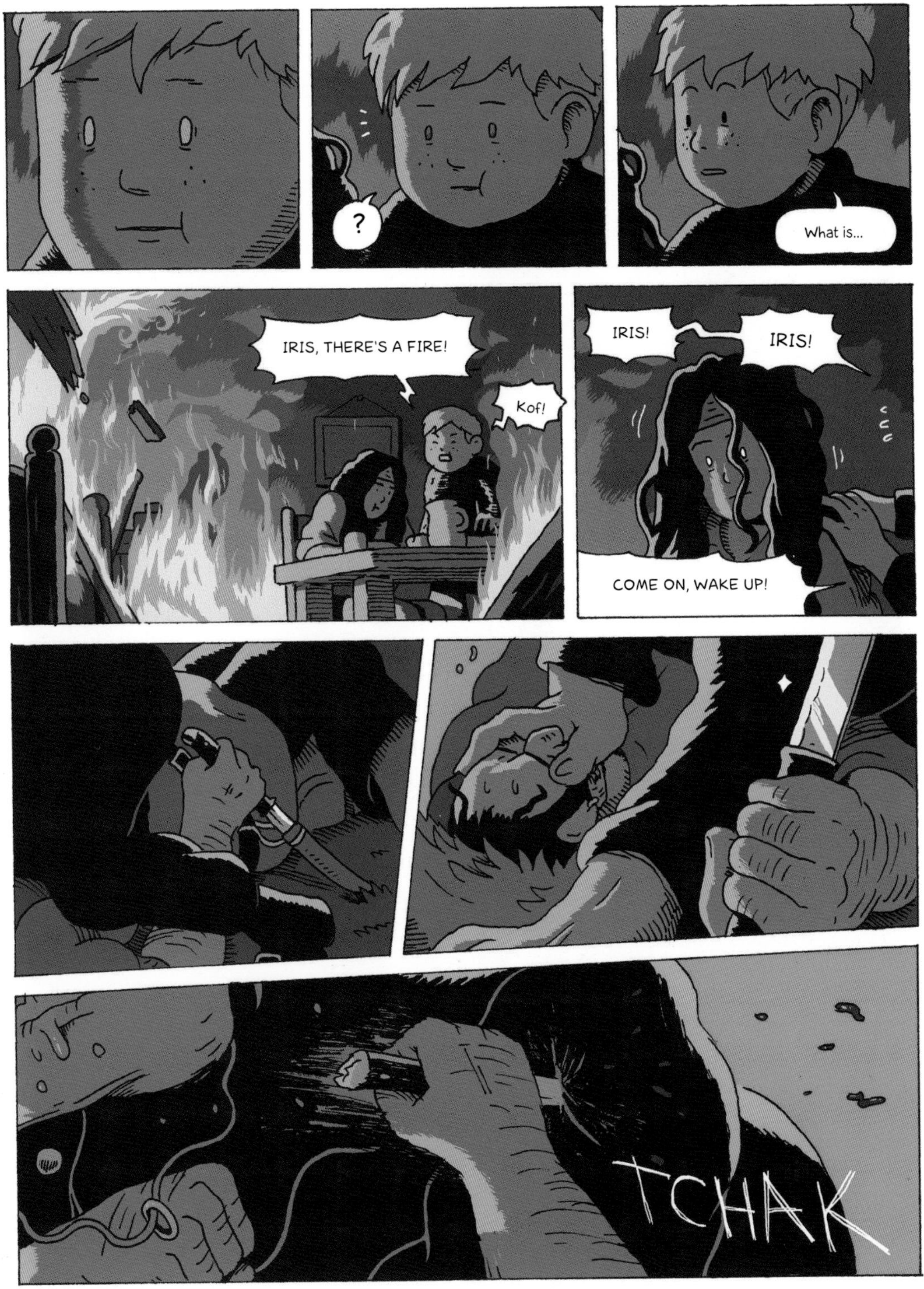

?
What is...
IRIS, THERE'S A FIRE!
Kof!
IRIS!
IRIS!
COME ON, WAKE UP!
TCHAK

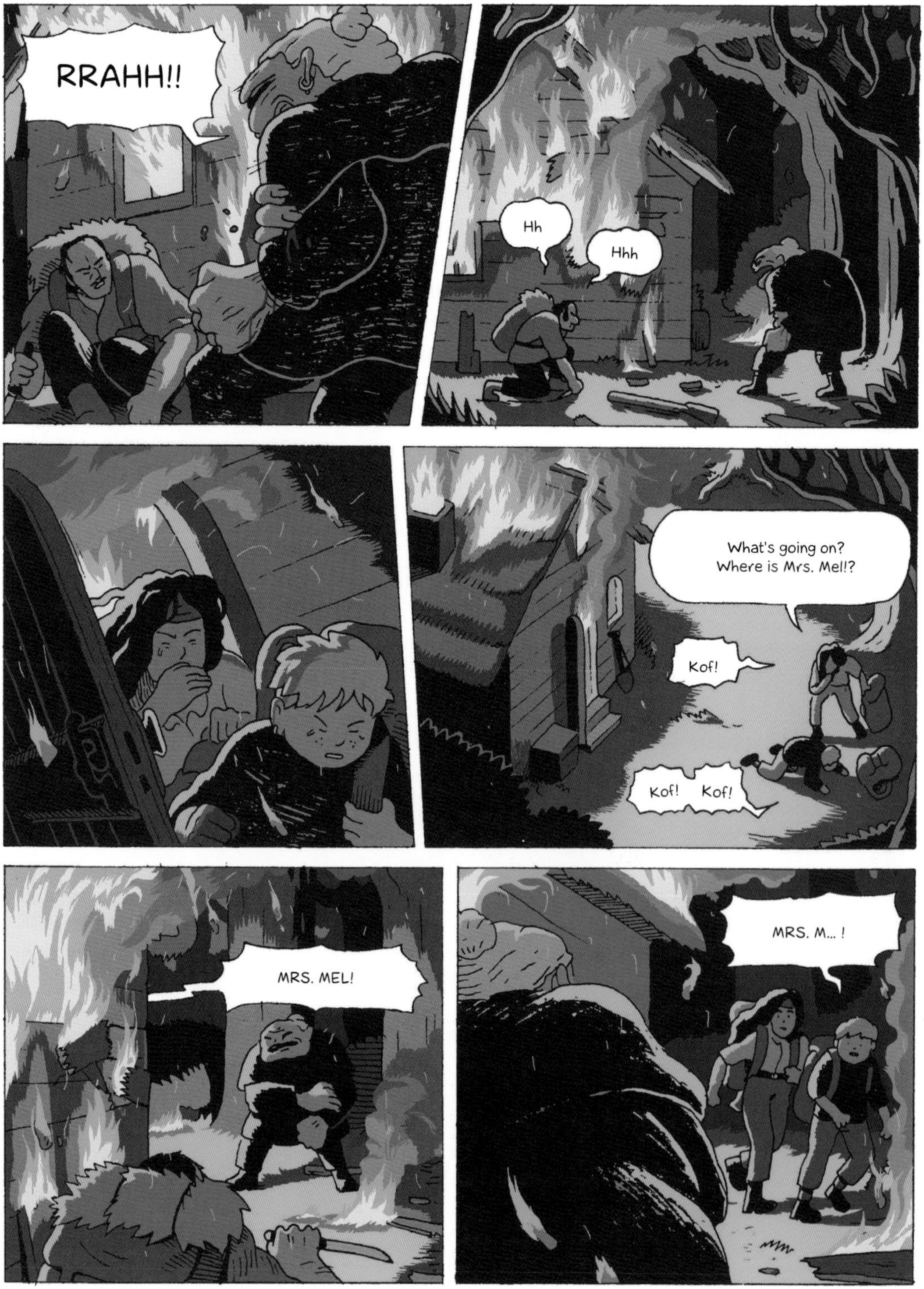
RRAHH!!
Hh
Hhh
What's going on?
Where is Mrs. Mel!?
Kof!
Kof! Kof!
MRS. MEL!
MRS. M... !

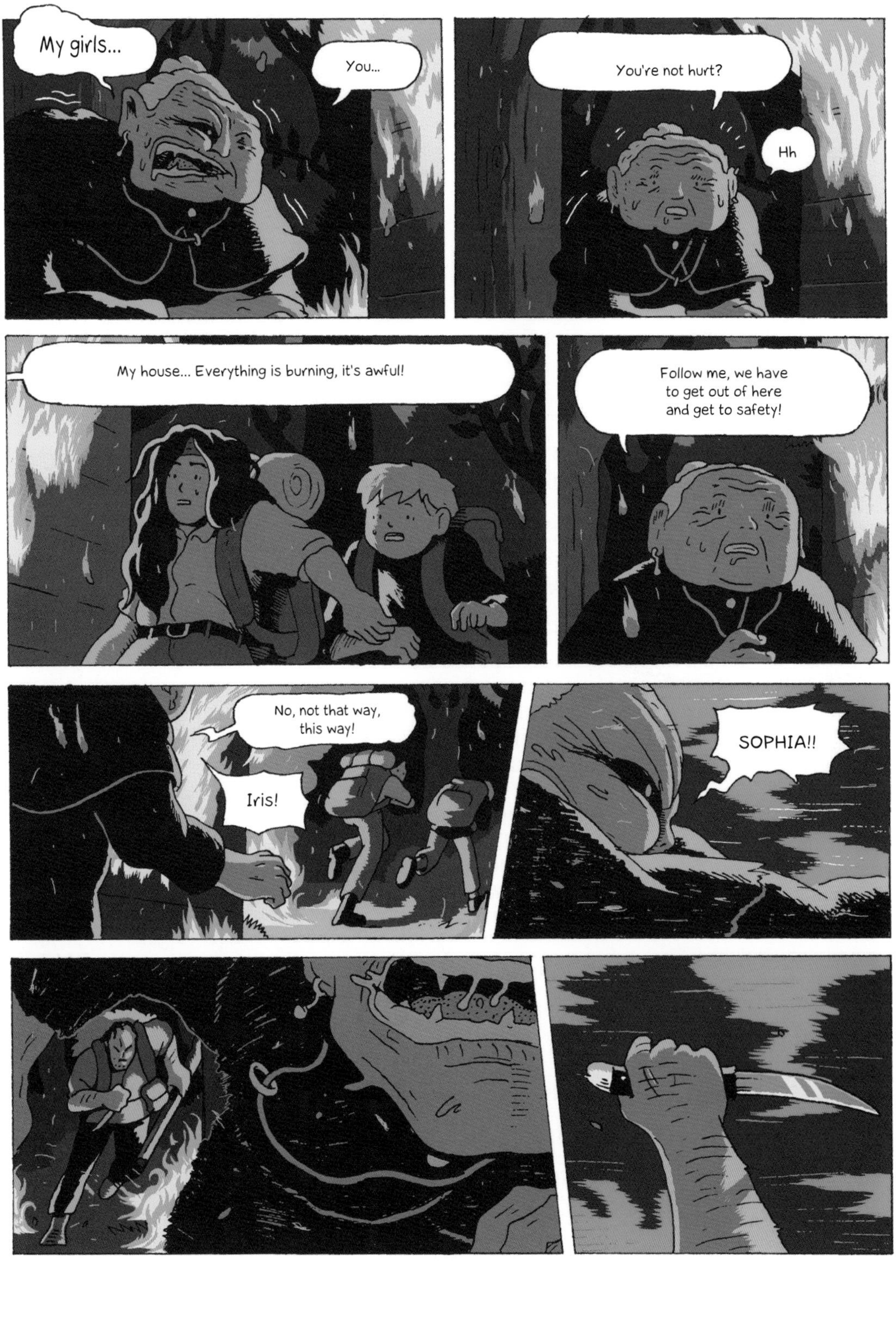
My girls...
You...
You're not hurt?
Hh
My house... Everything is burning, it's awful!
Follow me, we have to get out of here and get to safety!
No, not that way, this way!
Iris!
SOPHIA!!

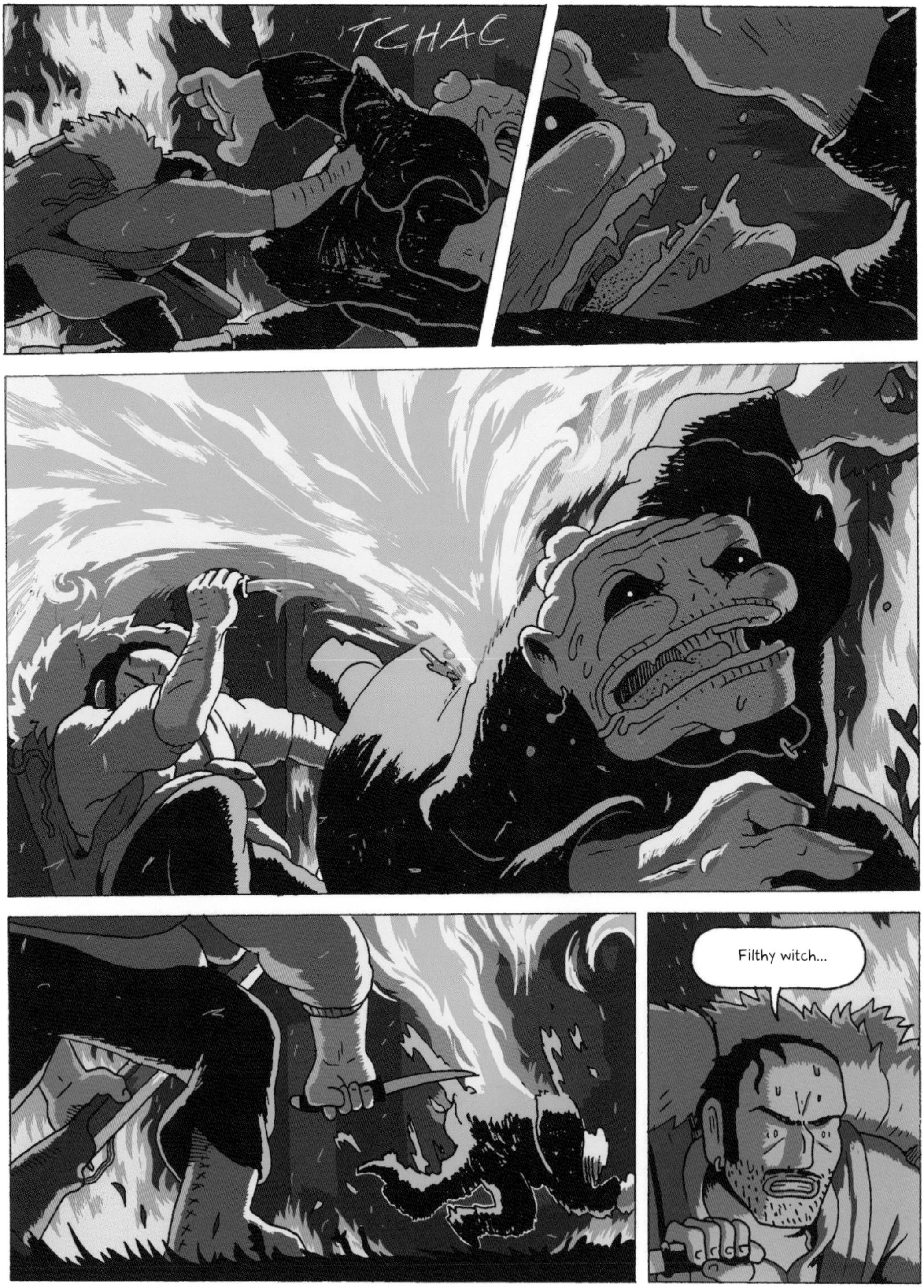
TCHAC
Filthy witch...

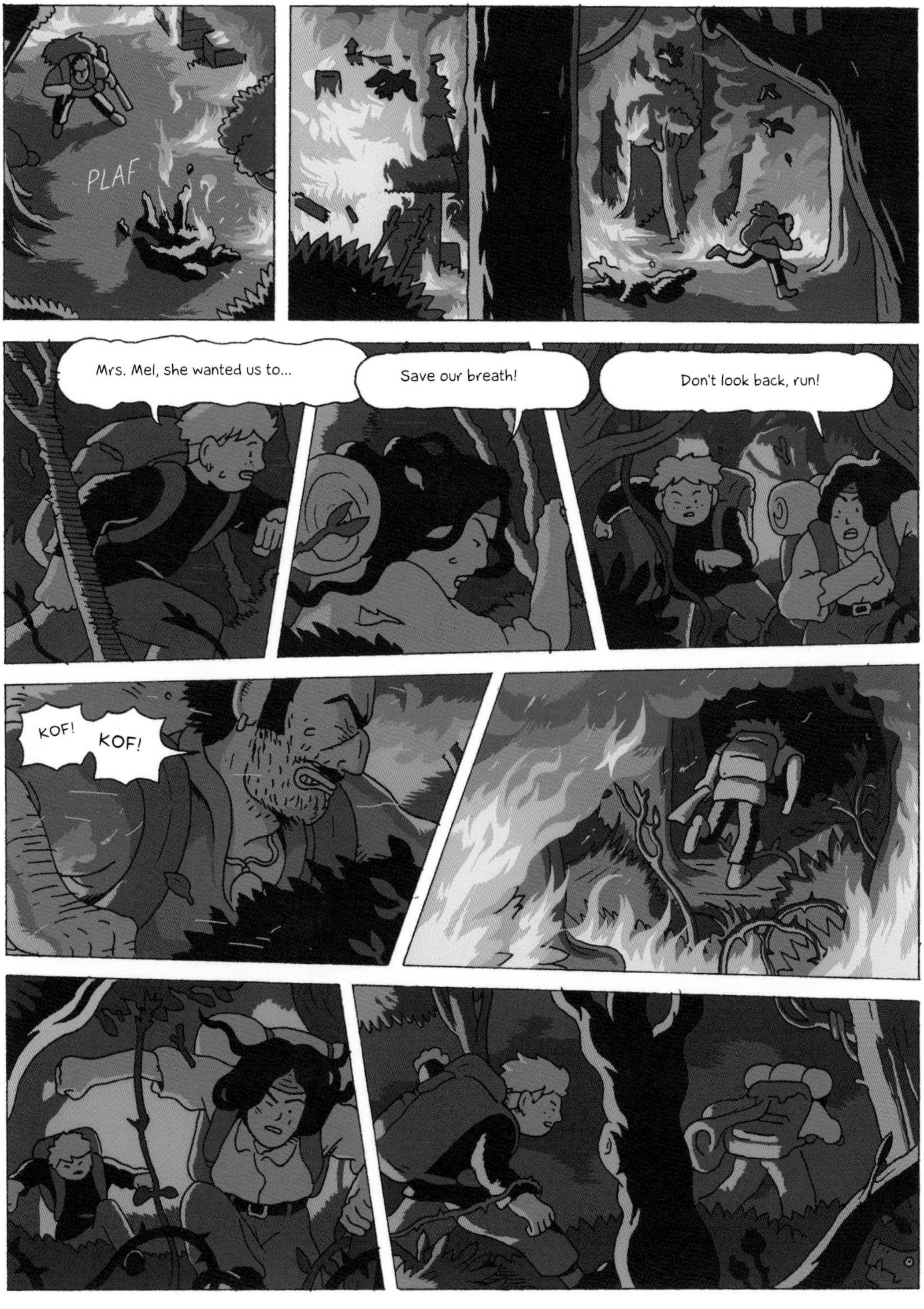
PLAF
Mrs. Mel, she wanted us to...
Save our breath!
Don't look back, run!
KOF!
KOF!

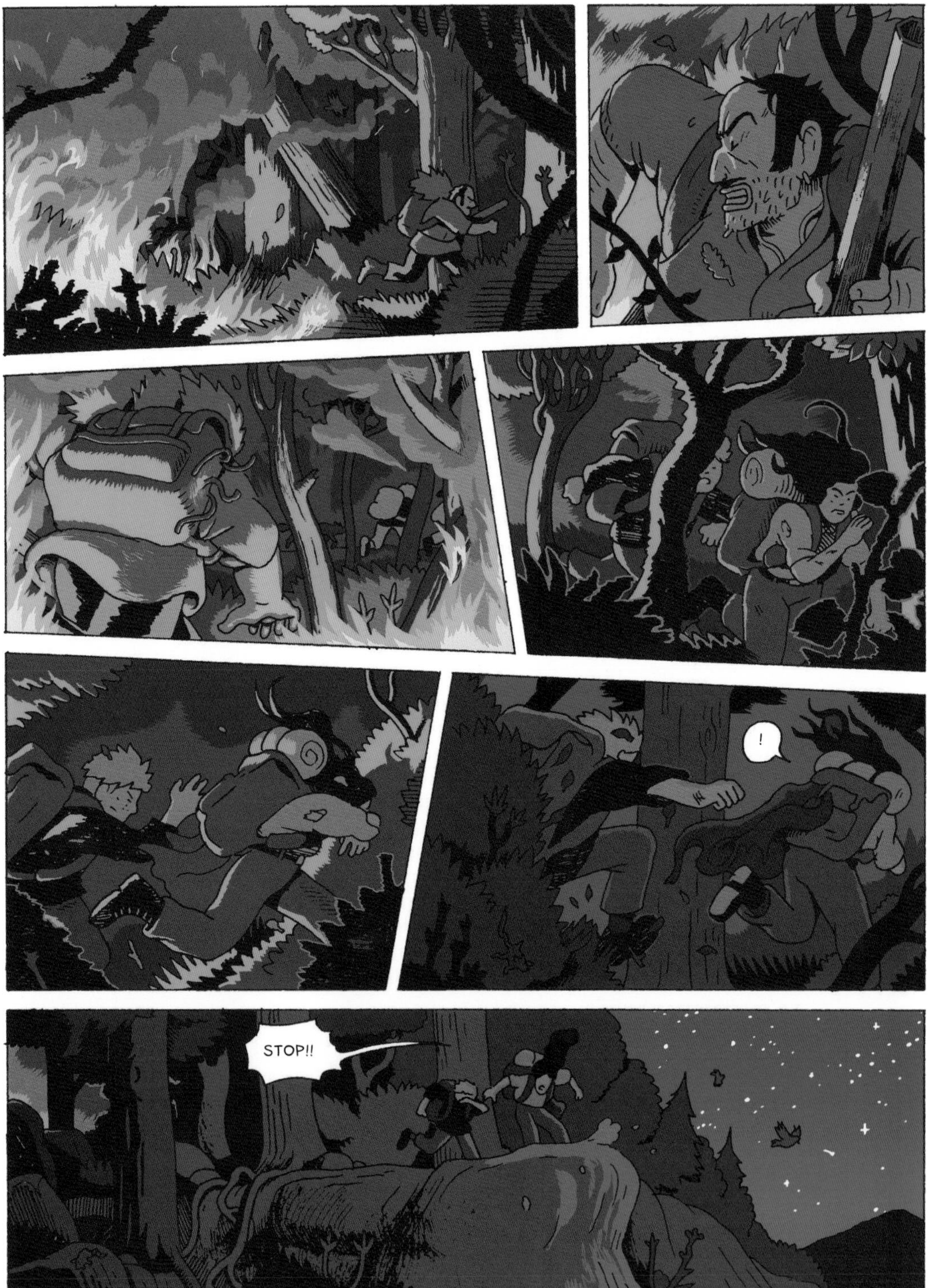
!
STOP!!

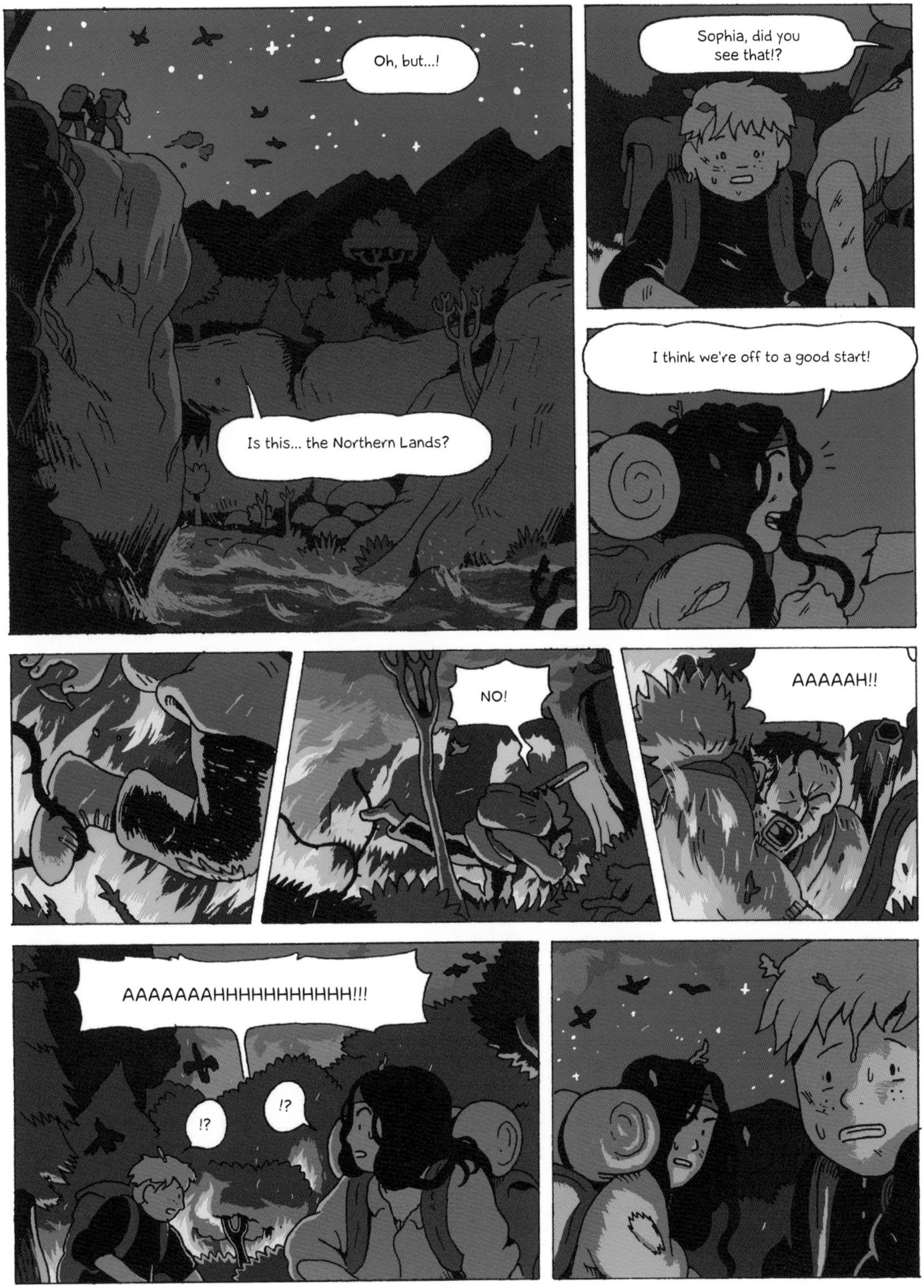

Oh, but...!
Is this... the Northern Lands?
Sophia, did you see that!?
I think we're off to a good start!
NO!
AAAAAH!!
AAAAAAAHHHHHHHHHHHH!!!
!?
!?

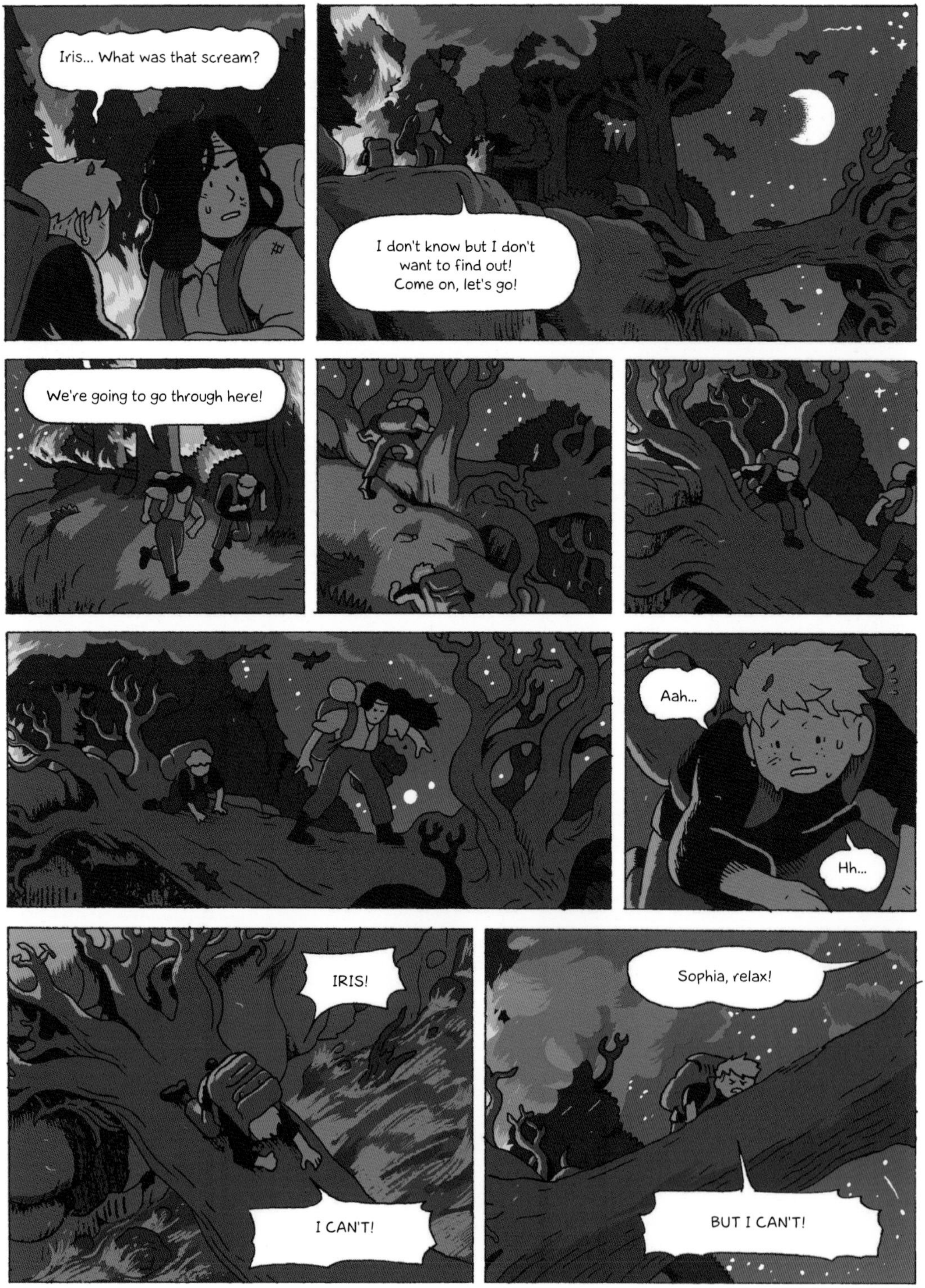
Iris... What was that scream?
I don't know but I don't want to find out! Come on, let's go!
We're going to go through here!
Aah...
Hh...
IRIS!
I CAN'T!
Sophia, relax!
BUT I CAN'T!

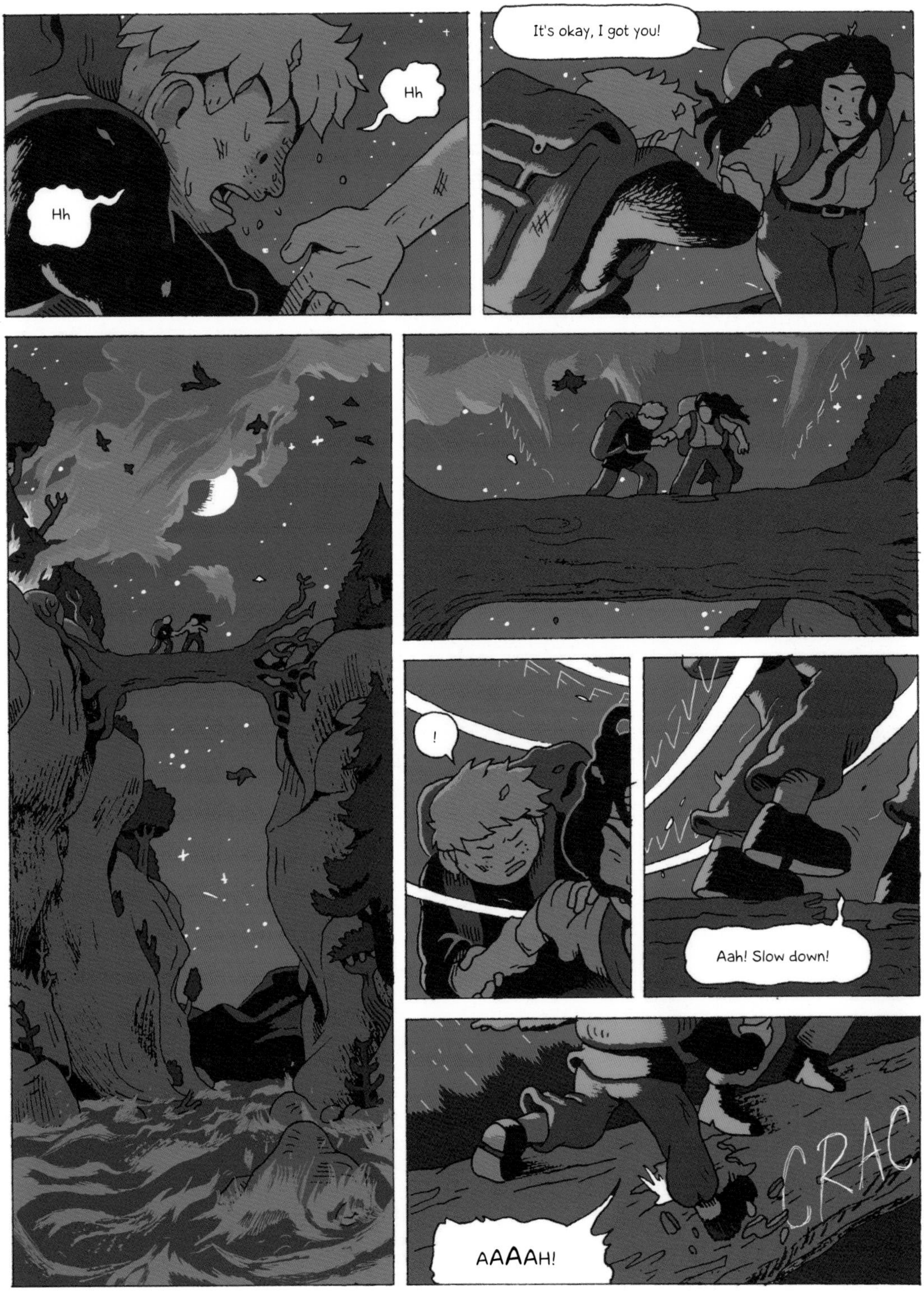
Hh
Hh
It's okay, I got you!
!
Aah! Slow down!
AAAAH!
CRAC

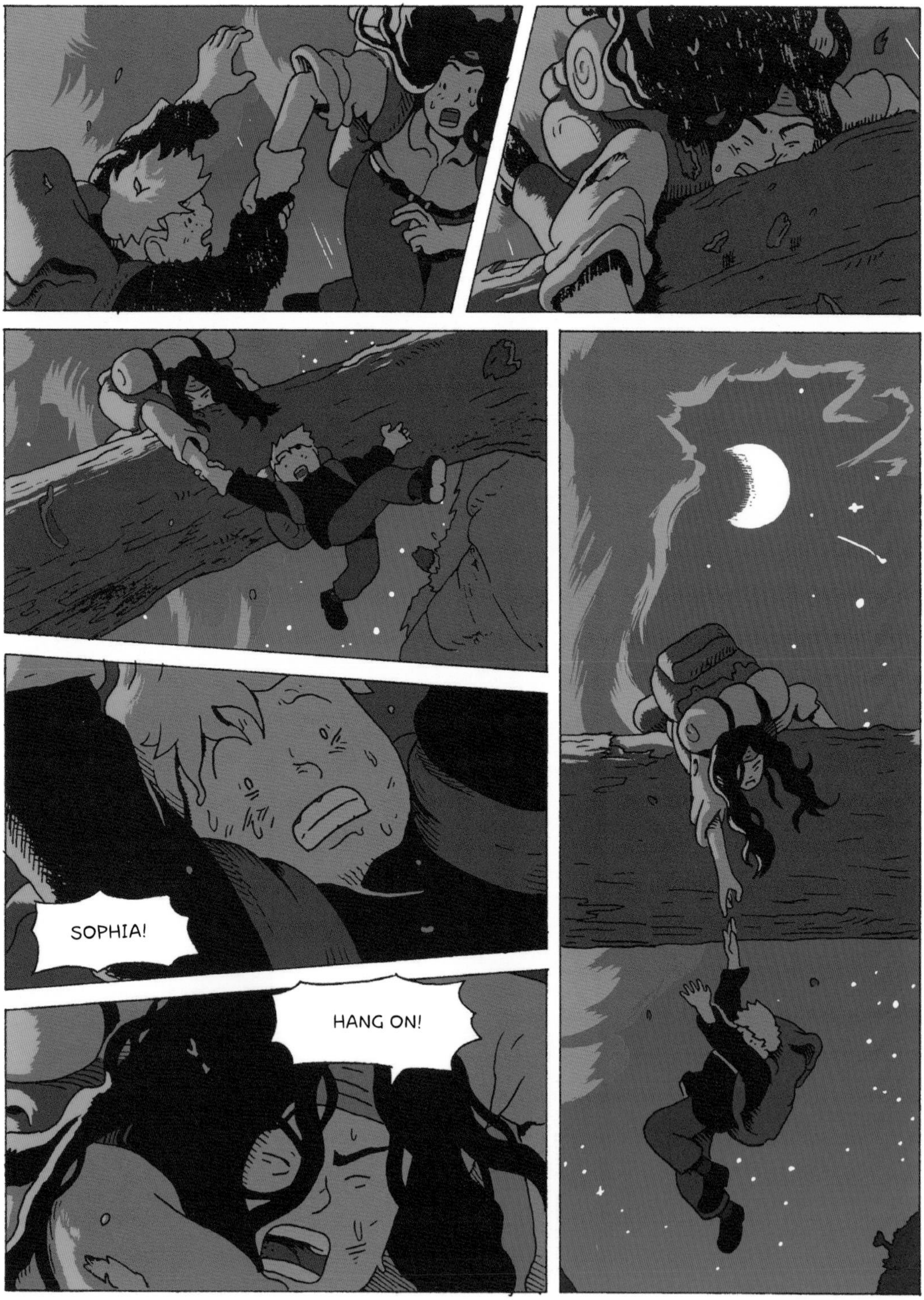
SOPHIA!
HANG ON!

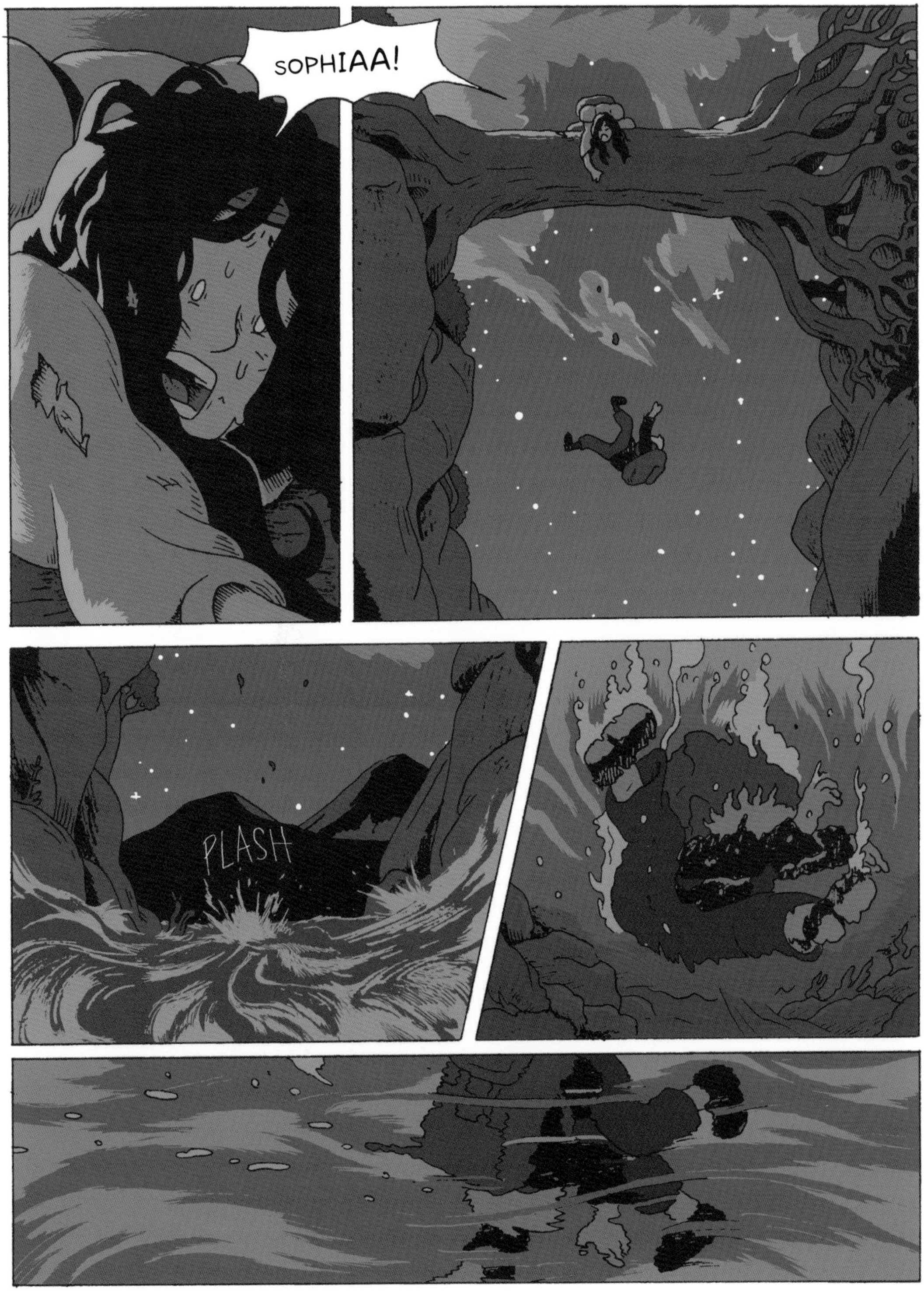
SOPHIAA!
PLASH

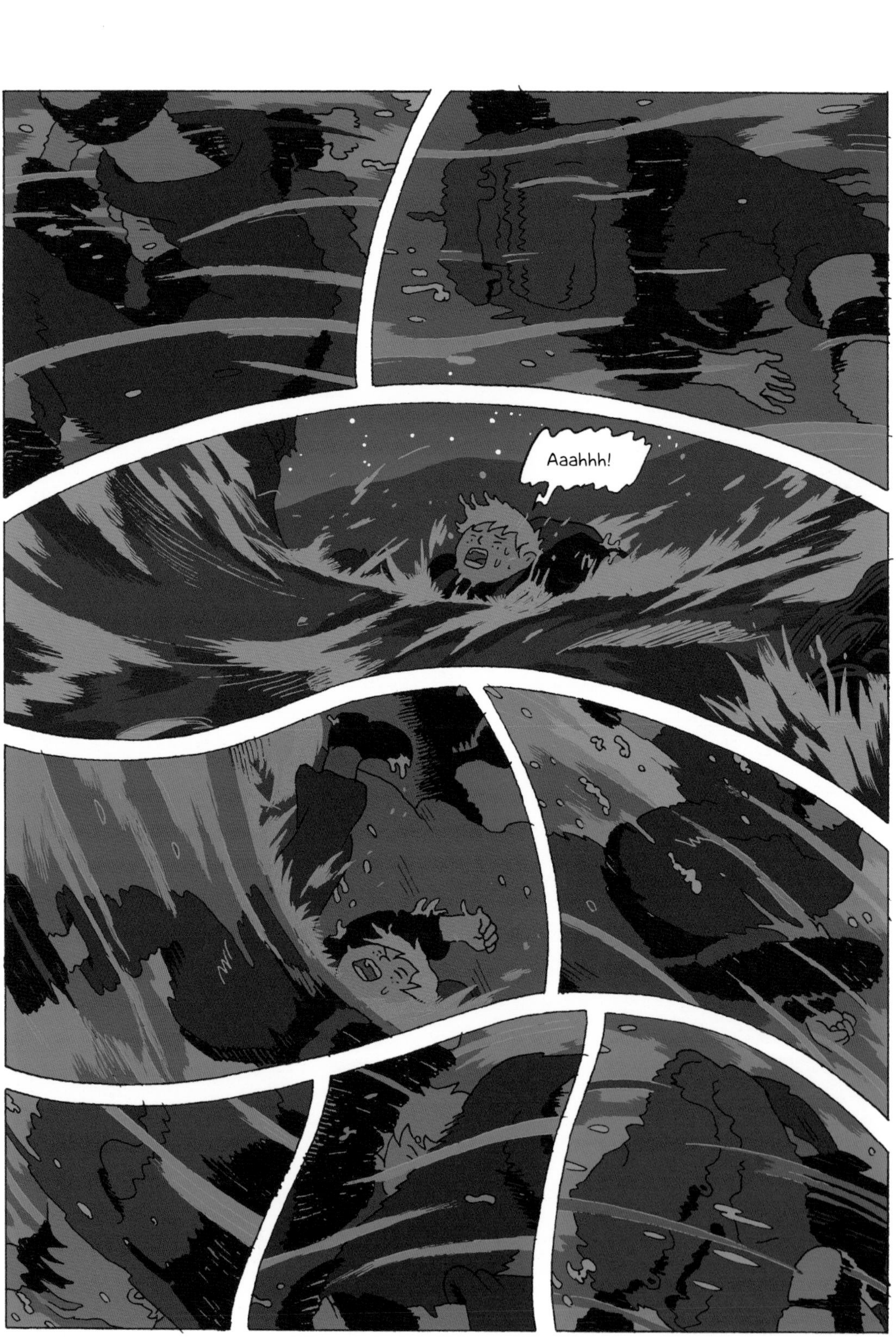
Aaahhh!

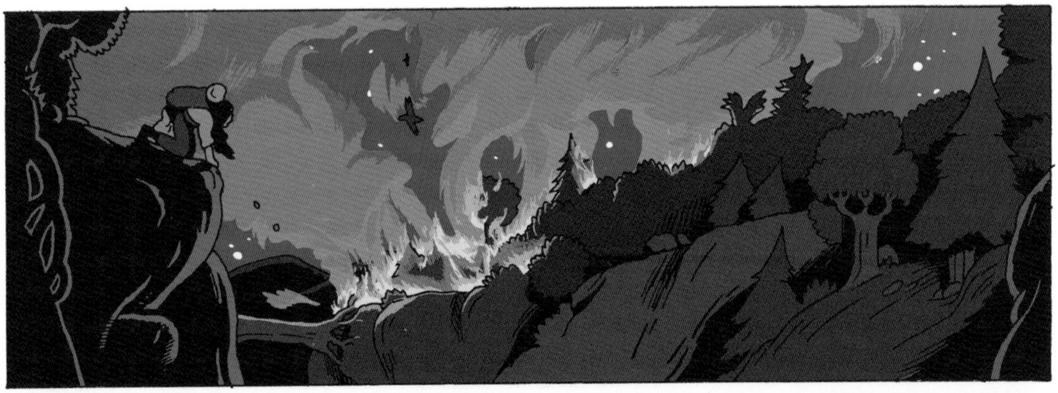

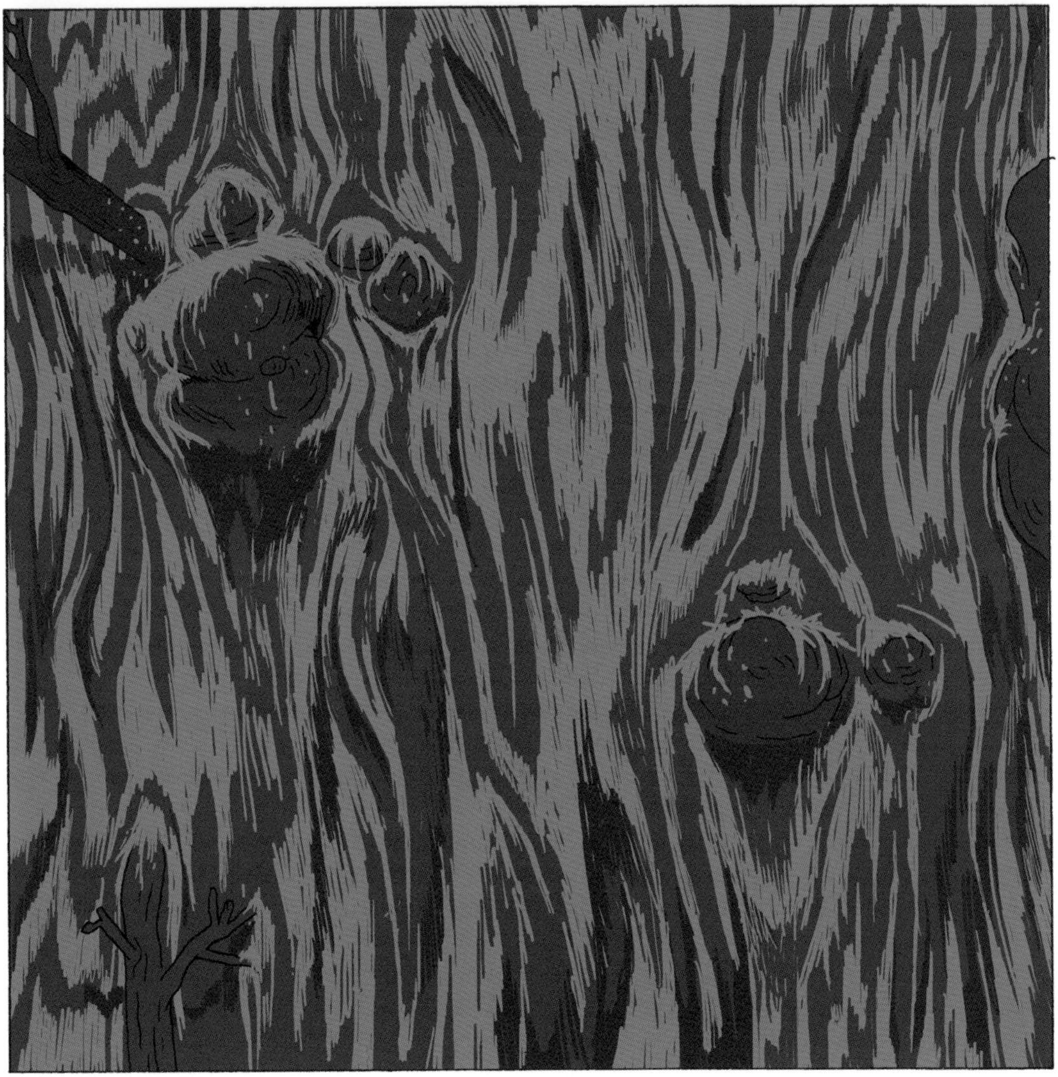

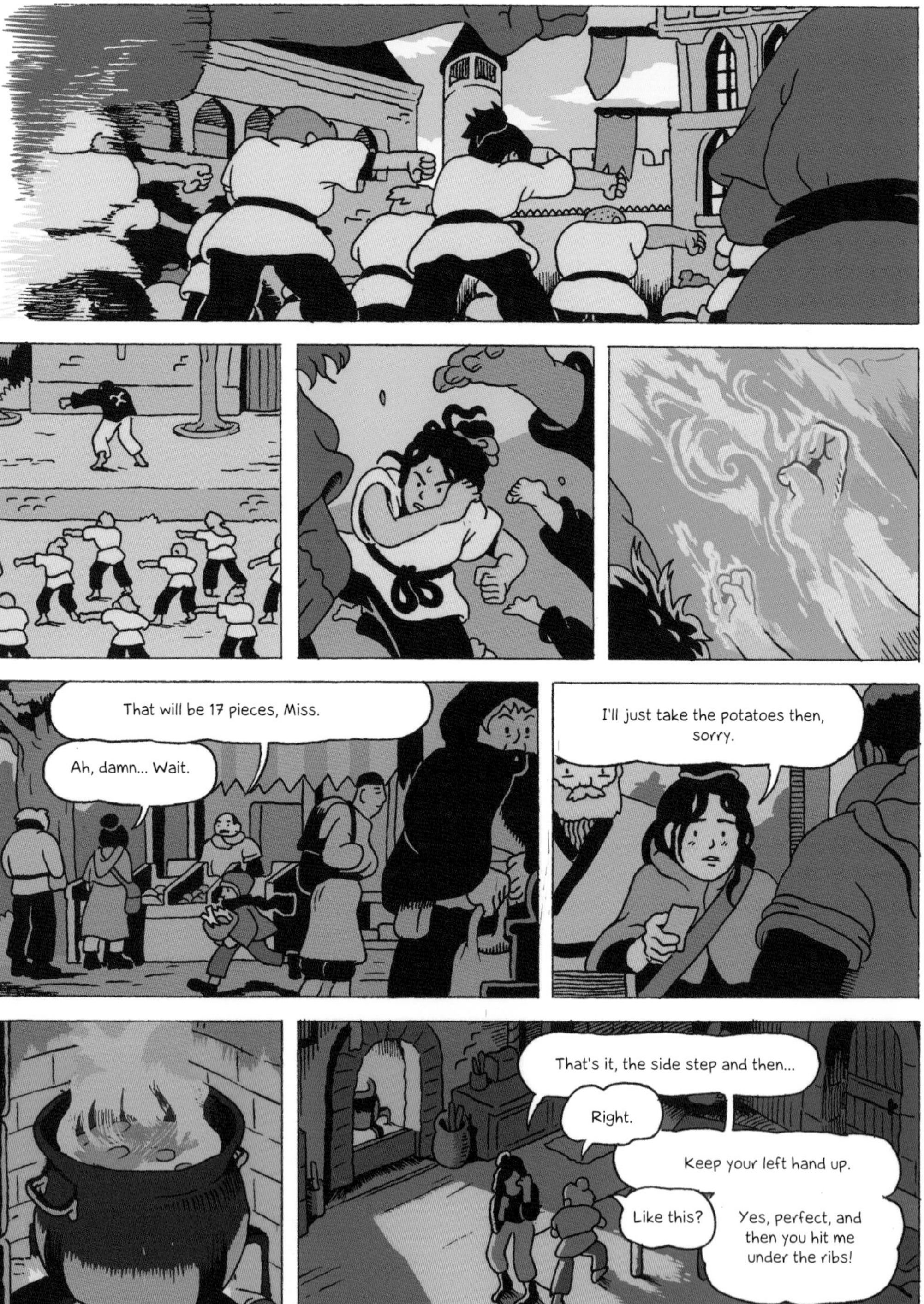
That will be 17 pieces, Miss.
Ah, damn... Wait.
I'll just take the potatoes then, sorry.
That's it, the side step and then...
Right.
Keep your left hand up.
Like this?
Yes, perfect, and then you hit me under the ribs!

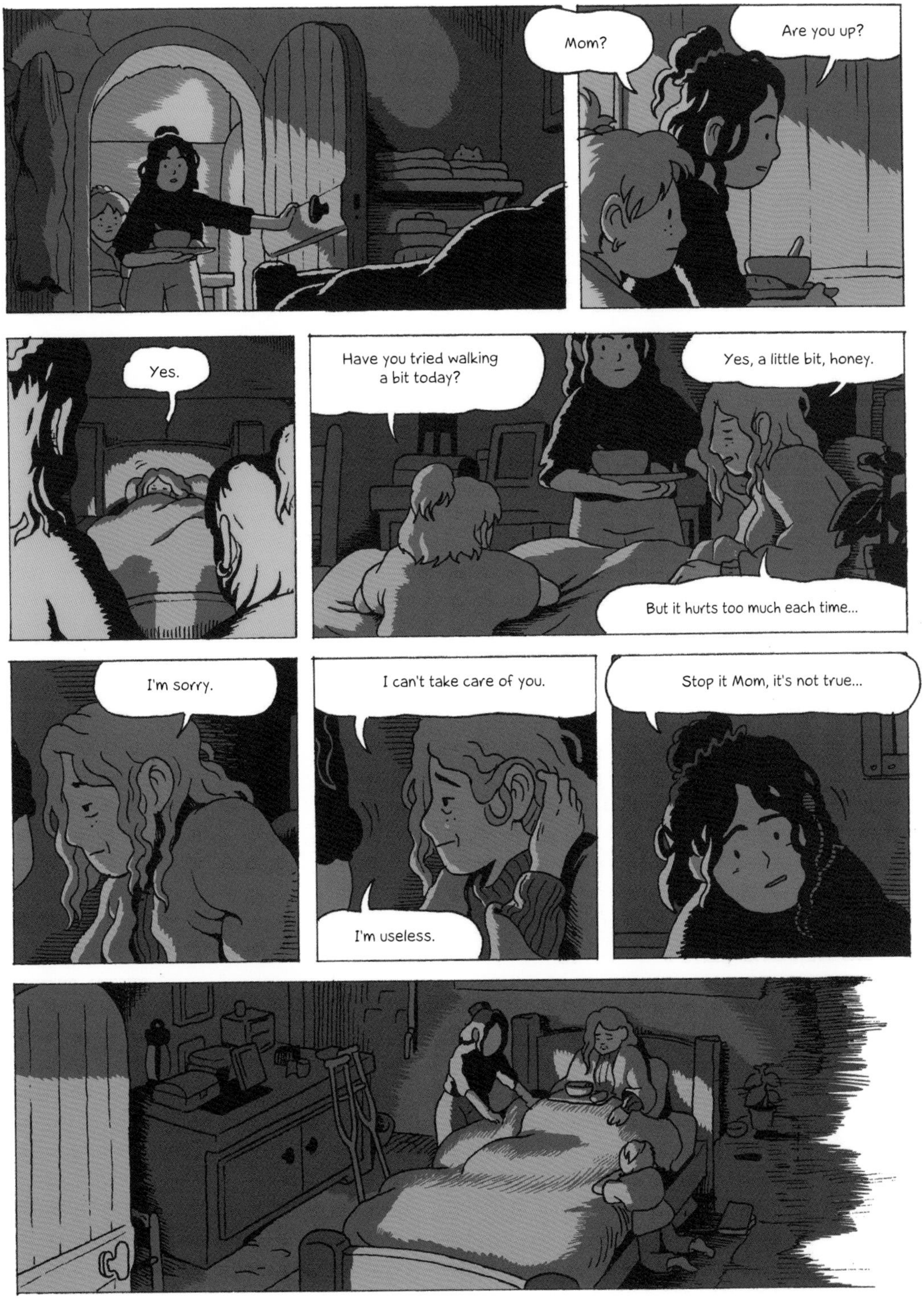

Mom?
Are you up?
Yes.
Have you tried walking a bit today?
Yes, a little bit, honey.
But it hurts too much each time...
I'm sorry.
I can't take care of you.
I'm useless.
Stop it Mom, it's not true...

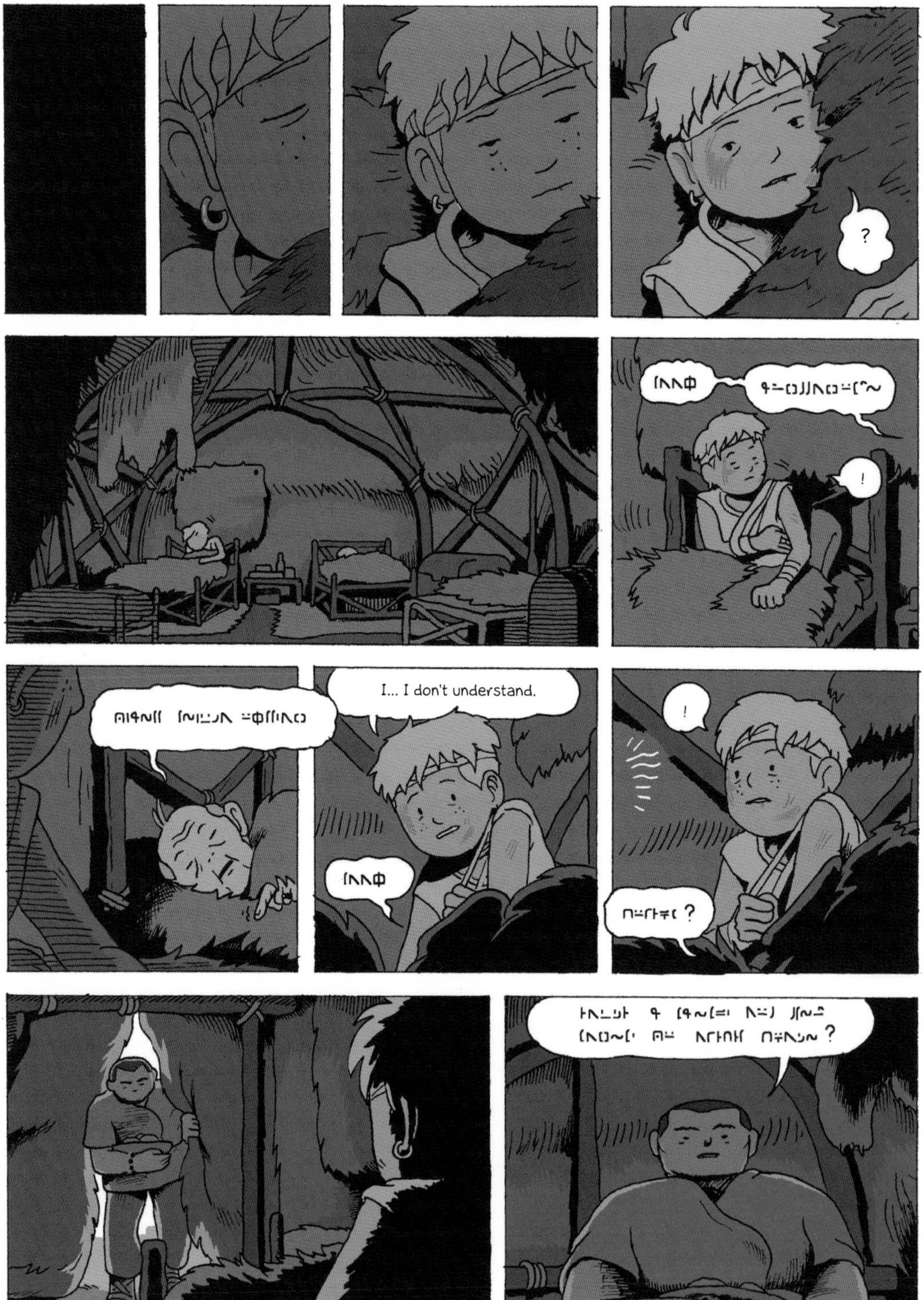
?
!
I... I don't understand.
!
?
?

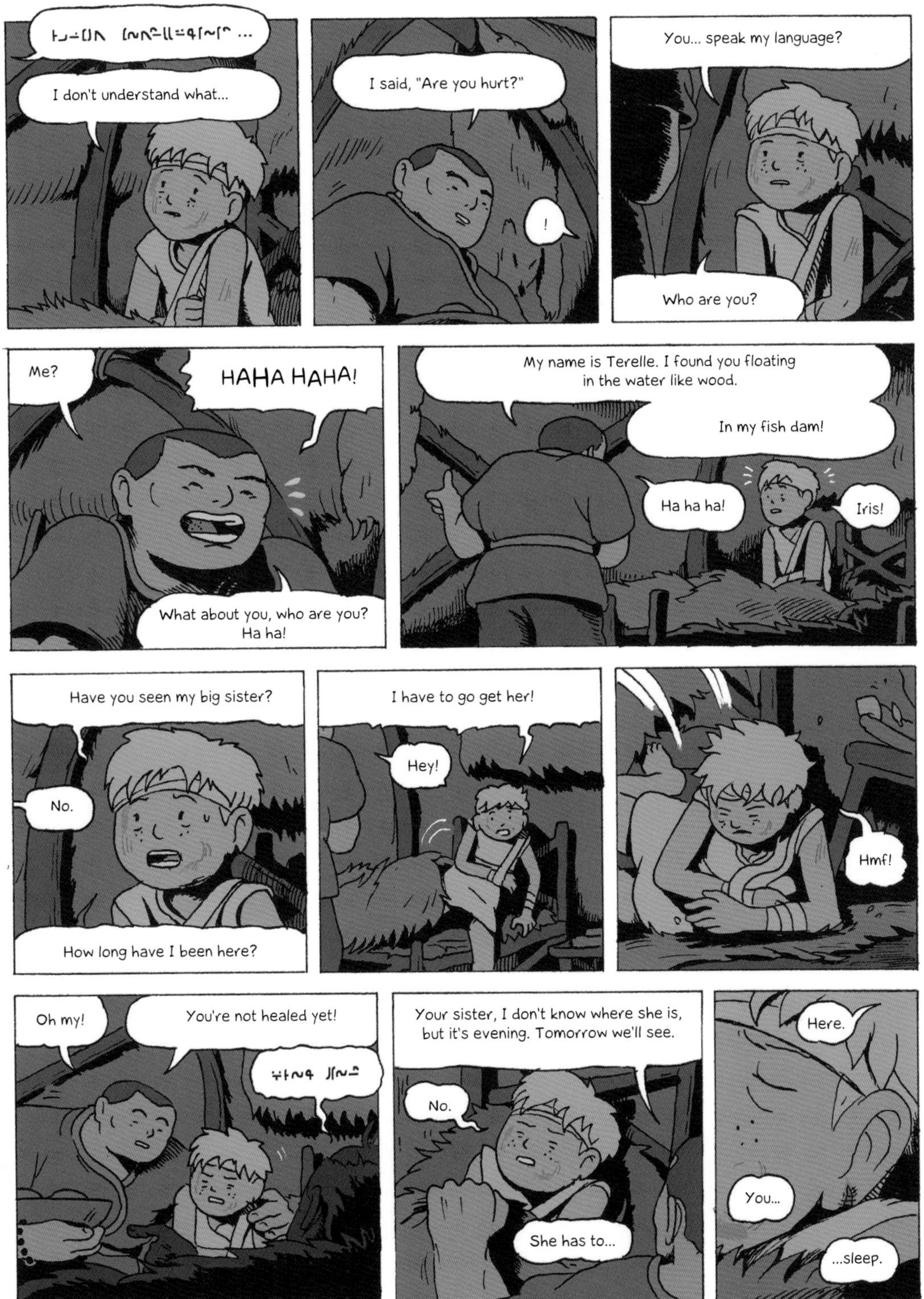

I don't understand what...
I said, "Are you hurt?"
!
You... speak my language?
Who are you?
Me?
HAHA HAHA!
What about you, who are you? Ha ha!
My name is Terelle. I found you floating in the water like wood.
In my fish dam!
Ha ha ha!
Iris!
Have you seen my big sister?
No.
How long have I been here?
I have to go get her!
Hey!
Hmf!
Oh my!
You're not healed yet!
Your sister, I don't know where she is, but it's evening. Tomorrow we'll see.
No.
She has to...
Here.
You...
...sleep.

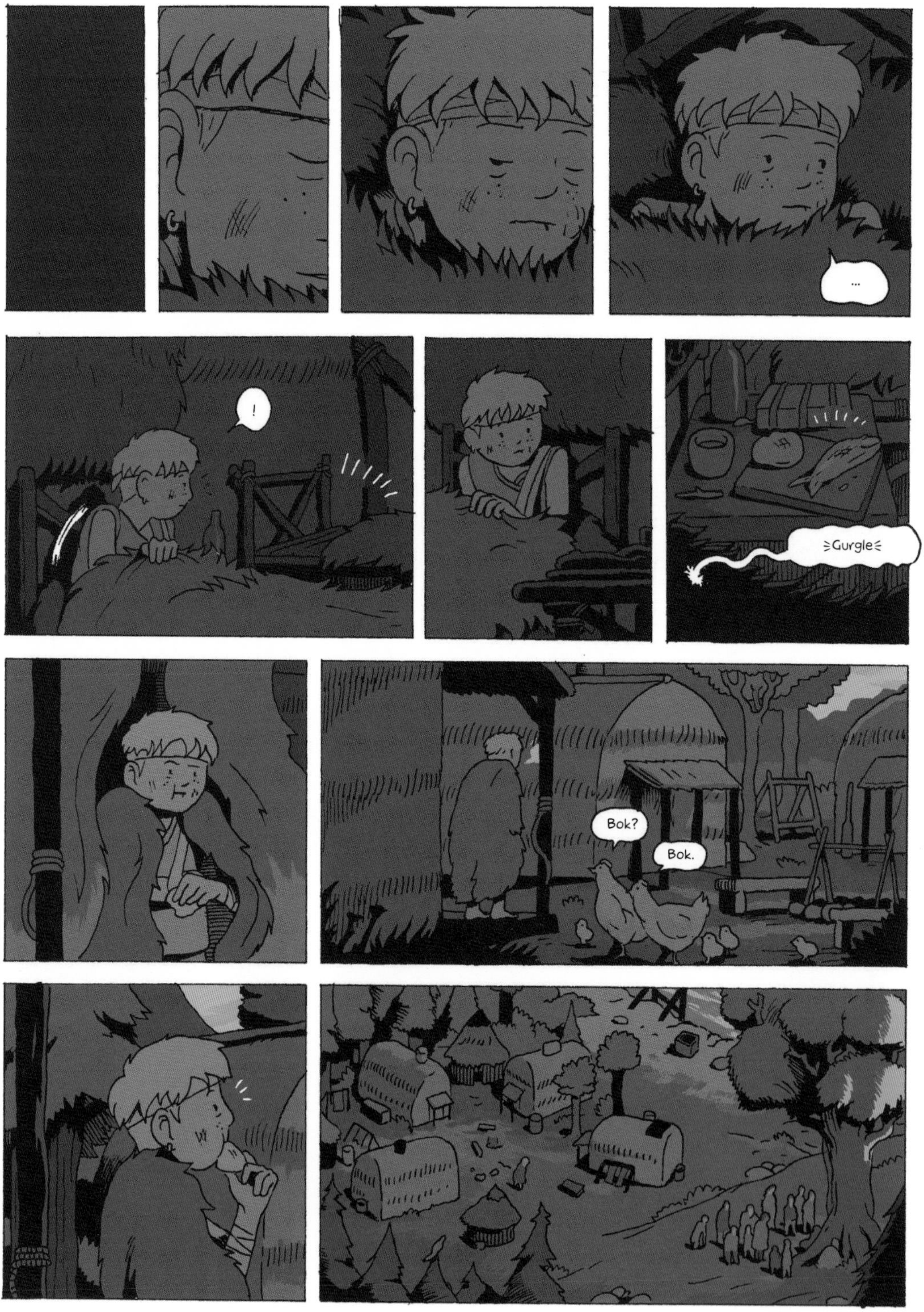
...
!
Gurgle
Bok?
Bok.

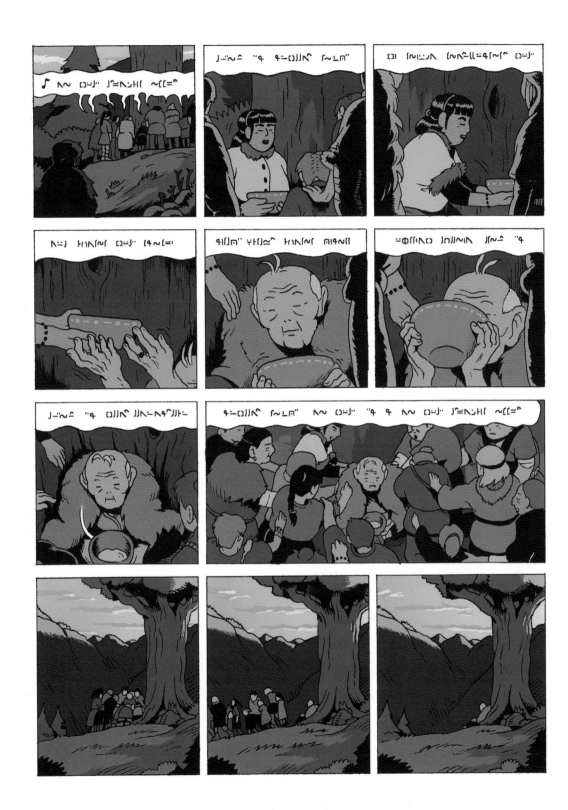

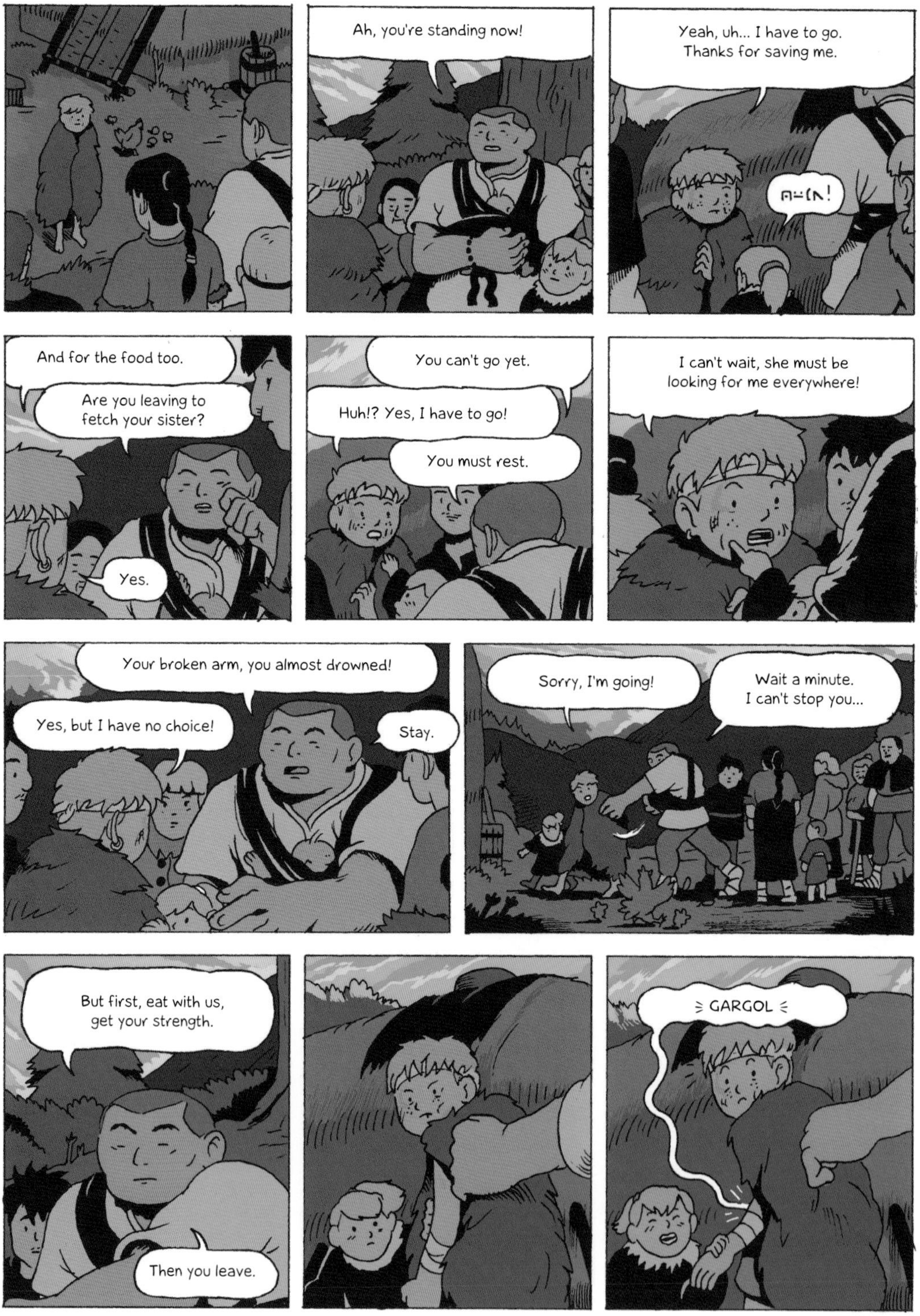
Ah, you're standing now!
Yeah, uh... I have to go.
Thanks for saving me.
And for the food too.
Are you leaving to fetch your sister?
Yes.
You can't go yet.
Huh!? Yes, I have to go!
You must rest.
I can't wait, she must be looking for me everywhere!
Your broken arm, you almost drowned!
Yes, but I have no choice!
Stay.
Sorry, I'm going!
Wait a minute.
I can't stop you...
But first, eat with us, get your strength.
Then you leave.
GARGOL

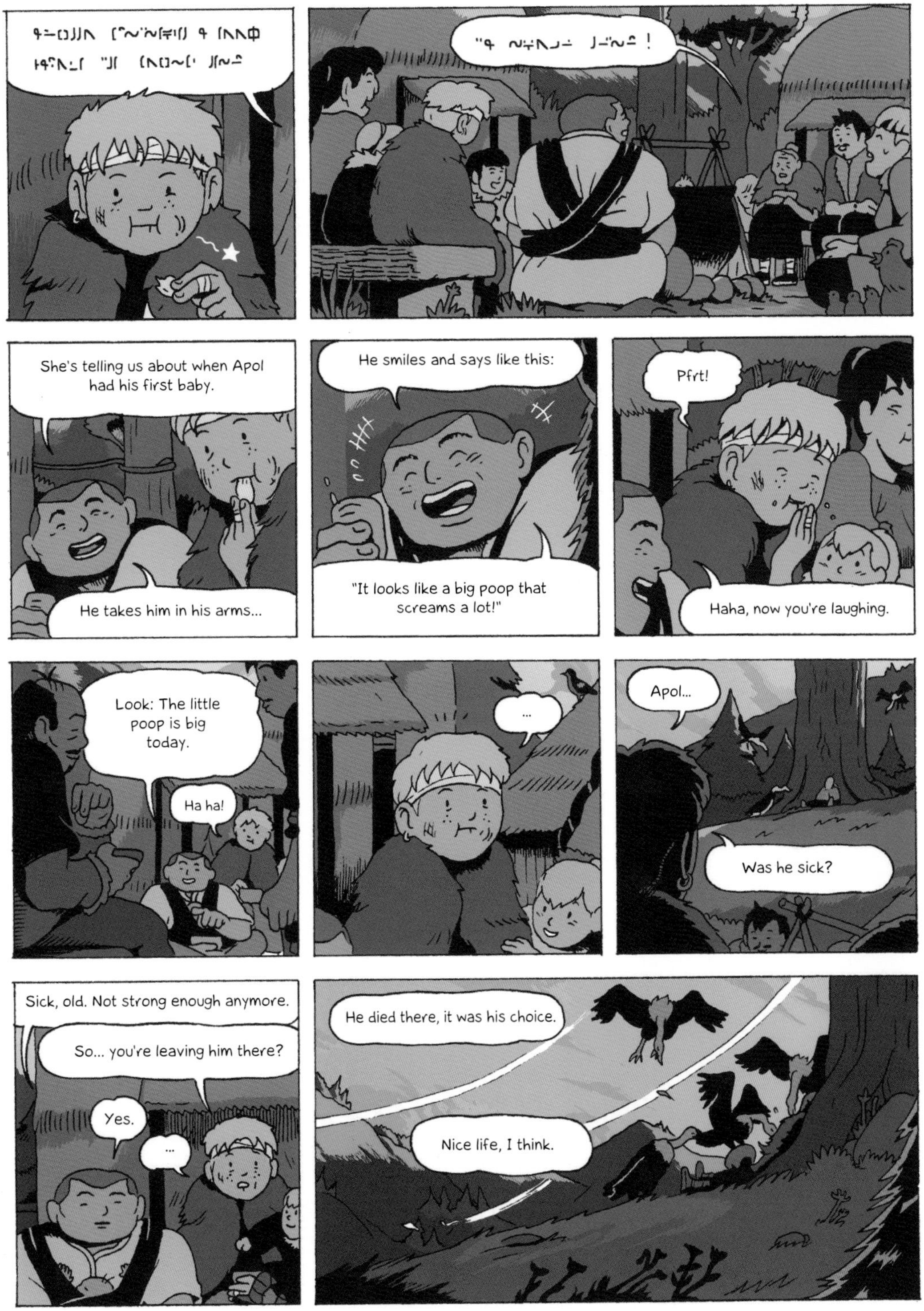
She's telling us about when Apol had his first baby.
He takes him in his arms...
He smiles and says like this:
"It looks like a big poop that screams a lot!"
Pfrt!
Haha, now you're laughing.
Look: The little poop is big today.
Ha ha!
...
Apol...
Was he sick?
Sick, old. Not strong enough anymore.
So... you're leaving him there?
Yes.
...
He died there, it was his choice.
Nice life, I think.

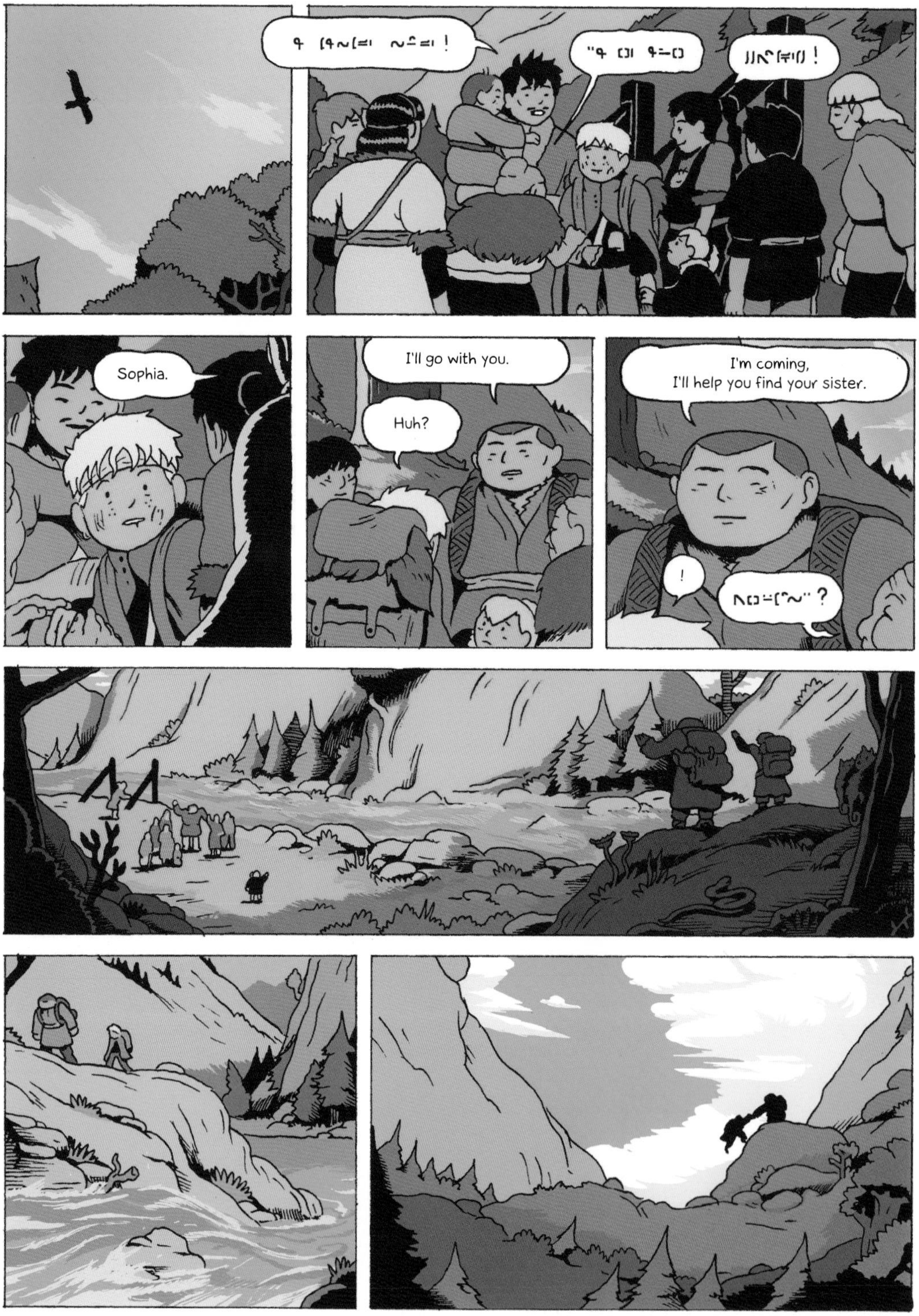
Sophia.
I'll go with you.
Huh?
I'm coming,
I'll help you find your sister.
!

Terelle?

What?

Thanks for looking after me.

And continuing to help me.

You're still hurt, that's why.

Terelle...

Do you know the legend of the Giants?

And their breath?

Do you know if they exist?

Sllllluuuuuuuuuuuuurrrrppp...

...

Aaaaah...

...

Terelle, did you understand what...

At home, we say:

ᕼᐃᐃᐢᐅᐢ ᒥᐃᐃᐃᐢ ᐦᒍ ᐃᐢᗷᒥᒥᐃᐊᐅ
ᐸᐅ ᐊᒥᕼᐊᕼ ᗭᐃ ᕿᕼᐃᒥᒥᐢ

"Death is life."

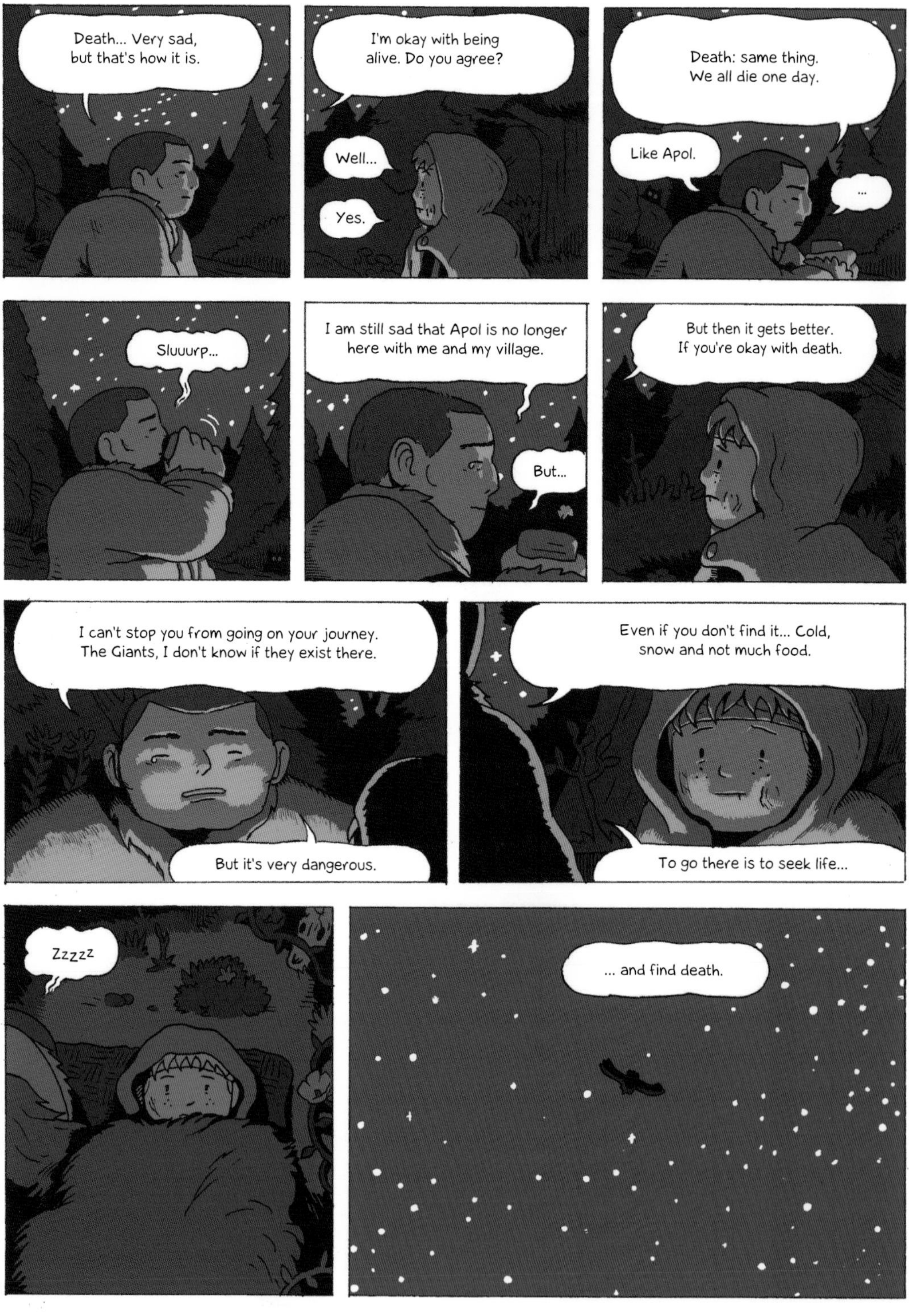
Death... Very sad, but that's how it is.
I'm okay with being alive. Do you agree?
Well...
Yes.
Death: same thing. We all die one day.
Like Apol.
...
Sluuurp...
I am still sad that Apol is no longer here with me and my village.
But...
But then it gets better. If you're okay with death.
I can't stop you from going on your journey. The Giants, I don't know if they exist there.
But it's very dangerous.
Even if you don't find it... Cold, snow and not much food.
To go there is to seek life...
Zzzzz
... and find death.

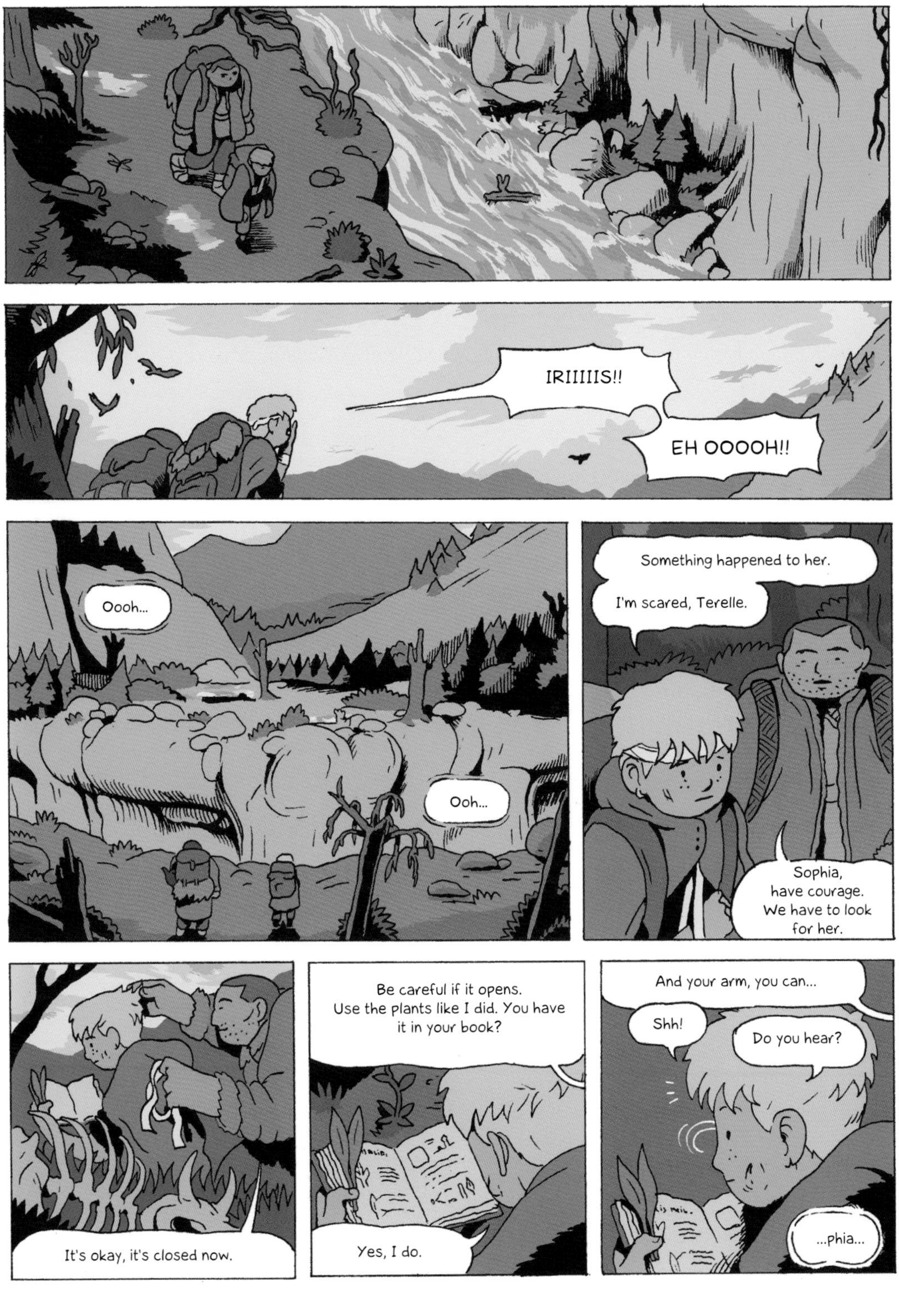
IRIIIIIS!!
EH OOOOH!!
Oooh...
Ooh...
Something happened to her.
I'm scared, Terelle.
Sophia, have courage. We have to look for her.
It's okay, it's closed now.
Be careful if it opens. Use the plants like I did. You have it in your book?
Yes, I do.
And your arm, you can...
Shh!
Do you hear?
...phia...

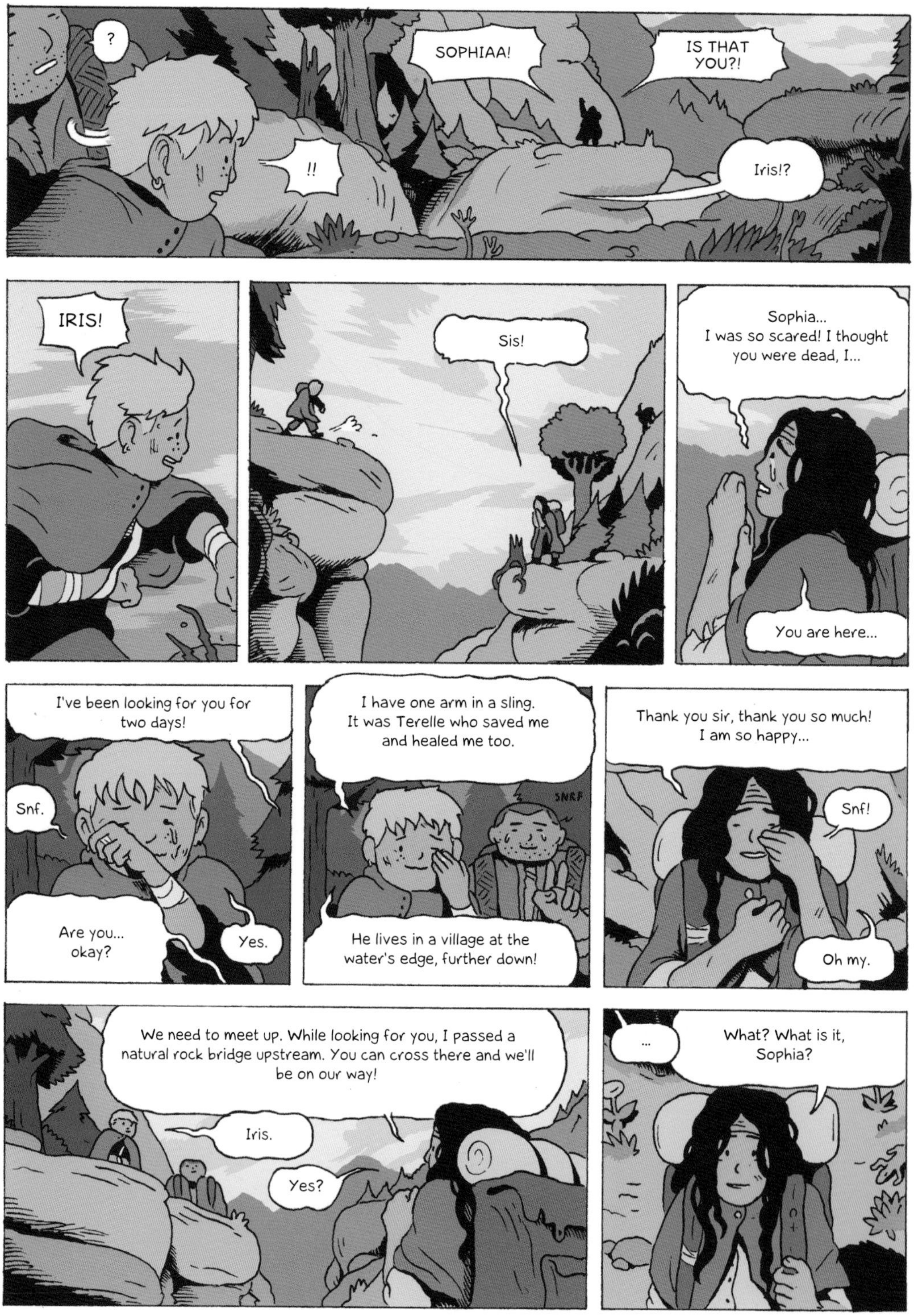
?
!!
SOPHIAA!
IS THAT YOU?!
Iris!?
IRIS!
Sis!
Sophia... I was so scared! I thought you were dead, I...
You are here...
I've been looking for you for two days!
Snf.
Are you... okay?
Yes.
I have one arm in a sling. It was Terelle who saved me and healed me too.
SNRF
He lives in a village at the water's edge, further down!
Thank you sir, thank you so much! I am so happy...
Snf!
Oh my.
We need to meet up. While looking for you, I passed a natural rock bridge upstream. You can cross there and we'll be on our way!
Iris.
Yes?
...
What? What is it, Sophia?

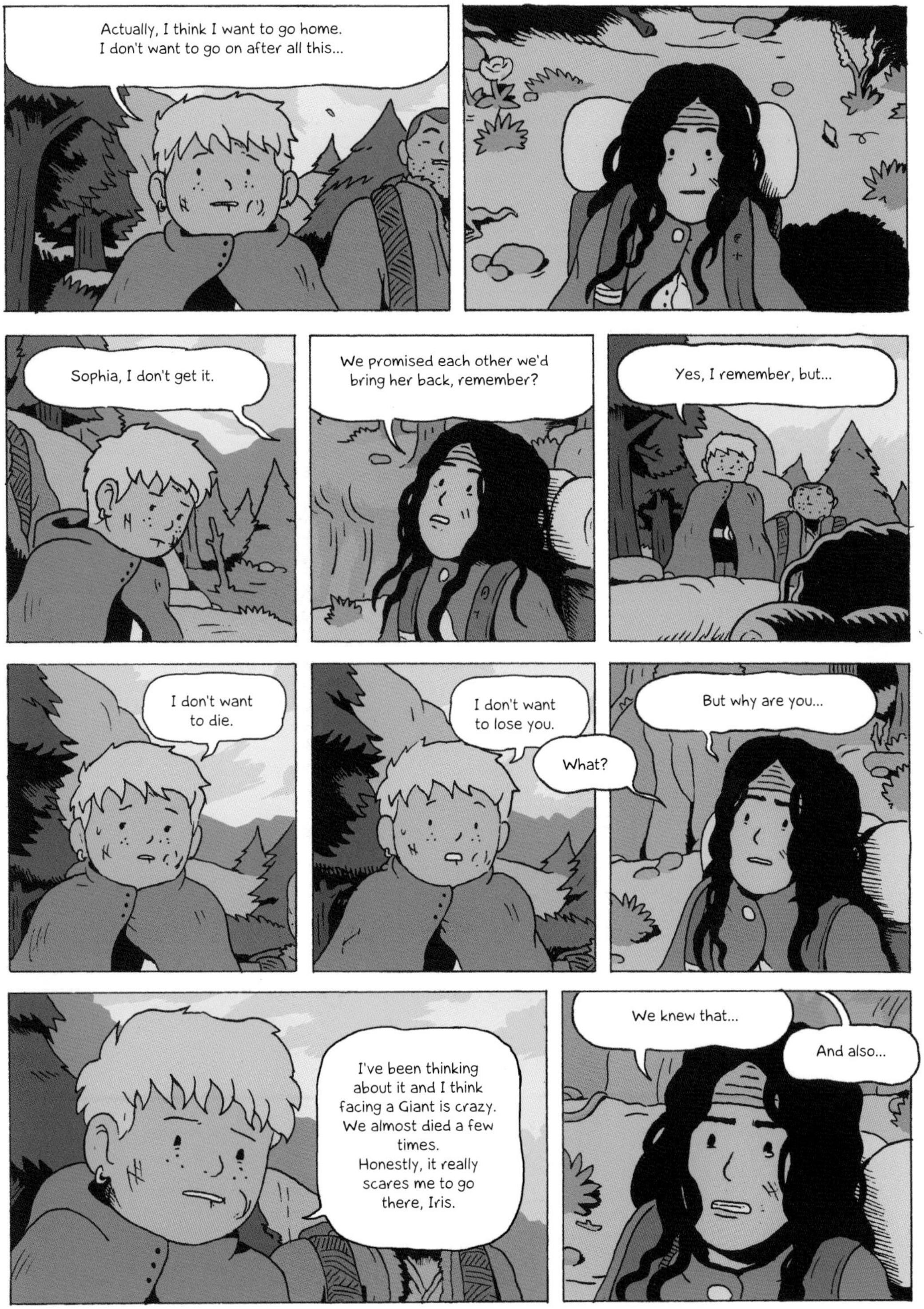
Actually, I think I want to go home.
I don't want to go on after all this...
Sophia, I don't get it.
We promised each other we'd bring her back, remember?
Yes, I remember, but...
I don't want to die.
I don't want to lose you.
What?
But why are you...
I've been thinking about it and I think facing a Giant is crazy. We almost died a few times. Honestly, it really scares me to go there, Iris.
We knew that...
And also...

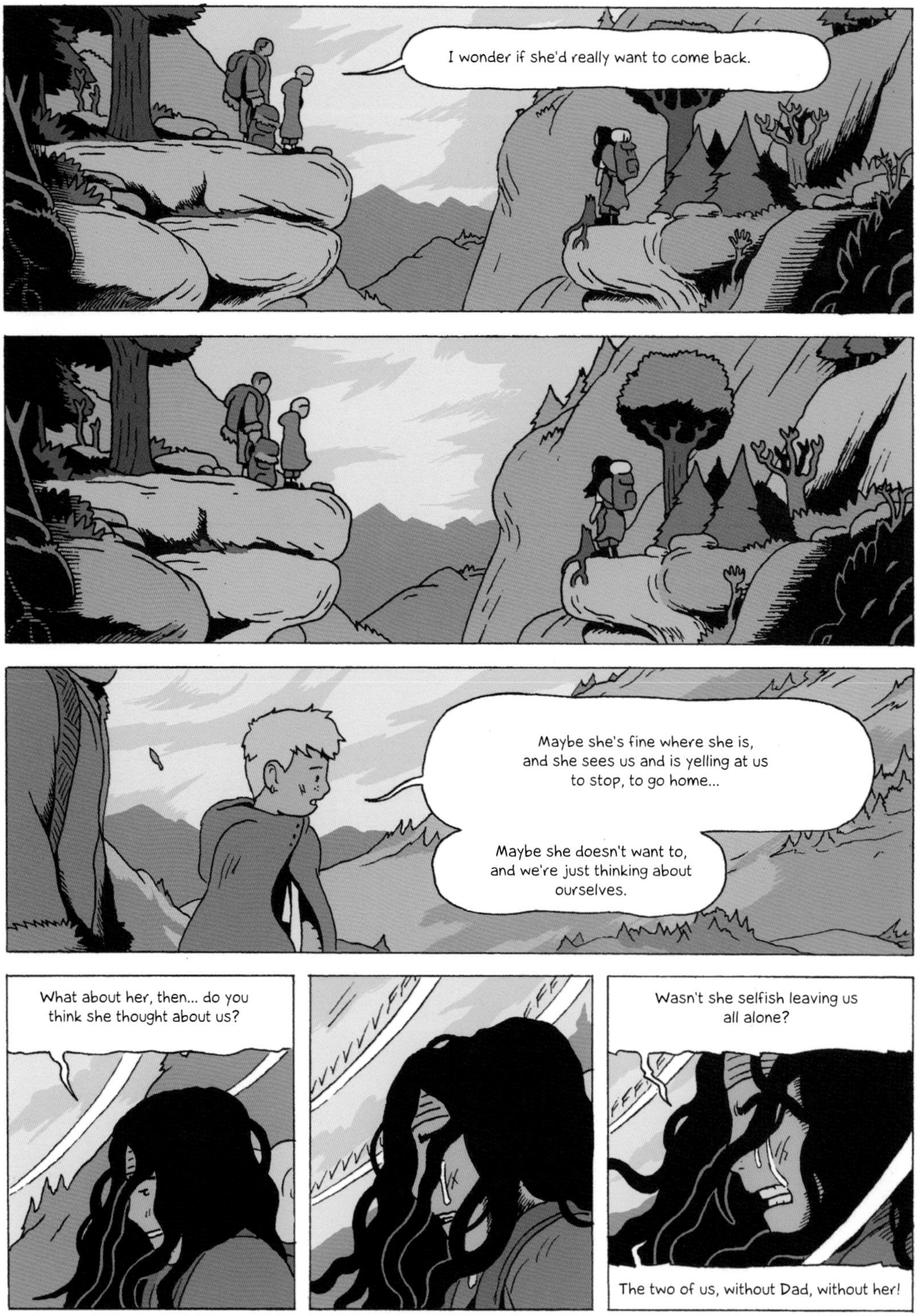
I wonder if she'd really want to come back.
Maybe she's fine where she is, and she sees us and is yelling at us to stop, to go home...
Maybe she doesn't want to, and we're just thinking about ourselves.
What about her, then... do you think she thought about us?
Wasn't she selfish leaving us all alone?
The two of us, without Dad, without her!

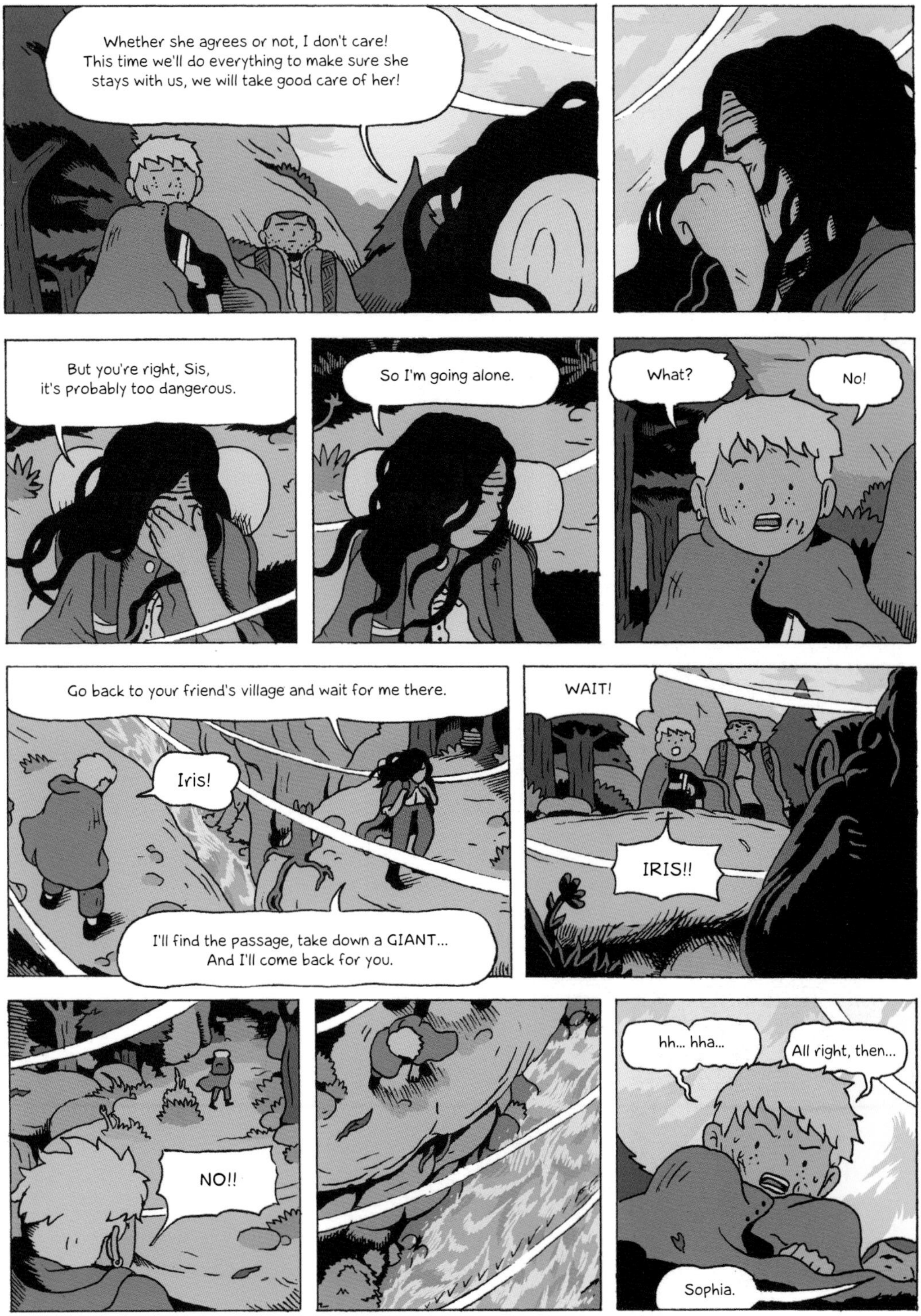
Whether she agrees or not, I don't care!
This time we'll do everything to make sure she stays with us, we will take good care of her!
But you're right, Sis, it's probably too dangerous.
So I'm going alone.
What?
No!
Go back to your friend's village and wait for me there.
Iris!
I'll find the passage, take down a GIANT... And I'll come back for you.
WAIT!
IRIS!!
NO!!
hh... hha...
All right, then...
Sophia.

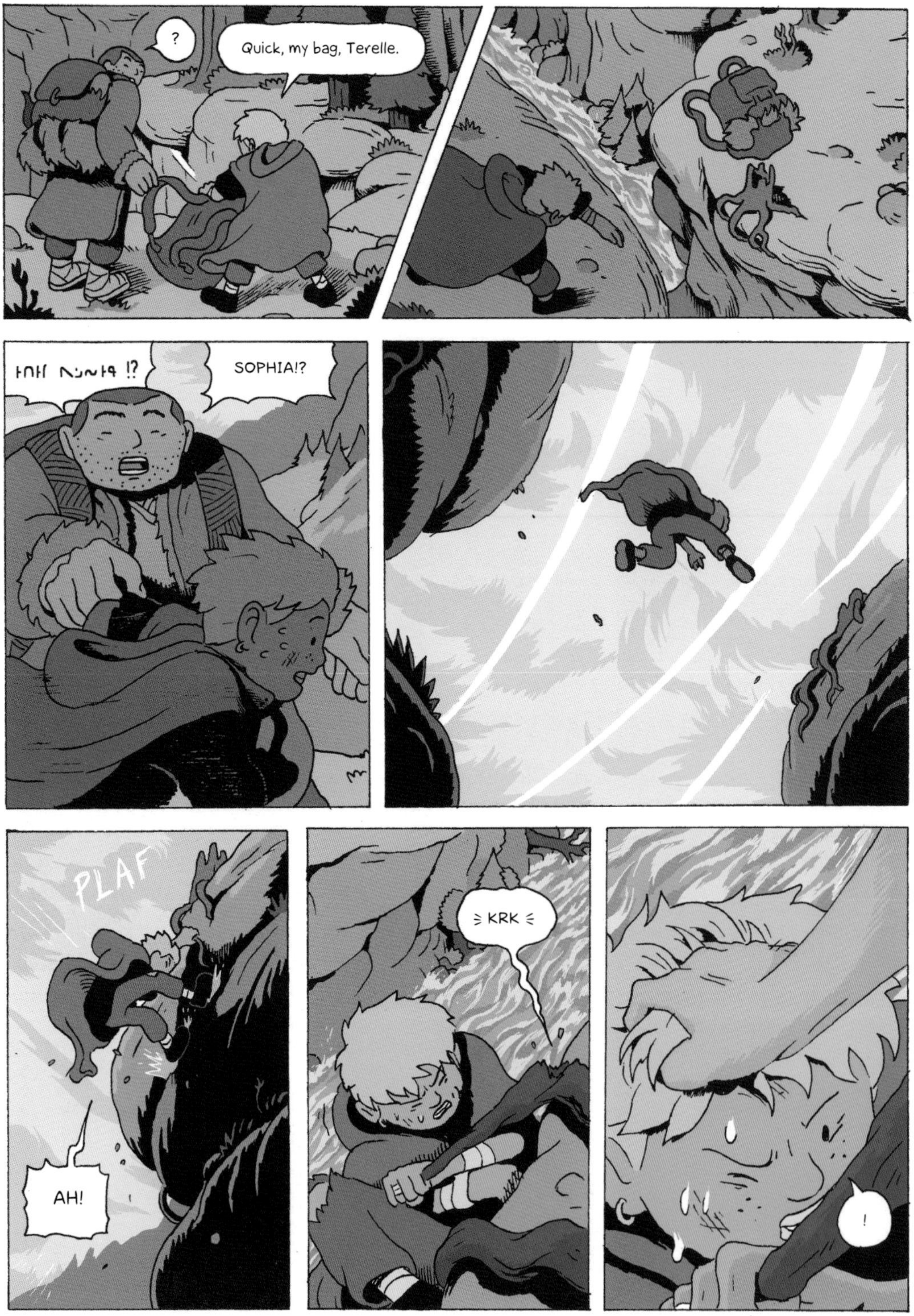
?
Quick, my bag, Terelle.
!?
SOPHIA!?
PLAF
AH!
KRK
!

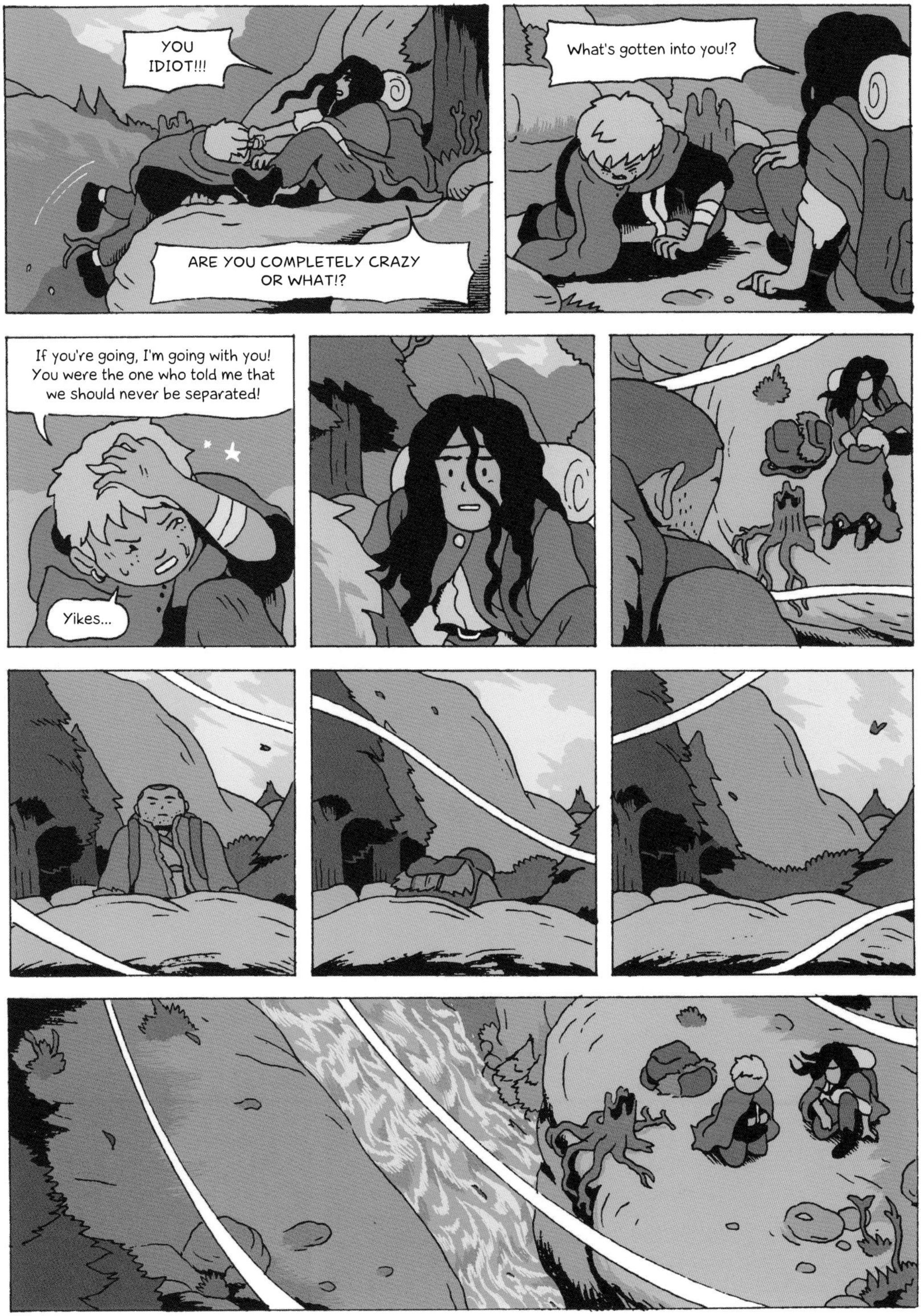
YOU IDIOT!!!
ARE YOU COMPLETELY CRAZY OR WHAT!?
What's gotten into you!?
If you're going, I'm going with you! You were the one who told me that we should never be separated!
Yikes...

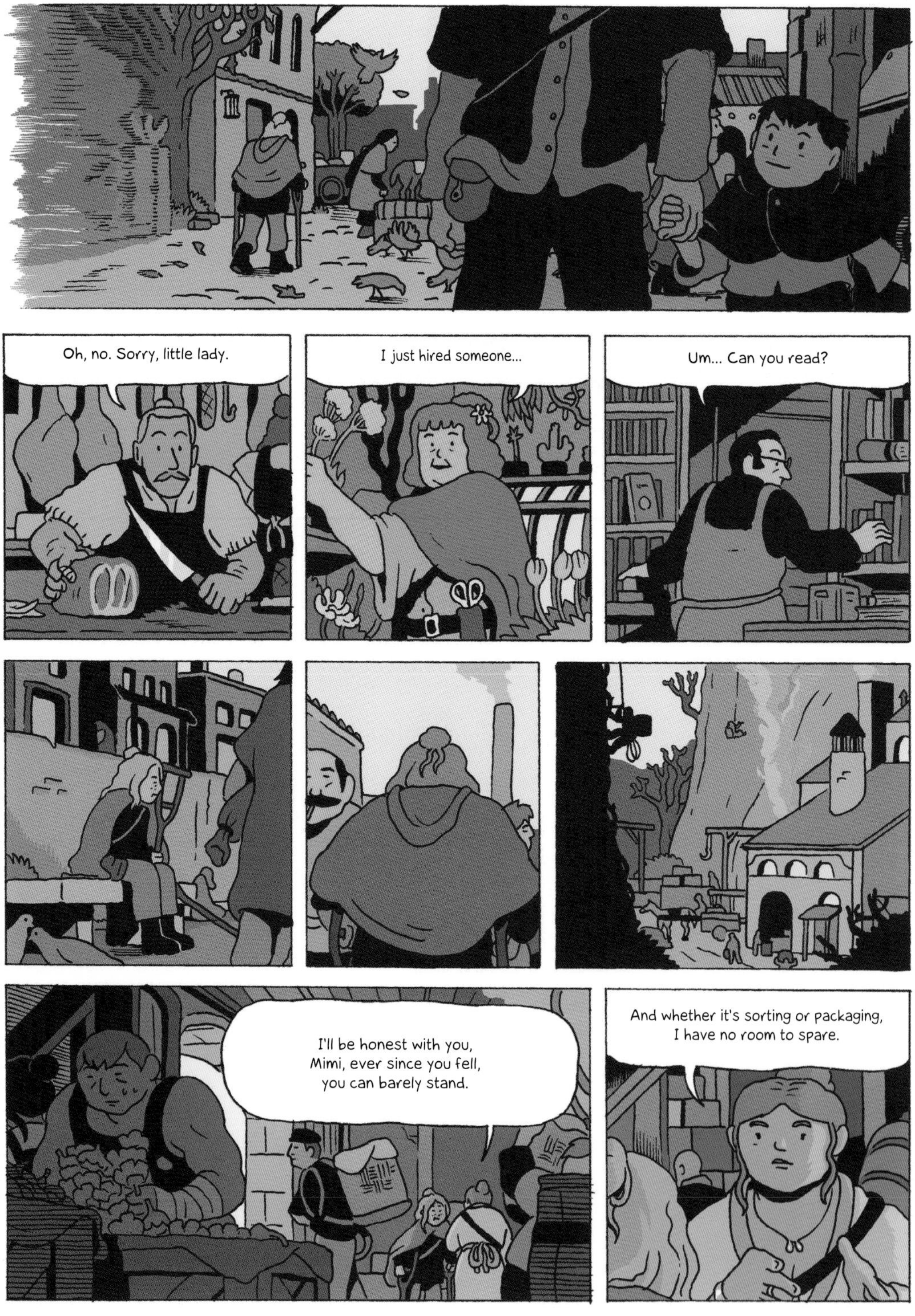

Oh, no. Sorry, little lady.
I just hired someone...
Um... Can you read?
I'll be honest with you, Mimi, ever since you fell, you can barely stand.
And whether it's sorting or packaging, I have no room to spare.

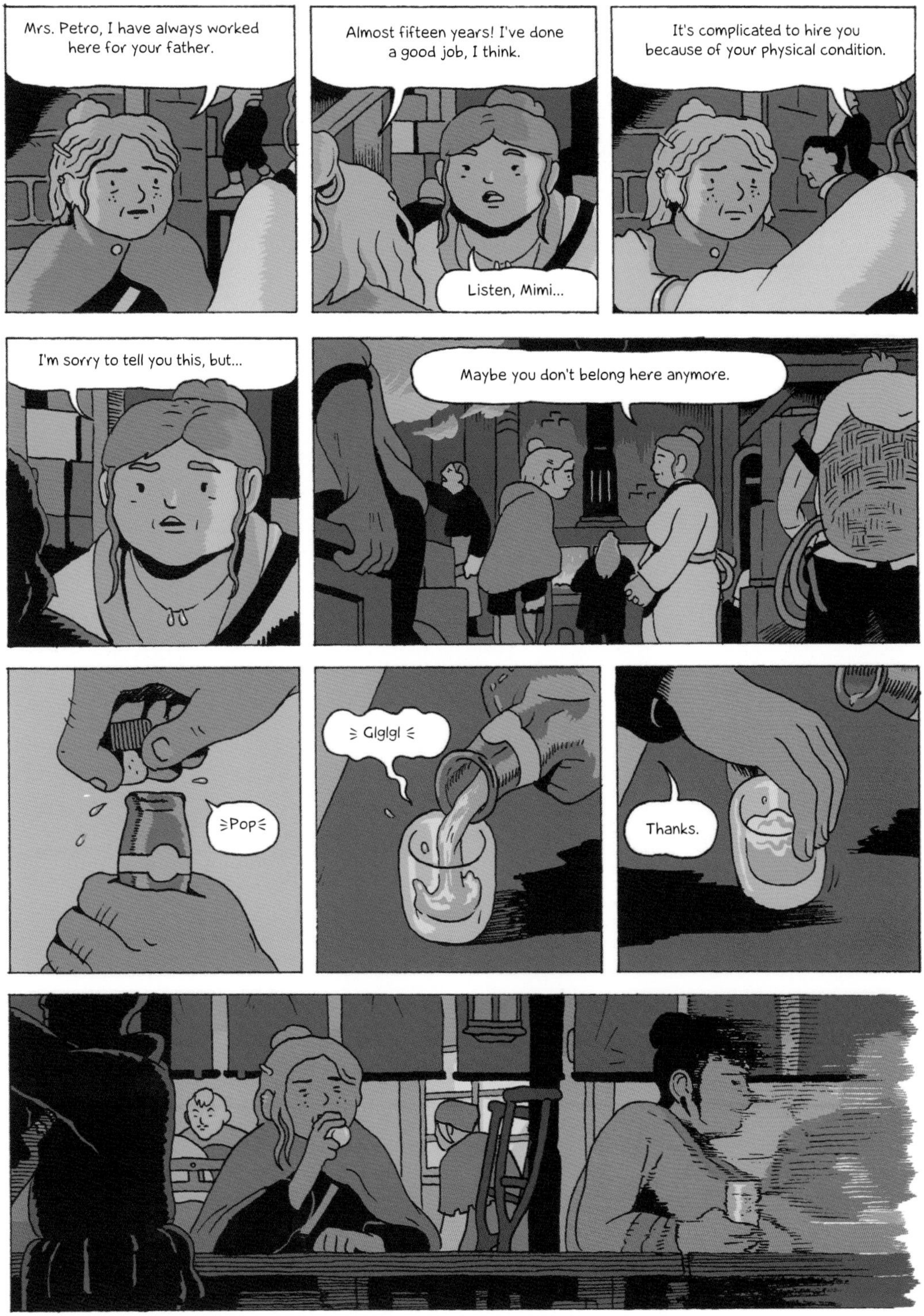
Mrs. Petro, I have always worked here for your father.
Almost fifteen years! I've done a good job, I think.
Listen, Mimi...
It's complicated to hire you because of your physical condition.
I'm sorry to tell you this, but...
Maybe you don't belong here anymore.
Pop
Glglgl
Thanks.

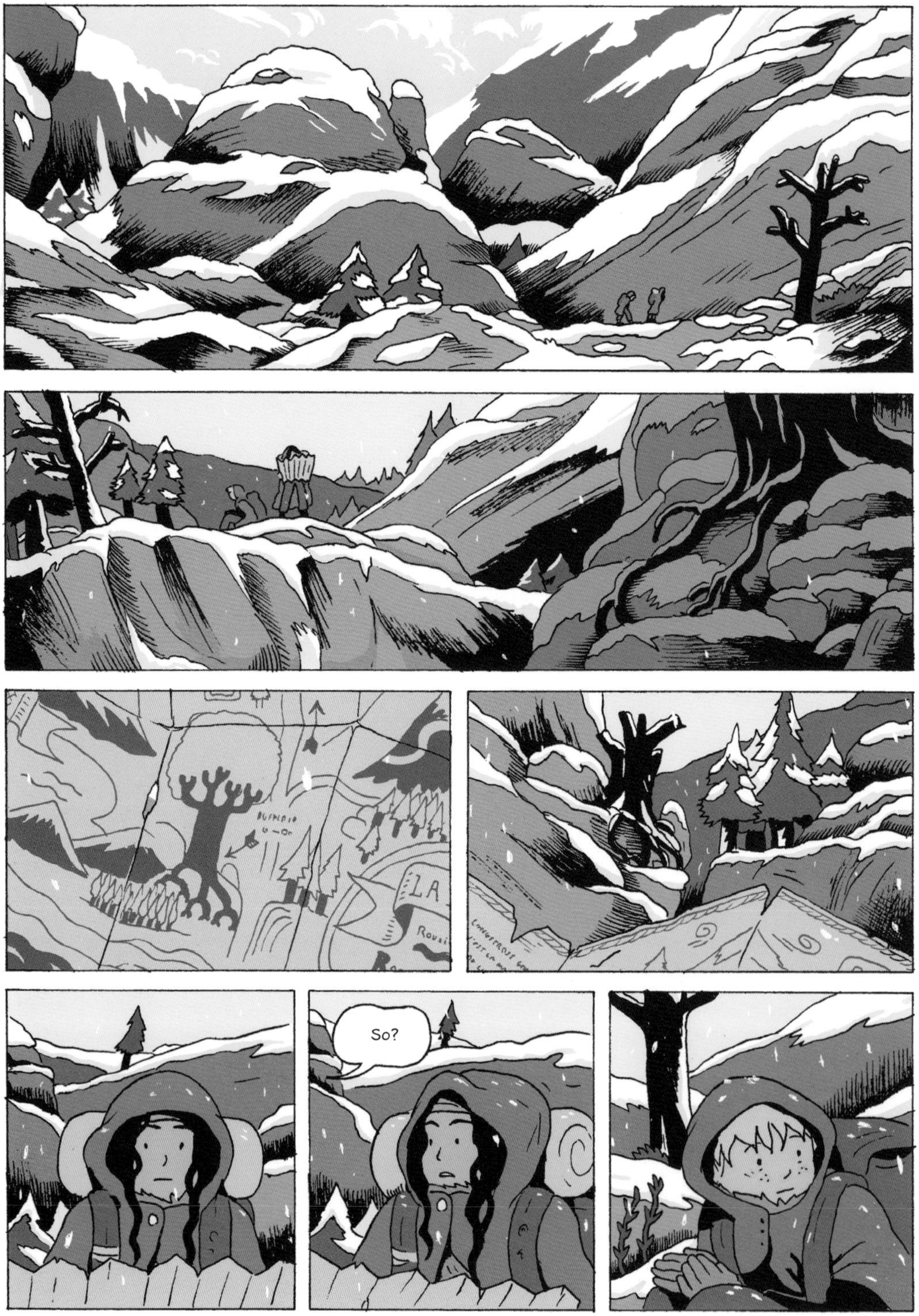
LA
So?

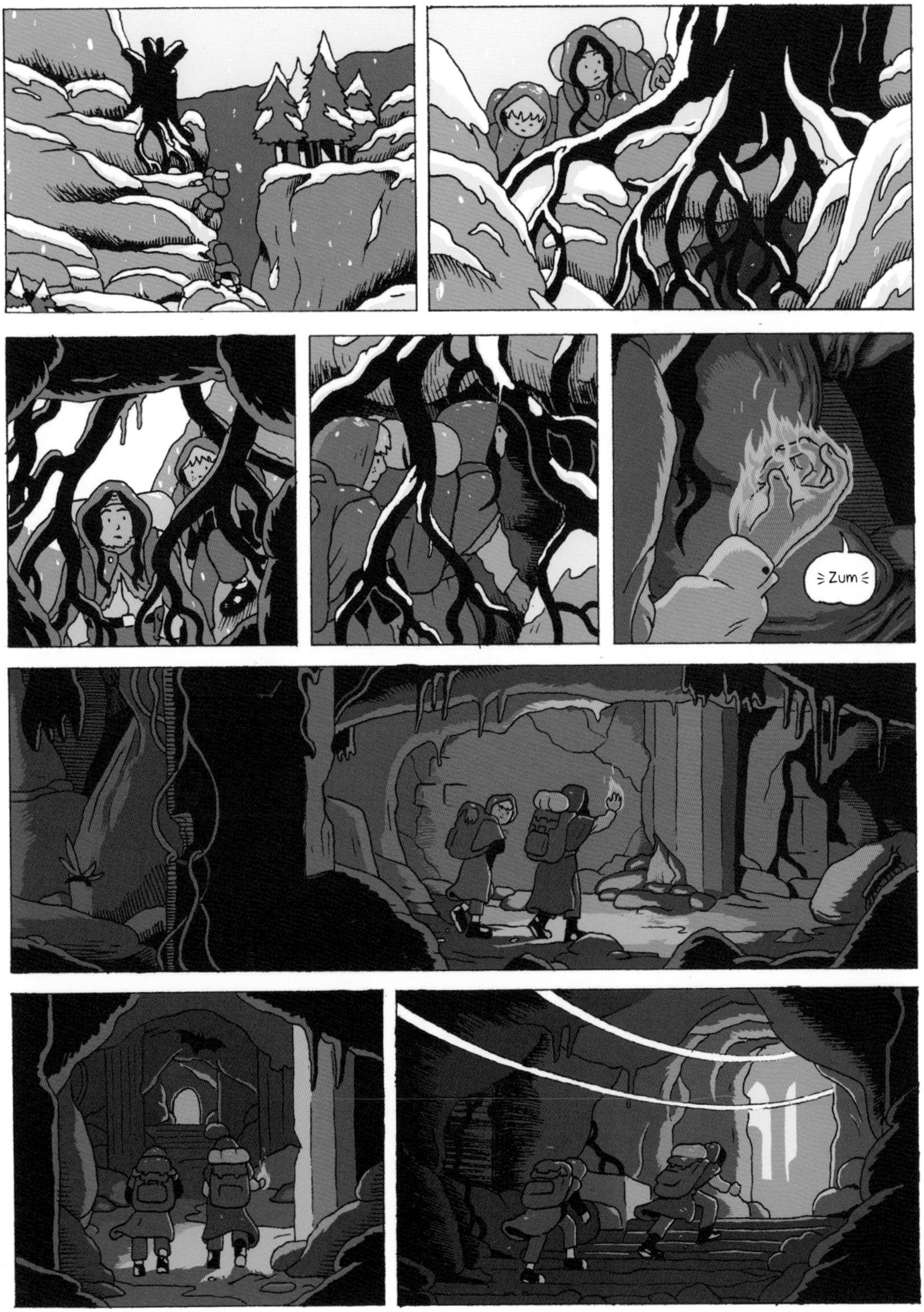
Zum

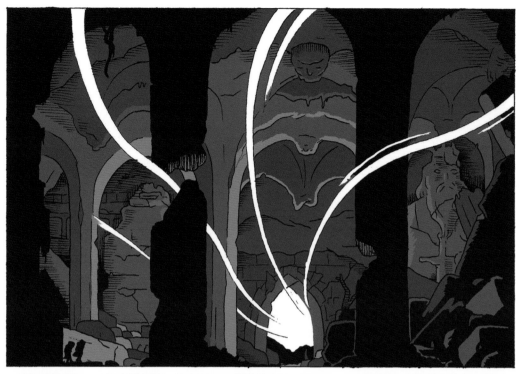

This is it, Sophia. This is it.

Yes.

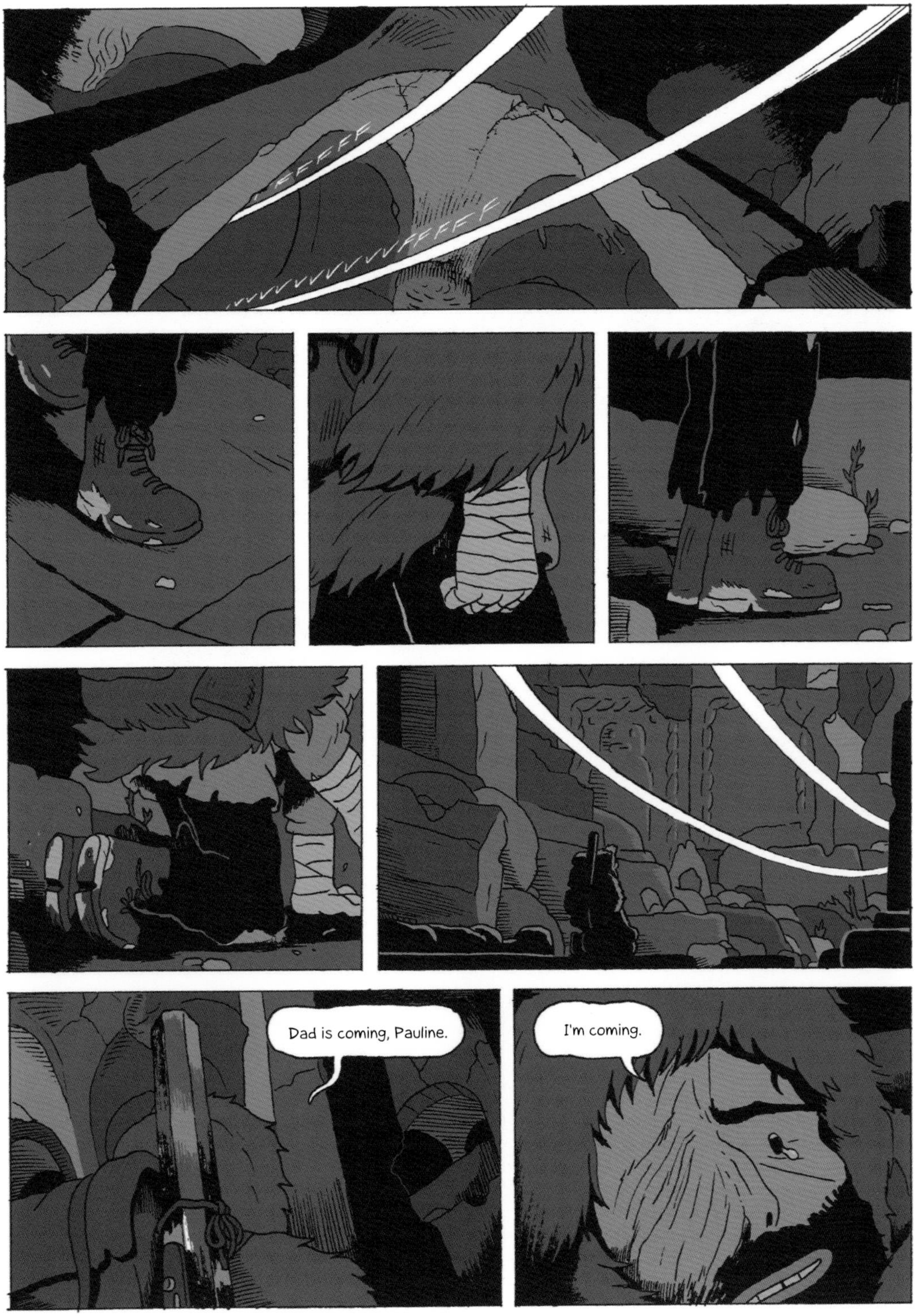
FFFFFF
VVVVVVVVVVVFFFFF
Dad is coming, Pauline.
I'm coming.

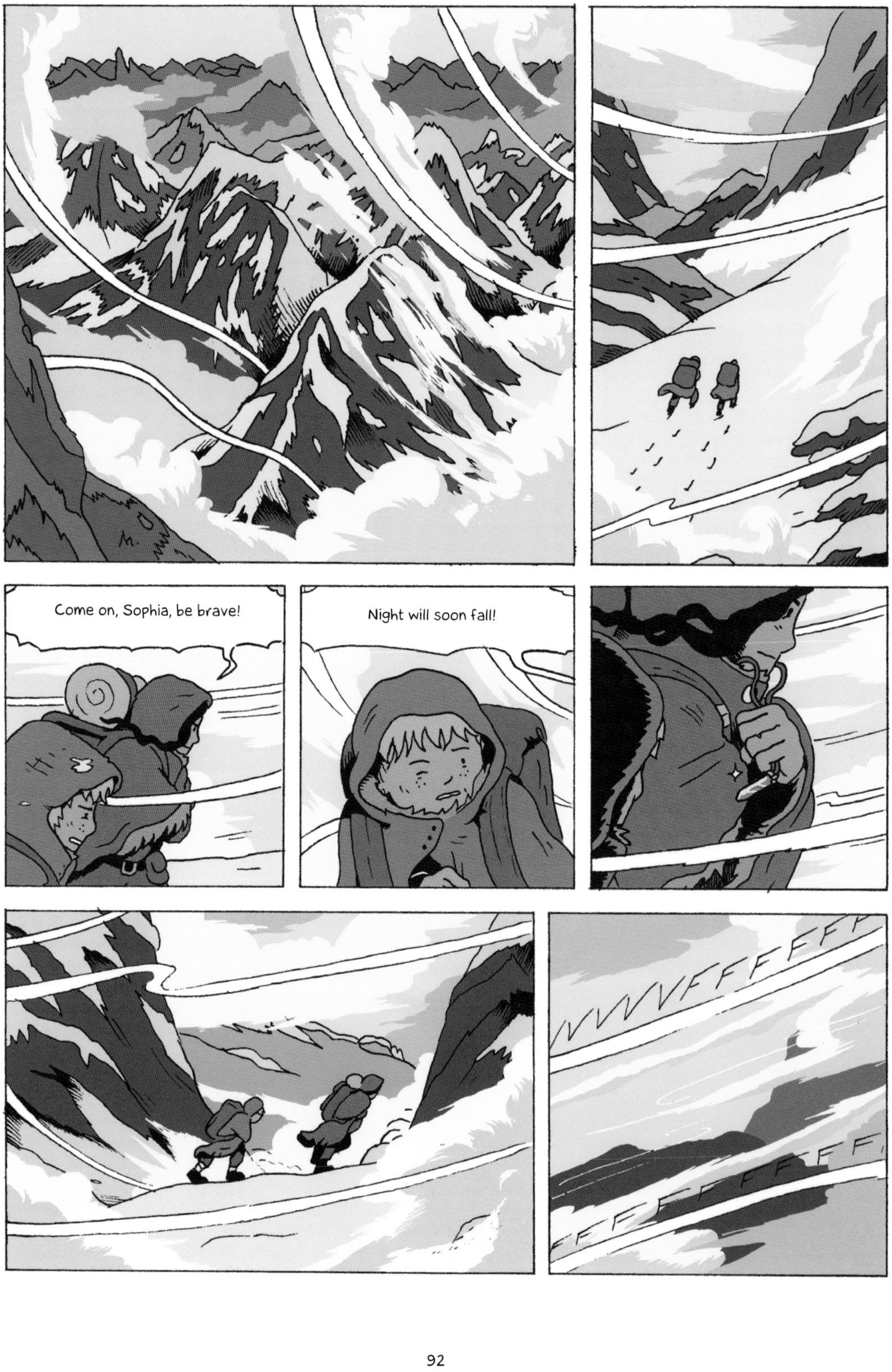
Come on, Sophia, be brave!
Night will soon fall!

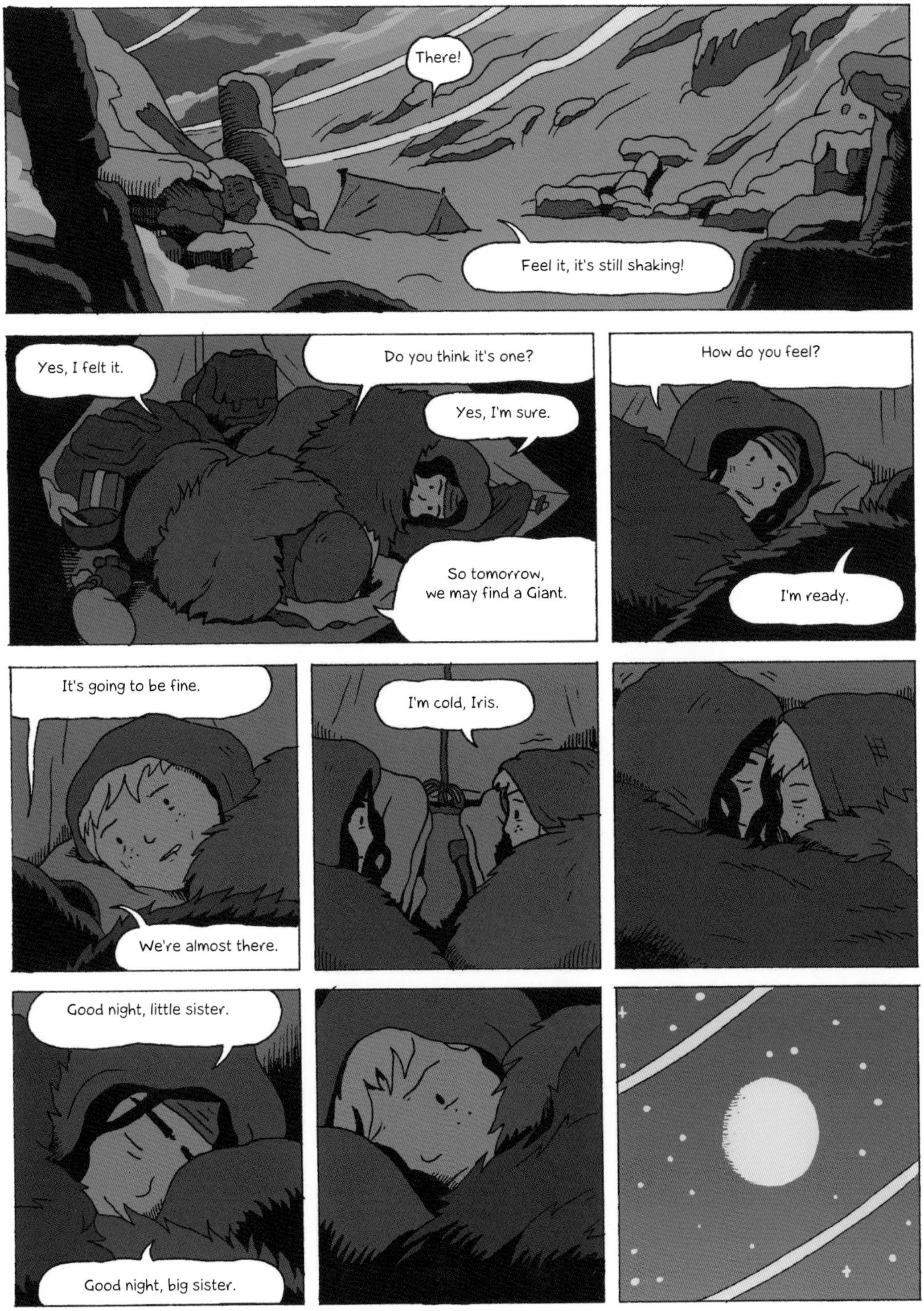
There!
Feel it, it's still shaking!
Yes, I felt it.
Do you think it's one?
Yes, I'm sure.
So tomorrow, we may find a Giant.
How do you feel?
I'm ready.
It's going to be fine.
We're almost there.
I'm cold, Iris.
Good night, little sister.
Good night, big sister.

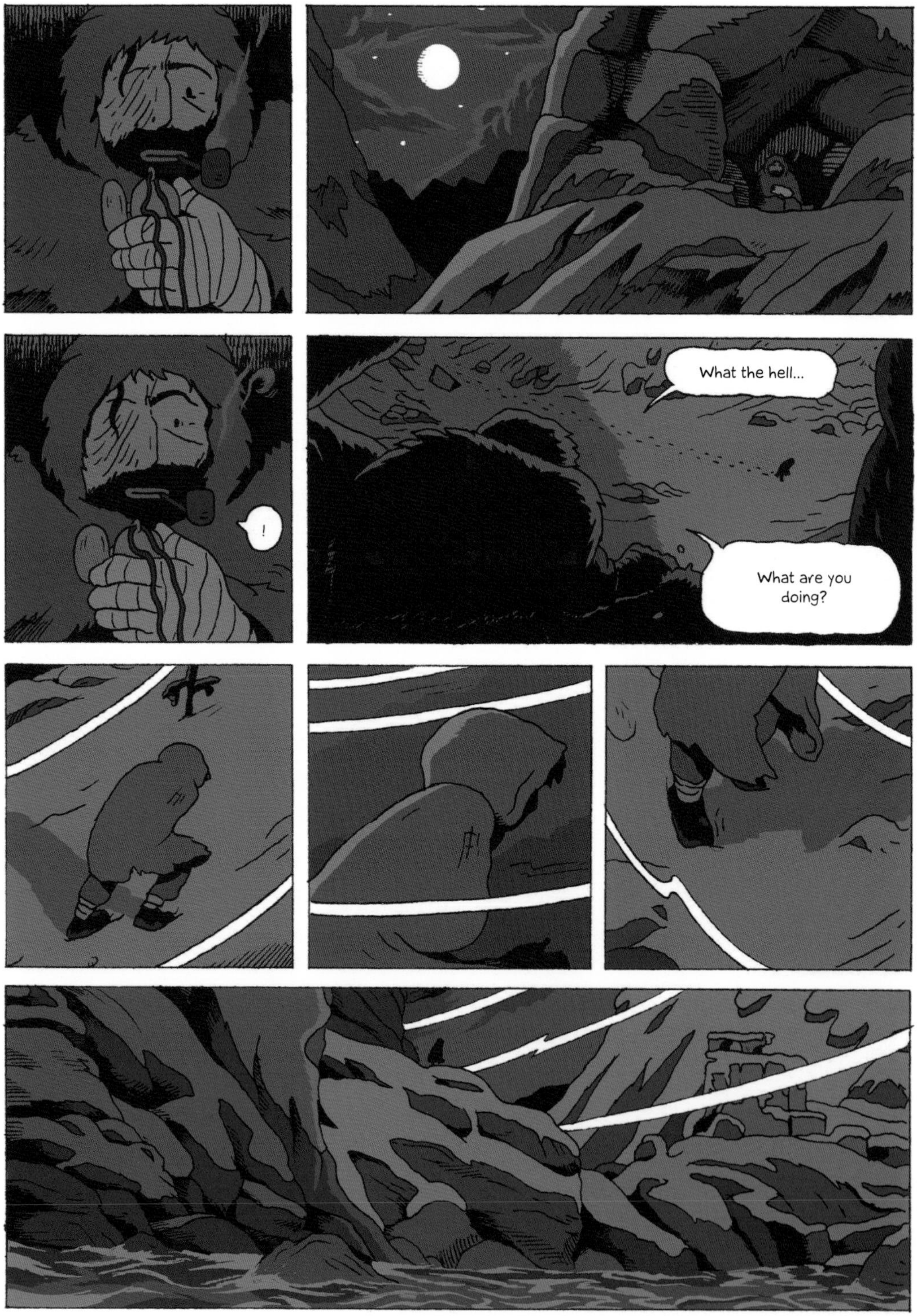
!
What the hell...
What are you doing?

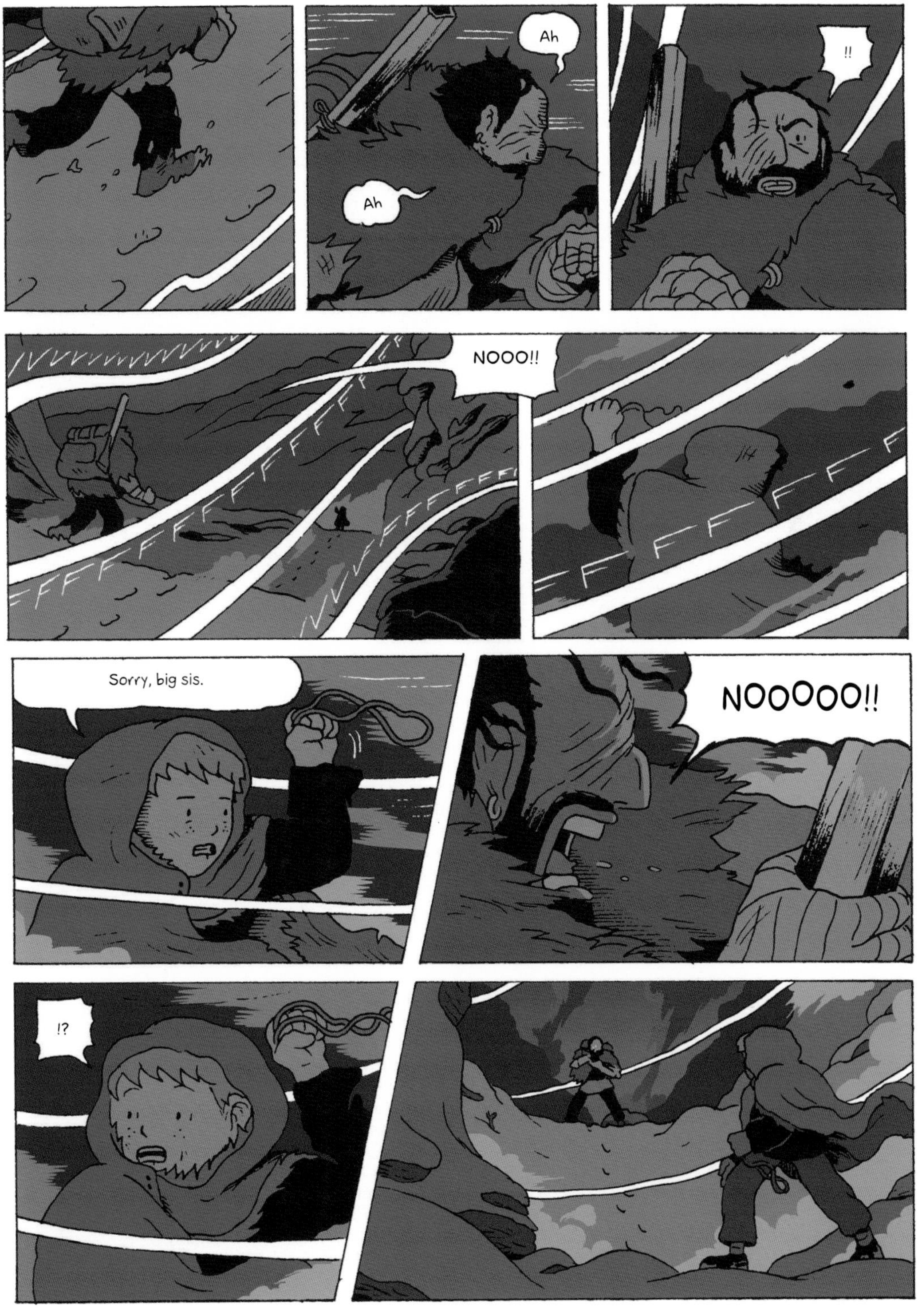
Ah
Ah
!!
NOOO!!
Sorry, big sis.
NOOOOO!!
!?

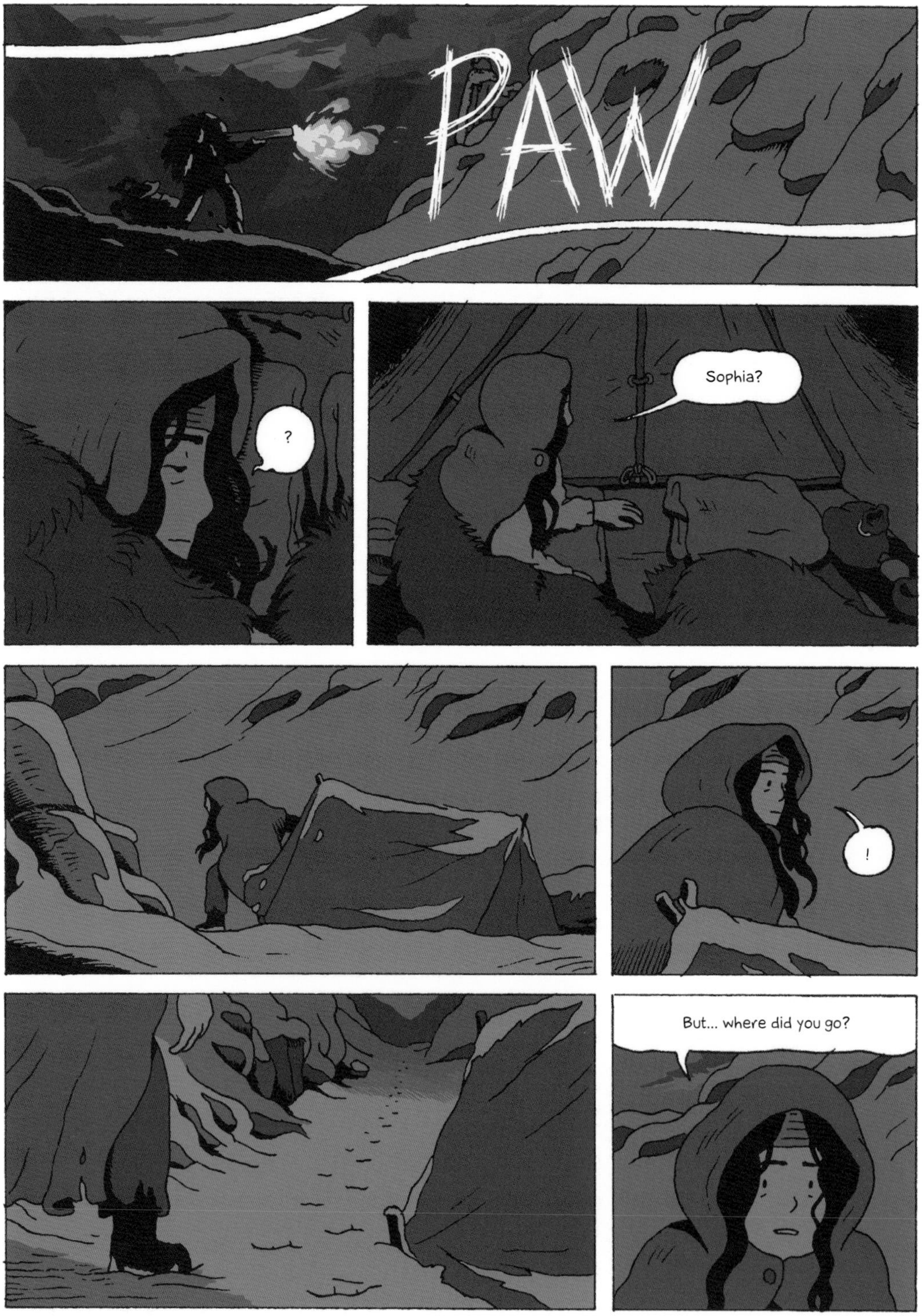
PAW
?
Sophia?
!
But... where did you go?

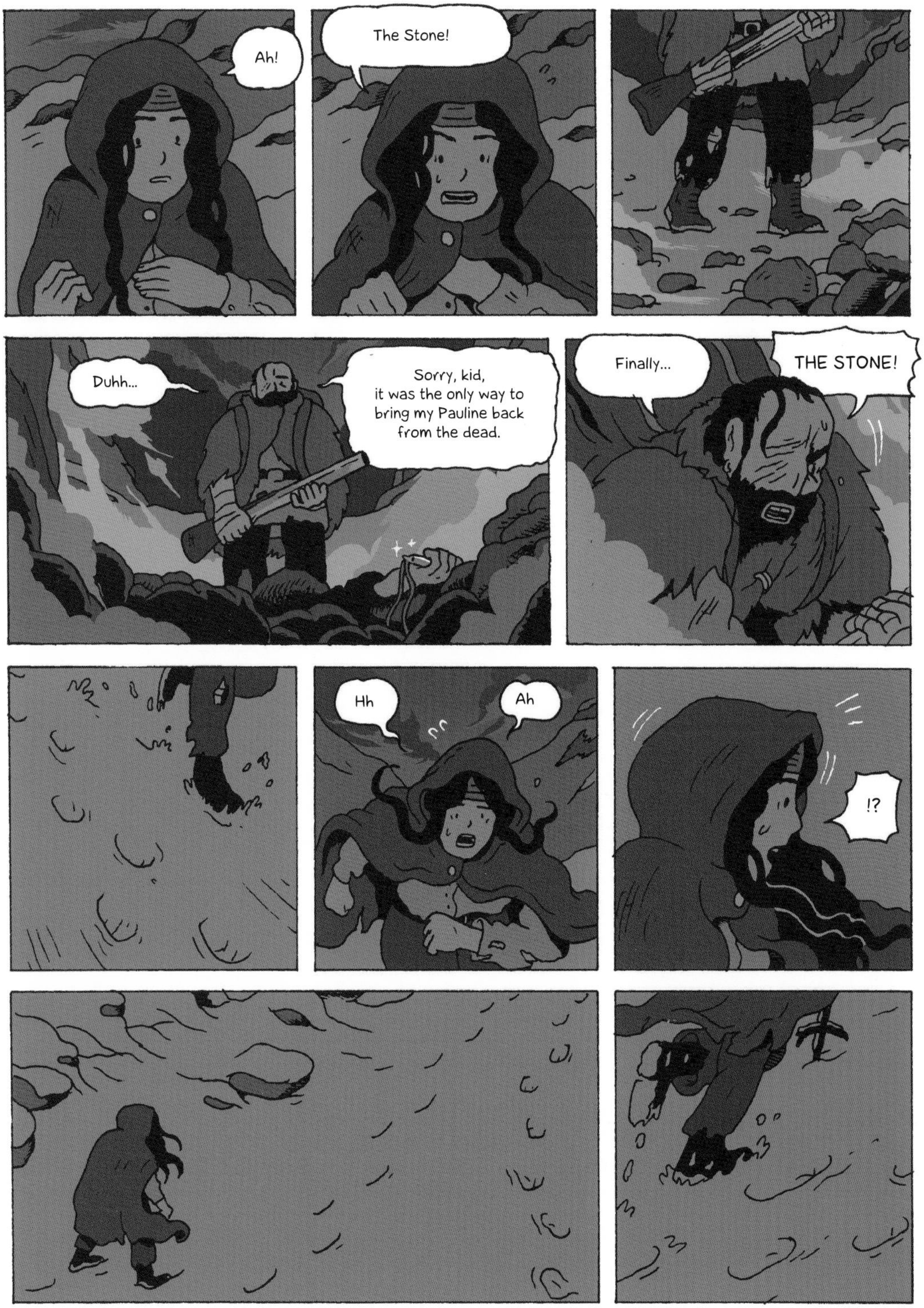
Ah!
The Stone!
Duhh...
Sorry, kid, it was the only way to bring my Pauline back from the dead.
Finally...
THE STONE!
Hh
Ah
!?

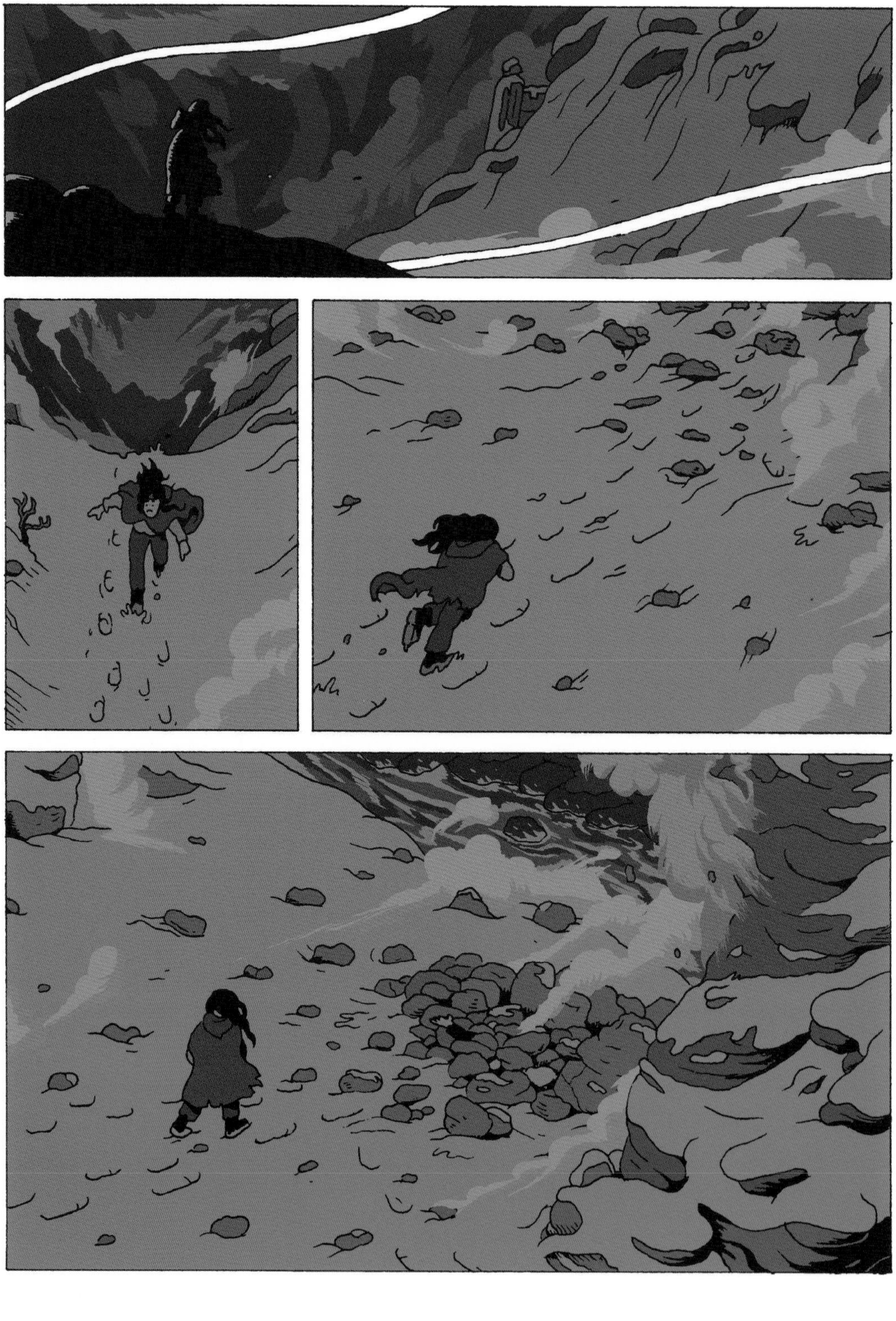

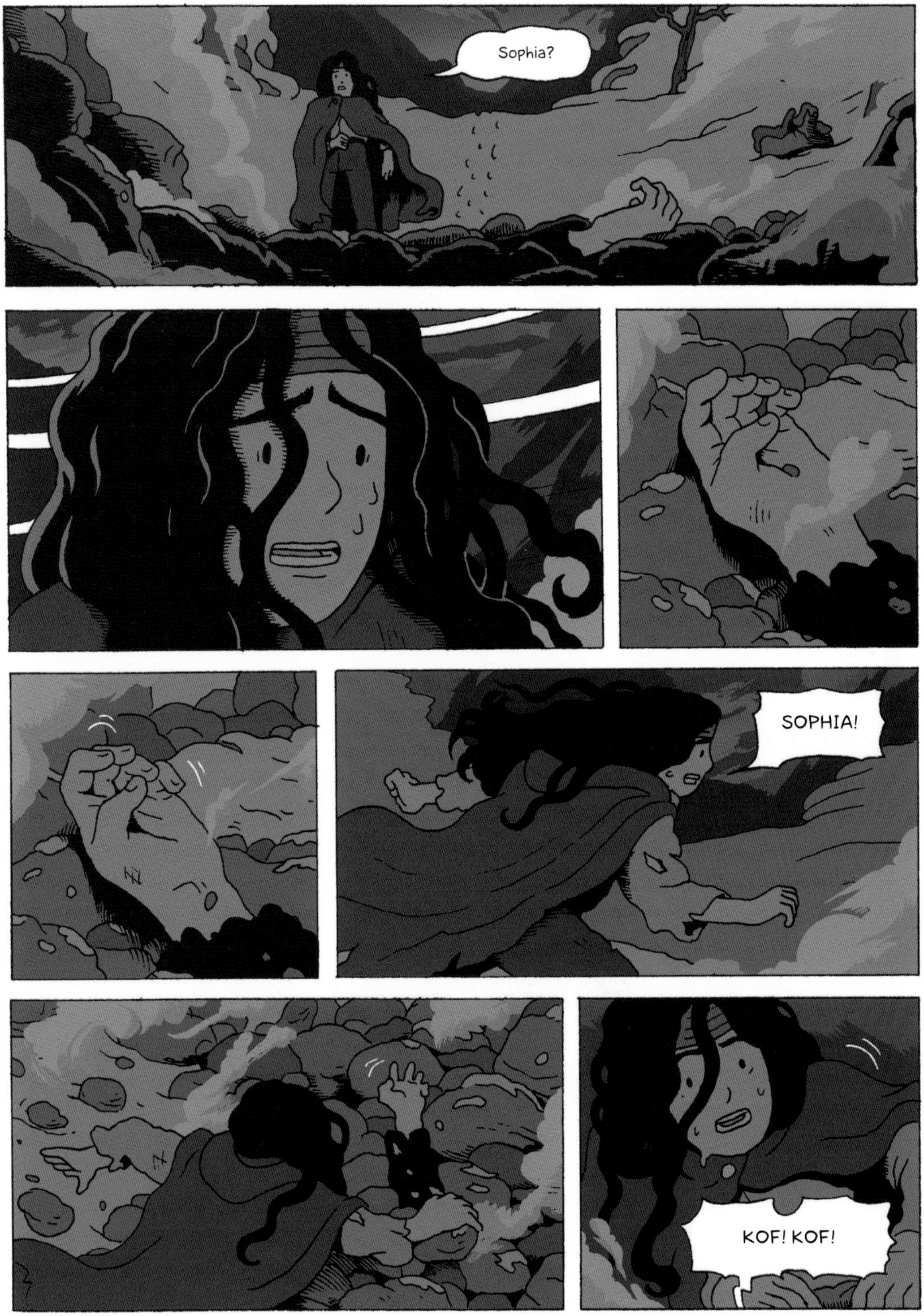
Sophia?
SOPHIA!
KOF! KOF!

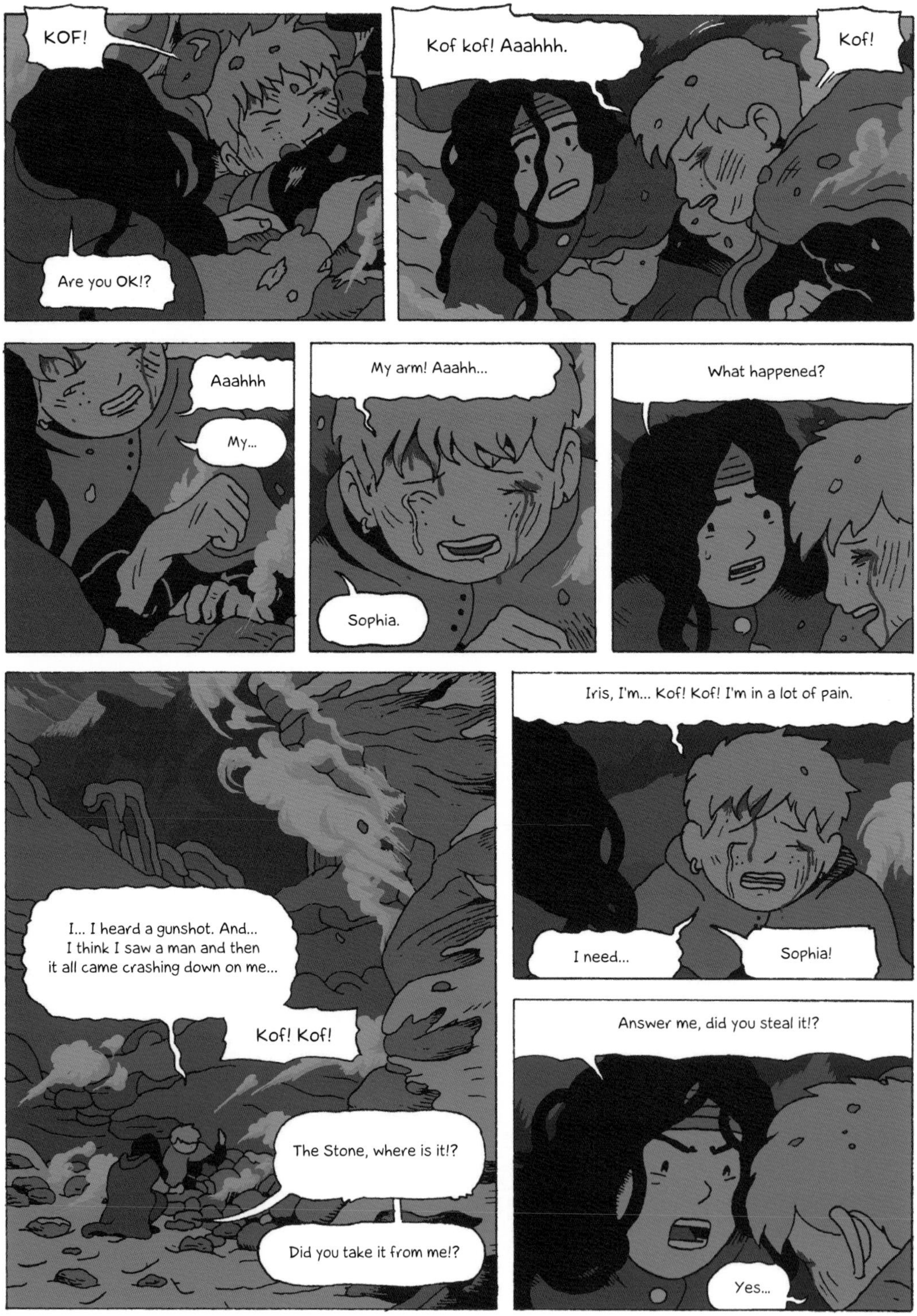
KOF!
Are you OK!?
Kof kof! Aaahhh.
Kof!
Aaahhh
My...
My arm! Aaahh...
Sophia.
What happened?
Iris, I'm... Kof! Kof! I'm in a lot of pain.
I need...
Sophia!
I... I heard a gunshot. And...
I think I saw a man and then
it all came crashing down on me...
Kof! Kof!
The Stone, where is it!?
Did you take it from me!?
Answer me, did you steal it!?
Yes...

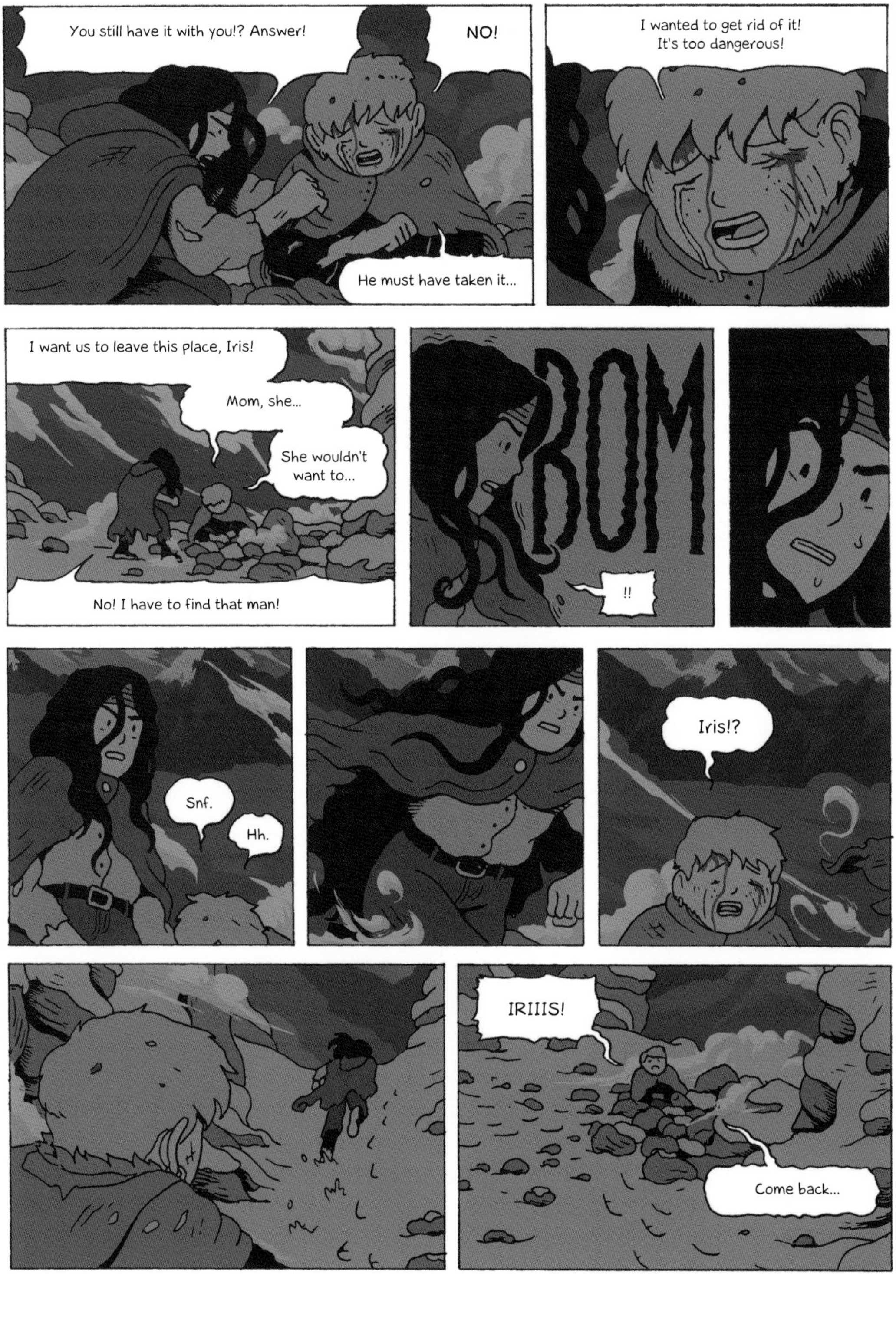
You still have it with you!? Answer!
NO!
He must have taken it...
I wanted to get rid of it!
It's too dangerous!
I want us to leave this place, Iris!
Mom, she...
She wouldn't want to...
No! I have to find that man!
BOM
!!
Snf.
Hh.
Iris!?
IRIIIS!
Come back...

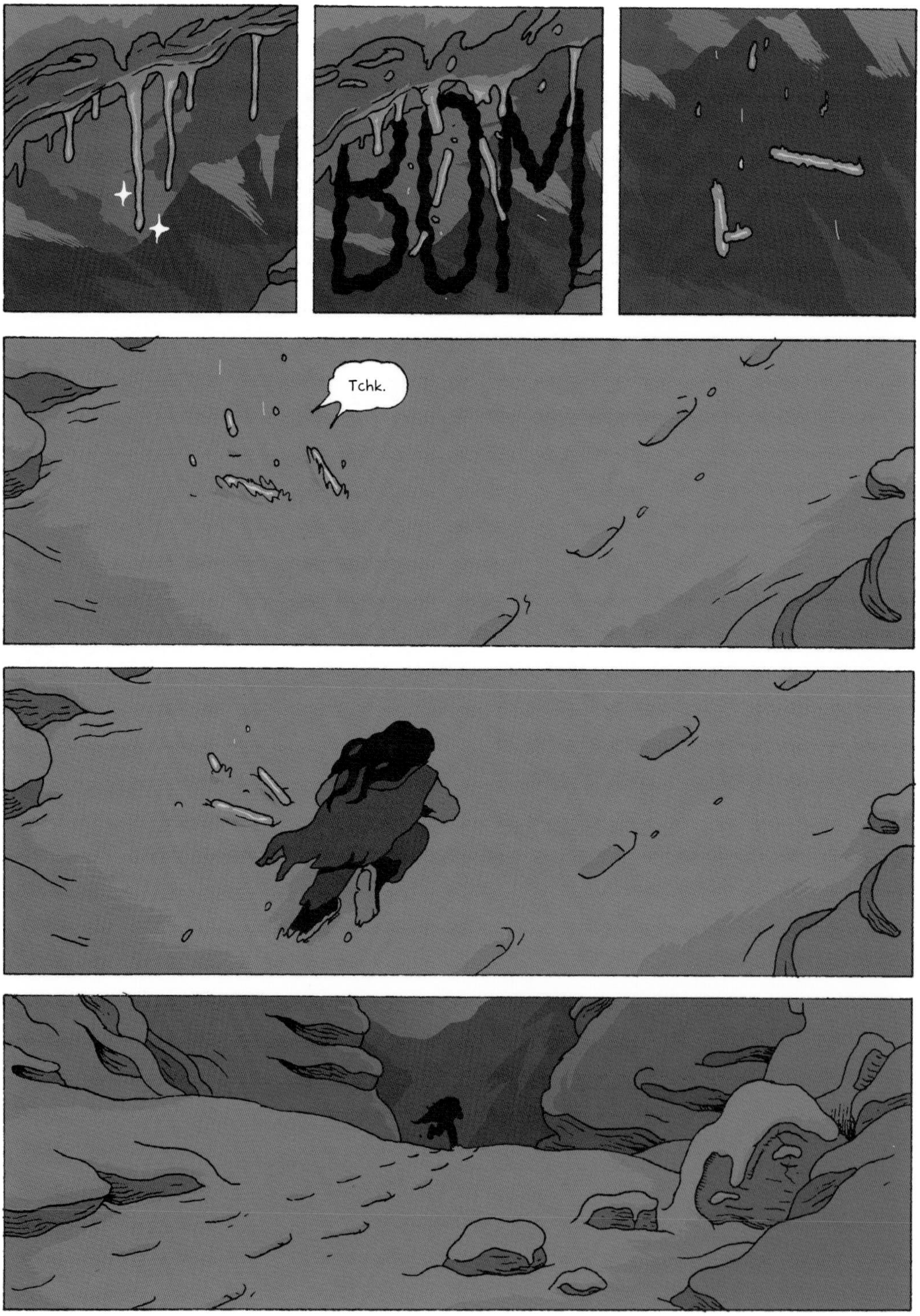
BOM
Tchk.

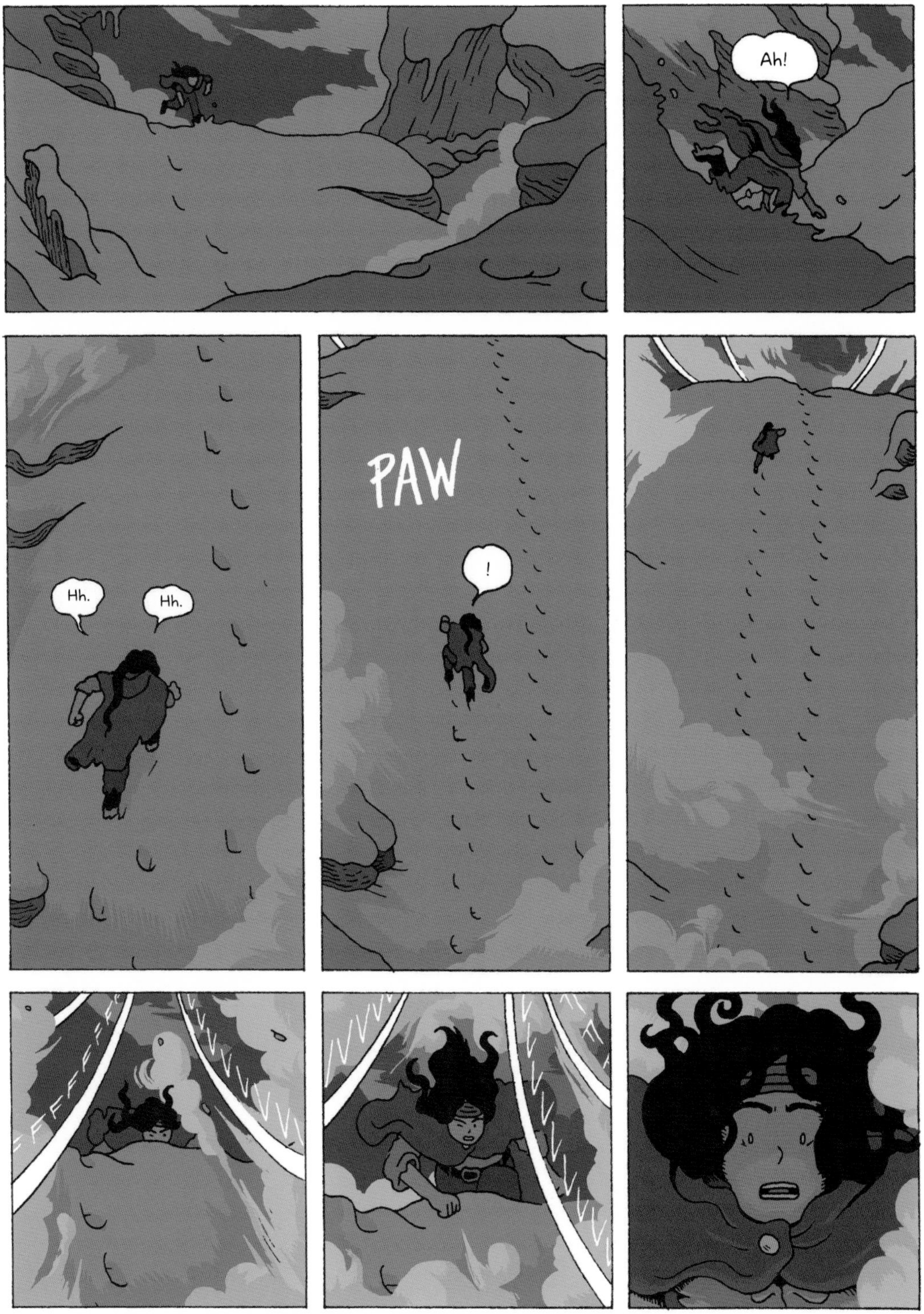
Ah!
Hh.
Hh.
PAW
!

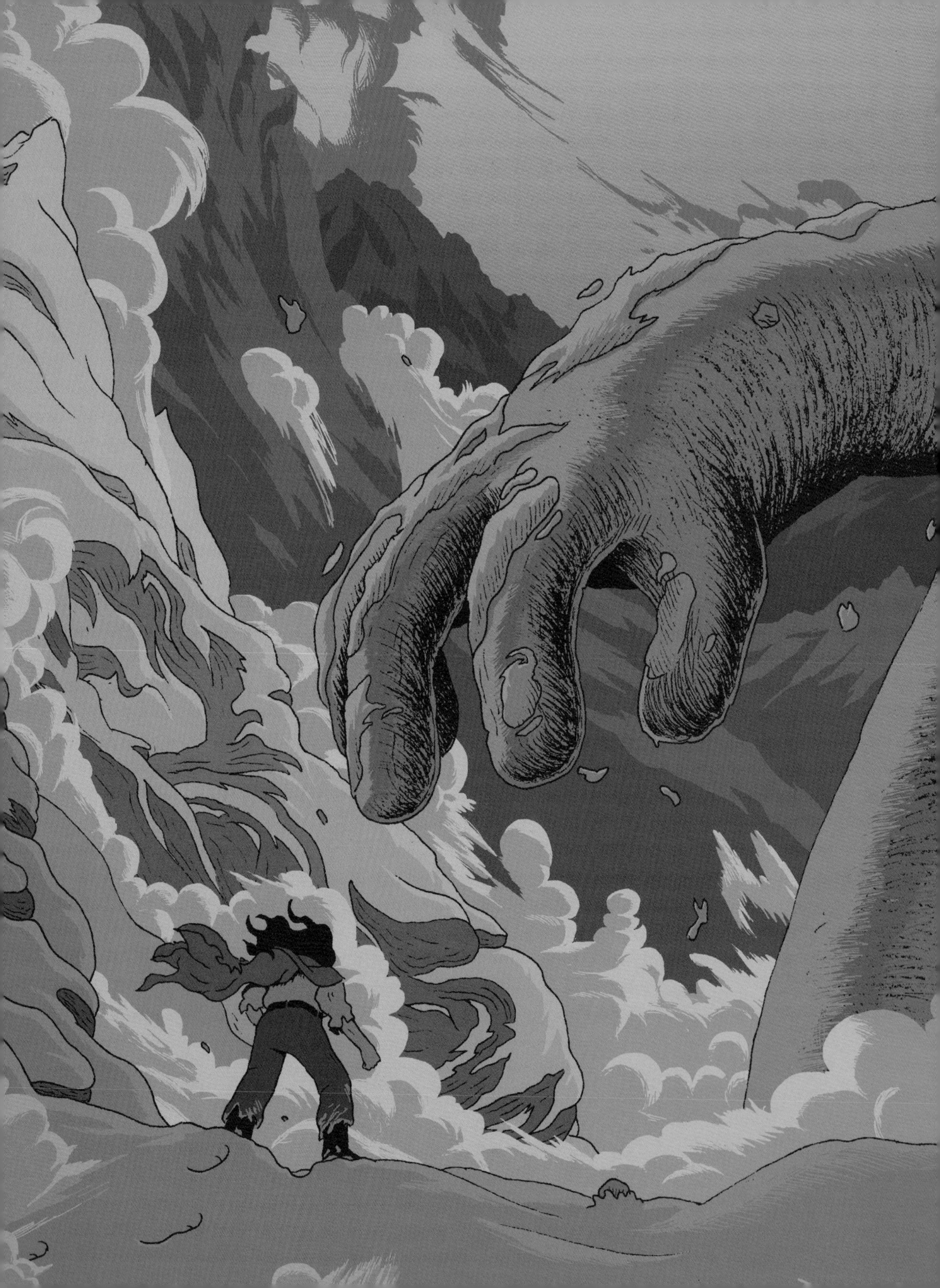

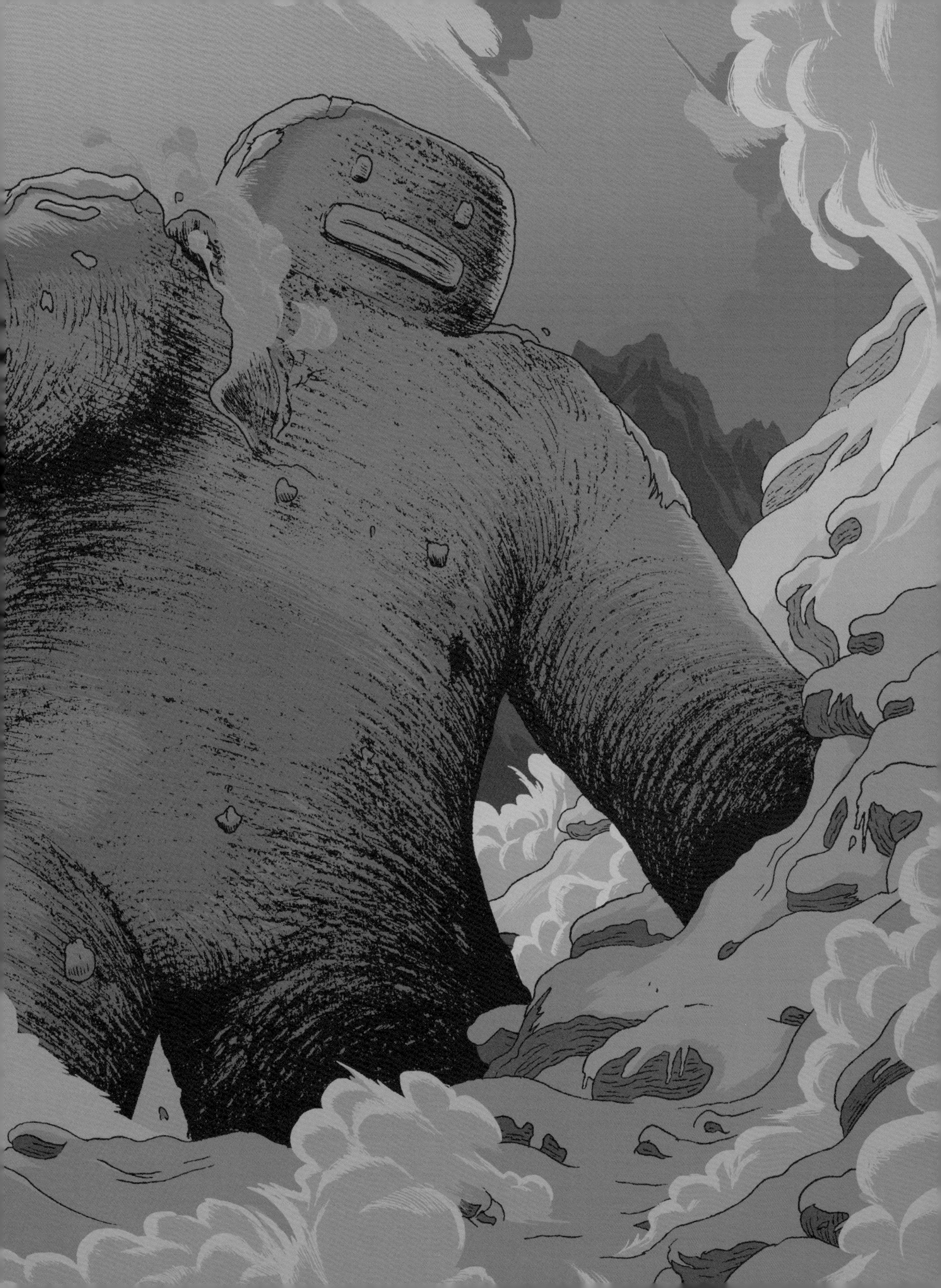

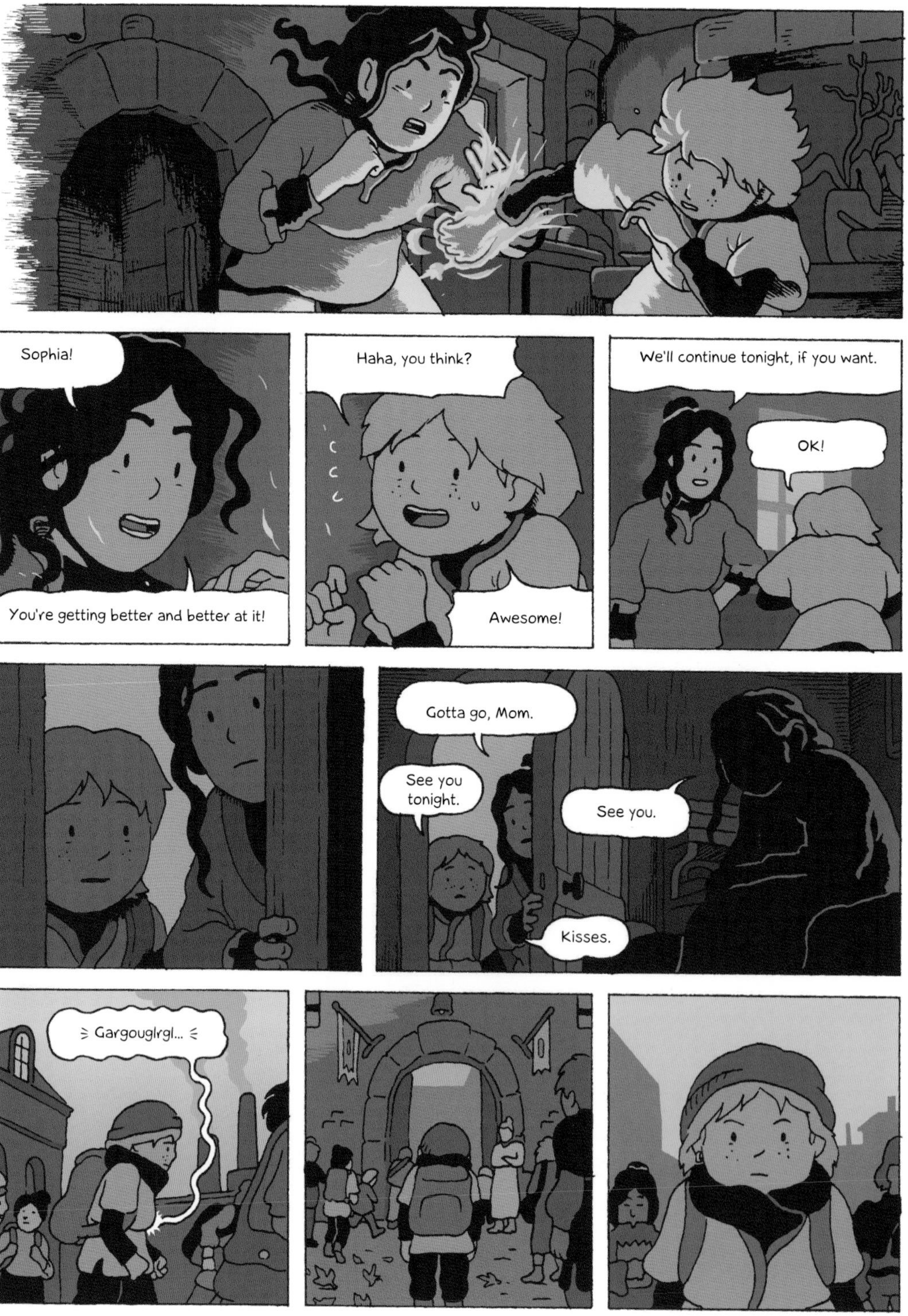
Sophia!
You're getting better and better at it!
Haha, you think?
Awesome!
We'll continue tonight, if you want.
OK!
Gotta go, Mom.
See you tonight.
See you.
Kisses.
Gargouglrgl...

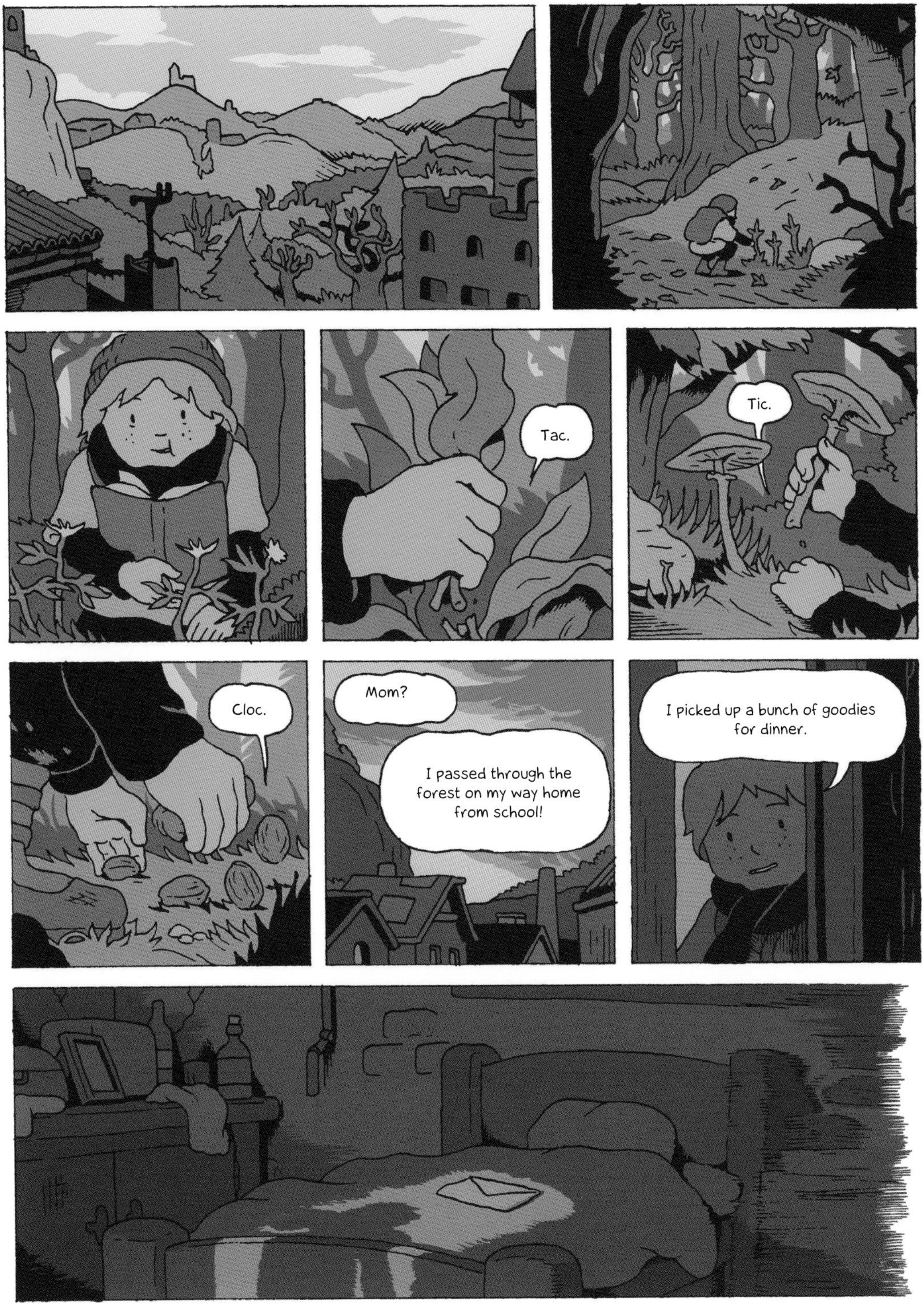
Tac.
Tic.
Cloc.
Mom?
I passed through the forest on my way home from school!
I picked up a bunch of goodies for dinner.

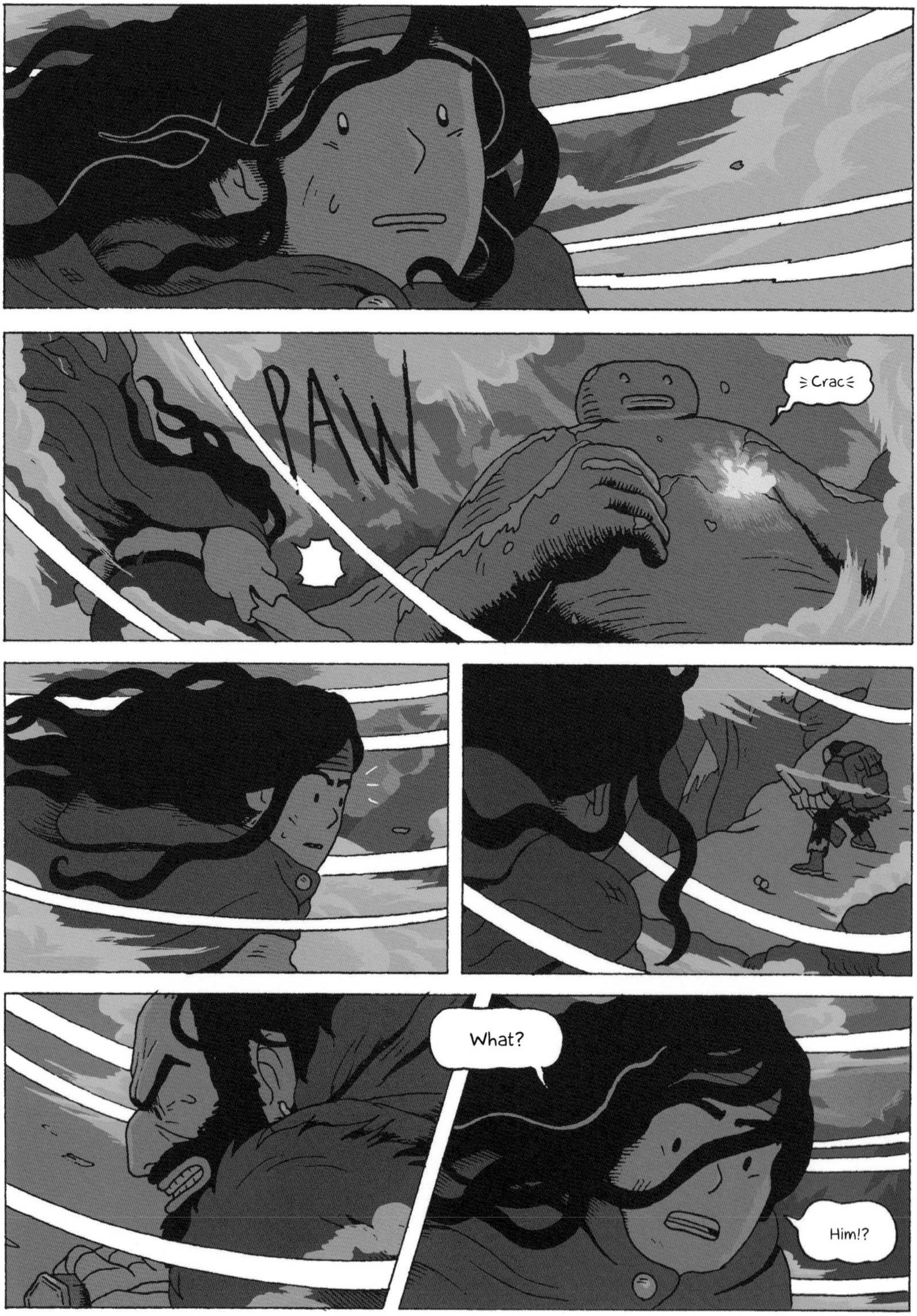
PAW
Crac
What?
Him!?

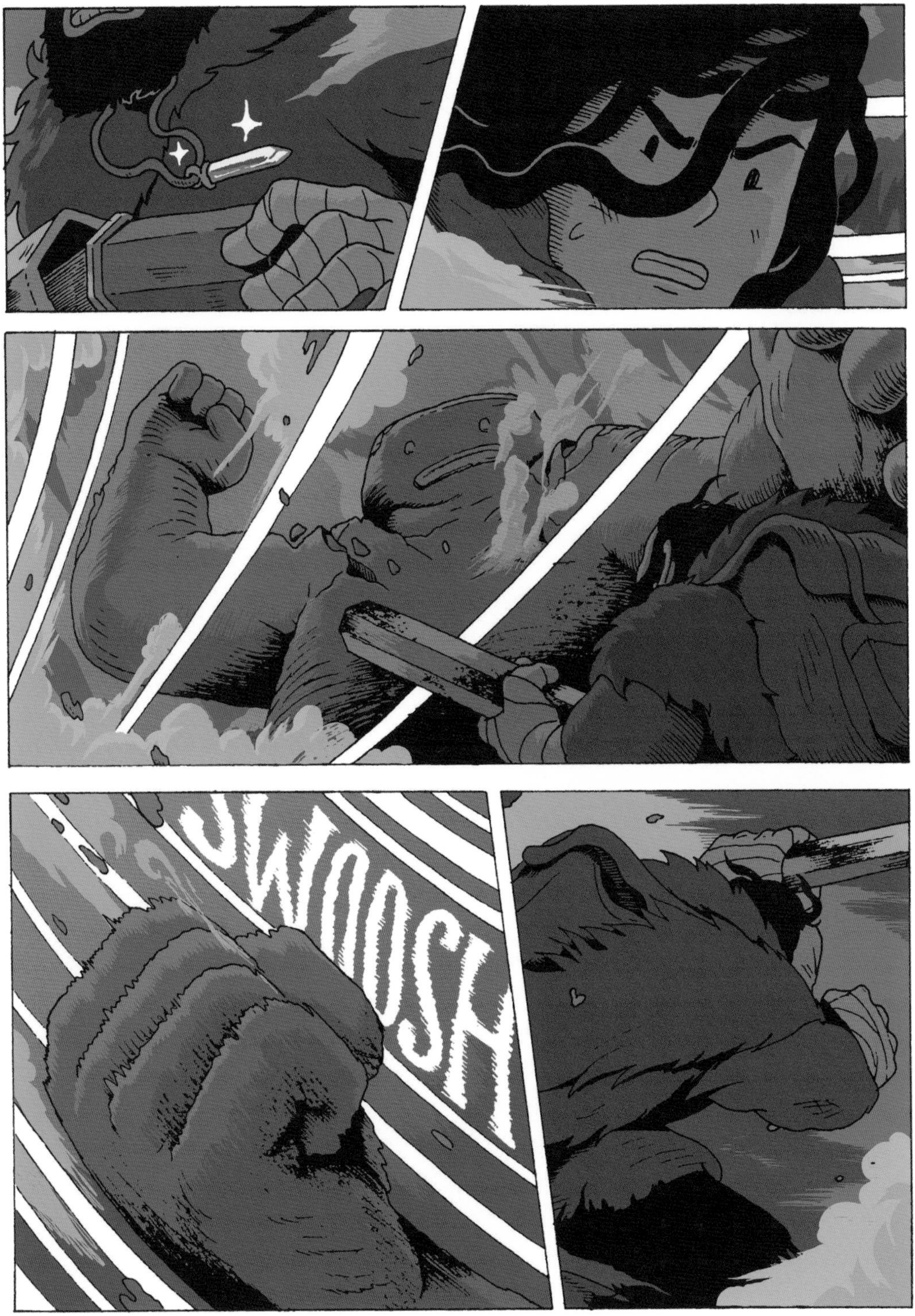
SWOOSH

BAMM
Pshhhh
PAW

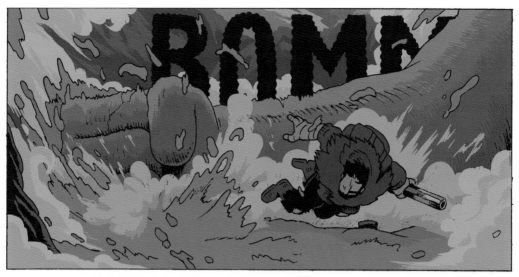

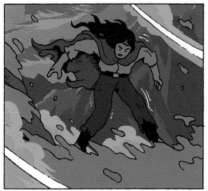

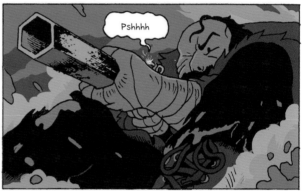

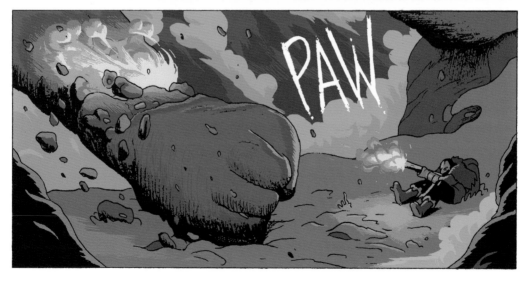

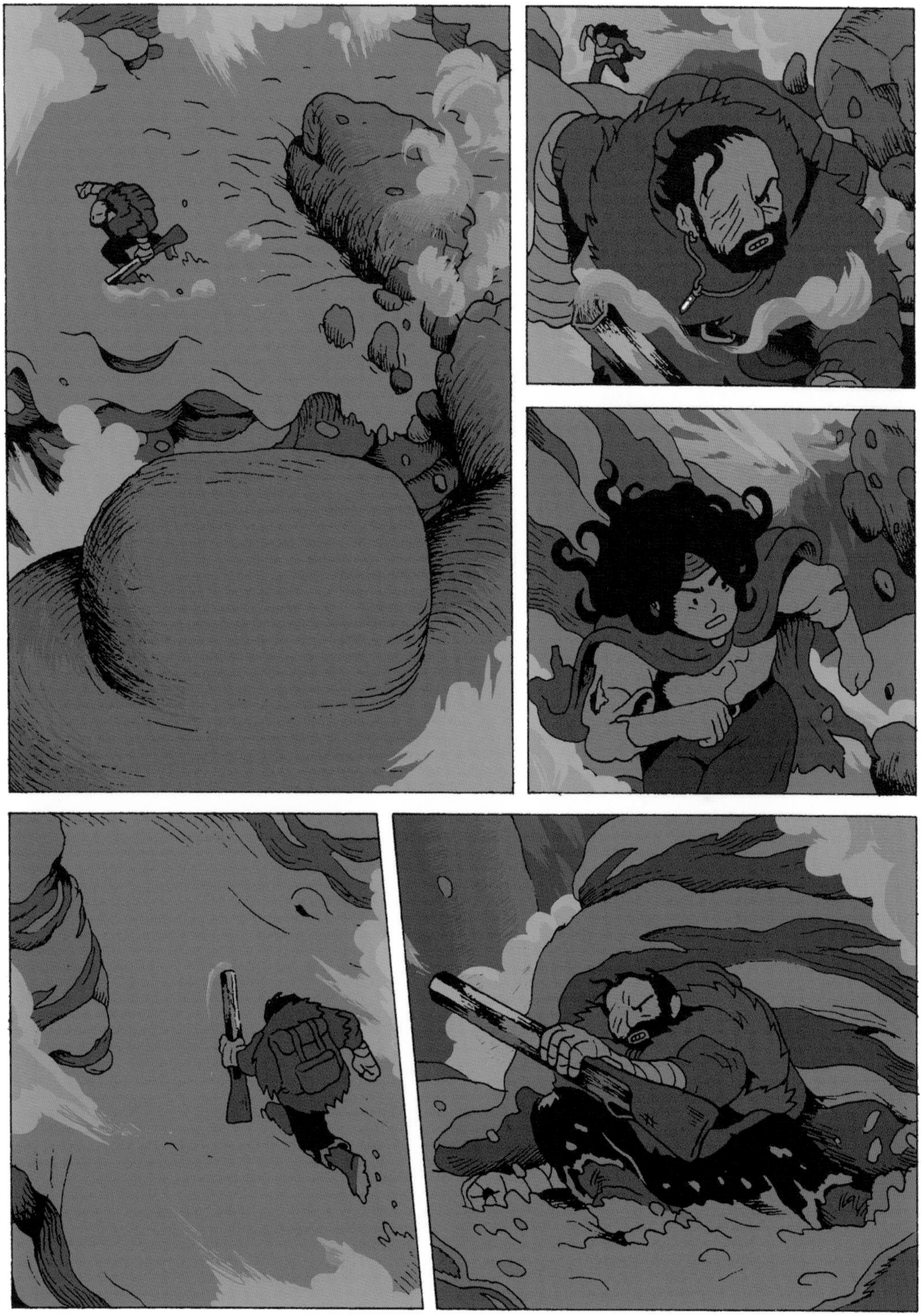

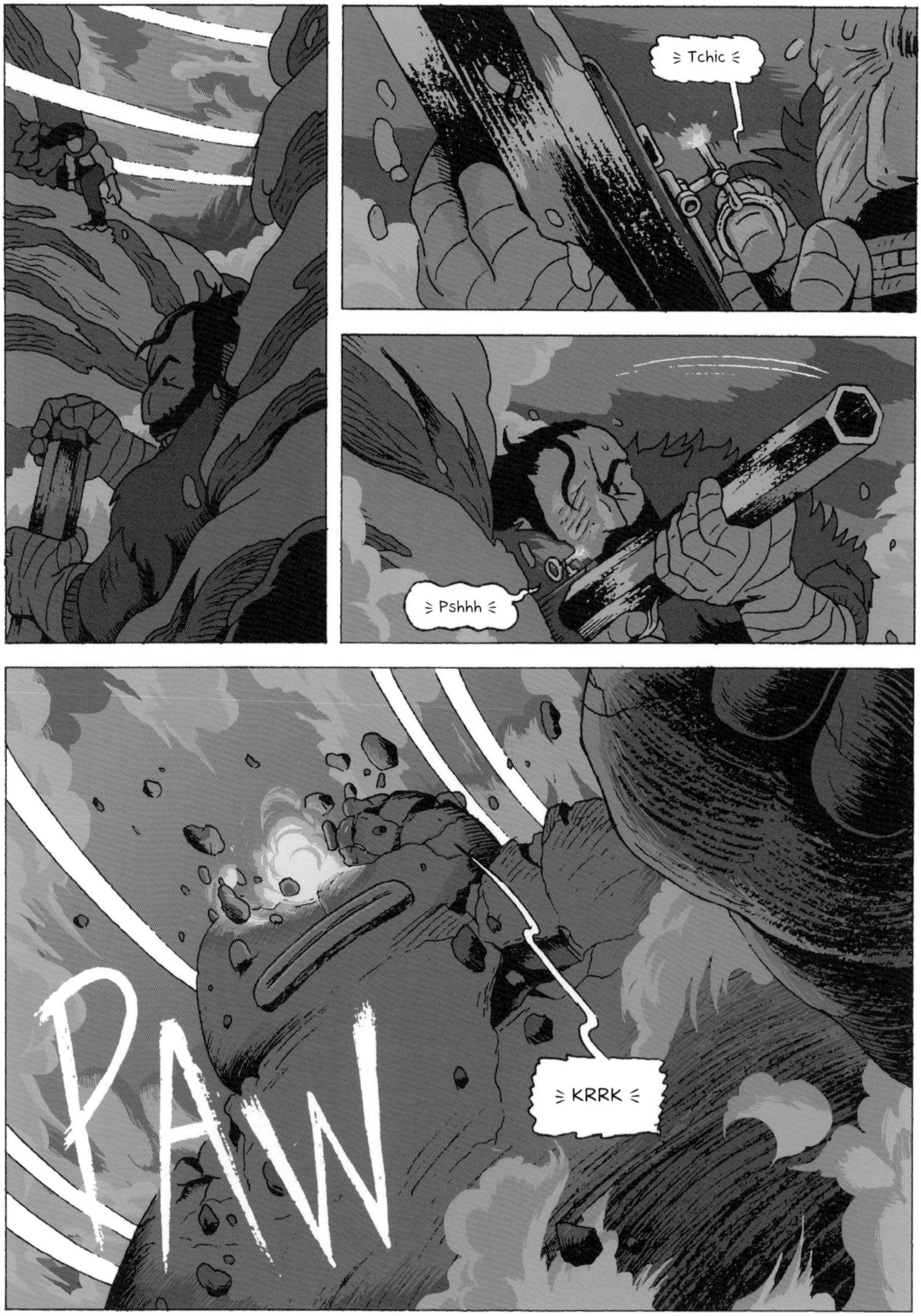
Tchic
Pshhh
PAW
KRRK

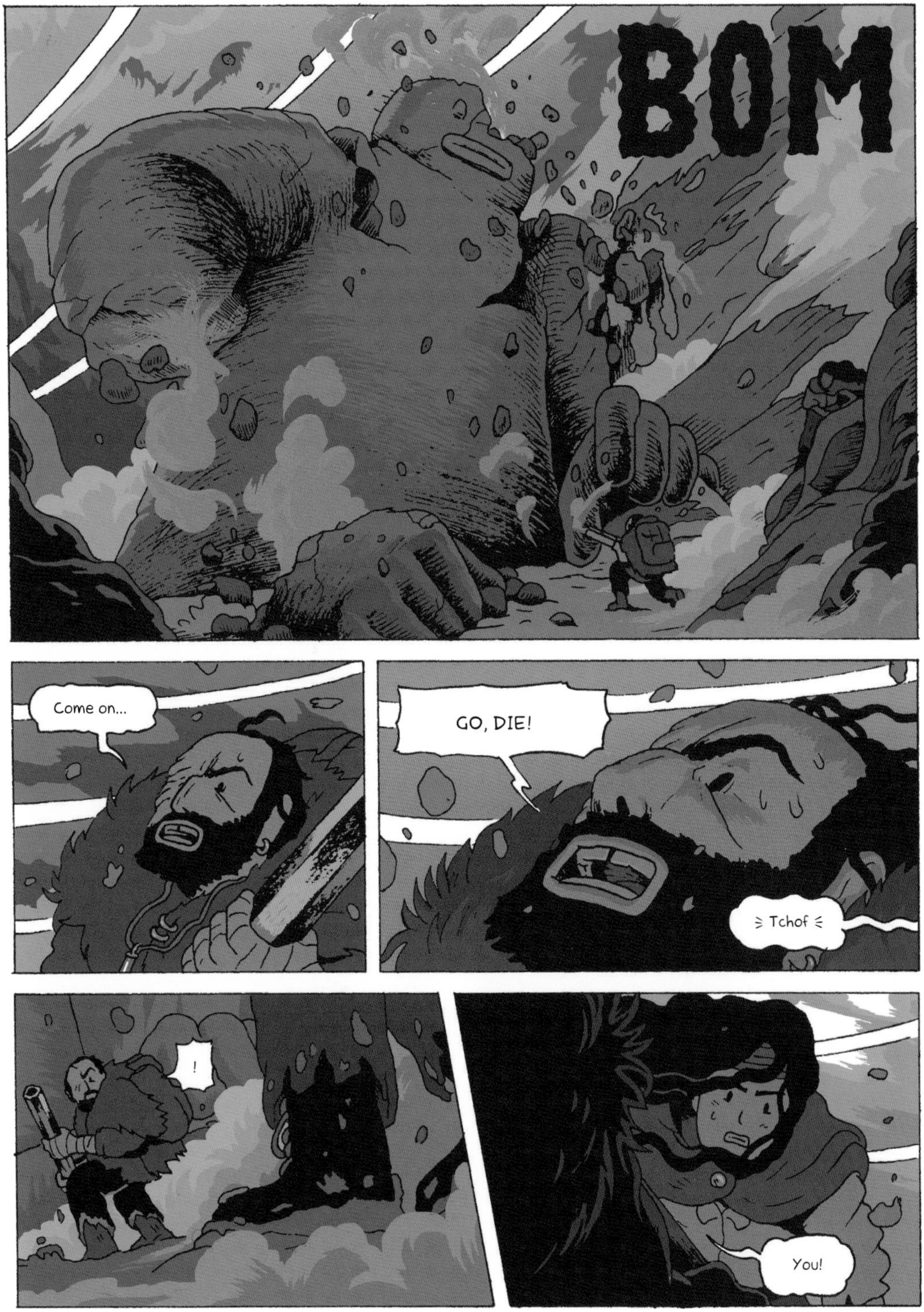
BOM
Come on...
GO, DIE!
Tchof
!
You!

KRKRRR!

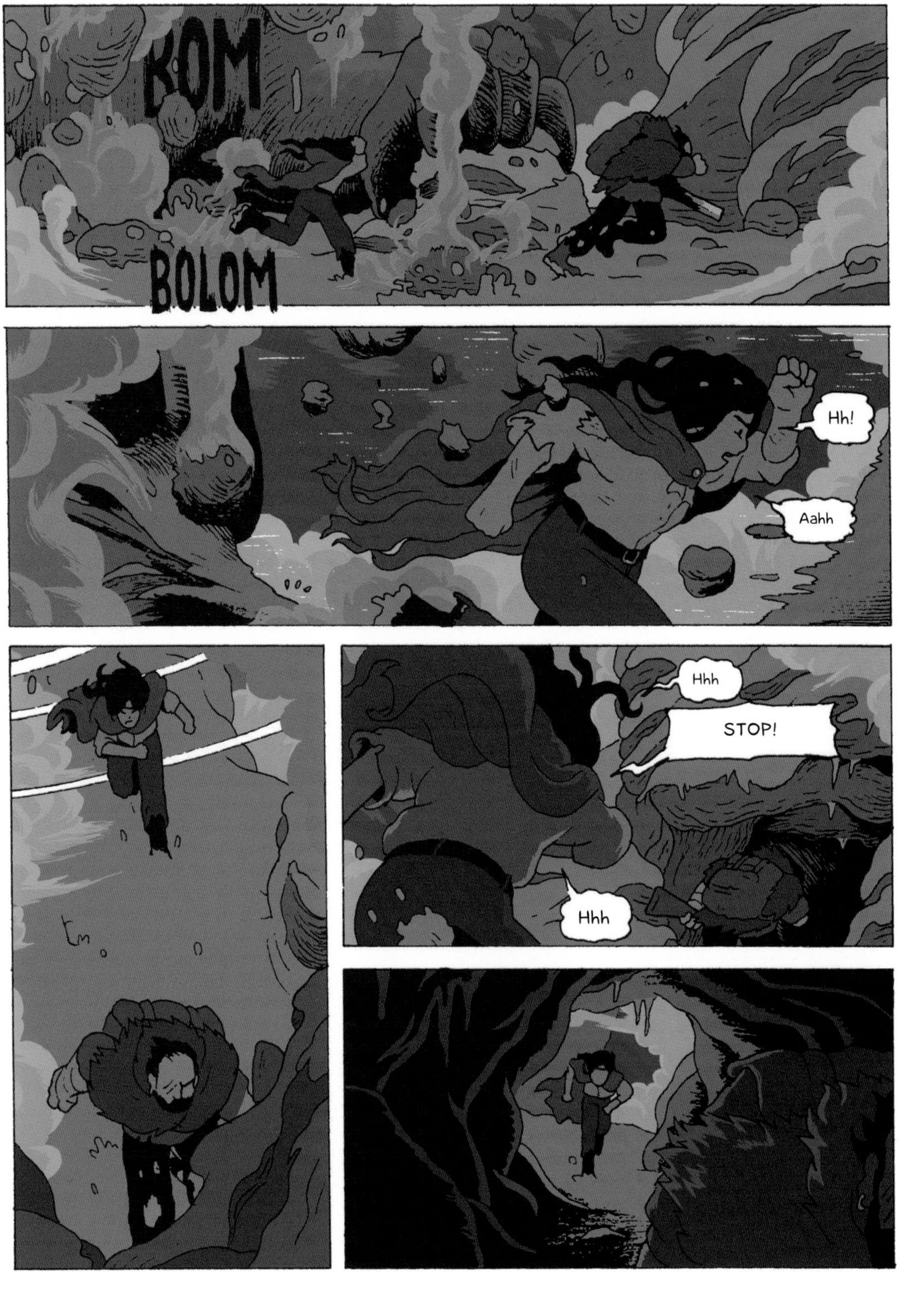
KOM
BOLOM
Hh!
Aahh
Hhh
STOP!
Hhh

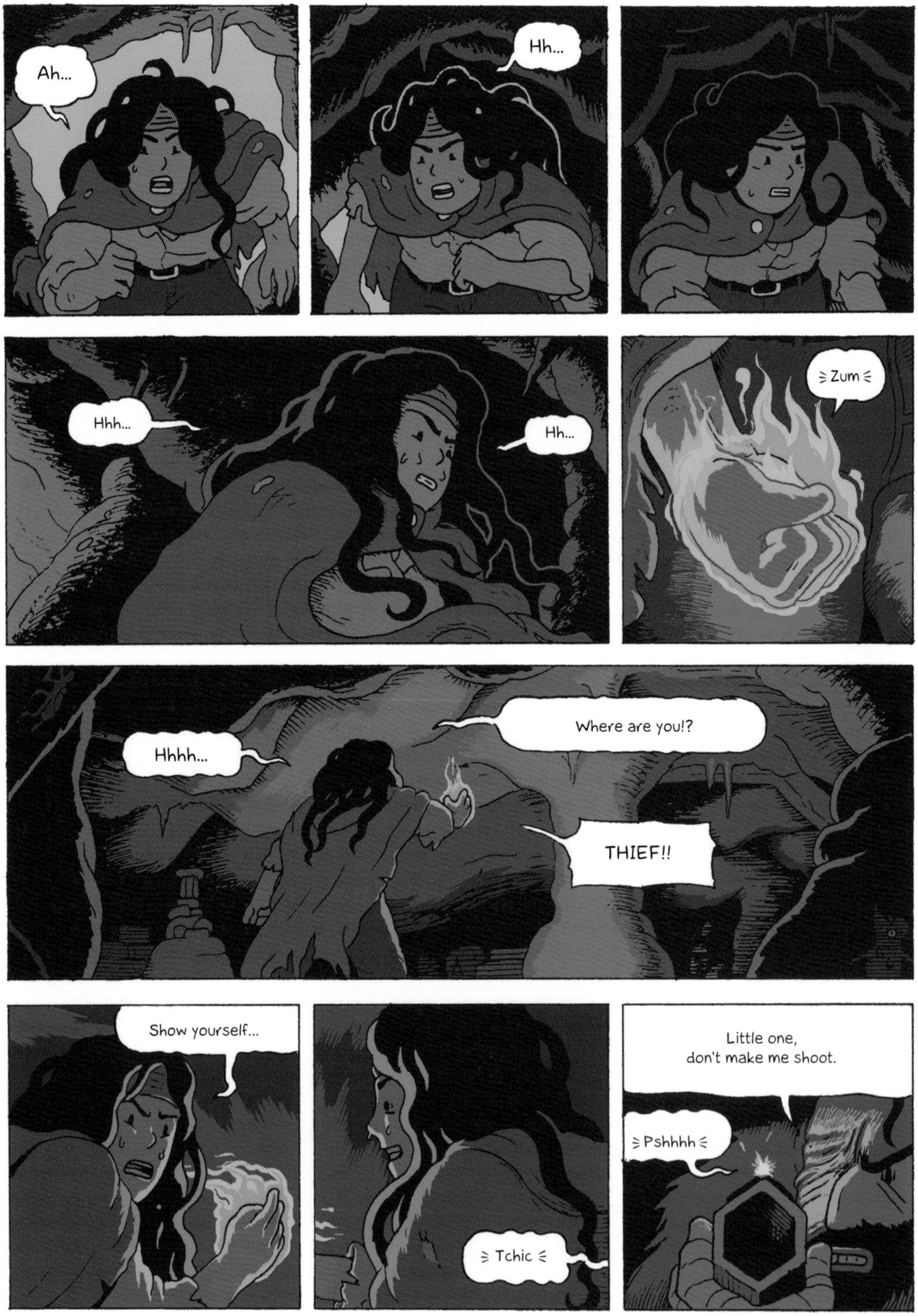
Ah...
Hh...
Hhh...
Hh...
Zum
Hhhh...
Where are you!?
THIEF!!
Show yourself...
Tchic
Little one, don't make me shoot.
Pshhhh

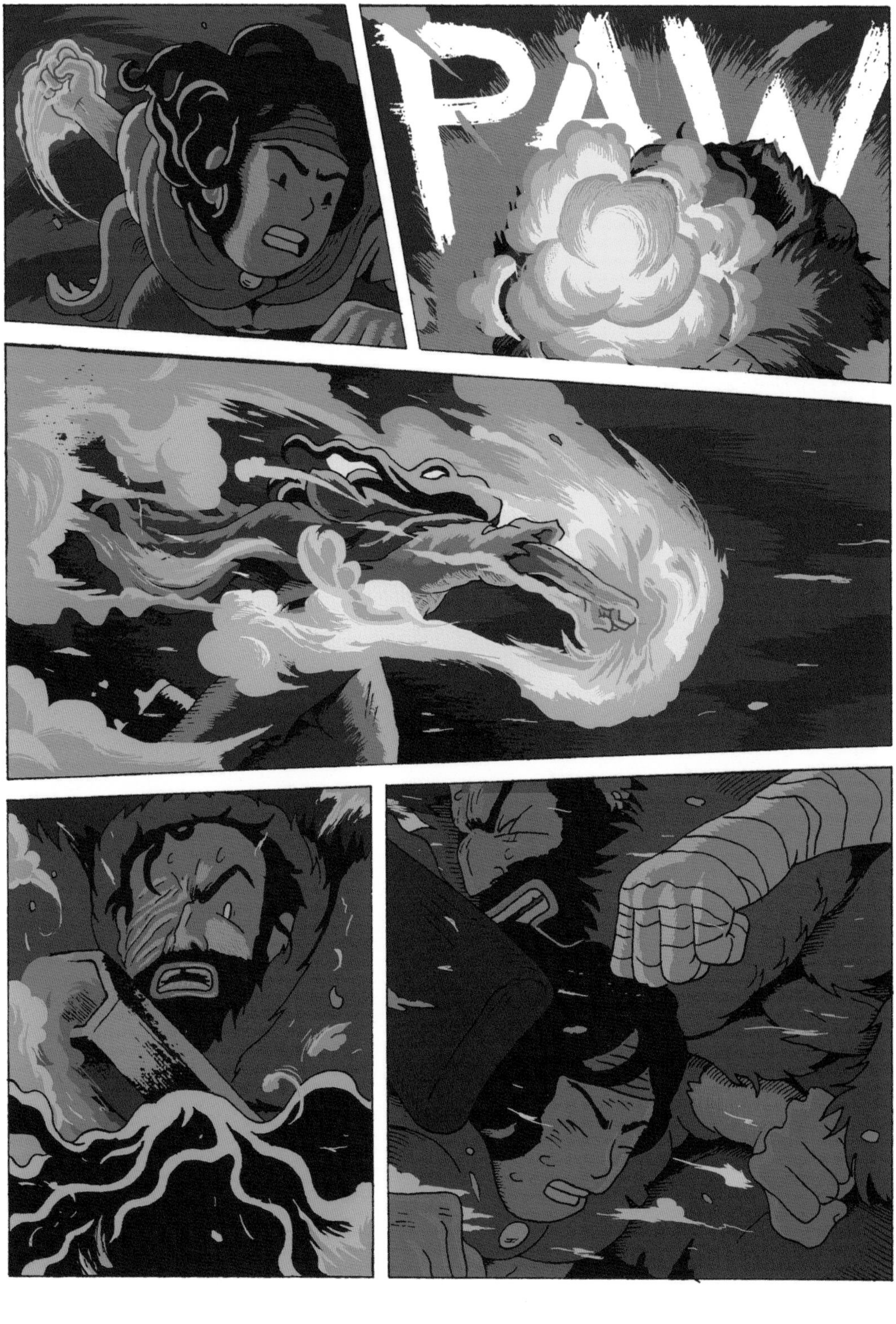
PAW

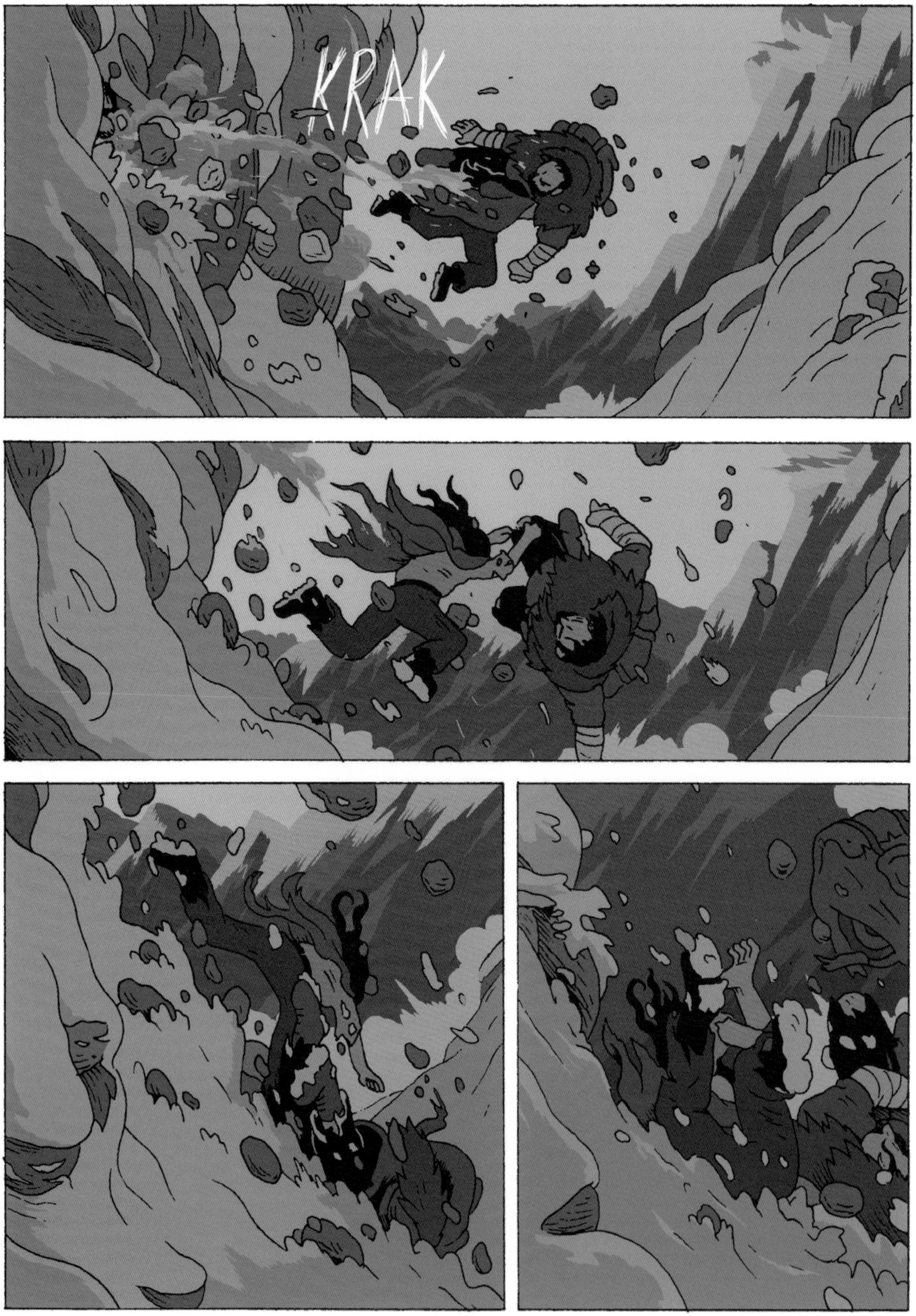
KRAK

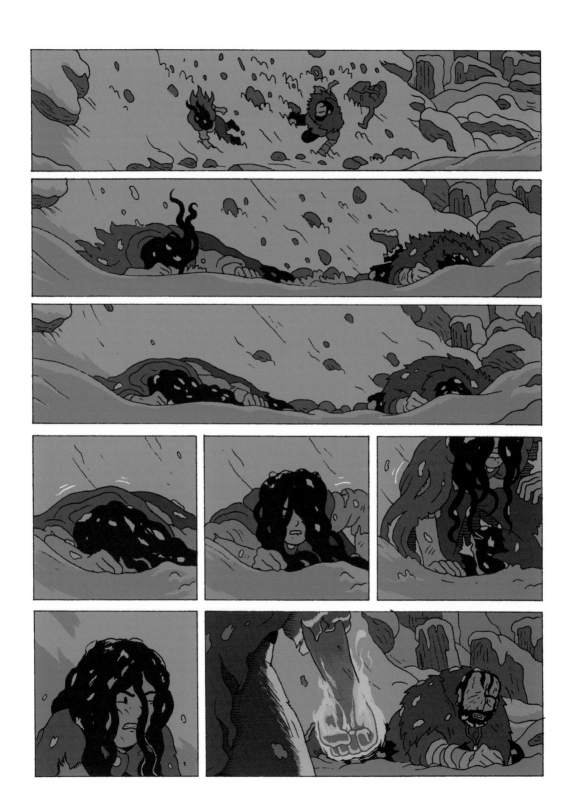

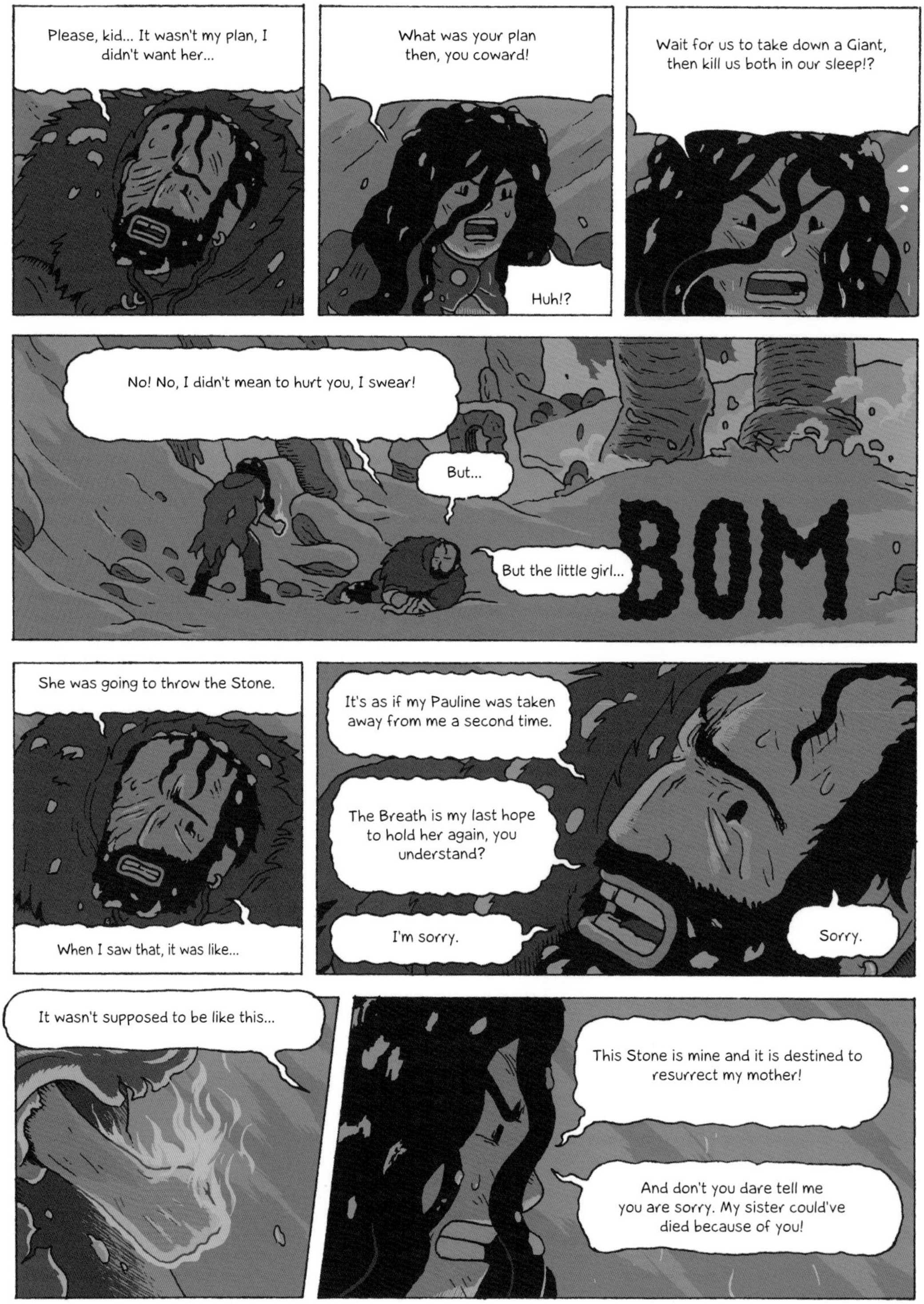
Please, kid... It wasn't my plan, I didn't want her...
What was your plan then, you coward!
Huh!?
Wait for us to take down a Giant, then kill us both in our sleep!?
No! No, I didn't mean to hurt you, I swear!
But...
But the little girl...
BOM
She was going to throw the Stone.
When I saw that, it was like...
It's as if my Pauline was taken away from me a second time.
The Breath is my last hope to hold her again, you understand?
I'm sorry.
Sorry.
It wasn't supposed to be like this...
This Stone is mine and it is destined to resurrect my mother!
And don't you dare tell me you are sorry. My sister could've died because of you!

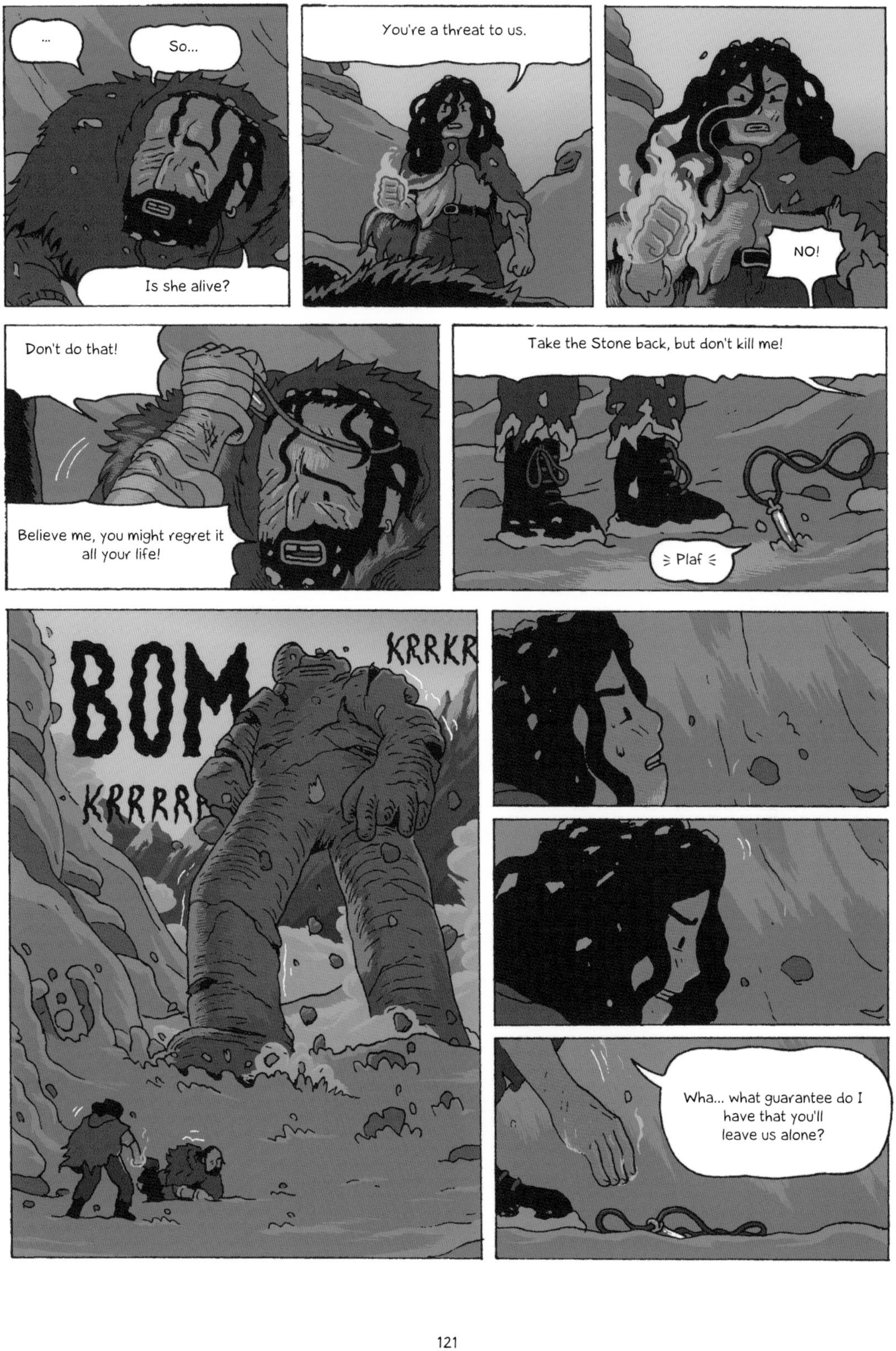
...
So...
Is she alive?
You're a threat to us.
NO!
Don't do that!
Believe me, you might regret it all your life!
Take the Stone back, but don't kill me!
Plaf
BOM
KRRKR
KRRRR
Wha... what guarantee do I have that you'll leave us alone?

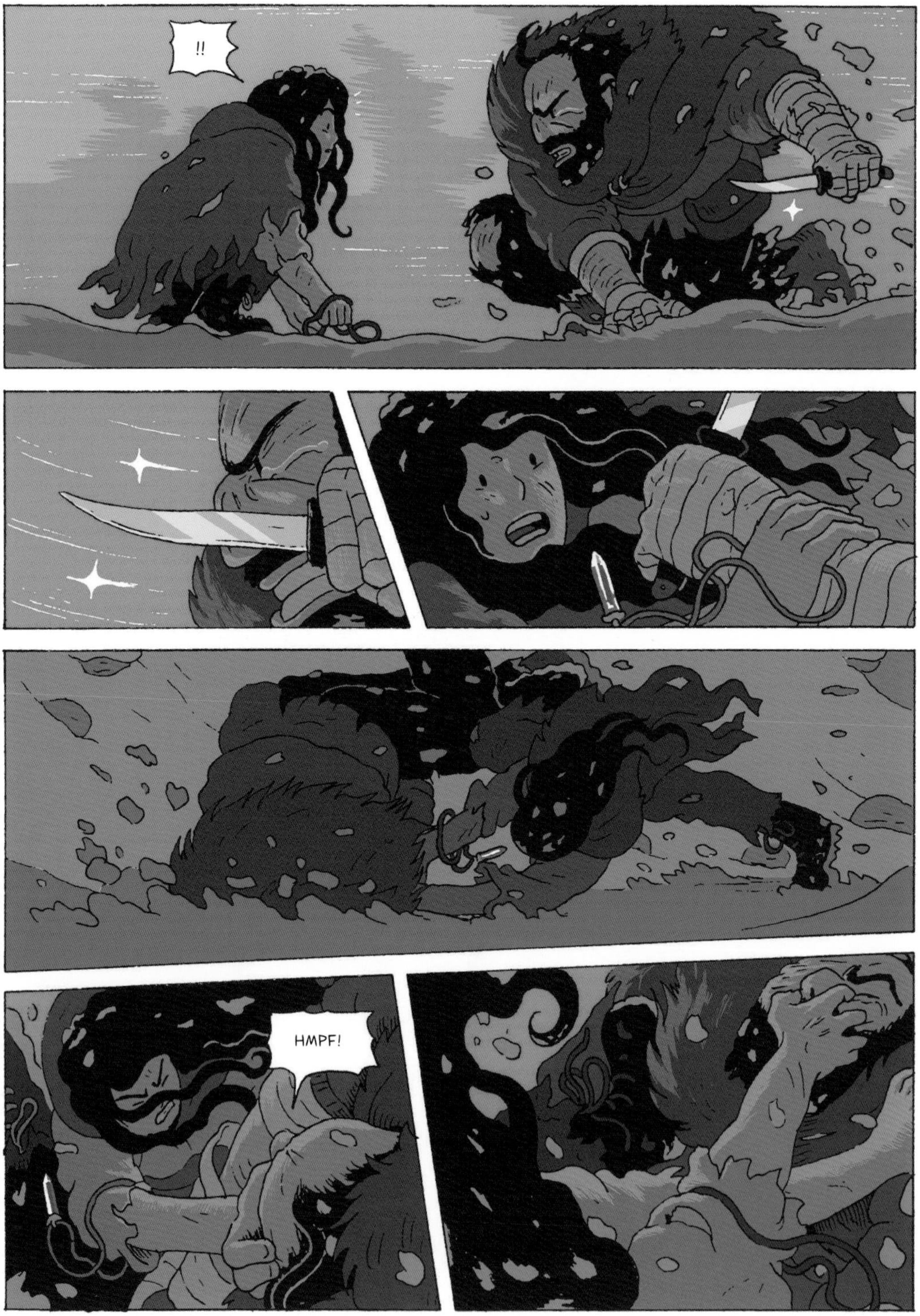
!!
HMPF!

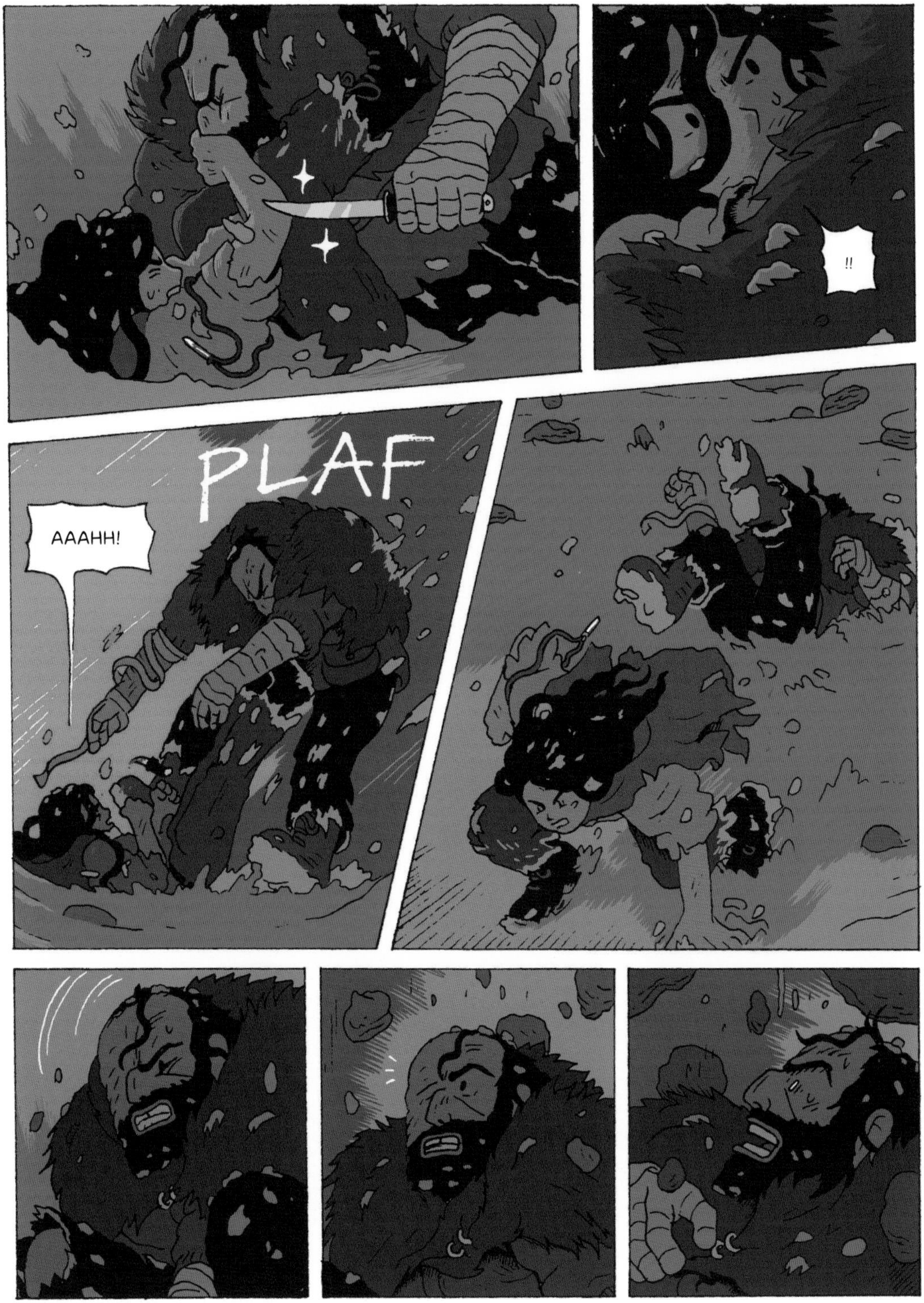
!!
PLAF
AAAHH!

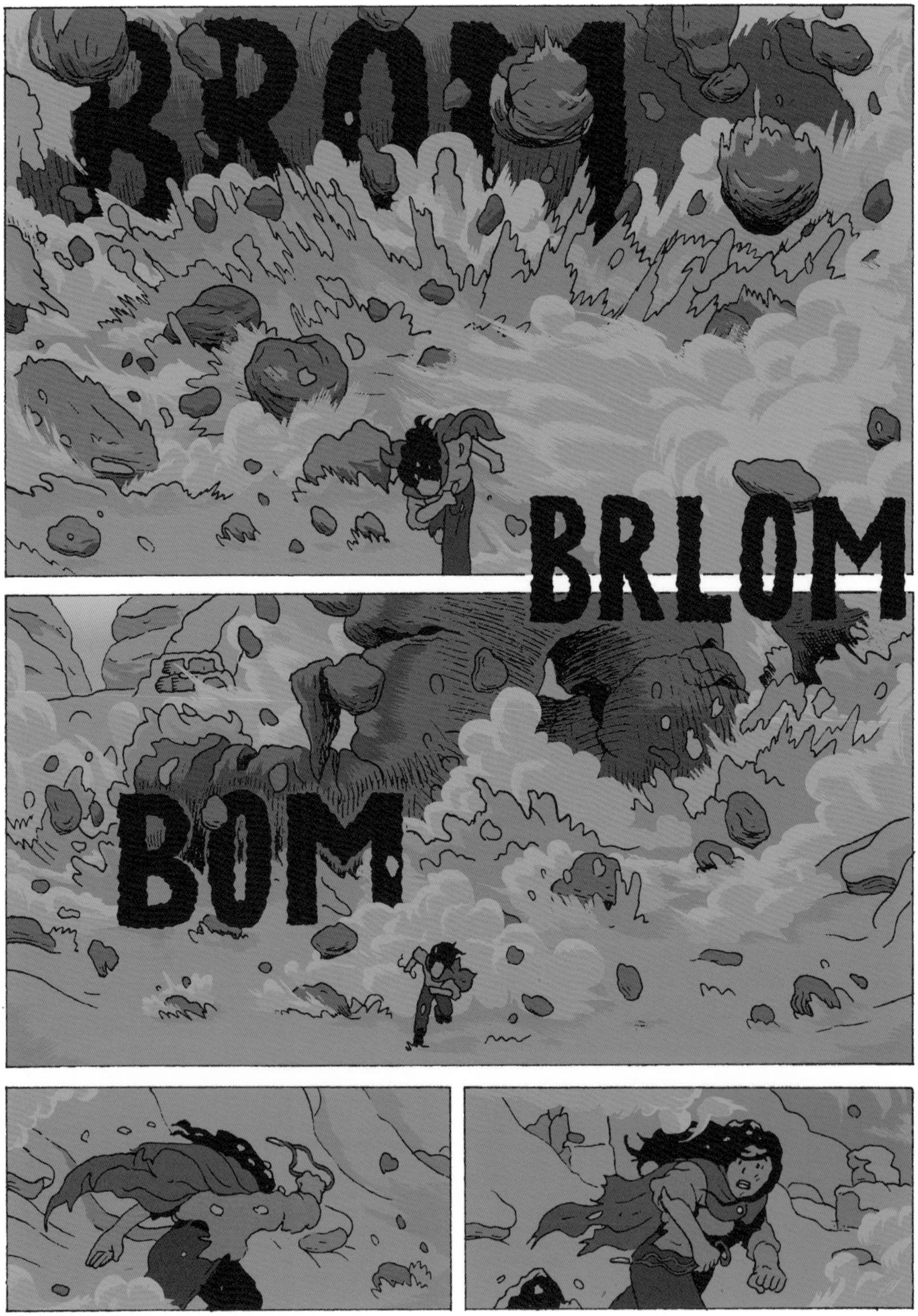
BROM
BRLOM
BOM

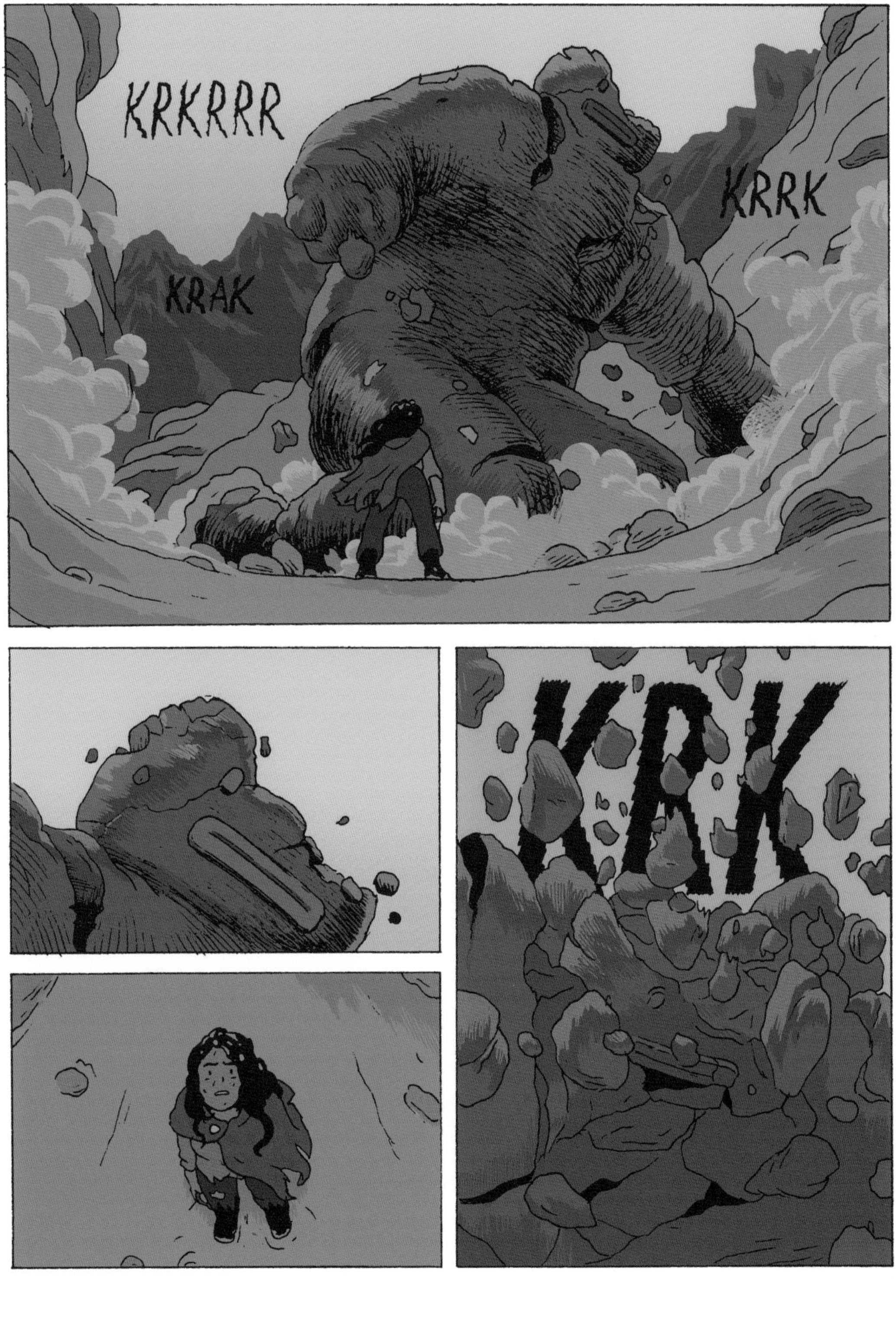
KRKRRR
KRAK
KRRK
KRK

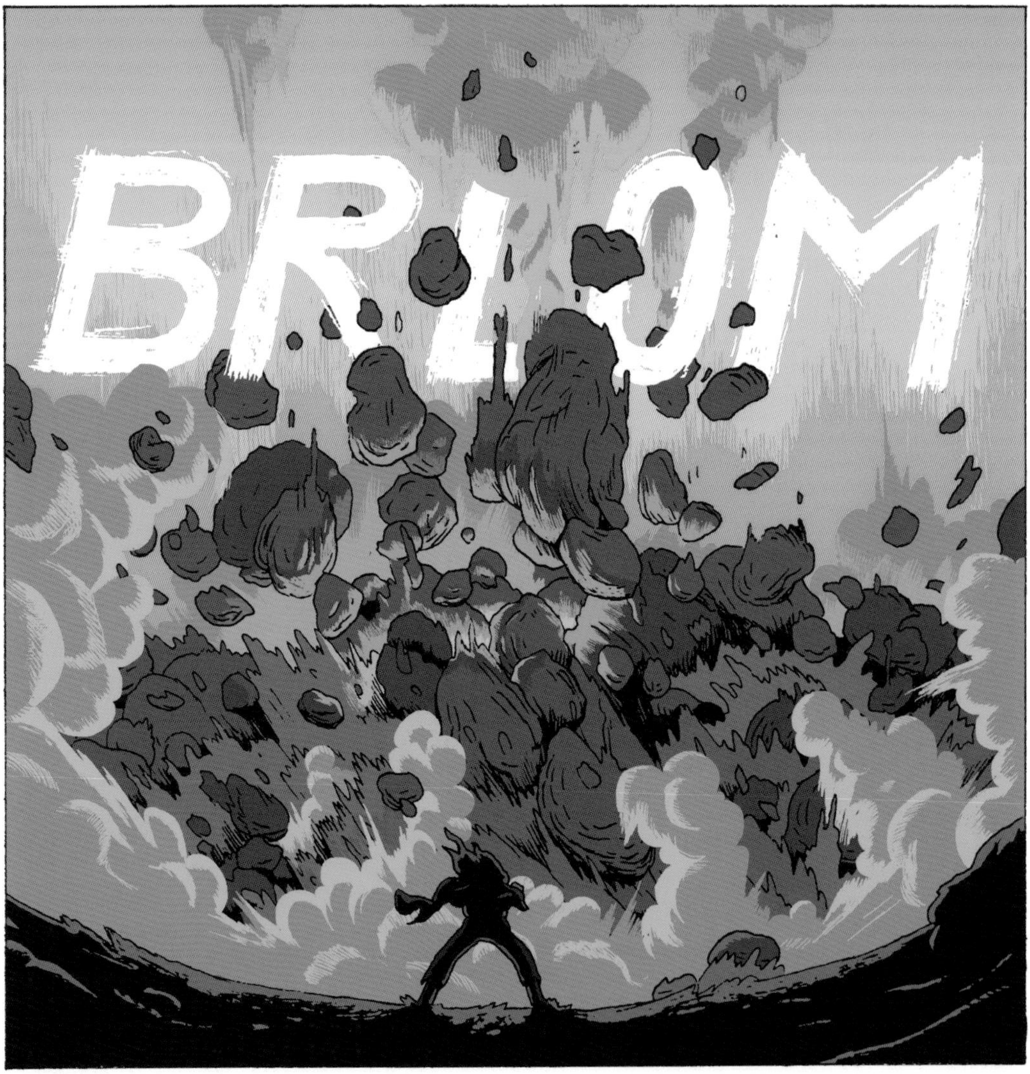
BRLOM

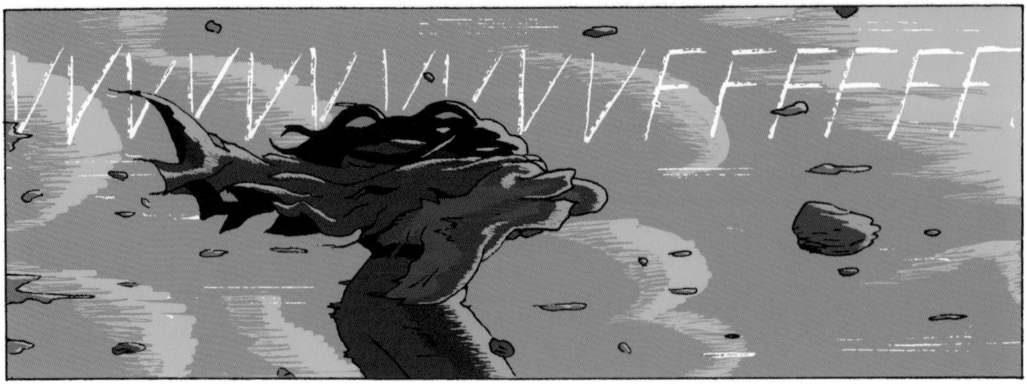
VVVVVVVVVVFFFFFF

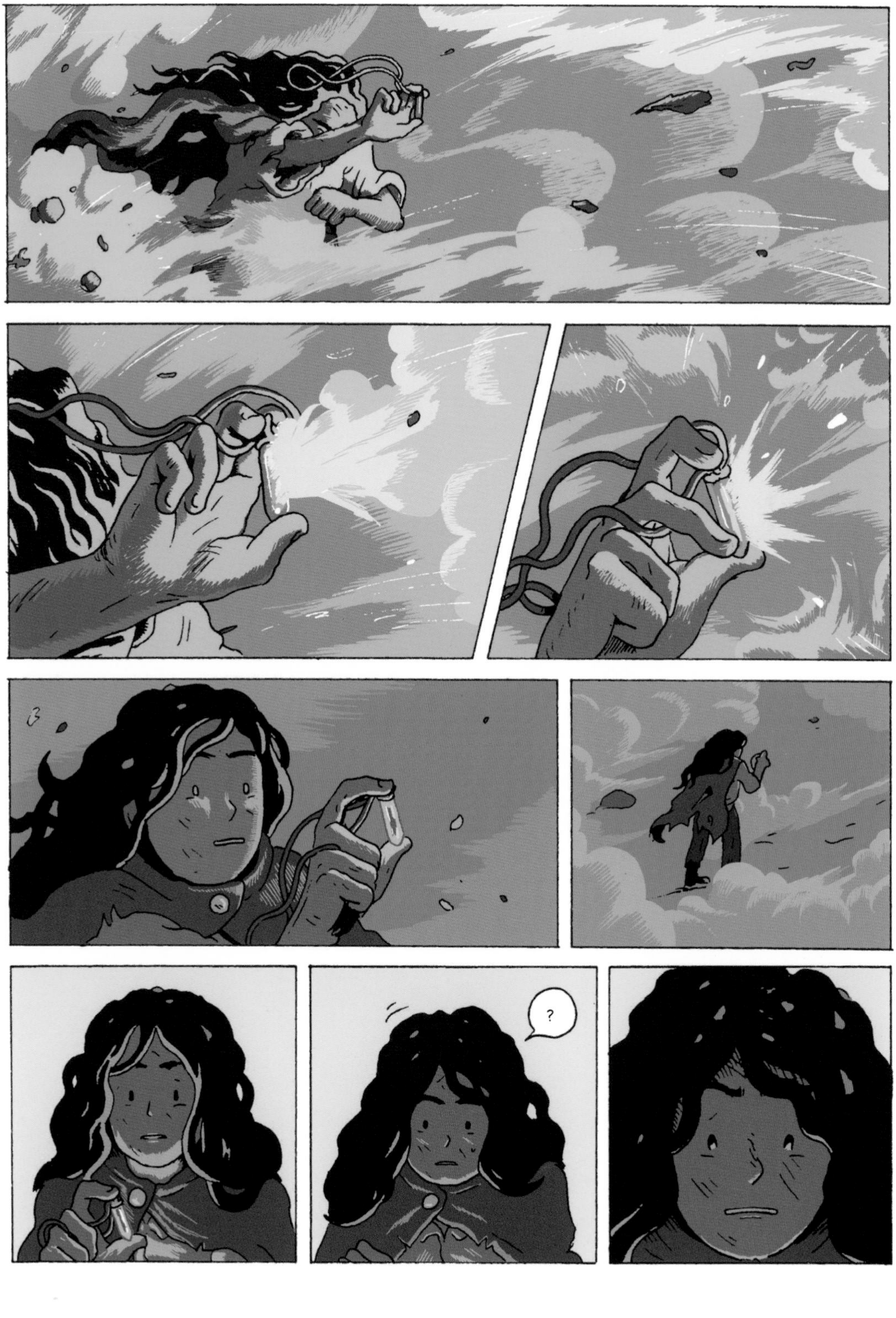
?

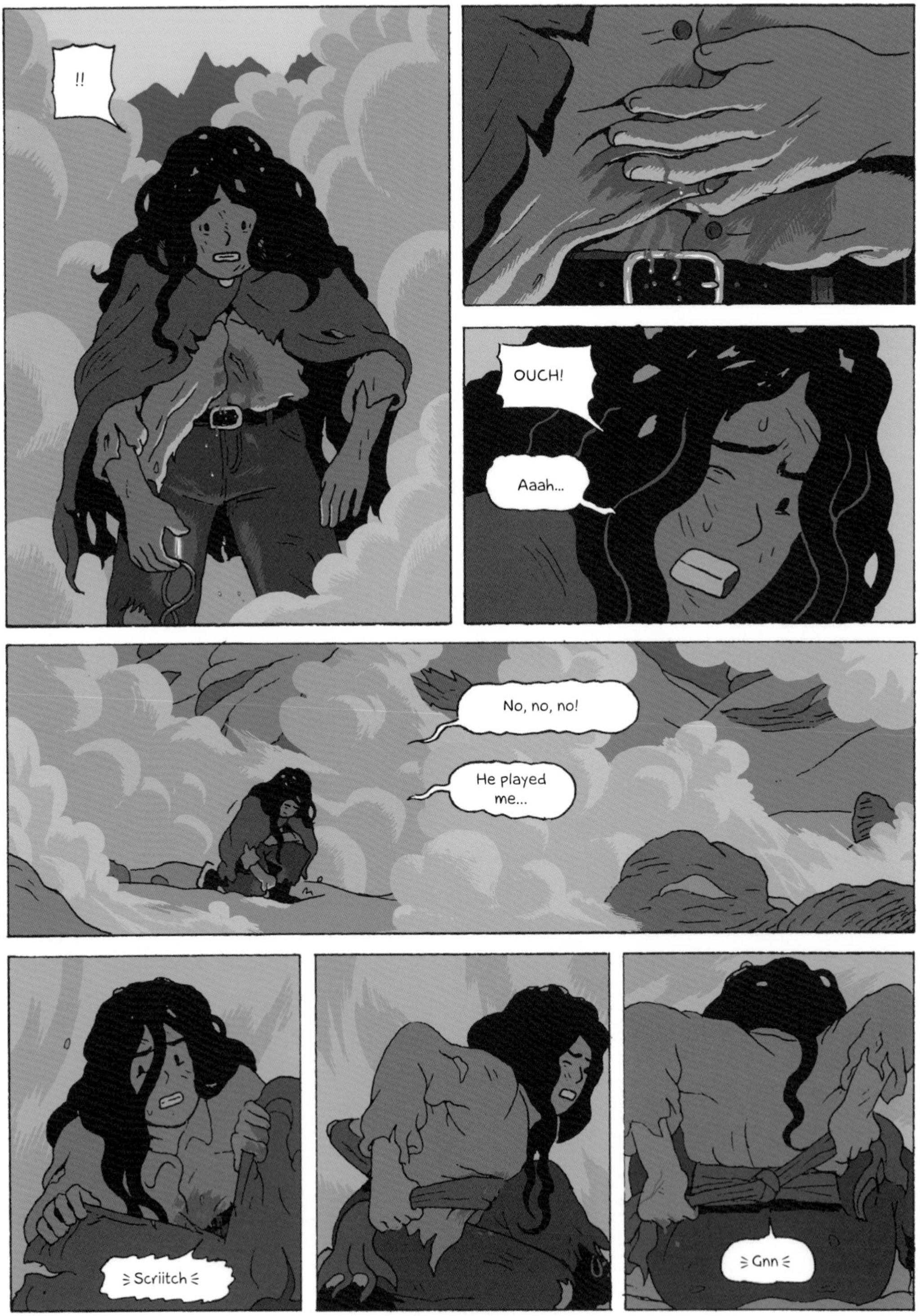
!!
OUCH!
Aaah...
No, no, no!
He played me...
Scriitch
Gnn

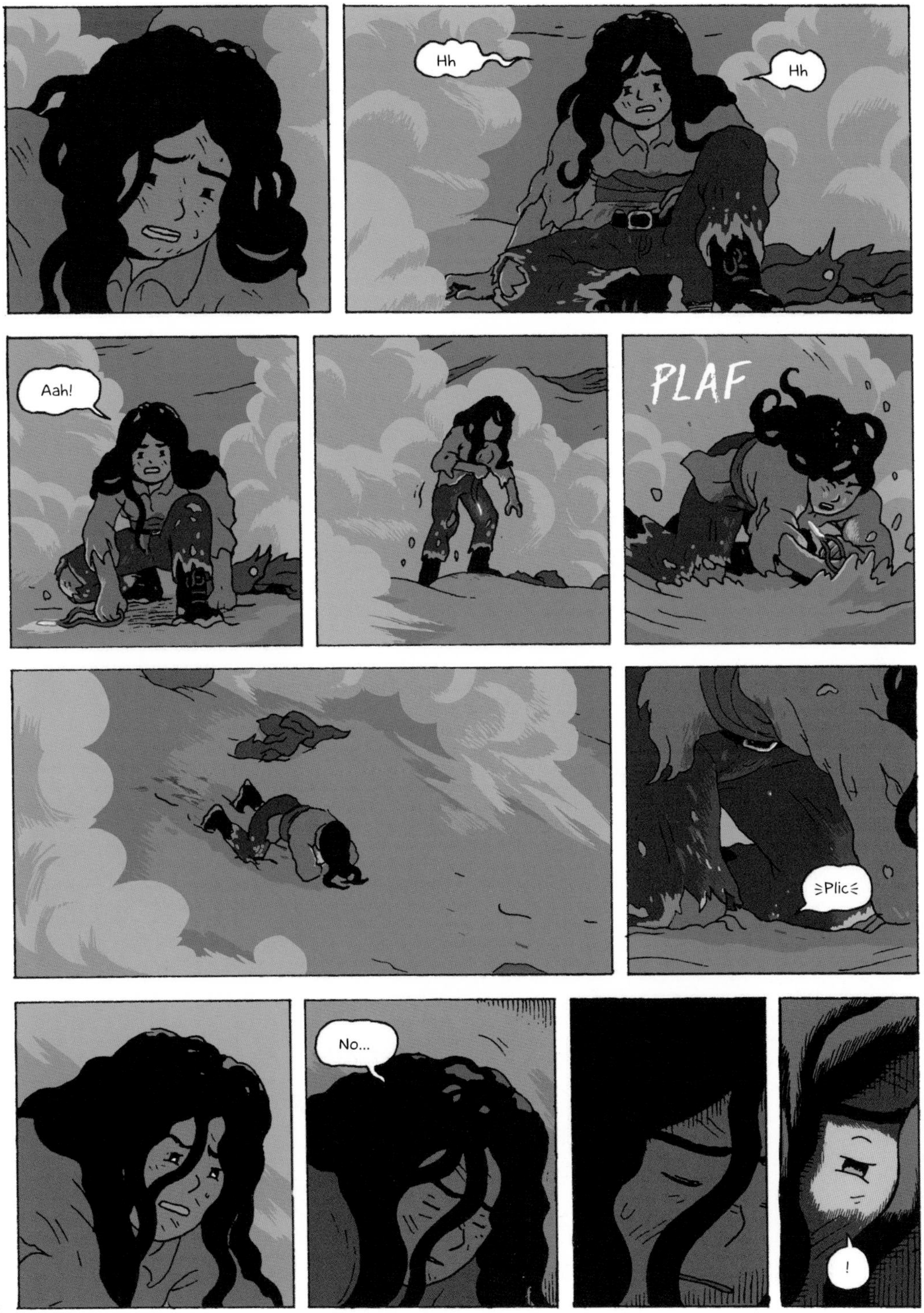
Hh
Hh
Aah!
PLAF
Plic
No...
!

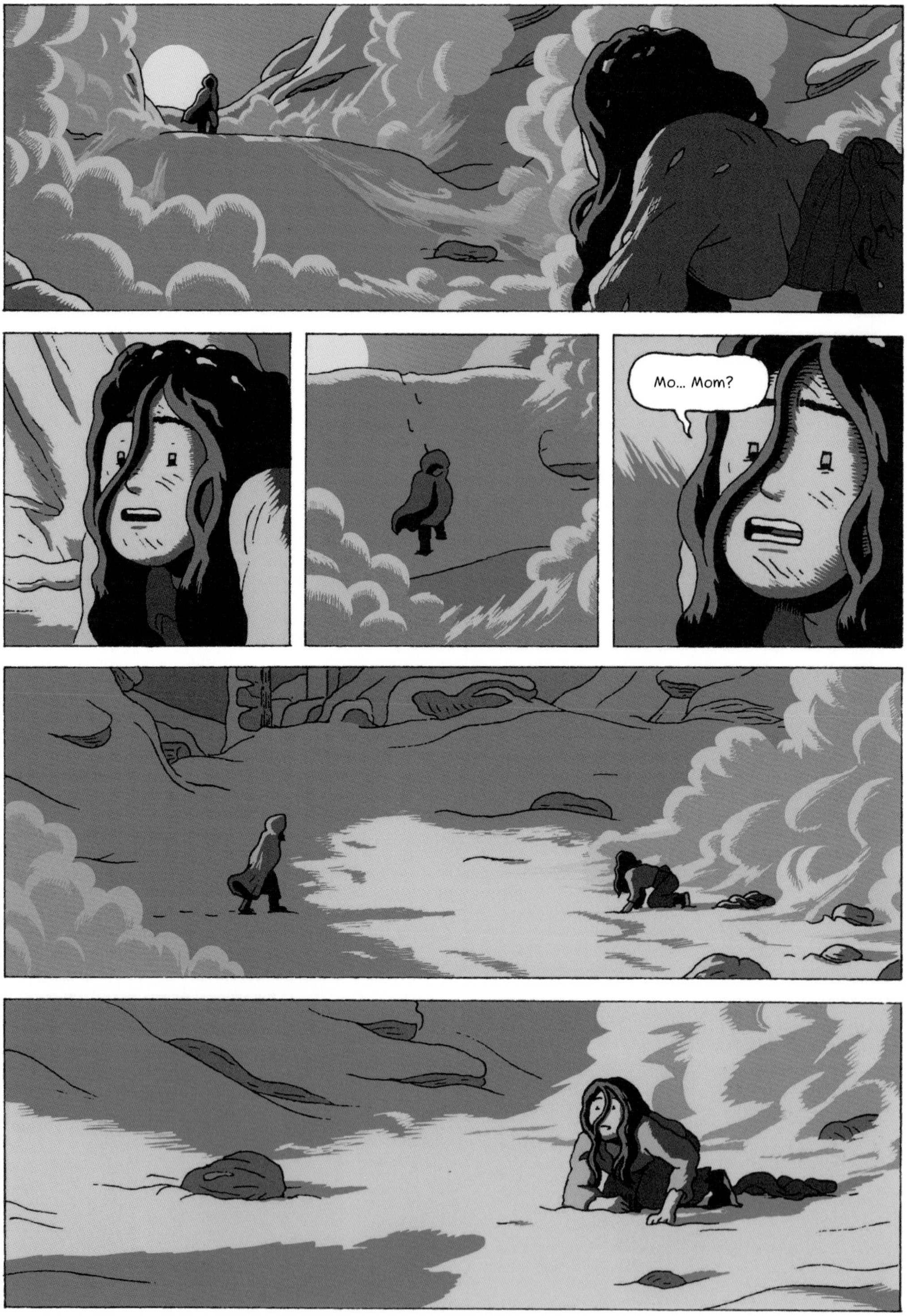
Mo... Mom?

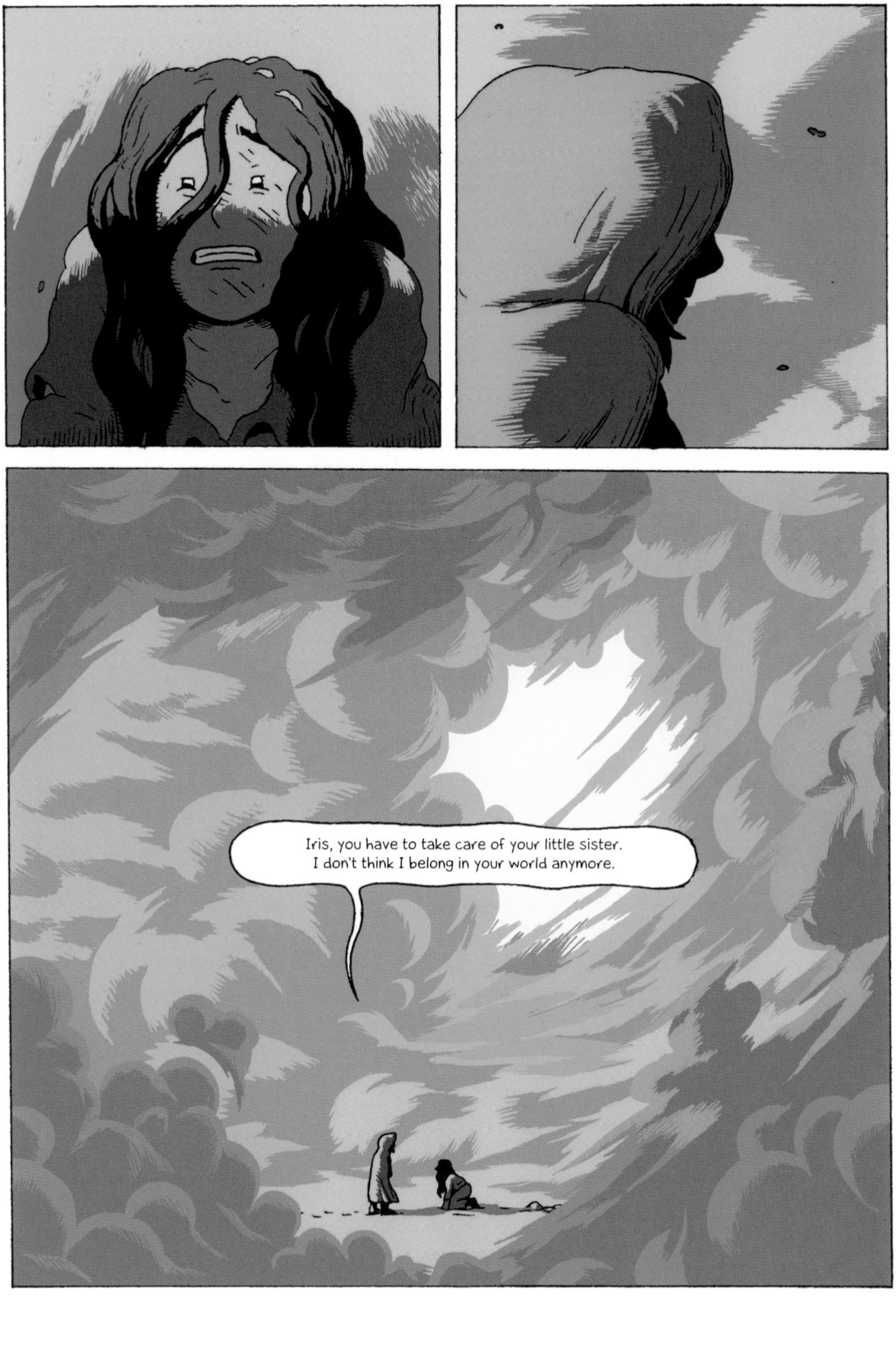
Iris, you have to take care of your little sister.
I don't think I belong in your world anymore.

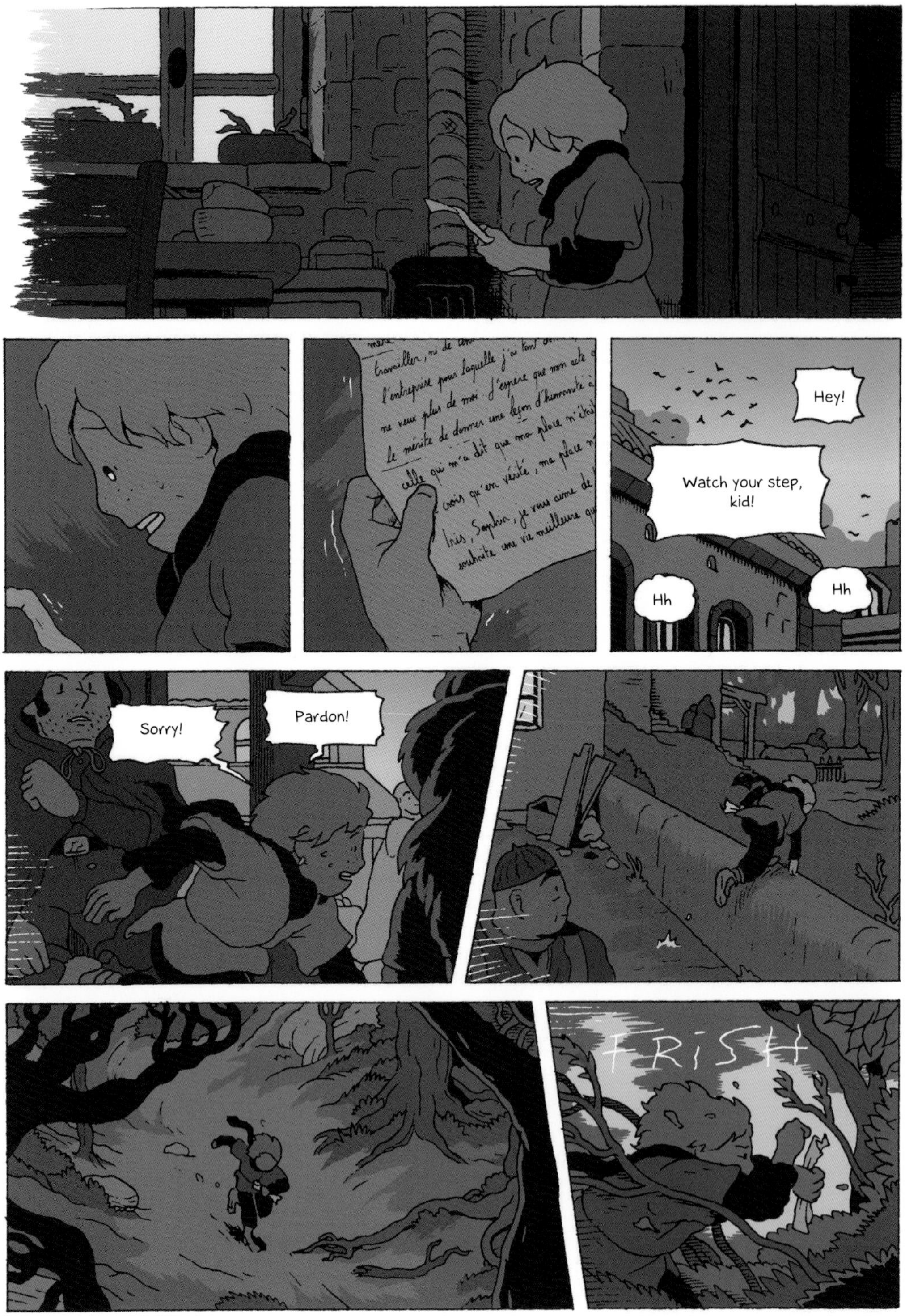
travailler, ni de
l'entreprise pour laquelle j'ai tant
ne veux plus de moi. J'espère que mon acte
le mérite de donner une leçon d'humanité à
celle qui m'a dit que ma place n'était
crois qu'en vérité, ma place
Iris, Sophia, je vous aime de
souhaite une vie meilleure qu
Hey!
Watch your step, kid!
Hh
Hh
Sorry!
Pardon!
FRISH

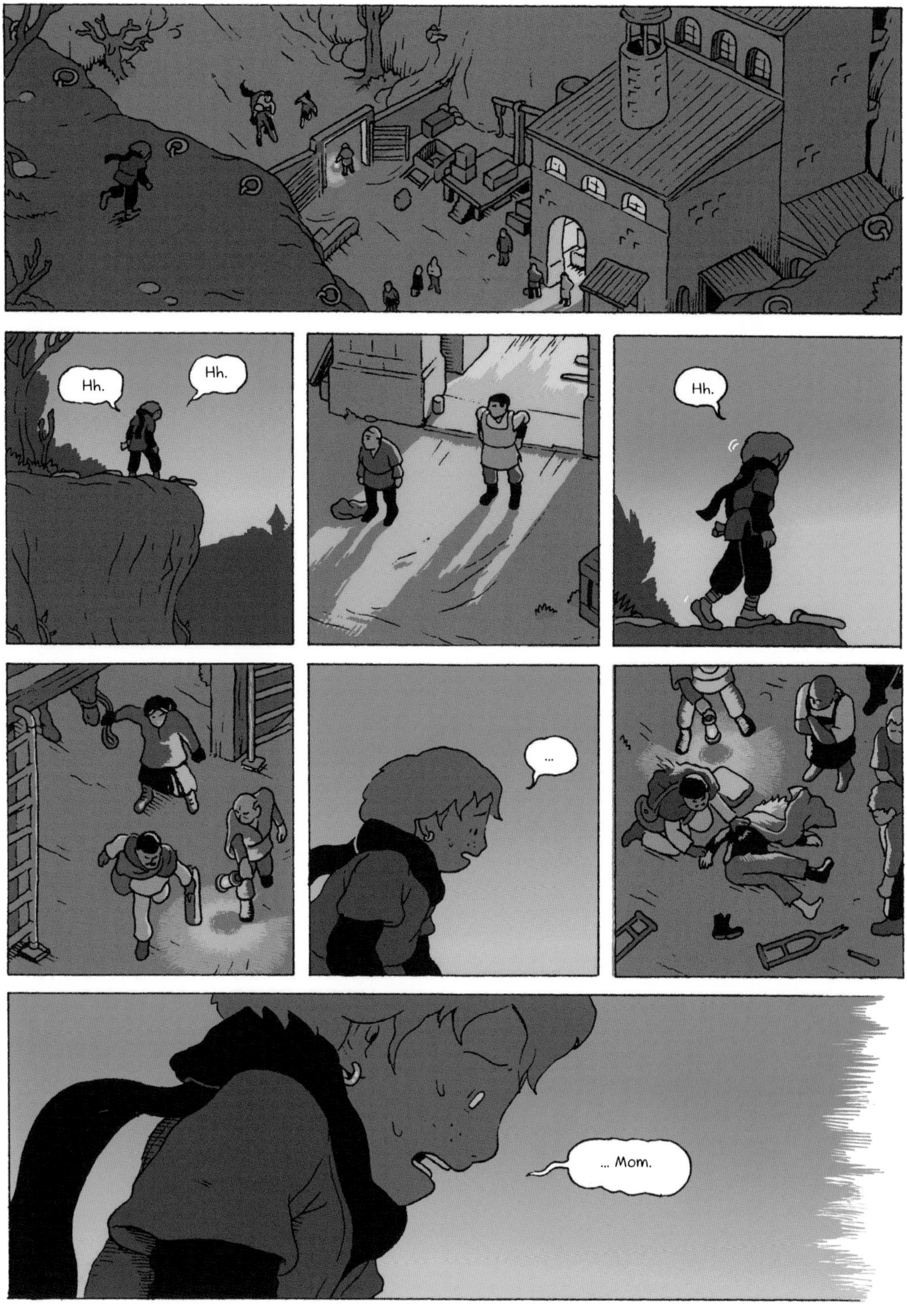
Hh.
Hh.
Hh.
...
... Mom.

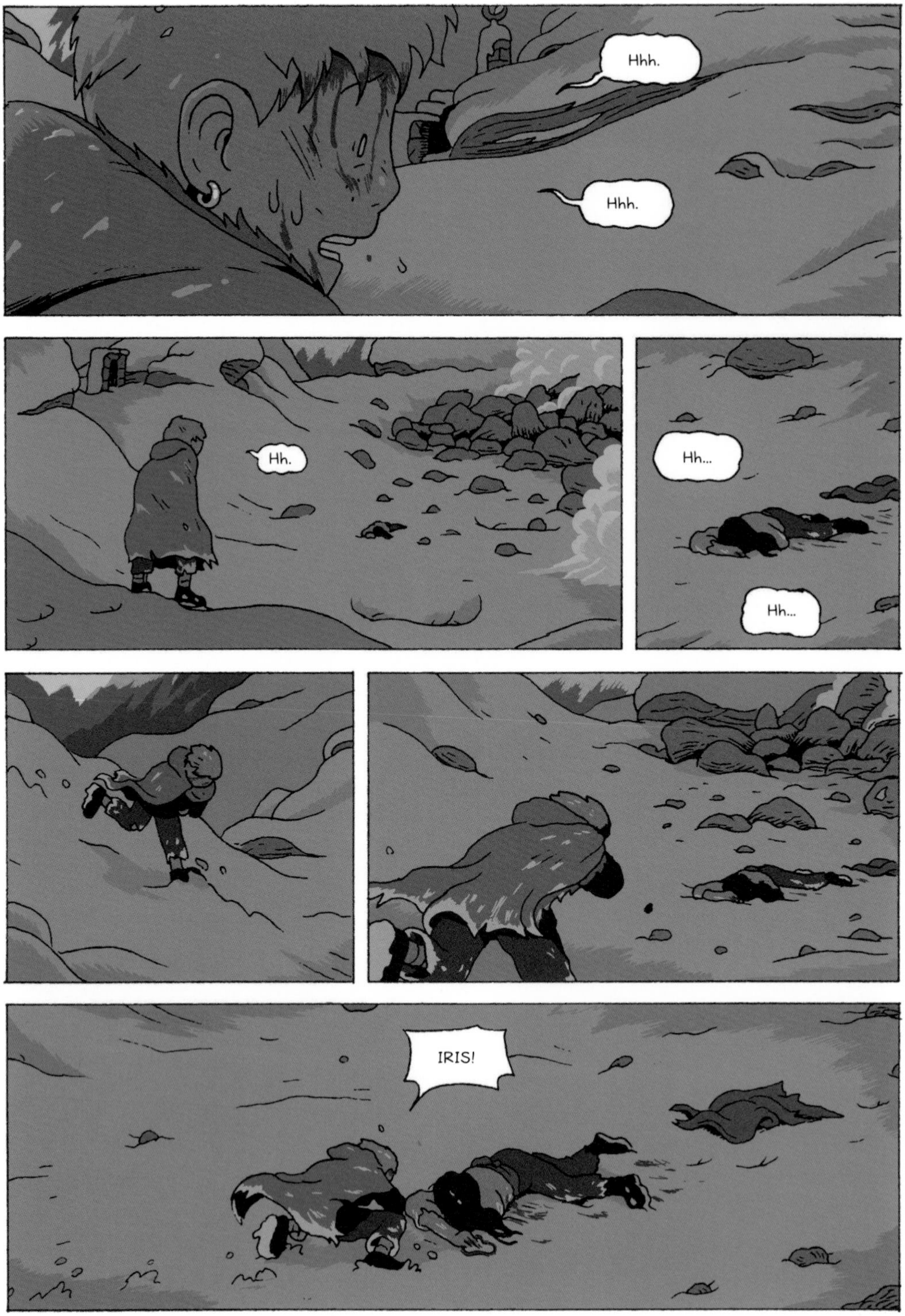
Hhh.
Hhh.
Hh.
Hh...
Hh...
IRIS!

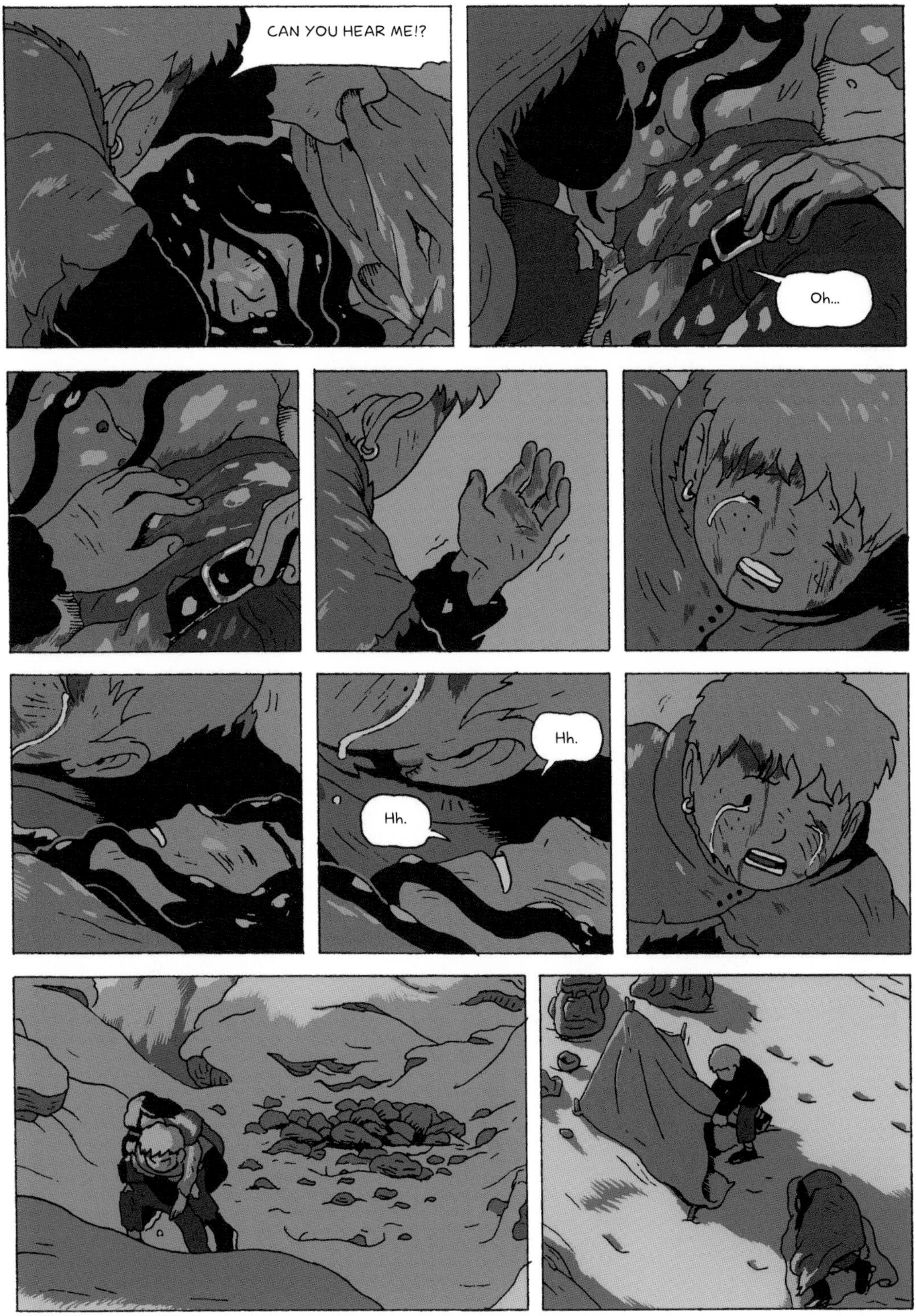
CAN YOU HEAR ME!?
Oh...
Hh.
Hh.

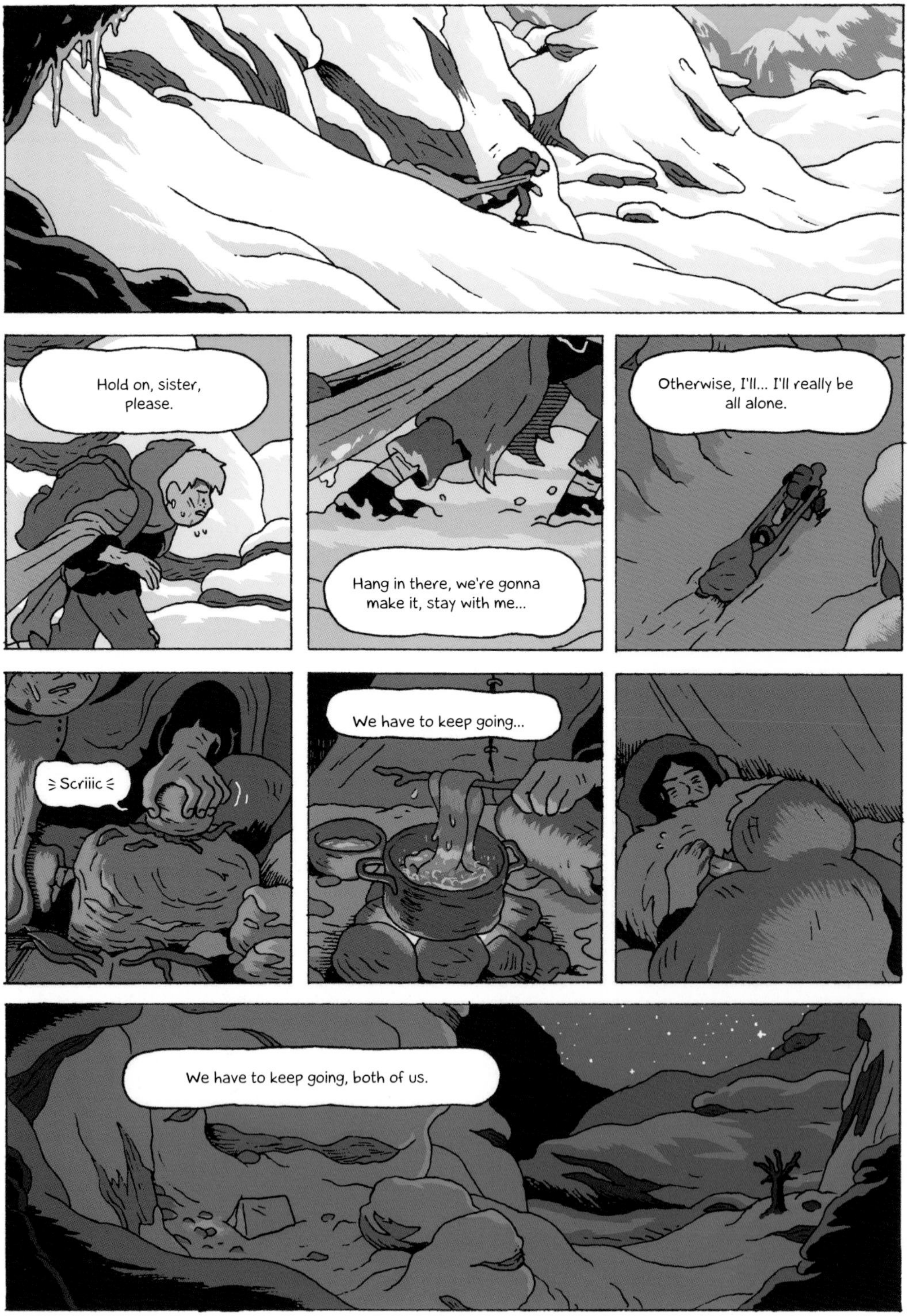
Hold on, sister, please.
Hang in there, we're gonna make it, stay with me...
Otherwise, I'll... I'll really be all alone.
Scriiic
We have to keep going...
We have to keep going, both of us.

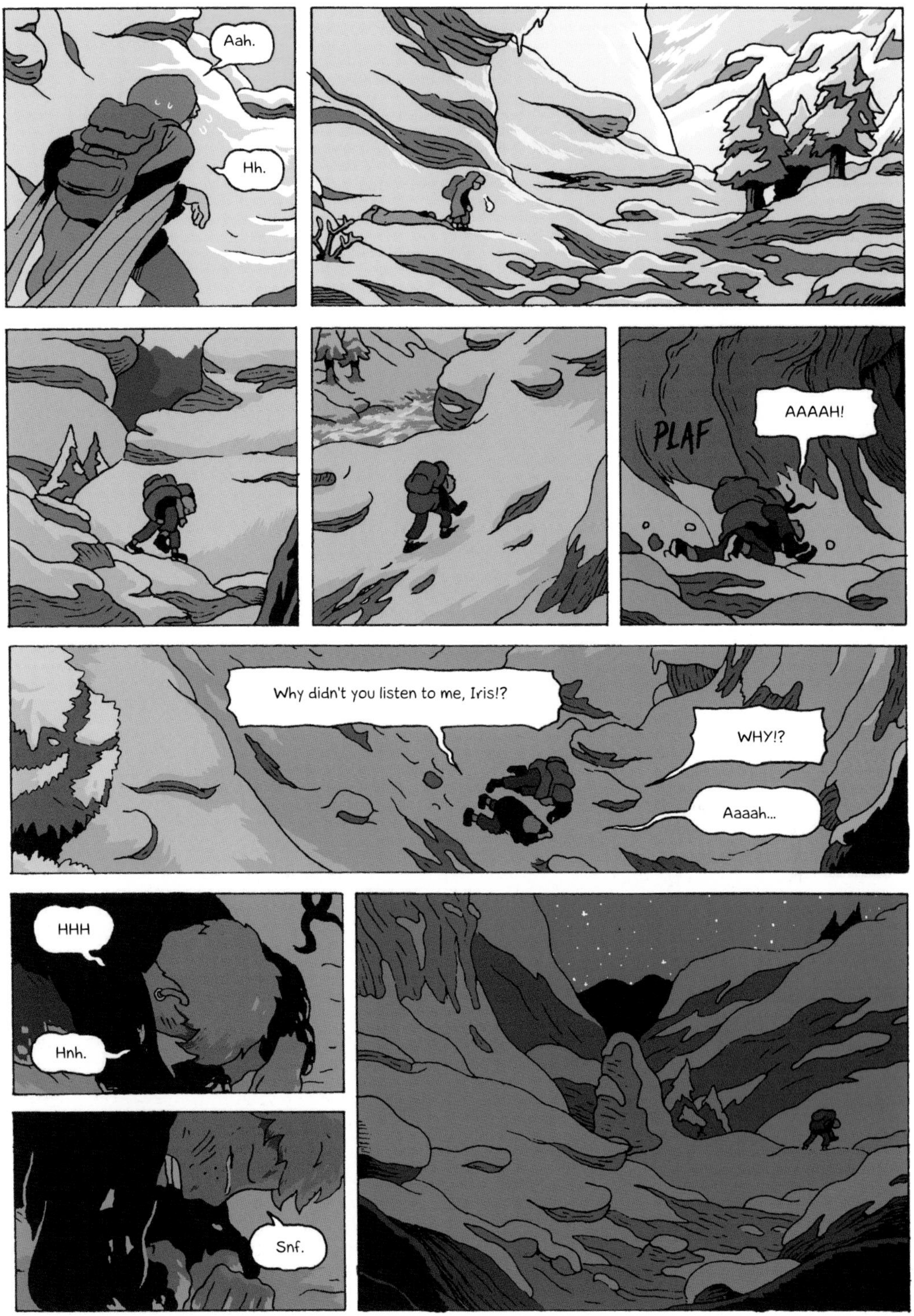
Aah.
Hh.
PLAF
AAAAH!
Why didn't you listen to me, Iris!?
WHY!?
Aaaah...
HHH
Hnh.
Snf.

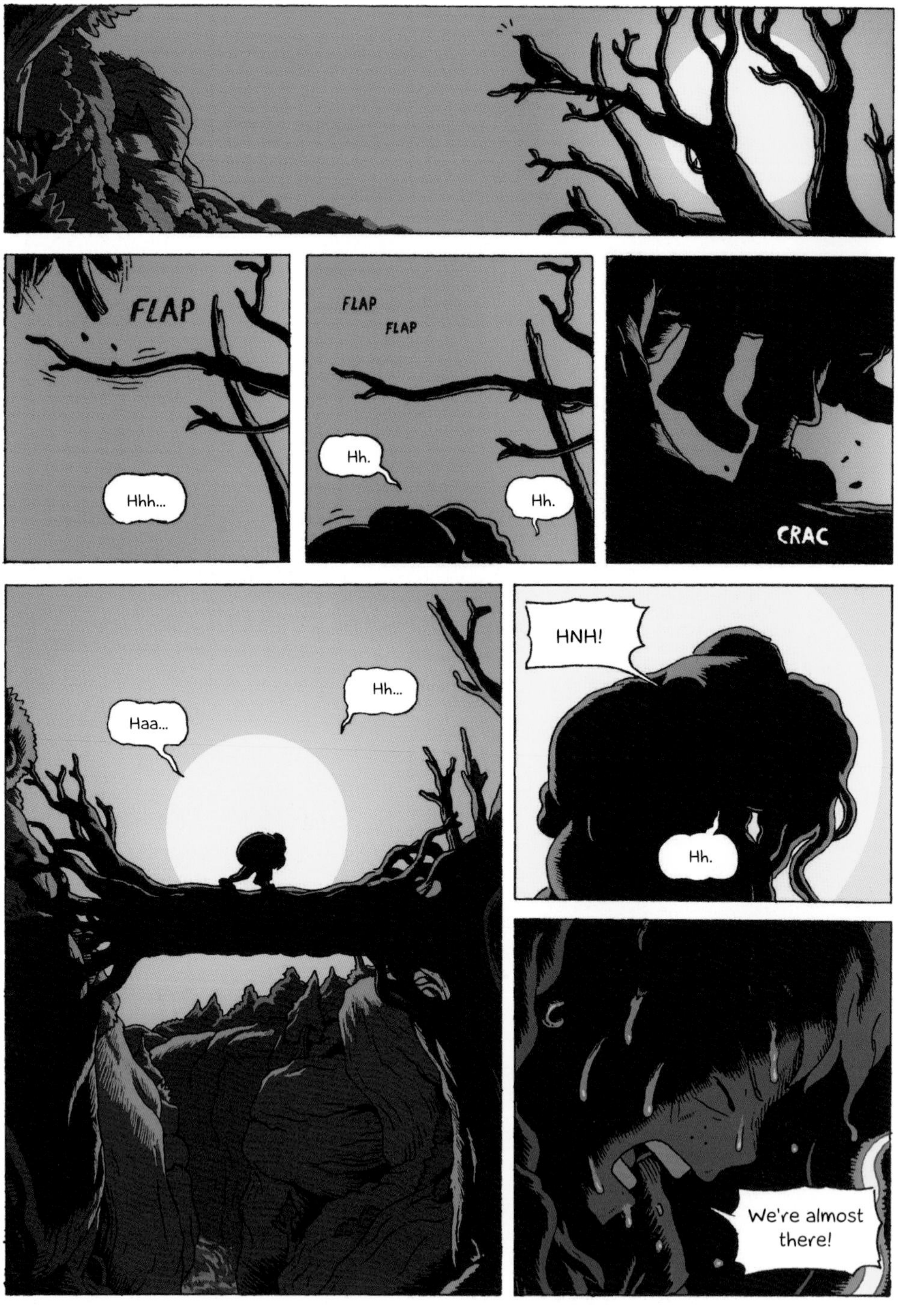
FLAP
Hhh...
FLAP
FLAP
Hh.
Hh.
CRAC
Haa...
Hh...
HNH!
Hh.
We're almost there!

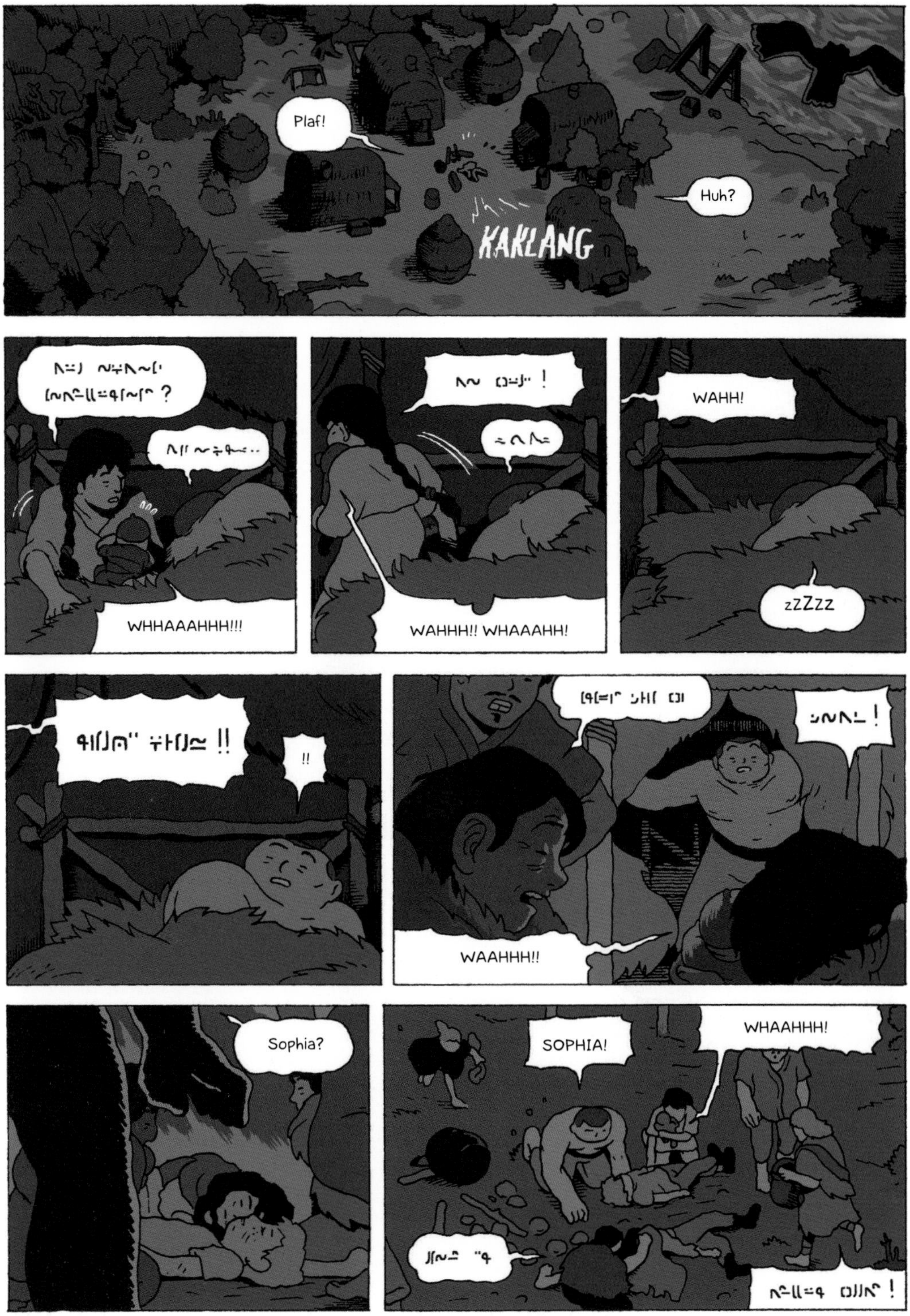
Plaf!
KAKLANG
Huh?
WHHAAAHHH!!!
WAHHH!! WHAAAHH!
WAHH!
zZZzz
!!
WAAHHH!!
Sophia?
SOPHIA!
WHAAHHH!

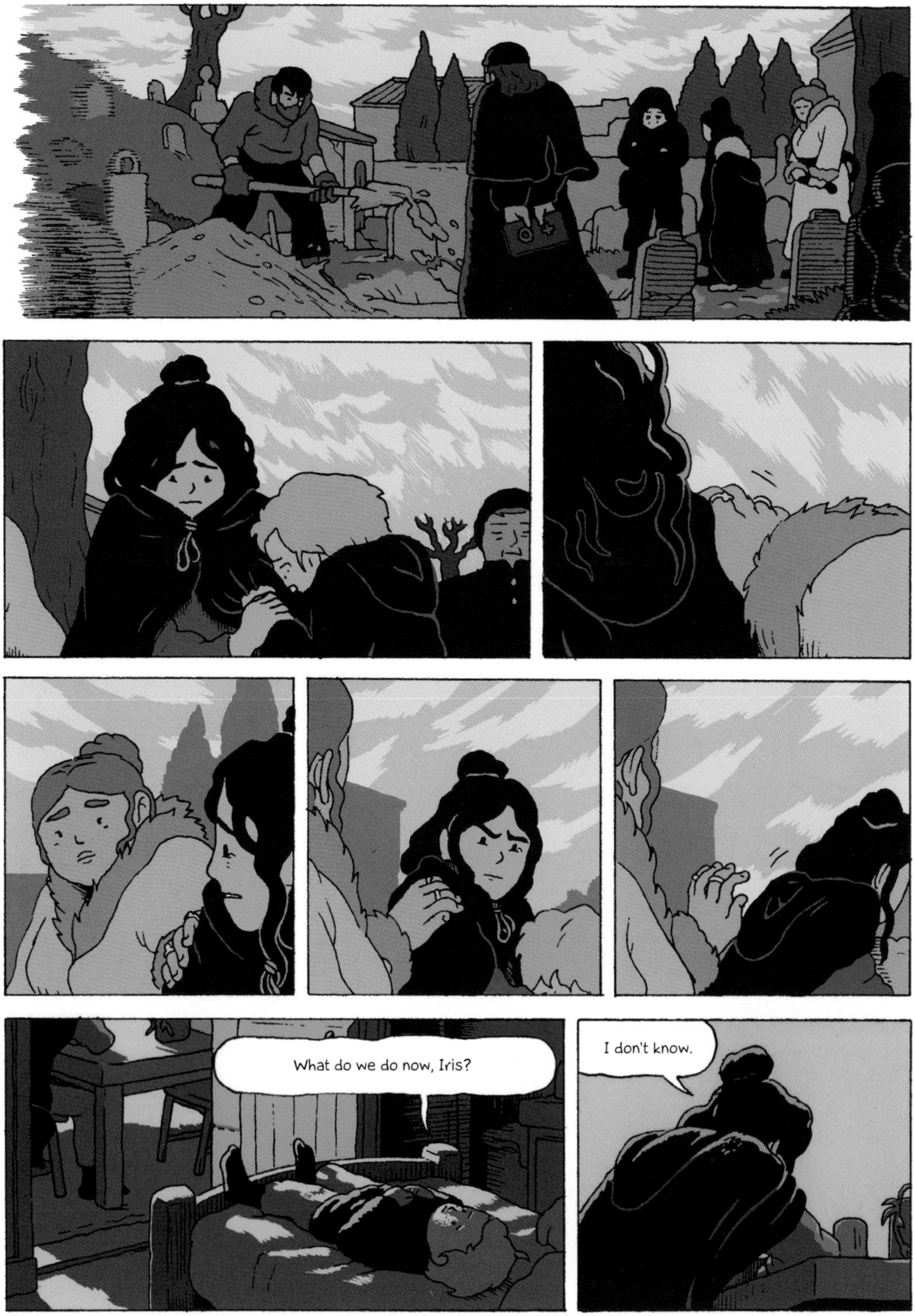
What do we do now, Iris?
I don't know.

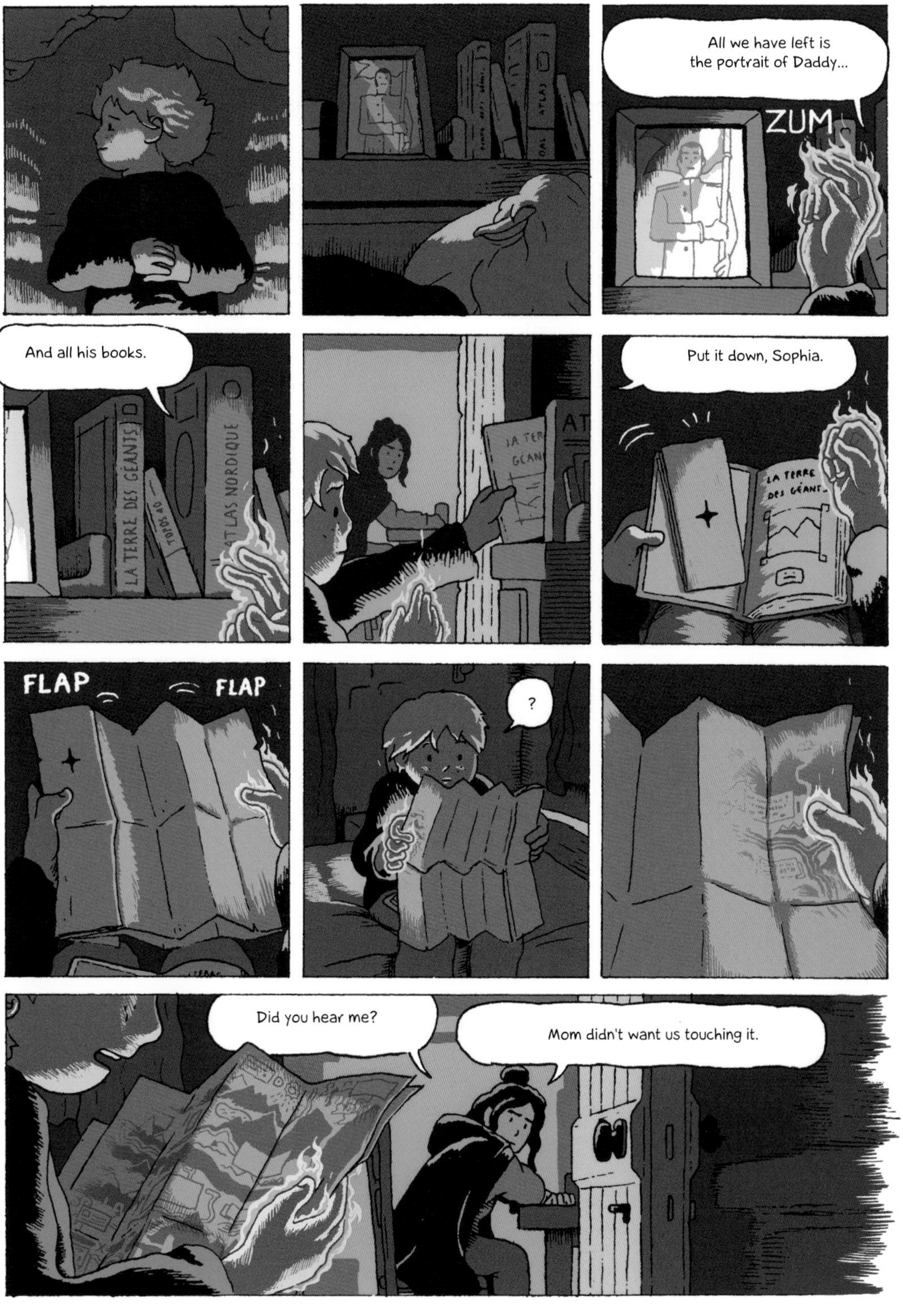
All we have left is the portrait of Daddy...
ZUM
And all his books.
LA TERRE DES GÉANTS
TOPOS 40
ATLAS NORDIQUE
Put it down, Sophia.
LA TERRE DES GÉANTS
FLAP FLAP
?
Did you hear me?
Mom didn't want us touching it.

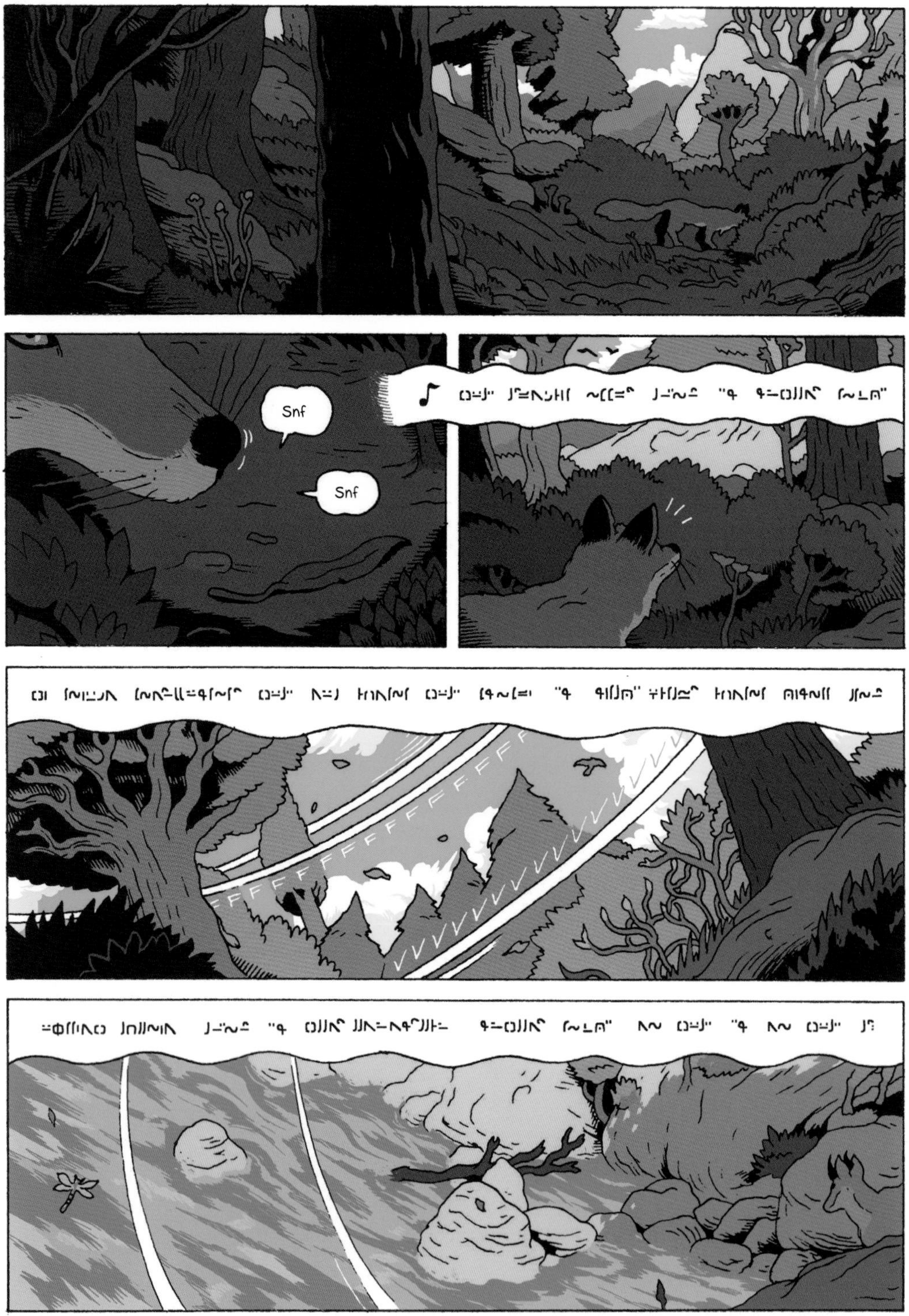
Snf
Snf

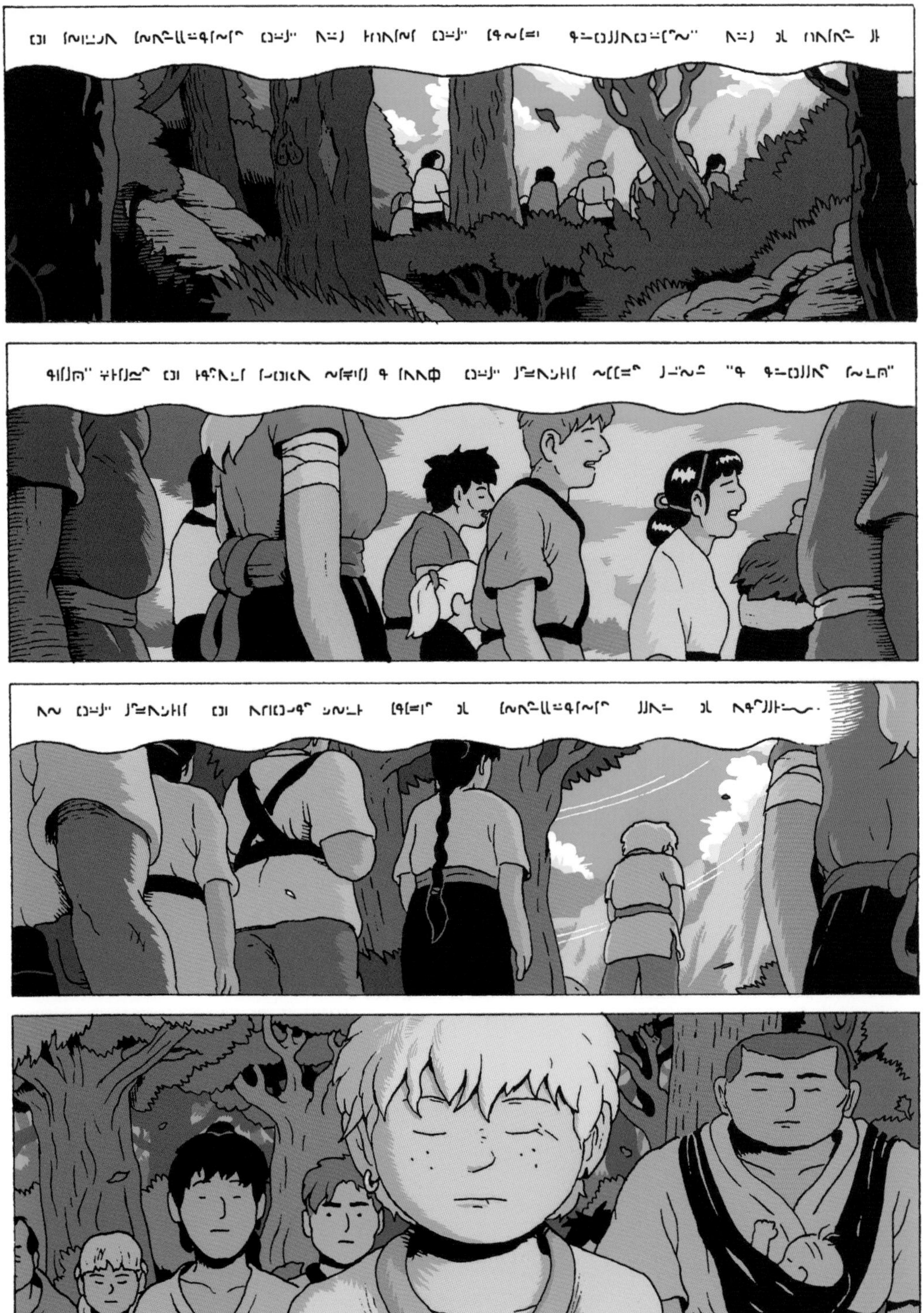

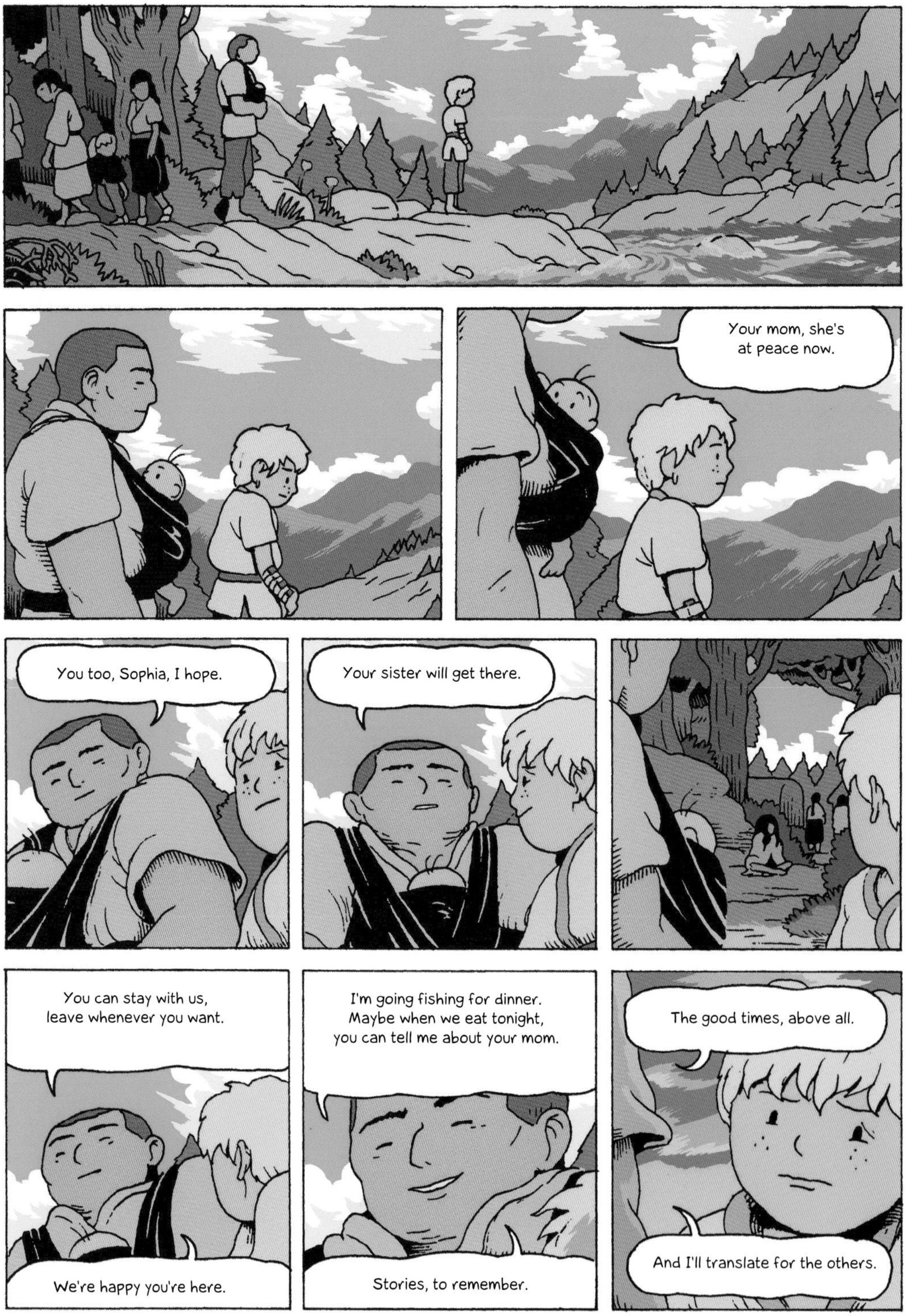
Your mom, she's at peace now.
You too, Sophia, I hope.
Your sister will get there.
You can stay with us, leave whenever you want.
We're happy you're here.
I'm going fishing for dinner. Maybe when we eat tonight, you can tell me about your mom.
Stories, to remember.
The good times, above all.
And I'll translate for the others.

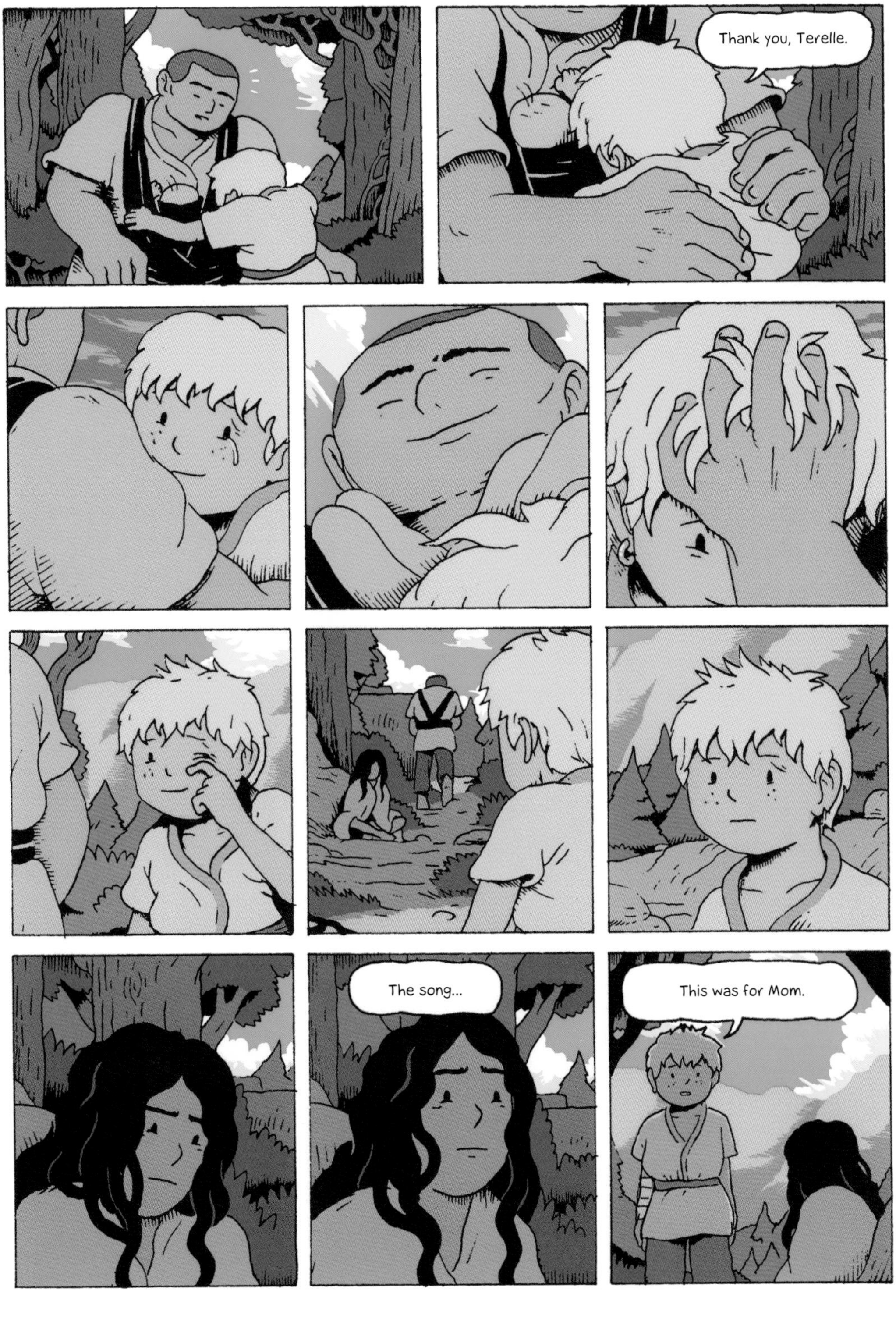
Thank you, Terelle.
The song...
This was for Mom.

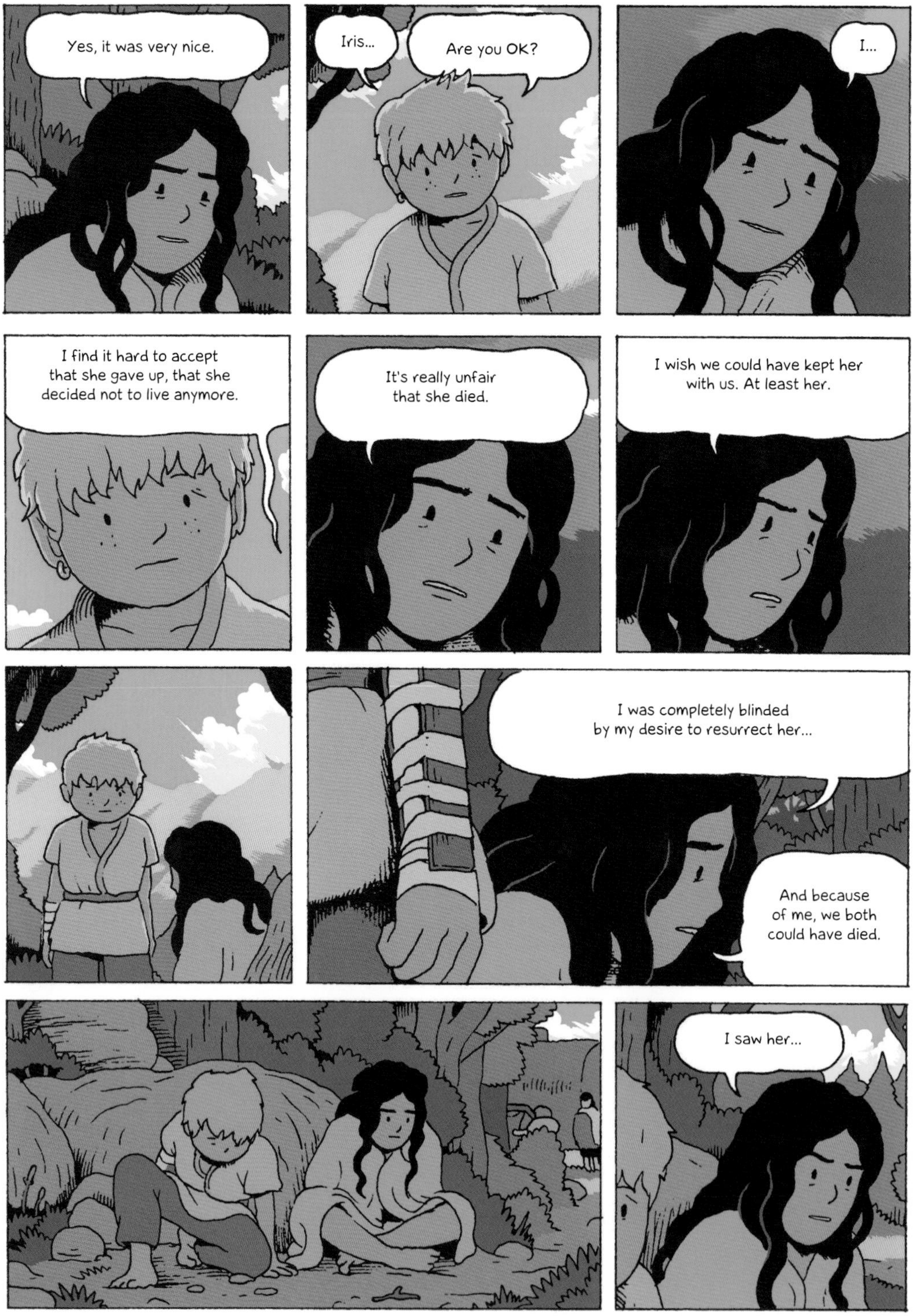
Yes, it was very nice.
Iris...
Are you OK?
I...
I find it hard to accept that she gave up, that she decided not to live anymore.
It's really unfair that she died.
I wish we could have kept her with us. At least her.
I was completely blinded by my desire to resurrect her...
And because of me, we both could have died.
I saw her...

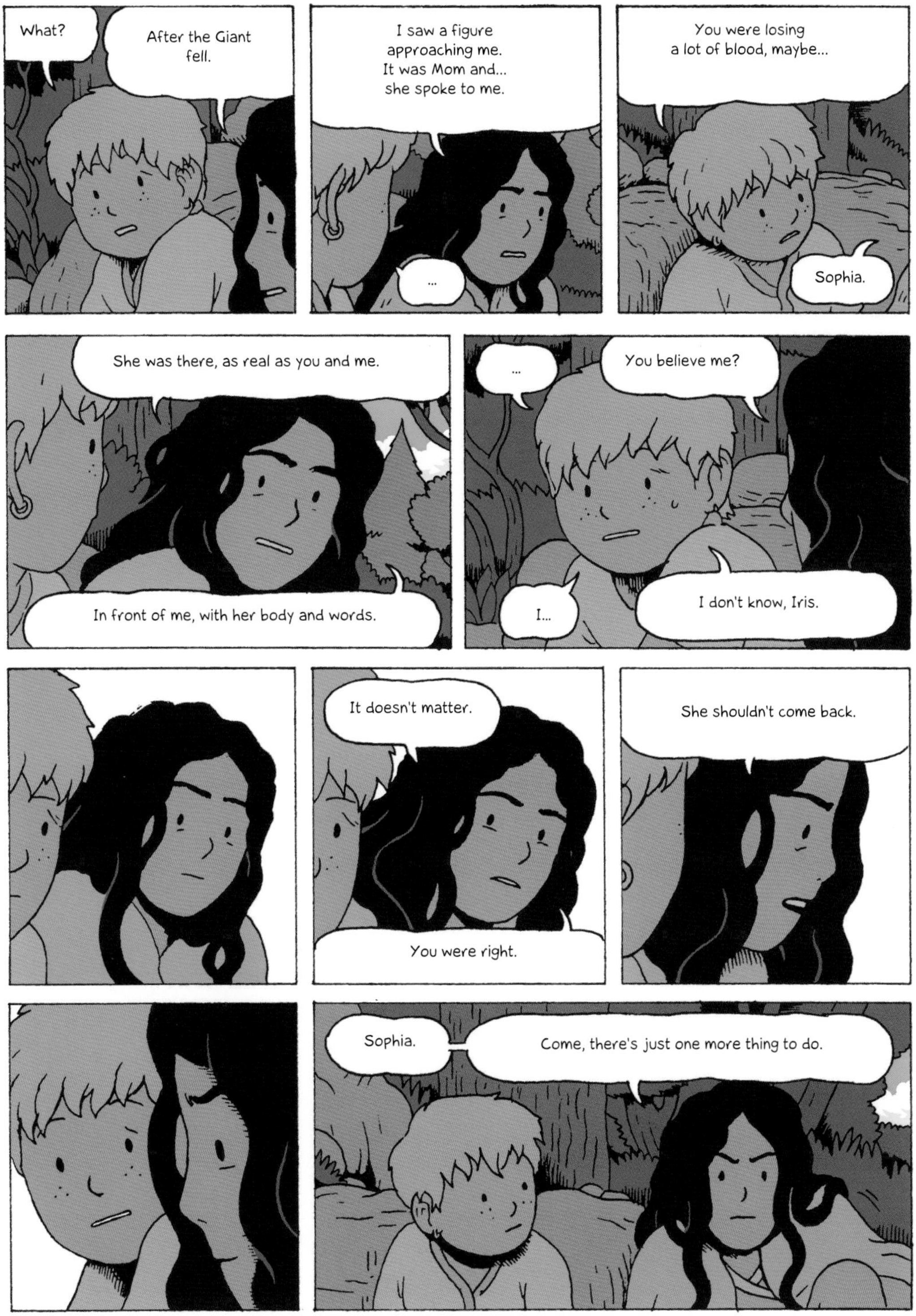
What?
After the Giant fell.
I saw a figure approaching me. It was Mom and... she spoke to me.
...
You were losing a lot of blood, maybe...
Sophia.
She was there, as real as you and me.
In front of me, with her body and words.
...
You believe me?
I...
I don't know, Iris.
It doesn't matter.
You were right.
She shouldn't come back.
Sophia.
Come, there's just one more thing to do.

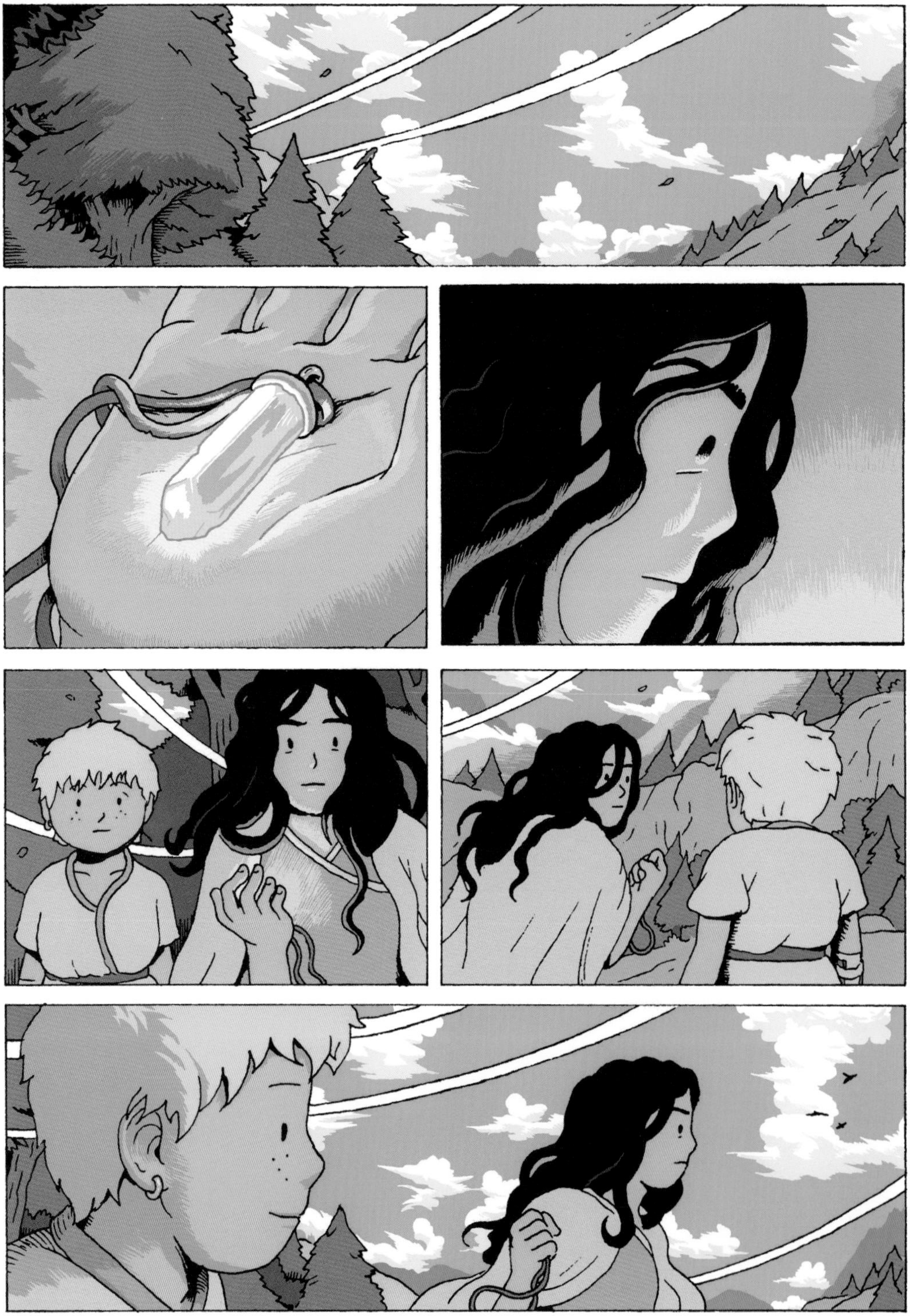

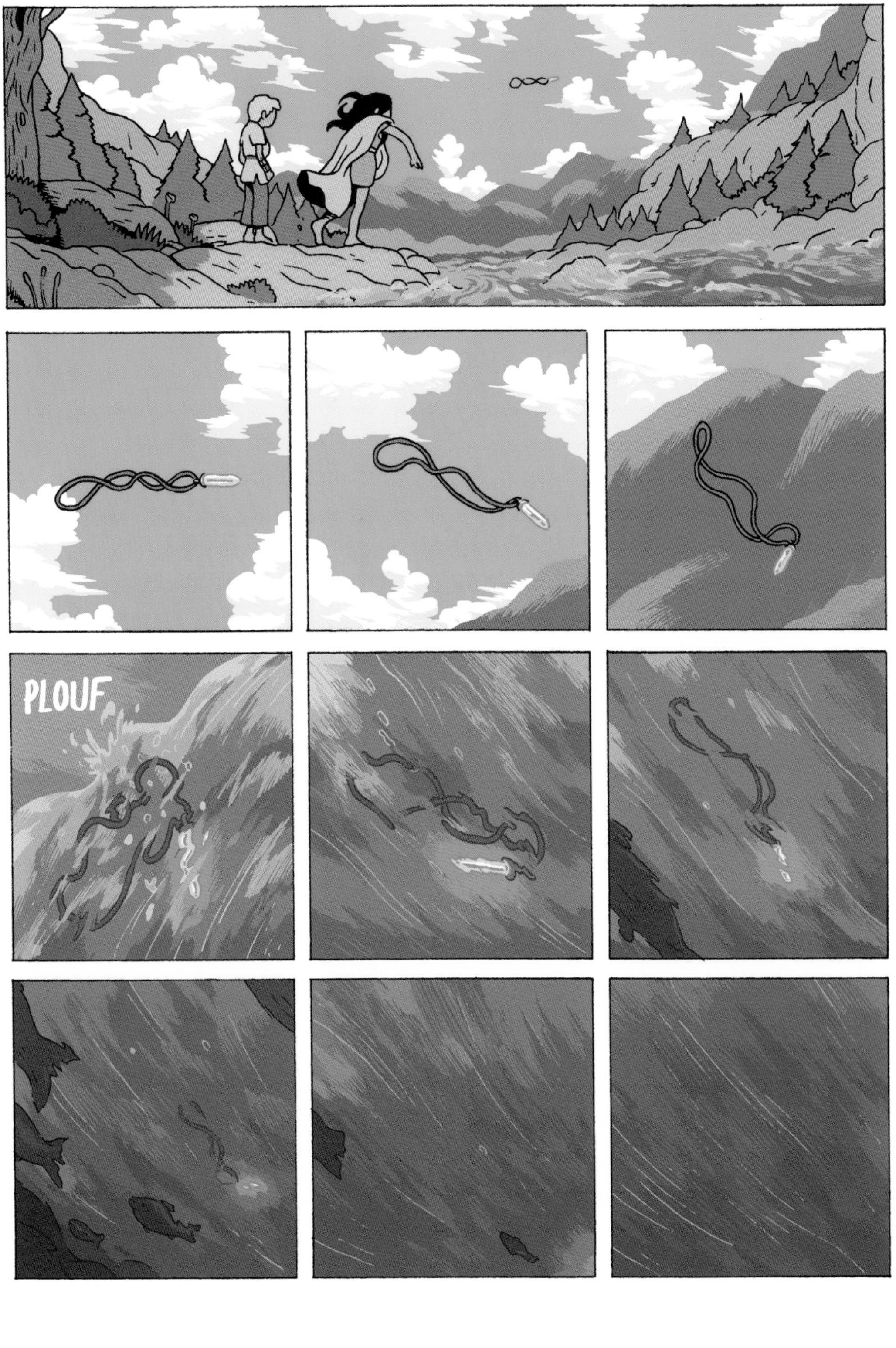
PLOUF

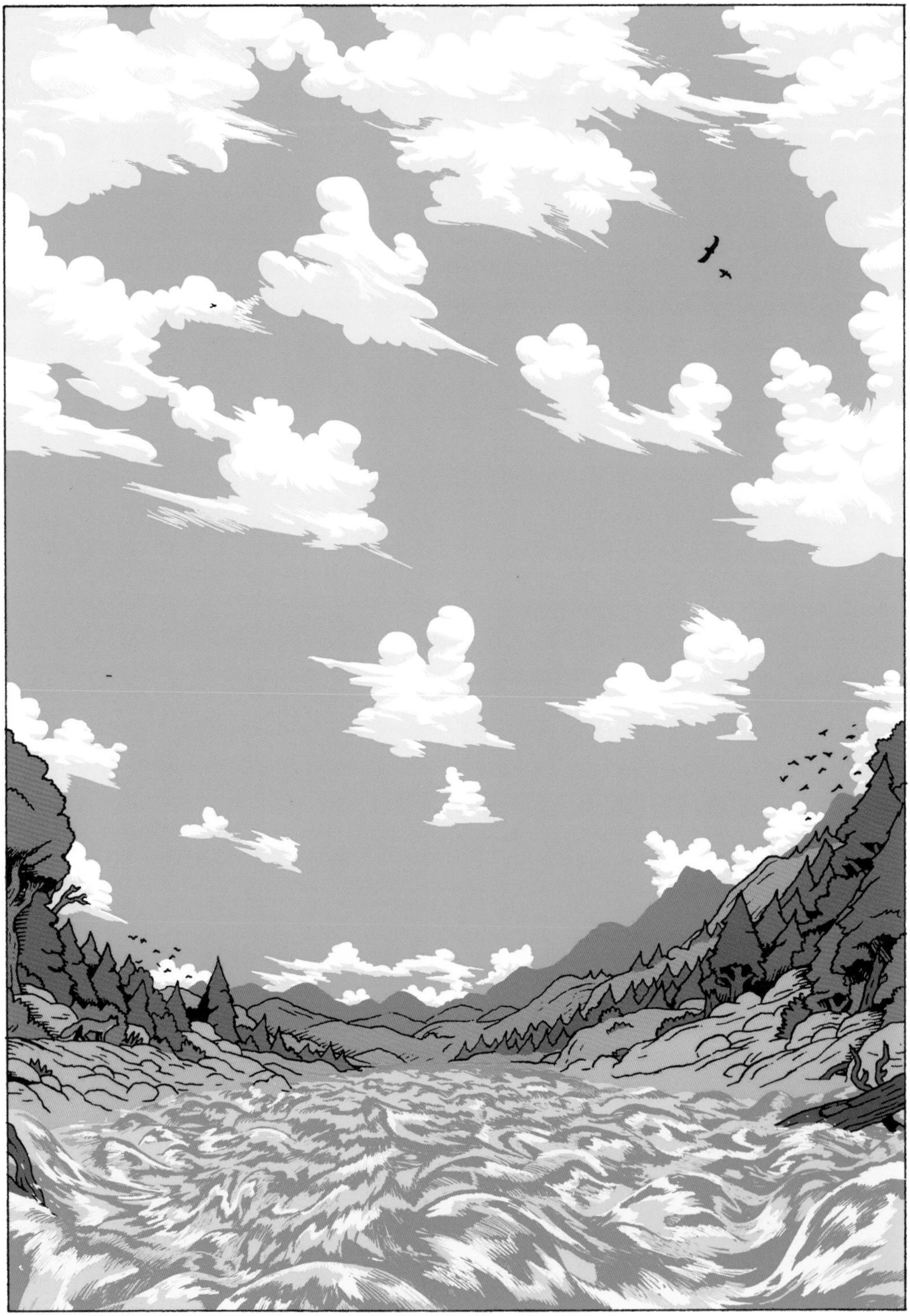

JUST LIKE SOPHIA AND IRIS, IT'S BEEN QUITE A JOURNEY TO CREATE BREATH OF THE GIANT. CREATOR TOM AUREILLE AGREED TO LET US TAKE A PEEK AT HIS SECRET FILES!

# TOM'S Secret Lair

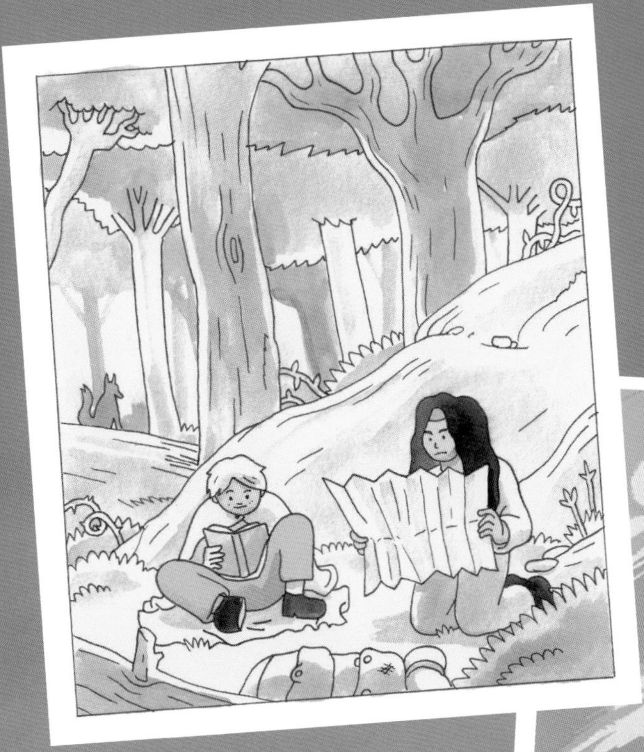

## testing waters

A graphic novel like this one starts with sketches, research and preliminary drawings. Tom Aureille has experimented with colors, moods and various techniques in order to get the right style for the story.

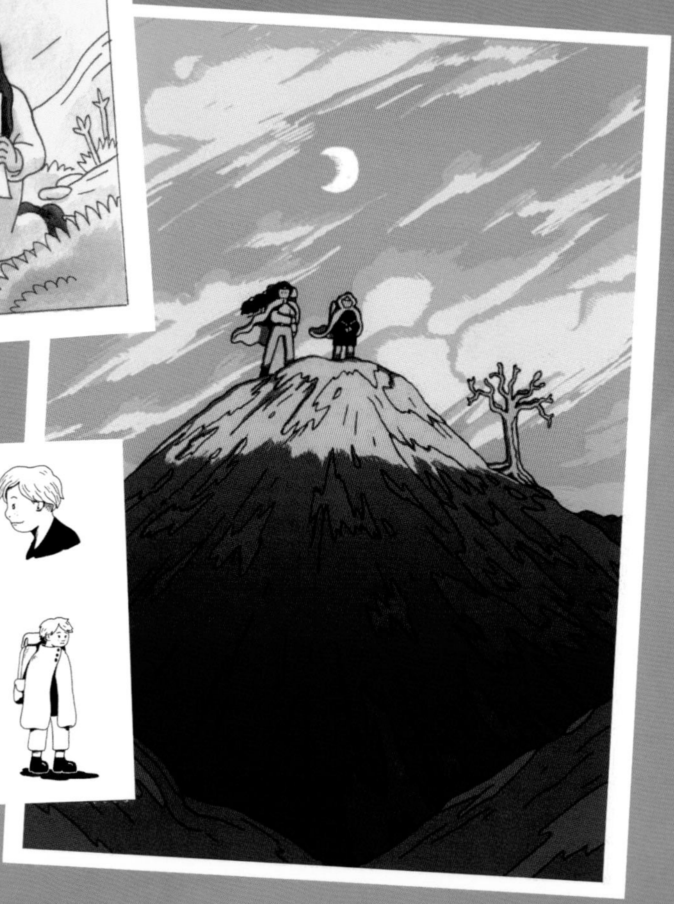

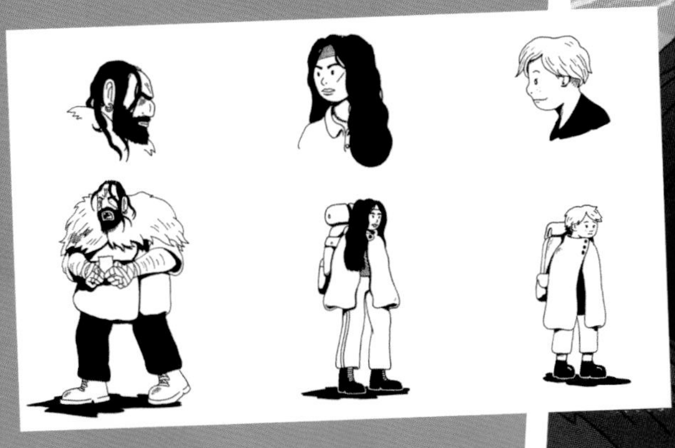

## Sketch a sketch

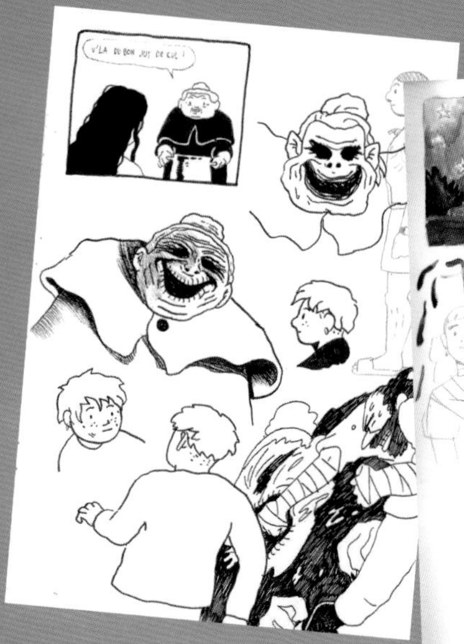
V'LA DU BON JUS DE CUL !

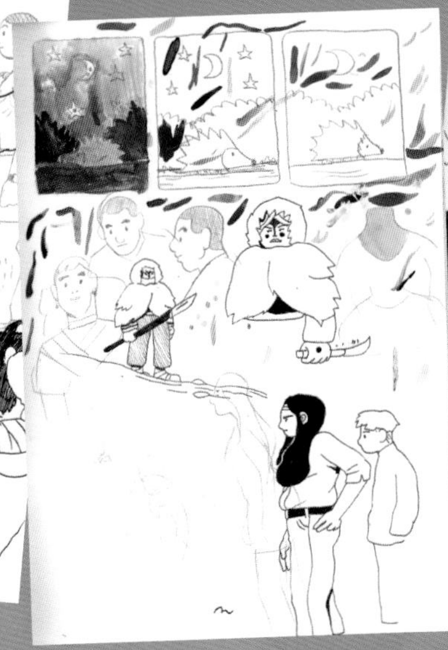

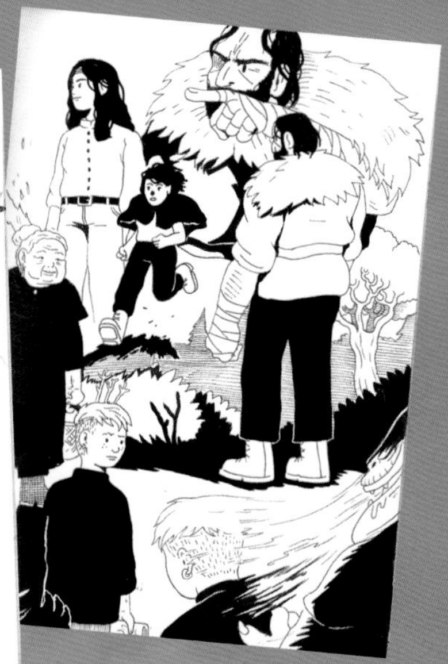

Above are excerpts from Tom's personal sketchbook. This is where the story and the panels were born. Before he laid out any page. Below is one of his first versions of the giant.

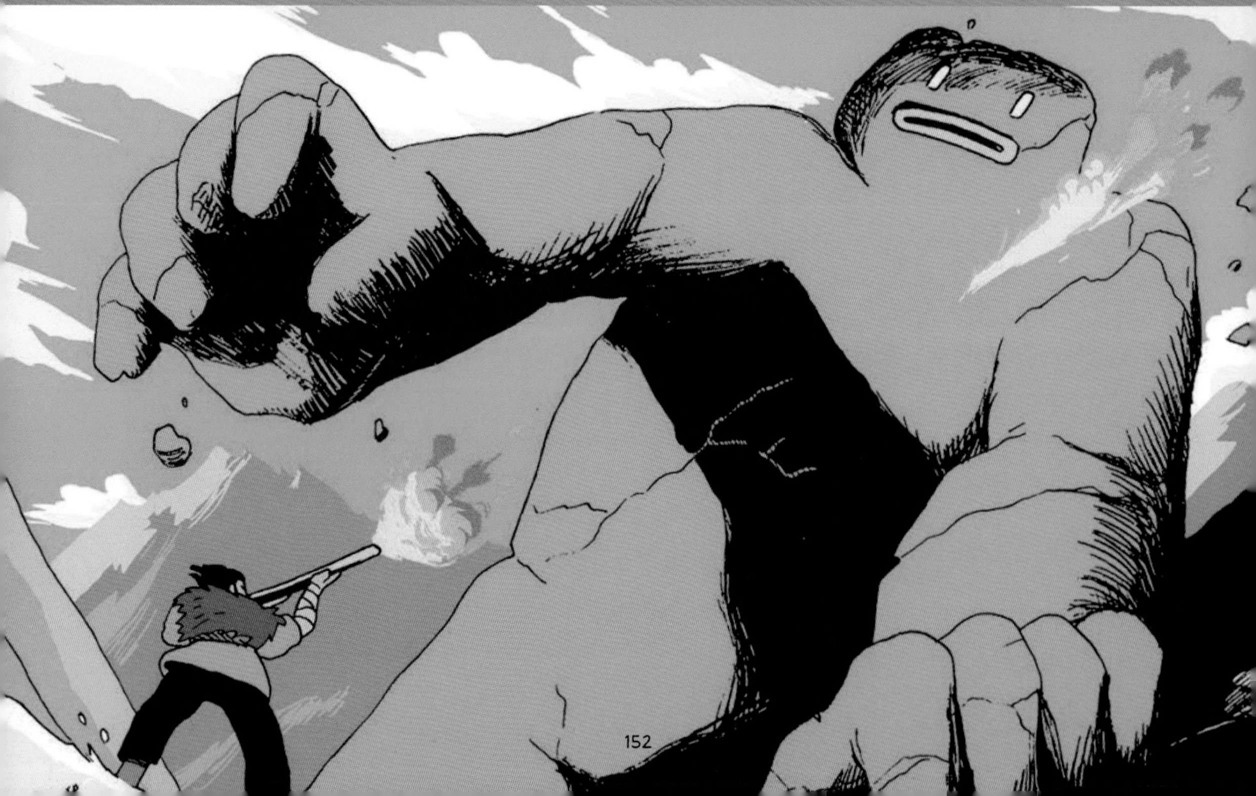

Tom Aureille tried a lot of different options for the cover of this graphic novel for its first publication, in France. What's your favorite? We like them all!

## Covering the Giant

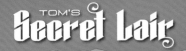

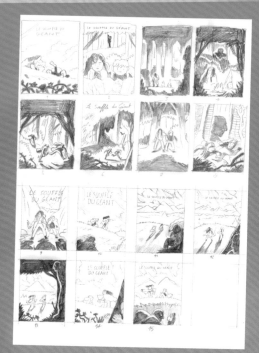

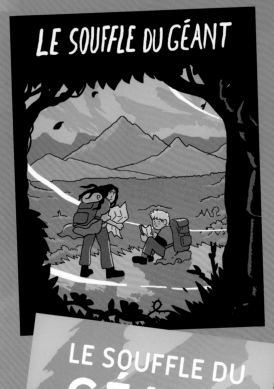

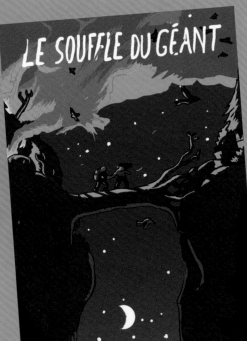

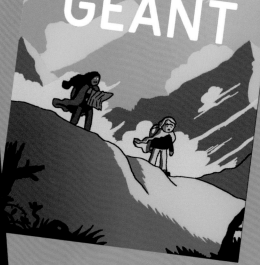

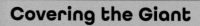
Finally, Tom and the original editor went for this version...Well. Not exactly.
Can you spot the difference with the final cover?